Healing the Rift
A Physician's Insight into Medical Negligence – Past, Present, and Paths to Progress

Don't Honour me Please understand m

Dr. Yogesh A Gupta

Ukiyoto Publishing

All global publishing rights are held by

Ukiyoto Publishing

Published in 2024

Content Copyright ©Dr. Yogesh A Gupta

ISBN 9789360495039

Edition 1

www.ukiyoto.com

Dedication

In heartfelt gratitude and profound love, I dedicate this book to my cherished family, with special appreciation for my wife, Dr. Geeta Gupta, and our two beloved daughters, Manya and Arayna. This work is a testament to the unwavering support and understanding they have showered upon me.

This book is a tribute to the dedicated physicians who tirelessly pursue their noble calling, driven by a singular mission to alleviate the suffering of patients. Amidst their selfless efforts, many find themselves unjustly entangled in cases of medical negligence, enduring a harrowing journey through the labyrinth of legal procedures that often shatters their confidence.

A poignant acknowledgement extends to the patients and their families who have endured genuine acts of commission, enduring the painful wait for justice that stretches across years. This book stands as a testament to their resilience and unwavering pursuit of truth.

To the pillars of justice, the judiciary, and the valiant officers who navigate the intricate complexities of medical science, I offer this dedication. Your tireless efforts to understand and resolve the challenges faced by healthcare professionals do not go unnoticed.

Finally, this book is a tribute to the spirit of India, poised to leap into a new era of healthcare. May the collective aspirations and efforts propel us toward a future where compassion, understanding, and justice prevail in the realm of medicine."

Preface

King vs. Doctor

All the patient are king and all the healers are doctor.

In a kingdom called Earth, there reigned a powerful and authoritative ruler named Mr. Powerful. He believed in his own infallibility and passed judgments on his subjects with ease, either rewarding them or punishing them as he saw fit. His dominion was vast, and his word was law.

One fateful day, however, King Powerful fell ill. Afflicted with fever, vomiting, and abdominal pain, he summoned his trusted doctor to attend to him. The doctor, diligent and dedicated, immediately left all his tasks to cater to the needs of the ailing king.

After a thorough examination and a series of inquiries, the doctor discovered that the king's deteriorating health was a consequence of an unhealthy lifestyle. King Powerful indulged in consuming a variety of detrimental foods, partook in daily alcohol consumption, and neglected to follow the prescribed medication regimen provided by the doctor.

Advising the king to adhere to a disciplined routine, the doctor prescribed medication based on his diagnosis. However, the king, with a mindset of his own, chose to selectively follow the advice that suited his desires. He continued his excessive drinking, justified by its perceived necessity in social and official gatherings, and dismissed the importance of dietary restrictions.

Ignoring certain medications for conditions like high blood pressure and diabetes, the king, in his royal arrogance, believed that such ailments were beneath him. "How can my sugar be uncontrolled?" he thought, asserting his regal stature.

As the king persisted in his chosen course of action, the initial simple fever escalated into a grave illness. The once trivial ailment gained the support of compromised kidney and liver functions, exacerbating the severity of the condition. The king's health deteriorated rapidly, and it took the doctor 15 days to stabilize him. An additional three months were required for the king to regain his former strength under the care of his family.

Upon his return to the royal council, instead of expressing gratitude to the doctor, the ministers criticized and blamed him for the king's suffering. Succumbing to the prevailing sentiments, King Powerful ordered his Defense minister to apprehend the doctor and bring him before the throne.

Chained and escorted by soldiers, the doctor faced the wrath of the citizens who, influenced by the prevailing sentiment, cursed and even physically attacked him. The doctor, despite his desire to defend his actions, knew that his words would fall on deaf ears. His attempts to proclaim his role in saving lives and aiding the community in times of crisis seemed futile, drowned out by the overwhelming condemnation that surrounded him.

Interaction of Doctor with Public:

(The doctor, shackled and escorted by soldiers, walks through the enraged crowd.)

Citizen 1: (Shouting) "You failed to cure the king! You should be ashamed!"

Doctor: "Citizens, please understand, I did my best to treat the king's illness."

Citizen 2: (Hurling an insult) "Best? You call this your best? Our king almost died because of you!"

Doctor: "I assure you, I worked tirelessly to bring him back to health. His choices contributed to his condition".

Citizen 3: (Throwing a stone) "We trusted you, and you betrayed us!"

Doctor: "I never intended harm. His refusal to follow medical advice worsened the situation."

Citizen 4: (Pointing accusingly) "You're a disgrace to your profession!"

Doctor: "I've dedicated my life to healing. I plead for a fair hearing."

Citizen 5: (In anger) "Fair hearing? You deserve to be punished for what you did to our king!"

Doctor: "Punishment won't change the truth. I saved many lives; I'm not your enemy."

Citizen 6: (Sarcastically) "Oh, a savior, aren't we lucky to have you?"

Doctor: "My duty is to heal, not to harm. I stand by my commitment to the well-being of the people."

(The doctor continues to walk amidst the hostile crowd, attempting to convey his perspective despite the overwhelming anger and condemnation.)

So, finally, he was brought in front of the king. The king had the help of his legal team, defense ministers, and other intelligent council of ministers. They all hurled abuses at the doctor and asked many questions. When the doctor stated that it was the lifestyle of the king that led to his sufferings, everyone got angry. The defense minister shouted, "How dare you say this? Who are you to say what lifestyle is right? Do you even know how the king works and how important his decisions are?"

For the first time, the king spoke, "You are putting blame on me when it was you who did not diagnose the correct reason for my disease. Because of the delay in the right medicine, I suffered. Instead of accepting that, you are blaming me."

The doctor responded, "Sir, when I saw you, I diagnosed the disease according to symptoms. We have to decide between all the possible diagnoses and take a call. Your symptoms best suited the diagnoses I made. I have even explained to you about the possibility of alternate diagnoses. I have also told you to take certain medicines. I have been telling you to stop alcohol and bad food for so many years."

Now the king got angry, "I don't want to listen to anything, doctor. Accept that you were wrong. Because your diagnosis was wrong, I suffered. I am not the only one who drinks or eats bad food. How many have suffered when they have similar symptoms? You are negligent."

All the council ministers concurred with what their king said. The doctor still tried to defend himself, "Sir, look into my long experience and long service. I have helped so many patients save their lives and have relieved them of their sufferings. I have been wrong many times in my diagnoses, but I am not God."

The defense minister said, "We don't care whether you have served well or not. You have done wrong here, and so you are negligent."

The doctor responded, "But sir, I am not God."

One of the council ministers added, "We don't know that. But we come to you thinking that you are God."

The doctor continued, "But sir, is this my fault that people consider me as a God? And sir, even your wishes are not fulfilled by God. Will you punish him also for your suffering? God has preached not to sin, not to drink alcohol, and to live a healthy lifestyle. So will you blame God also?"

Almost all started shouting, "Don't say so. You are insulting our Gods and abusing our faith in God. Why should we punish God? Who are we to punish God?"

The doctor almost lost his cool but was very frightened, "Sir, then why are you punishing me if you are thinking of me as a God."

The king shouted, "How dare you call yourself God? I am sitting here. I am the judge, and I am God in this kingdom. If you say one more word, I will punish you with jail time for insulting me and my court." The doctor was now confused but knew it was his life on the line.

So, he continued with his argument. He said, "Sir, I can only say I tried my level best, just like any other doctor. I had no intention to harm you, and moreover, please remember when your condition deteriorated, it was my efforts that saved you." But the king said, "I don't care whether you saved me afterward, but it was you who led to all this. I would have died. But it was my luck that I survived. Otherwise, through your negligence, you almost killed me."

The doctor responded, "Sir, but that's how doctors work. We try our level best to provide relief from sufferings. In some cases, we succeed, in some, we fail. But then we never intend to harm." The king still was not impressed. He and his council of ministers had already made up their minds. He said, "Nothing you say can convince us. We know you were negligent. So I order you to be stripped of your degree, and from now on, you will not be allowed to practice medicine. If anyone sees you giving medicine, you will be jailed."

The doctor was angry, but he knew he could not say anything to the king because then the king would get angry, and for contempt of the king, he would be jailed or may even be hanged. Still, he cursed the king and the kingdom of Earth, stating that since the people don't treat their doctors well, a time would come when they would have no good doctors to treat them.

Now just put any patient or lawyer or judge or media in place of king and put any doctor in place of the doctor in the story.

A Doctor's Frustration: Bear With Me

Hypocritic World: We Are Not Healers Or Warriors But Expendable Force

In 1999, our country faced a terrorist attack from a neighboring nation. During the winter, they attempted to encroach on our land near Jammu and Kashmir. These terrorists were supported, funded, and weaponized by the Pakistani army. Our intelligence team and army discovered this, leading to a war famously known as the Kargil War.

While we emerged victorious, we lost many soldiers, and some citizens were also injured. The terrorists, who were not claimed by Pakistan, were considered enemies due to their infiltration. Our army faced challenges during the conflict, dealing with outdated equipment, corruption in the defense sector, and a lack of protective gear and protocols for fighting in difficult terrain.

Additionally, certain media personnel, whether knowingly or unknowingly, televised our movements, weapons, and plans, aiding the enemy. This compromised the element of surprise and contributed to casualties. The opposition, though seemingly united, used the situation to criticize the government, even accusing the most honest politicians of corruption in purchasing coffins.

Now, fast-forward to 2023 and the battle against the novel coronavirus. We faced a formidable enemy, unfamiliar to our immune system, with its own set of weapons. Our healthcare infrastructure was unprepared for such an attack. Despite the challenges, the government took charge of policy-making, determining admission criteria, investigations, discharges, and even attributing causes of death. The healthcare workers found themselves in a position where decisions were influenced by both government policies and the financial conditions of the patients.

The media, relentless in its coverage, reported incidents of violence against doctors, sealing of hospitals, reprimands for non-compliance, and controversies over bills. Hospitals, facing an infrastructure crunch, were compelled to redesign their premises for more beds and ICUs, resulting in unfortunate fires and subsequent legal actions. The healthcare sector found itself under intense scrutiny and criticism during the battle against the pandemic.

Until Covid persisted, the government was aware of the crucial role that doctors and healthcare infrastructure played. They acknowledged the scarcity and their negligence in developing this sector at various levels. Realizing that without the contribution of the private sector, doctors, and staff, the battle would be lost before it began, they initially attempted to sideline this sector, considering the situation as a minor scare that would pass in a few days. Protocols were designed to allow only government hospitals and health centers to manage the situation. College hostels and certain hotels were converted into Covid care centers, lacking full-time, round-the-clock doctors.

As the Covid situation prolonged for more than two years, the government eventually opened up the private sector, albeit with strict regulations.

In March 2023, a doctor practicing in Baroda for 20 years received a court notice. A patient treated by him two years ago during Covid times had filed a case, citing the doctor's actions during that period as the cause of mental harassment for the patient and relatives.

A doctor practicing in Surat received a summons, accusing him of negligence while treating a Covid patient. The patient was given unnecessary medicines, specifically HCQS, which, as everyone now knows, has no effect on Covid.

An elderly clinician and a well-known face in Ahmedabad received a notice stating that, although the patient had died of Covid, there was no mention of Covid on the diagnosis paper, leading to allegations of negligence. The doctor recalled that during Covid, doctors were not responsible for preparing the discharge summary or death summary, following government guidelines.

A hospital was sealed during Covid because a doctor chose to administer Remdesivir to a patient strongly suspected to have

Covid, despite negative test reports. The doctor, aware of international articles indicating that a percentage of patients could test negative, made a decision to save the patient's life. However, someone complained, and the media created breaking news, leading the corporation to seal the hospital. The incident raises questions about who should decide what is best for a critically ill patient – a policy maker with no medical knowledge or a doctor?

There are thousands of cases ongoing in courts and consumer courts, involving allegations of substandard care, delayed injections, early discharge, late discharge, and more investigations by doctors and hospitals. Doctors who worked during Covid, following protocols, are now fearing such cases being filed against them.

Due to a lack of hospital beds and the enormity of the catastrophe, the government declared that it would pay for the bills, announcing packages for services and strictly regulating the same. Hospitals initially protested but, due to the enforcement of the Epidemic Act, media pressure, and an increased patient influx, they ultimately agreed. Despite the pandemic being declared over, payments to the majority of hospitals have not been made. Committees are examining bills, and commission agents are extorting money in the name of bill processing. The accumulated amounts for these hospitals run into crores. As a result, hospitals are closing, and doctors are left unpaid. Protesting against this leads to accusations of being "lootera" (looters) from politicians and the media.

During a live TV debate, the topic was that doctors were negligent during Covid, prescribing unnecessary medicines and conducting trials, leading to suffering, deaths, and ongoing suffering. As a doctor on the panel, I faced criticism from the anchor, politicians, activists, and an eminent lawyer.

The anchor asked, "So, Dr., what are your views on these accusations?" I responded, "All the accusations are correct. We doctors were completely unfamiliar with the disease, investigations, and medicines. So, we did what you are accusing."

This statement surprised them, blunting their attack. The anchor shouted, "So, you are accepting that doctors were negligent?" I clarified, "No, I don't accept that accusation."

They were back in the game, asking what I meant. I continued, "Will you all agree that this was a novel virus? Meaning that no country, no doctor, and no scientist in the world knew about this virus." The lawyer agreed, and I further asked if the government knew what to do when the news first came in. The opposition party person criticized the government, and the anchor tried to intervene, saying, "Sir, your turn will come."

The ruling party politicians said, "What are you talking about, doctor? We did not know about the virus, but we knew what to do. We were the ones who went for the longest lockdown. See how we increased the healthcare infrastructure in a short time."

I asked, "But were you sure your steps would work? Did you have any knowledge that lockdown, isolation, quarantine would work?"

The anchor said, "What are you talking about, doctor? How can they know such things? This was the first time such an attack has happened, so they tried. Failure or success is on fate."

I said, "Wah, you are so intelligent." This irked the anchor. He got the sarcasm and said, "Dr., why don't you answer about your accusations?"

I said, "Oh, it looks like your intelligence is only for politicians and not doctors. So let me say directly." I continued, "When this disease started, we doctors did not know anything about the disease and its whole style of damage. And so it is called novel. Then, as different countries started fighting, we started devising the fight. In this fight, our hands were further tightened by policies made. We were not given a free hand to decide on investigations and medicines. We accepted this as it was a pandemic, and the government, with the help of an expert team, made certain policies."

"Now let me ask you a pointed question. When the Kargil war happened, did our soldiers know the enemy? They were sent to battle with whatever equipment we had, knowing the poor defense structure till then. They fought and got killed. The enemy was sitting on higher ground and could easily target us, and we were like sitting ducks. So should we blame our soldiers for the loss and sufferings?"

The politicians, both in unanimity, shouted, "How dare you insult our soldiers? Who are you to insult them? They protected our motherland, and you are questioning them." The anchor said, "I request the public to understand that these views are personal. This has nothing to do with the channel."

I did not stop, "Our soldiers went in with full force, unknown to the enemy and with substandard and ill-equipped weapons. So, is it their fault?" I continued, "During the Mumbai attack, so many civilians were trapped inside the Taj hotel. The enemy had the upper hand. When NSG commandos and police came, did they know where they were stationed inside and what weapons they had?"

The anchor said, "Again, sir, you are going in the wrong direction." I said, "Just tell me, did they know?" He said, "No." So when our NSG and police went in and attacked from all sides, there were many civilian casualties. So were they responsible for the sufferings and killings?"

The politicians were now angry and yelling at me, "You have lost your mind, they are soldiers, and if a few are lost to save many, then it is called collateral damage. Why should they be responsible?"

I then said, "Sir, when Covid came, it was an unknown enemy. We fought with whatever we were given as weapons. We did not know which report would help and which medicine would work. So, when we fought with medical science initially, many medicines did not work. Even to date, we don't have any sure medicine for that. But did we do that knowingly? No, it was the only weapon available. So yes, we failed, but no, we were not negligent."

The lawyer said, "It is easy for you to say this, but doctors should be tried in court for all the negligence complaints." I said, "Yes, you can, and the judiciary is already doing that. But just tell me, will you try soldiers also for negligence after a war?"

He shouted back, "Doctor, you are not a soldier. You are a doctor."
I said, "Wah, when you all were facing devastation due to the Covid pandemic, you did that thalis and talis and called us corona warriors. We left everything and jumped into the war without thinking for our life. Then where was this arrogance?"

Now the debate was heating up. I was in no mood to let them off the hook. I said, "Did we make the policy whom to investigate? Did we make the policy when to investigate? Did we make the policy when to admit and when to discharge? Did we make the policy which drug to give and when to give? Did we decide which hospital is Covid and which is not?"

The anchor knew I was talking sense, so he tried to cool me down. He said, "Doctor, I agree with what you are saying. But see, patients felt let down, they suffered, and so they are blaming you."

I said, "I have no complaints towards patients. They have the right to blame us as we were the direct face for them. But my complaint is against the government and the judiciary."

The lawyer jumped, "How come you are blaming the judiciary?"

I said, "Why don't you listen to everything I say? You listen only to what you want. I have blamed the government." I continued, "Let me ask you, sir, do you agree that it was a once-in-a-hundred-year event?"

He said yes. I asked, "Do you agree this was bigger than world wars, an enemy so cruel that it destroyed lives over the globe?" He said yes. I asked again, "So you agree it was worse than a war?" He said yes.

I again asked, "Do you agree, on a larger perspective, that doctors, nurses, ward boys, and other healthcare personnel were frontline workers who came directly face to face with the enemy?"

He said yes. I asked, "Was there not an epidemic act in action or not?" He said yes. Now he was irritated. He said, "Doctor, come to the point, please."

I said laughingly, "Sir, since you are a lawyer, I thought you would like to go point by point. Still, please help me understand, should the judiciary and government not take steps to protect us healthcare people from such frivolous complaints?"

He knew I was right, but still, he did not speak a single word.

I said, "Sir, let me tell you one fact. The next pandemic is around the corner. Let me see who will come forward when the doctor knows that our judiciary is not going to protect us. We are just called soldiers, but like soldiers, we are not protected from the acts of ours that we do during these wars."

I finally said, "Don't worry; we will fight the cases you and your friends file against us. We will keep working for the service of patients. But the trust in the judiciary and government is at the bottom." It looked like today they had no points to counter me. They knew healthcare did protect the larger population in a country like India.

But for some unsatisfactory people, a country cannot allow doctors to face the law on such absurd grounds. If this is the case, then make policymakers, media, and judiciary also party to the crime. Let us all stand in the guilty box.

Faced with recurrent medical malpractice crises, we would do well to recall the words of

Albert Einstein:

"The formulation of a problem is often more essential than its solution, which may be merely a matter of mathematical or experimental skill.

To raise new questions, new possibilities, to regard old problems from a new angle, requires creative imagination and marks real advance."

Contents

When Business Enters Healthcare   176

Solution   211

Epilogue   262

If We Don't Know The History We Will Not Know The Problem

Introduction

Medical negligence, also known as medical malpractice, has a long and complex history that has evolved over centuries. The concept of holding medical practitioners accountable for their actions dates back to ancient civilizations, but formalized legal systems to address medical negligence began to emerge in the 19th century. Here is a brief historical background of medical negligence:

1. Ancient Civilizations:

   - In ancient civilizations such as Mesopotamia, Greece, and Rome, there were early forms of medical codes and ethical guidelines. However, the concept of legal liability for medical errors was not well-established.

2. Hippocratic Oath (5th Century BCE):

   - The Hippocratic Oath, attributed to the ancient Greek physician Hippocrates, emphasized ethical principles for physicians, including a commitment to "do no harm." While not a legal document, it laid the foundation for medical ethics.

3. Middle Ages:

   - During the Middle Ages, medical practices were often intertwined with religious institutions. The Church had a significant influence on healthcare, and there were limited legal frameworks for addressing medical errors.

4. Rise of Medical Professionalism (17th-18th Centuries):

- The establishment of medical colleges and professional societies in Europe marked a shift toward formalized medical education and standardized practices. However, legal recourse for patients harmed by medical negligence remained limited.

5. 19th Century:

- With advancements in medical science and the rise of modern medicine, the need for legal accountability became more apparent. The first recorded medical malpractice case in the United States was in 1794 (Parsons v. Winchell), but it was in the 19th century that legal precedents and statutes addressing medical negligence began to emerge.

6. Flexner Report (1910):

- The Flexner Report in the United States recommended higher standards for medical education, leading to increased professionalization and a focus on competency. This period saw the development of medical licensing boards and the integration of medical ethics into medical education.

7. 20th Century:

- Medical malpractice litigation increased during the 20th century, reflecting societal changes and the growth of the healthcare industry. Landmark cases, such as Salgo v. Leland Stanford Jr. University Board of Trustees (1957), helped shape the legal standards for medical negligence.

8. Modern Era:

- In the late 20th and early 21st centuries, medical malpractice laws continued to evolve.

Different countries have developed their own legal frameworks to address medical negligence, incorporating principles of compensation, patient rights, and quality improvement in healthcare.

Medical negligence cases today are complex and often involve multiple stakeholders, including healthcare providers, insurers, legal professionals, and regulatory bodies. The ongoing development of medical and legal standards reflects society's ongoing efforts to balance patient rights with the challenges faced by healthcare professionals.

Ancient Times, Middle Ages, Churches, Middle East And Even The King

A Healer's Dilemma - A Mesopotamian Tale

Characters:

- Eshnunna (Healer)

- Nisaba (Patient)

- Elders of Ur

(The scene opens in the ancient city of Ur, where the ziggurats dominate the skyline. Eshnunna, a skilled healer, is tending to patients in his modest clinic.)

Eshnunna: (Speaking to a patient) Fear not, my friend. With the blessings of the gods, we shall overcome your ailment.

(Word reaches Eshnunna about Nisaba, who has suffered unexpected harm following his treatment. The elders summon Eshnunna and Nisaba to the court.)

Elder 1: "Eshnunna, you stand accused of mala praxis - a breach of trust that has harmed Nisaba. What say you?"

Eshnunna: (Humbly) "Elders, I sought only to heal. The gods bear witness to my intentions."

Nisaba: (With concern) "My condition worsened, honored elders. I seek justice."

Elder 2: (Deliberating) "The Code of Ur-Nammu demands retribution, but healing is our pursuit. How do we reconcile?"

(The elders contemplate, reflecting on the delicate balance between justice and the complexities of healing.)

Elder 3: "Eshnunna, you shall not face punishment that mirrors the harm caused. We aim for healing, not vengeance".

Eshnunna: (Gratefully) "Thank you, wise elders. I accept your judgment".

(The elders decree that Eshnunna shall serve the community, channeling his healing skills for the greater good.)

Elder 1: "Let this be a lesson - a path to redemption, not only for Eshnunna but for us all."

(Months pass, and Eshnunna dedicates himself to service. The community witnesses the positive impact of his redemption.)

Nisaba: (Observing) "Eshnunna's service has brought healing not only to me but to our entire community".

Elder 2: "The gods' mercy shines upon a just resolution. Eshnunna's path to redemption is a testament to the wisdom of our elders."

A Healer's Redemption - A Medieval Tale

Characters:

- Gareth (Healer)

- Eleanor (Patient)

- Village Elders

(The setting is a medieval village surrounded by towering castles. Gareth, a skilled healer, tends to patients in his modest dwelling.)

Gareth: (To a patient) Worry not, good friend. The herbs and tinctures I provide will mend your ailments.

(News spreads of Eleanor, whose health deteriorated unexpectedly after Gareth's treatment. The village elders summon Gareth and Eleanor to the courtyard.)

Village Elder 1: "Gareth, you are accused of malpractice – a breach of trust that has harmed Eleanor. How do you respond?"

Gareth: (With humility) "Elders, I meant only to heal. Mayhaps the spirits were not with me that day."

Eleanor: (Expressing concern) "My condition worsened, honorable elders. I seek justice."

Village Elder 2: (Contemplating) "In these medieval times, justice must be tempered with mercy. Gareth, explain your actions."

(Gareth recounts his efforts to heal Eleanor and the uncertainties of medieval medicine. The elders deliberate on the delicate balance between justice and the healer's intent.)

Village Elder 3: "Gareth, we recognize the complexities of healing in these times. Punishment must be just, not vengeful."

Gareth: (Gratefully) "I am at your mercy, wise elders".

(The elders decide that Gareth shall dedicate himself to serving the village, utilizing his skills for the greater good.)

Village Elder 1: "Let this be a lesson - a path to redemption, not only for Gareth but for our medieval village."

(Time passes, and Gareth dedicates himself to the well-being of the village. The community witnesses positive changes brought about by his redemption.)

Eleanor: (Observing) "Gareth's service has brought healing not only to me but to our entire medieval village."

Village Elder 2: "The balance of justice and mercy has been achieved. Gareth's journey toward redemption is a tale for our medieval times."

A Healer's Redemption - A Tale of Church and Compassion

Characters:

- Brother Gabriel (Healer)

- Isabella (Parishioner)

- Ecclesiastical Elders

(The scene is set in a monastery with Brother Gabriel, a skilled healer, attending to the ailments of the parishioners.)

Brother Gabriel: (To a parishioner) Fear not, dear friend. The healing balm and prayers shall bring solace to your afflictions.

(News spreads of Isabella, who faced unexpected complications following Brother Gabriel's treatment. The ecclesiastical elders summon Brother Gabriel and Isabella to the hallowed halls of the monastery.)

Ecclesiastical Elder 1: "Brother Gabriel, you stand accused of a breach of trust, a mala praxis that has brought harm to Isabella. How do you respond?"

Brother Gabriel: (With piety) "Elders, I only sought to be an instrument of God's healing. The outcome pains my soul."

Isabella: (With concern) "My suffering deepened, honorable elders. I seek solace in the embrace of the Church."

Ecclesiastical Elder 2: "In these sacred halls, healing is intertwined with divine providence. Brother Gabriel, elucidate your actions."

(Brother Gabriel recounts his endeavors to heal Isabella and expresses the uncertainties inherent in divine healing. The ecclesiastical elders deliberate on the delicate balance between justice and divine intervention.)

Ecclesiastical Elder 3: "Brother Gabriel, we acknowledge the complexities of healing in the divine light. Our judgment must be tempered with mercy."

Brother Gabriel: (With humility) "I submit to the wisdom of the Church, venerable elders."

(The ecclesiastical elders decree that Brother Gabriel shall undertake a pilgrimage, dedicating himself to serve the needy along the sacred journey.)

Ecclesiastical Elder 1: "Let this be a pilgrimage of redemption, Brother Gabriel. May your actions bring solace not only to Isabella but to all who seek healing."

(Months pass, and Brother Gabriel embarks on his pilgrimage. The Church witnesses positive changes as his healing touch extends beyond the monastery.)

Isabella: (Observing) "Brother Gabriel's pilgrimage has brought divine healing to me and our sacred community."

Ecclesiastical Elder 2: "The Church's wisdom prevails. Brother Gabriel's pilgrimage is a testament to the compassion and redemption found in divine service."

A Balance of Justice - An Ancient Tale

Characters:

- Malik (Injured Party)

- Jamila (Accused)

- Elders of the Oasis

(The scene unfolds in a peaceful oasis in ancient Arabia. Malik, a member of the community, has suffered an injury, and the elders are summoned to address the matter.)

Malik: (Addressing the elders) "Elders, I have suffered harm at the hands of Jamila. I seek justice for the pain inflicted upon me."

(Jamila stands solemnly, acknowledging the accusations. The elders gather under the shade of the palm trees to deliberate.)

Elder 1: "Malik, what transpired that led to this injury?"

Malik: "We had a dispute over the boundaries of our land. Words were exchanged, and in the heat of the moment, harm befell me."

Jamila: (With remorse)" Elders, I did not intend for this to happen. The dispute escalated beyond my control."

(The elders contemplate the ancient principle of "an eye for an eye" as they seek a fair resolution.)

Elder 2: "Our ancestors believed in a balance of justice. Malik, what say you? Should we follow the ancient principle?"

Malik: (Reflecting) "Elders, while my pain is great, I understand that balance is crucial. I do not seek vengeance but a fair resolution."

Elder 3: (Addressing Jamila) "Jamila, the balance must be restored. What would you offer as compensation for the harm caused?"

Jamila: "I am willing to provide compensation in the form of resources to Malik. I wish to mend the harmony of our oasis."

(The elders and the community witness an agreement where Jamila provides compensation to Malik for the injury caused. The ancient principle is upheld, and a sense of balance is restored.)

Elder 1: "Let this be a lesson to our oasis. Our ancient principles guide us towards harmony and justice, ensuring the balance is maintained."

Ancient Mesopotamia:

In ancient Mesopotamia, where the concept of justice was deeply rooted in the idea of reciprocity and communal well-being, medical negligence was addressed through a system that valued compensation and community service. When a healer's negligence led to harm, the community sought redress by ensuring the healer compensated the affected individual. The emphasis was on restoring balance rather than punitive measures. The community-oriented approach aimed at maintaining the healer's role in serving society, acknowledging the importance of their contributions.

Middle Ages and Church Involvement:

During the Middle Ages, with the influence of the Church, medical negligence cases were often dealt with by ecclesiastical authorities. The Church played a pivotal role in overseeing medical practices and ensuring ethical conduct among healers. Punishments varied, including penance, fines, or community service. The Church's involvement reflected a moral and spiritual perspective on healing, intertwining faith and medicine. The emphasis on repentance and community service aimed to redeem the healer and reaffirm their commitment to serving the community in a more responsible manner.

Ancient Middle East and "Eye for an Eye":

In ancient times in the Middle East, where the principle of "eye for an eye" prevailed, a story unfolded where medical negligence resulted in severe consequences. When a healer's actions led to harm, the legal system should have applied the same harm to the healer as a form of retribution. This approach would have showcased a stringent adherence to reciprocal justice, emphasizing proportional punishment. But even there the elders decided that healer is important for the larger good and so the punishment was tweaked. The story highlights how severe can be the consequences for medical negligence in a society where strict retributive measures are integral to the legal framework.

Common Theme:

Across these stories, a common theme emerges - the recognition of the healer's crucial role in society and the efforts to ensure their continued service. Whether through compensation, community service, or retributive measures, the underlying goal was to maintain the healer's responsibility toward the well-being of the community. **The emphasis on community service as a form of redress not only addressed the harm caused but also aimed to channel the healer's skills and knowledge for the greater good, reinforcing the societal role of healers in various historical contexts.**

So even those days they understood the medical complexities and so the punishment were kept in such a way that the healers could become more productive for the communities. **JUST REMEMBER THIS IDEA OF MAKING HEALERS MORE PRODUCTIVE FOR THE SOCIETY**. Punishing them and taking revenge is like EYE FOR AN EYE. And this cannot be good for the society.'

Code of Hammurabi

There were some who had stringent laws in medical negligence. So civilization had two path to follow. One was of the compassion and another was law.

The code offers the founding statement of medical malpractice law, reading "If the doctor has treated a gentlemen with a lancet of bronze and has caused the gentleman to die, or has opened an abscess of the eye for a gentleman with a bronze lancet, and has caused the loss of the gentleman's eye, one shall cut off his hands."

The passage appears to be a part of the "Code of Hammurabi," one of the earliest and most complete written legal codes, dating back to ancient Mesopotamia. The Code of Hammurabi is associated with the Babylonian King Hammurabi, who ruled from 1792 BCE to 1750 BCE. It is inscribed on a stele, a large stone monument, and contains a set of laws and punishments governing various aspects of Babylonian society.

The specific passage you mentioned is a punitive measure for a doctor's actions that resulted in the death of a patient or the loss of their eye. It reflects the severity of consequences in ancient Mesopotamian law for medical practitioners whose negligence or actions led to harm or injury to their patients. The cutting off of hands in such cases was a form of retribution, reflecting the principle of "eye for an eye" that was prevalent in the legal systems of that time.

While the Code of Hammurabi predates the British colonial era by thousands of years, I can create a fictional story set in ancient Mesopotamia, involving a medical case where the Code of Hammurabi is applied. Keep in mind that this is a creative narrative and not based on historical events.

In the bustling city of Babylon, where the laws of King Hammurabi reigned supreme, there lived a skilled healer named Enlil. Enlil was renowned for his knowledge of herbal remedies and surgical skills, using his bronze lancet to heal various ailments. One day, a nobleman named Ur-Nammu sought Enlil's expertise to treat a persistent ailment.

Ur-Nammu, suffering from a mysterious illness, placed his trust in Enlil's hands. The healer, confident in his abilities, decided to perform a procedure to extract what he believed to be the root cause. Unfortunately, the treatment took an unexpected turn, and Ur-Nammu succumbed to the healer's efforts.

News of Ur-Nammu's demise reached the ears of the city elders, invoking the Code of Hammurabi to address this tragic event. Enlil found himself summoned to the court, facing the stern judgment of the King's law.

As Enlil stood before the court, he knew that his fate rested on the principles outlined in Hammurabi's Code. The king, known for his commitment to justice, presided over the case. The grieving family of Ur-Nammu demanded retribution, invoking the law that stipulated an eye for an eye or, in this case, a life for a life.

Enlil, aware of the gravity of the situation, defended himself. He argued that he had followed the best practices known to him at the time and that the outcome was unforeseen.

Ultimately, King Hammurabi, guided by the principles of code rendered a decsions which was to cut the hands of the healer as punishment.

So humanity had another aspect in ancient time which believed that law is above all other things and it was not ready to accept the complexities of medicine and human body.

So if go through all this stories arguably majority of the countries of world choose the punitive action for medical negligence while only few like New Zealand and Sweden took a more compassionate path.

History: The Term "Mala Praxis"

In 1768, Sir William Blackstone authored Commentaries on the Laws of England, where he introduced the Latin term "mala praxis" to delineate the concept of professional negligence, or 'tort' in contemporary language. Blackstone observed that mala praxis "breaks the trust which the party had placed in his physician, and tends to the patient's destruction." The term 'malpractice' itself was coined subsequently, drawing from Blackstone's seminal work.

Whether the justice system that ensued restored trust or undermined the backbone of healthcare is for you to decide. Nevertheless, history remains an unerring guide, offering insights into the evolution of legal concepts like malpractice and their implications for the healthcare landscape.

The historical context highlighted is indeed fascinating. The introduction of the term "mala praxis" by Sir William Blackstone in the 18th century represents a significant step in the evolution of legal language, particularly in relation to professional negligence. The term eventually evolved into "malpractice," a term widely used today in various fields, including medicine.

The concept of malpractice, as described by Blackstone, emphasizes the breach of trust between a professional and their client or patient, recognizing the potential harm or destruction that can result from such breaches. This legal concept reflects an important recognition of the duty professionals have towards those they serve.

In the realm of healthcare, the concept of malpractice has played a crucial role in defining the standards of care, ensuring accountability, and safeguarding the rights of patients. While the legal system has sought to bring justice and compensation to those who have suffered harm due to professional negligence, it's also true that the evolution of malpractice laws has been complex.

On one hand, malpractice laws are designed to hold healthcare professionals accountable and provide a means for patients to seek redress for injuries caused by negligence. This can contribute to building trust by establishing a system that demands accountability and fairness.

On the other hand, there are debates about the potential impact of malpractice litigation on the healthcare system. Concerns include the rise of defensive medicine (where practitioners may order unnecessary tests or procedures to avoid legal liability), increased healthcare costs, and potential impacts on the doctor-patient relationship.

History indeed provides valuable insights into the development of legal concepts like malpractice, and understanding this evolution helps inform ongoing discussions about the balance between accountability, justice, and the effective delivery of healthcare services. It's a complex interplay between the legal system, healthcare professionals, and the broader societal expectations for fairness and safety.

Then It All Began

Setting: America, 1794. A small medical board room with Mr. and Mrs. Stellar, Senior Surgeon Dr. Dale, and members of the medical board.

Act 1: The Assurance

Scene 1: Dr. Dale's Office

- Mr. and Mrs. Stellar anxiously enter Dr. Dale's office.

Mr. Stellar: "Doctor, are you confident in your skills? We've heard great things about you."

Dr. Dale: (smiling) "Mr. Stellar, I assure you, I've performed many successful surgeries. I'll do my best for your wife."

Mrs. Stellar: "Please, be careful. I'm nervous."

Dr. Dale: (soothingly) "Mrs. Stellar, you're brave. Trust me, I'll give my hundred percent."

Act 2: The Tragedy Unfolds

Scene 2: The Operating Theater

The surgery is underway, but complications arise.

Dr. Dale: (concerned) "This wasn't anticipated. Hand me that tool."

Tension fills the room as the surgery takes an unexpected turn.

Act 3: Seeking Justice

Scene 3: The Medical Board Room

Mr. Stellar, grief-stricken, confronts the medical board.

Mr. Stellar: "My wife trusted Dr. Dale's expertise, and now she's gone. This is medical negligence!"

Dr. Dale defends his actions, emphasizing the complexities of medical procedures.

Dr. Dale: "Certain things are beyond our control. I informed them of the risks involved."

Act 4: The Verdict

Scene 4: The Verdict Day

The medical board delivers its decision.

Board Member: "After careful consideration, we find that Dr. Dale didn't meet the expectations set during the consultation. Mr. Stellar, you shall be compensated."

Mr. Stellar is awarded 40 English pounds.

Summary:

This dramatic representation captures the tragic tale of Mrs. Stellar's surgery, where Dr. Dale, despite his assurance, faced unforeseen complications. Mr. Stellar, seeking justice, claimed medical negligence. The medical board, considering the breach of expectations, awarded compensation. This early case marked a shift towards punitive justice in medical negligence, emphasizing the importance of meeting promises made during medical consultations. The verdict set a precedent for future cases, shaping the evolving landscape of medical malpractice justice.

INDIA IN 1794: Beginning of loss of identity and laws

Just to make readers understand the scenario in India in those times when world has already started discussing about such punitive action against the healers we Indians were going through wars and loot. Something sinister was happening in Indian subcontinent. A colony was going to infest the country and later leave a vast web of its own legal laws which would finally come to haunt the Indian doctors of future.

In the annals of American legal history, the year was 1794, and a landmark case unfolded, marking the inception of the first-ever medical malpractice litigation in the United States. The intricacies of this case set the stage for the evolution of medical ethics and legal accountability within the rapidly advancing field of healthcare.

Meanwhile, across the vast expanse of the Indian subcontinent, in the region of Padmanabham, situated within the Visakhapatnam district of modern-day Andhra Pradesh, a parallel but dramatically different narrative was unfolding. It was on the 10th of July in that same year that the Battle of Padmanabha transpired, a tumultuous clash between the Zamindari of Vizianagaram, led by Vijayram Raj II, and the formidable forces of the East India Company's Madras Presidency, commanded by Colonel Pendargast on behalf of the British Governor of Madras, Sir Charles Oakly.

The battlefield, strewn with the echoes of cannon fire and the clash of swords, bore witness to a fierce struggle for supremacy. The British forces, representing the expanding dominion of the East India Company, sought to consolidate their authority over the region. On the opposing front, the Zamindari of Vizianagaram fiercely resisted the encroachment, embodying a struggle against colonial dominance.

As the dust settled and the echoes of gunfire subsided, the British emerged victorious, securing their dominance in the aftermath of the Battle of Padmanabha. However, this victory came at a cost. In the midst of the ferocious battle, the Zamindar, a prominent figure in the resistance, met his demise, succumbing to the fatal shot fired by an adversary's musket.

The events of the Battle of Padmanabha, though a testament to the might of colonial powers, inadvertently underscored the grim realities of armed conflicts in the 18th century. In this chaotic environment, the intricacies of medical surgeries and concerns about medical malpractice were relegated to the shadows, overshadowed by the immediate urgency of survival and geopolitical struggles.

The stark contrast between the unfolding legal developments in the United States and the harrowing battlegrounds of Padmanabham serves as a poignant reminder of the diverse challenges faced by societies during this tumultuous period in history. While one frontier grappled with the nuances of medical malpractice, the other bore witness to the clash of empires, where the stakes were measured not in legal precedents but in the lives lost and the destinies altered on the battlefield. But because this events happened we lost our own identity of compassion and just laws.

The Story Is Going To Become Murkier: It Was Gradual Though

Part 1: Emergence of Distrust (Mid-1800s - Late 1800s)

As days turned into years in the United States, a disconcerting trend began to emerge - a rising sense of distrust between doctors and patients. Over the span of approximately 50 years, from the mid-1800s to the late 1800s, the nation witnessed a surge in cases involving abuses, fights, and outright violence within the realm of healthcare. The intricacies of the doctor-patient relationship became entangled in a web of bitterness, contributing to a growing atmosphere of animosity.

Part 2: The Unraveling Thread of Trust (Mid-1800s - Late 1800s)

During this tumultuous period, numerous battles unfolded within the healthcare landscape, each exacerbating the already strained relationship between medical practitioners and the public. Stories of conflicts, both verbal and physical, added layers to the prevailing narrative of distrust. The lack of a standardized approach to medical practice further fueled the flames, with orthopedic malpractice cases and deformations arising from poorly executed amputations becoming commonplace.

Story Interlude: A Tale of Bitterness

In the midst of this turmoil, one story stands out - that of a patient who, having undergone a supposedly routine surgical procedure, found themselves facing unexpected complications. The resultant dispute escalated into a heated altercation, emblematic of the growing discord between physicians and those they were entrusted to care for. Such narratives became emblematic of a healthcare system teetering on the edge of chaos.

Part 3: The American Medical Association's Ascent (1847)

To address the escalating crisis, the American Medical Association (AMA) was founded in 1847. The primary objectives were to promote standardization within the medical profession and elevate the societal standing of physicians. However, despite these noble intentions, the AMA faced an uphill battle in restoring trust. The aftermath of botched amputations continued to haunt medical practices, and the association found itself grappling with an increasingly complex and adversarial landscape.

Part 4: Escalation of Bitterness and Violence (Late 1800s - Early 1900s)

Contrary to expectations, the formation of the AMA did not herald an era of reconciliation. Instead, bitterness and violence escalated, creating a challenging environment for doctors and patients alike. Instances of blatant medical negligence, once clear-cut in nature, transformed into a spectrum of cases grounded in perceptions and probabilities of negligence.

Story Interlude: The Case of Shifting Perceptions

A pivotal case emerged, where what might have been deemed a straightforward instance of medical negligence became entangled in shifting perceptions. The blurred lines between actual negligence and perceived wrongdoing further muddied the waters, contributing to the pervasive climate of distrust.

Conclusion: The Complex Evolution of Doctor-Patient Dynamics

In tracing the trajectory of doctor-patient relations over these critical decades, a nuanced picture emerges. The evolution from outright abuses and violence to complex legal battles reflects the intricate dance between societal expectations, medical advancements, and the quest for accountability. The road ahead for the medical profession would prove challenging, as it navigated through an increasingly litigious landscape, striving to regain the trust that had eroded over time.

The Story Tells All: Patient Is The Ultimate King, They Are Allowed To Forget And Still Accuse.

In March 1857, amidst the bustling streets and markets of New York, a tragic incident unfolded. A massive crowd had gathered due to the day being a Sunday, creating an atmosphere of hustle and bustle. Under a building, a group of people stood enjoying their evening beer when suddenly, a colossal chimney collapsed, trapping Mr. Dove beneath its weight. The impact was severe, resulting in crushed legs and unconsciousness.

Promptly, Mr. Dove was rushed to a nearby hospital. During this era, the United States was slowly advancing in healthcare, witnessing the growth of corporate hospitals. In the emergency department, Dr. Dale and Dr. Dennis were on duty. After a preliminary examination, they concluded that the chances of surgical intervention for Mr. Dove were negligible. His crushed leg, shock, and the potential onset of other organ failures led them to decide against an operation.

Mrs. Dove, anxiously awaited any information on her husband's condition. In the emergency department, a palpable tension filled the air as Dr. Dale and Dr. Dennis discussed the severity of Mr. Dove's injuries.

Mrs. Dove, her eyes reflecting a mix of fear and hope, approached the doctors, seeking solace in their expertise. "Doctors, please tell me what's happening. How is my husband?" she pleaded, her voice trembling with worry.

Dr. Dale, with a gentle yet concerned demeanor, began to explain the critical situation. "Mrs. Dove, your husband has suffered significant injuries. His leg is crushed, and there's a risk of shock and potential organ failure. We're doing our best, but we must be honest with you – the chances of a surgical intervention seem negligible at this point."

Her eyes widened with concern, Mrs. Dove pressed for more information. "But what can be done? How can we help him?" she implored, desperately seeking a glimmer of hope.

Dr. Dennis, compassionate yet realistic, continued the dialogue. "We're considering options to stabilize him, given the risks involved in surgery.

At this point, our priority is to mitigate further complications. We believe applying splints to both legs is the best course of action. It won't be a cure, but it might prevent additional damage and, in good faith, alleviate some financial burden for your family."

Mrs. Dove, torn between the fear for her husband's life and the need to make practical decisions, nodded with a mixture of gratitude and trepidation. "Do whatever it takes to help him, doctors. We trust you," she whispered, her eyes expressing a silent plea for reassurance.

The doctors, recognizing the weight of the moment, shared a solemn nod with Mrs. Dove, acknowledging the shared responsibility in the challenging journey ahead. In those critical moments, trust became the anchor that held them together in the face of uncertainty.

Against the odds, Mr. Dove defied the grim prognosis. Gradually, he regained consciousness, started eating well, and gained strength. As his various organs improved, the day arrived when the doctors decided to remove the splint.

Throughout this ordeal, Dr. Dale and Dr. Dennis kept the family informed about Mr. Dove's health. They were aware that the avoided operation at the time of the accident could not be performed now.

When the splint was finally removed, Mrs. Dove, having witnessed her husband's survival against all odds, pondered the possibility of a corrective operation. However, Dr. Dennis explained that nearly two months had passed, and a routine operation might not be feasible. The extent of union and the potential for further intervention could only be determined after opening the splint and conducting x-rays.

Mrs. Dove, concerned about her husband's ability to walk, sought reassurance. Dr. Dale and Dr. Dennis, looking at each other, conveyed that the chances of Mr. Dove walking again were minimal. Despite the uncertainty, they emphasized taking one step at a time and suggested opening the splint first.

Mr. Dove's sudden outburst reverberated through the room, breaking the heavy silence that hung over the discussion about his recovery. He fixed his gaze on Dr. Dale with an intensity that demanded answers. "Tell me, doc. Can I walk again?" he demanded, his voice a mix of desperation and determination.

Dr. Dale, acknowledging the gravity of the question, met Mr. Dove's eyes with sincerity. "Mr. Dove, I'll be frank with you. Given the extent of the damage to your legs, the chances of walking again are quite slim. The impact on your limbs was severe, and we have to be realistic about the recovery prospects."

Mrs. Dove, standing by her husband's side, couldn't contain her concern. "But you were wrong about him not surviving the operation initially, weren't you?" she interjected, her eyes searching for a glimmer of hope.

Dr. Dale sighed, recognizing the weight of the moment. "Yes, we were wrong about the survival odds, and we are truly thankful that he pulled through. But the situation with his legs is different. The damage is extensive, and walking might be an uphill battle."

Mr. Dove, frustration evident in his voice, pressed on. "So, you're saying I'm stuck like this? I can't accept that. There must be something that can be done."

Mrs. Dove, torn between the harsh reality and her husband's unwavering spirit, sought clarification. "Doctors, is there no possibility of improvement? Could he not undergo some therapy or surgery to regain mobility?"

Dr. Dale exchanged a knowing glance with Dr. Dennis before responding, "Mrs. Dove, we understand your concern, but the reality is that the extent of the damage makes it highly improbable. We're here to support Mr. Dove in every way we can, but we have to be transparent about the challenges ahead."

Mr. Dove, frustrated yet determined, voiced his discontent. "So, I survive a falling chimney, only to be told I'll never walk again? What kind of life is that?"

Dr. Dennis, empathizing with his patient's plight, tried to convey a sense of understanding. "Mr. Dove, we're truly sorry for what you're going through. Survival is a remarkable feat, and we'll continue to do our best to assist you in this journey. Let's take one step at a time, and we can explore options for support and rehabilitation."

As the room filled with a heavy silence, the uncertainty of the future weighed on everyone. The delicate balance between hope and reality played out in the intense exchange between the doctors and the Doves, as they grappled with the profound implications of the challenges that lay ahead.Dr. Dennis attempted to explain, but the issue of potential mobility became a focal point now that survival was assured. As the splint was opened and x-rays conducted, the patient was discharged, and opinions were sought. The consensus was that an operation at this point would not be beneficial, and Mr. Dove would likely be unable to walk.

Dr. Shane, a new face in the medical narrative, entered the scene with a confident stride, his eyes scanning Mr. Dove's medical chart. Sensing the charged atmosphere, he cleared his throat before speaking. " May I offer a different perspective?"

Mr. Dove, his frustration apparent, turned his gaze toward Dr. Shane, a mix of curiosity and desperation in his eyes. "What do you have to say, Doc?" he inquired, his voice a blend of hope and skepticism.

Dr. Shane, undeterred by the weight of the moment, began to share his viewpoint. "In my professional opinion, considering the severity of Mr. Dove's injuries, early surgical intervention might have increased the chances of survival and a more favorable outcome. It's a delicate balance, and timing can play a crucial role."

Mrs. Dove, grappling with conflicting emotions, voiced her concerns. "But the other doctors said the risks were too high at that time. They were concerned about him not surviving the operation."

Dr. Shane, with a measured response, countered, "Understandable, but sometimes, taking calculated risks in surgery can be the turning point. Survival rates often improve with prompt action, and in Mr. Dove's case, it might have been worth considering."

Mr. Dove, caught in the crossfire of conflicting opinions, expressed his frustration. "So, what you're saying is they messed up by not operating early? I've been through enough already."

Dr. Shane attempted to clarify, "Mr. Dove, hindsight is always clearer. I'm not blaming anyone, but exploring surgical options early on might have presented a different set of challenges. It's a complex situation with no easy answers."

Mrs. Dove, torn between the different perspectives, sought assurance. "But is there anything that can be done now? Can we still consider surgery?"

Dr. Shane, maintaining his stance, responded, "It's not a straightforward decision. The window for early intervention has passed, and opening the possibility of surgery now comes with its own set of complications. It's a challenging scenario, and we must carefully evaluate the risks."

As the room absorbed the conflicting opinions, the frustration and confusion in Mr. Dove's eyes mirrored the complex reality they were navigating. The addition of Dr. Shane's perspective added a layer of uncertainty, leaving the Doves grappling with the difficult choices ahead.

Frustrated and determined, Mr. Dove decided to take legal action against Dr. Dale and Dr. Dennis. Dr. Shane characterized the situation as an act of commission, and Mr. Dove, armed with six attorneys, 15 physician witnesses, and 21 other witnesses, filed a lawsuit against the two physicians.

In the midst of the mid-1800s, a legal titan-to-be emerged, not in the courtroom but on the political stage – Abraham Lincoln. Before ascending to the presidency as America's 16th leader, Lincoln carved his legal path as a distinguished medical malpractice attorney. His prowess in the legal arena extended to cases involving both physicians and patients, showcasing his nuanced understanding of the complexities within the medical field.

In a twist of fate, Lincoln found himself representing two defendant physicians embroiled in a case linked to Mr. Dove, the unfortunate victim of a falling chimney. The small town buzzed with anticipation as Lincoln prepared to weave his legal magic in a courtroom drama that would test the boundaries of medical law during those bygone days.

With the town's only other 12 physicians as his clients, Lincoln embarked on a strategic legal journey. In a nod to the principles that would later form the foundation of modern statutes of limitations, Lincoln, with his keen legal acumen, recognized the importance of time in shaping the defense strategy. Like a chess grandmaster, he sought to leverage the passage of time and the acquisition of fresh and compelling evidence to bolster the physicians' case.

In a series of legal maneuvers, Lincoln obtained numerous postponements, deftly playing the legal chessboard to his advantage. The courtroom became a stage where he orchestrated the dance of litigation, each delay serving as a note in a symphony of legal tactics designed to tip the scales in his clients' favor.

As the trial unfolded, Lincoln skillfully navigated the nuances of medical malpractice law in an era where precedents were still being etched. He argued with eloquence and finesse, presenting a compelling case that left the jury hanging in suspense. The courtroom buzzed with the energy of legal theatrics, with Lincoln, the maestro of legal strategy, orchestrating a performance that would be remembered in the annals of legal history.

The complex dilemma faced by the surgeon in cases like Mr. Dove's is a reality. It underscores the intricate balance and risks involved for a surgeon dealing with critical patients where the decision to operate or not operate can have legal ramifications. On one hand, operating on a critically injured patient holds the risk of potential complications or even death on the table, which could lead to legal liability for the surgeon. On the other hand, refraining from immediate surgery to ensure the patient's survival first might be criticized as delayed treatment, also carrying legal consequences.

The irony lies in the patient's ability to file a case, often claiming a layman's understanding while navigating the legal complexities of medical decisions and outcomes. This case epitomizes the intricate legal and ethical tightrope that physicians walk when faced with critical medical situations, especially when the outcomes are uncertain or the risks of intervention are high.

India In 1857

FIGHT TO FINISH BEGAN. BUT BY NOW BRITISHERS HAVE INTRODUCED ALL THEIR LAWS IN INDIA.

In the annals of history, the mid-19th century marked a pivotal era, witnessing two contrasting narratives unfold on opposite sides of the globe. While America grappled with issues of medical negligence and the evolving discourse on human rights in healthcare, India found itself embroiled in a different struggle - a fight for overall human rights and freedom from the oppressive yoke of colonial rule.

As America dealt with the complexities of medical malpractice cases, India was entrenched in the midst of a political and social upheaval that would shape the course of its history. The year 1857 saw the eruption of the Indian Rebellion, a significant revolt against the British Empire, catalyzed by the actions of Mangal Pandey, an Indian sepoy in the British East India Company's army.

The catalyst for this rebellion lay in the British regimen's controversial use of ammunition rumored to be coated with cow and pig fat. For Hindus, the cow is considered sacred, and for Muslims, the pig is considered impure. The use of such bullets offended the religious sentiments of both communities, and this seemingly trivial yet deeply symbolic act became the spark that ignited a widespread revolt.

India, at that time, was still ensnared in the shackles of British colonial rule, and the people were grappling with a duality of oppression. On one front, they were subjugated by a foreign power that sought to exploit the resources of the land, and on another, they were forced to reconcile with actions that trampled upon their religious beliefs. The revolt of 1857, therefore, transcended a mere uprising against military policies; it was a manifestation of a deep-seated yearning for freedom and the restoration of basic human rights.

As the echoes of rebellion reverberated across the Indian subcontinent, a profound transformation was underway. What began as a protest against religious insensitivity evolved into a larger, fervent call for freedom and the recognition of the inherent human rights that were being systematically denied.

In stark contrast to the discourse on medical negligence and patient rights in the Western world, India's struggle for independence took center stage, fueling a movement that sought to break the chains of colonial oppression and reclaim the fundamental rights that had been trampled upon for far too long.

The narrative of this era is a poignant reminder that while the world elsewhere grappled with evolving notions of human rights within the confines of medical treatment, India was engaged in a battle that extended beyond healthcare - a battle for the holistic restoration of human rights and the triumph over a centuries-old imperialistic regime. The fight that began with the rebellion of 1857 sowed the seeds of a larger, more extensive movement that would culminate in India gaining its hard-fought independence in 1947. In the grand tapestry of history, these parallel struggles stand as testaments to the diverse battles humanity waged in pursuit of justice, freedom, and the universal recognition of the inherent rights of every individual.

From 1847 To 1970- They Should Have Done A Course Correction. But They Did Not....

The transformation of the medical profession in the 19th century ushered in a sea change in how society perceived doctors. Once revered as saviors and intellectuals dedicated to serving humanity, doctors found themselves cast as villains in the eyes of the public, the media, and even the political and judicial spheres. A profession once regarded as noble and virtuous suddenly became entangled in a web of suspicion and accusations.

The dawn of the 20th century brought significant upheaval to the American healthcare landscape.

In the early 1900s, amidst the backdrop of the industrial revolution, there was a concerted effort to organize healthcare. President Theodore Roosevelt recognized the importance of health insurance, asserting that the strength of a country was compromised when its people were sick and poor. However, attempts to implement compulsory health insurance faced staunch opposition from the American Medical Association and insurance companies, stalling its progress.

The subsequent decades, from 1910 to 1948, unfolded against the backdrop of World War I, the Great Depression, and World War II. World War I prompted efforts to provide healthcare to the military and veterans, setting the stage for a strained relationship between doctors and patients in the post-war era. The escalating costs of healthcare, coupled with economic downturns, intensified the debate on accessible healthcare for all.

Amidst the economic challenges of the 1930s, the Social Security Act of 1935 emerged as a pivotal development, creating a system to provide public support for the retired, elderly, unemployed, and disabled. However, it was during World War II in the early 1940s that significant shifts occurred. The war effort led to the emergence of employer-sponsored health insurance and the innovative prepaid insurance model introduced by Henry Kaiser. These developments became the precursors to the future healthcare system, establishing insurance structures that would shape the landscape for years to come.

Post-World War II, President Truman proposed the ambitious idea of Universal healthcare for all Americans, transcending social and economic boundaries. However, faced with resistance, this proposal was relegated to the back burner. The mid-20th century thus witnessed the evolution of the American healthcare system, shaped by a complex interplay of historical events, wars, economic challenges, and the dynamic relationship between healthcare providers, insurance structures, and government initiatives.

By this time, the trust between doctors and patients had reached its nadir, resulting in a surge of filed lawsuits that persisted for the next two decades. This trend was further exacerbated by another phase in the evolution of American healthcare, marked by significant progress from the 1950s onwards.

In 1950, amidst the backdrop of the Korean War, the third conflict in 40 years, the field of medicine continued to advance rapidly. The discovery of penicillin was a groundbreaking development, and in 1952, Jonas Salk's team at the University of Pittsburgh achieved a major milestone by creating an effective polio vaccine. Additionally, the first successful organ transplant took place when Dr. Joseph Murray and Dr. David Hume performed a kidney transplant between twin brothers. These medical breakthroughs continued to unfold, marking a period of remarkable progress.

However, this wave of advancement came at a significant cost for the American public. Healthcare expenses doubled and, in some instances, even tripled. The soaring costs left the American people apprehensive about falling ill and seeking medical attention. The exorbitant bills made affordable healthcare an elusive prospect. In response to this growing concern, the government intervened, and over the next 15 to 20 years, various administrations, through successive presidents, worked towards the implementation of the Social Security Act and the establishment of national health insurance.

By the 1960s and 1970s, the number of medical malpractice lawsuits had surged by an alarming 300 percent. Initially, these legal actions primarily stemmed from cases involving misdiagnosis or failure to diagnose, such as errors in reading X-rays, medication mistakes, and incorrect procedures. Physicians found themselves facing legal consequences for their actions, being sued for tangible errors they made.

However, a notable shift occurred, and doctors began facing lawsuits not just for what they did wrong but also for what they

failed to do right. Instances of litigation increased for failures in ordering crucial tests and diagnostic procedures, such as neglecting to request radiological reports or timely diagnose conditions like cancer. (A COMPLETE ANARCHY)

The legal landscape witnessed a notable uptick in jury verdicts and out-of-court settlements during the 1970s. Physicians found themselves financially liable, with plaintiffs being awarded millions of dollars due to the alleged negligence of doctors in omitting critical tests. The fear of lawsuits and the past experiences of legal action became powerful motivators for physicians to err on the side of caution and order more tests. This shift in practice was further reinforced by the insatiable demand from the public for both radiologic and non-radiologic tests, ranging from routine screenings to the investigation of minor symptoms or various medical conditions.

The looming threat of liability, rooted in concerns about errors of omission, began to exert a profound influence on the day-to-day practices of virtually all physicians. The landscape of medical care witnessed a paradigm shift, with the specter of legal repercussions shaping the decisions and actions of healthcare professionals as they navigated the delicate balance between ensuring thorough diagnostic procedures and meeting the public's demands for comprehensive medical assessments.

Deadly Combination: An Unsatisfied Patient And A Lawyer.

On January 1, 1951, Mrs. Smith sought the expertise of a skin specialist, Dr. Rice, for a wart on her thigh. Though not painful, its cosmetic appearance troubled her. Dr. Rice, upon examination, suggested removal and a subsequent biopsy. Concerned, Mrs. Smith questioned the need for a biopsy, preferring a straightforward removal. Dr. Rice explained the routine protocol of sending removed tissues for biopsy, eventually convincing Mrs. Smith to undergo the surgery.

Dr. Rice:" Good morning, Mrs. Smith. How can I help you today?"

Mrs. Smith: "Well, Dr. Rice, I have this wart on my thigh, and it's bothering me. Can you do something about it?"

Dr. Rice: "Of course, Mrs. Smith. Let me take a look." (examines the wart) "Ah, I see what you mean. It's not painful, but I understand the cosmetic concern."

Mrs. Smith: "Yes, exactly. Can't we just remove it? Why the need for a biopsy?"

Dr. Rice:" I appreciate your concern. Here's the thing – when we remove such growths, it's standard practice to send them for biopsy. It helps us understand the nature of the tissue and ensures we're not missing anything important."

Mrs. Smith: (worried) "But what if it's nothing serious? I don't want unnecessary tests."

Dr. Rice: "I completely understand. The biopsy is a precautionary measure. We want to rule out any potential issues and ensure we provide the best care."

Mrs. Smith: (hesitant) "I don't know, Dr. Rice. It seems like a lot for a simple wart."

Dr. Rice: "I assure you, Mrs. Smith, it's a routine procedure, and your well-being is our priority. It's better to be thorough and catch any potential problems early on."

Mrs. Smith: (pausing) "Well, if you say so, Dr. Rice. But I don't want anything unnecessary."

Dr. Rice:" I hear you, Mrs. Smith. We'll proceed with the removal, and I'll do my best to keep it as straightforward as possible."

The interaction concludes with Mrs. Smith agreeing to the procedure, albeit with lingering concerns about the necessity of the biopsy.

Post-surgery, the biopsy revealed Malignant Melanoma.

Dr. Rice: "Mrs. Smith, I understand this is a challenging situation, but the biopsy results indicate that the growth is malignant. We need to act swiftly to prevent it from spreading."

Mrs. Smith: (concerned) "Dr. Rice, I appreciate your concern, but I've heard stories about misdiagnoses. Are you absolutely sure about this?"

Dr. Rice:" I share your concern, Mrs. Smith, but these results are highly accurate. I wouldn't recommend further action if it wasn't crucial for your well-being."

Mrs. Smith: (skeptical) "Deeper excision sounds like a major surgery, Dr. Rice. I'm afraid of disfigurement."

Dr. Rice: "I understand your fear, Mrs. Smith. But a slightly deeper excision is necessary to ensure we remove any potentially affected tissue."

Mrs. Smith: (hesitant) "Can't we just monitor it? I don't want more surgeries unless we're absolutely certain."

Dr. Rice: (trying to reassure) " I wish it were that simple, Mrs. Smith, but this type of melanoma can be aggressive. I want to make sure we address it comprehensively."

After much back-and-forth, they reach a compromise for a slightly deeper excision.

Dr. Rice: "Thank you for understanding, Mrs. Smith. This will greatly reduce the risk of recurrence."

The subsequent biopsy, however, surprises both Dr. Rice and Mrs. Smith.

Dr. Rice: (amazed) "Mrs. Smith, the results came back benign. This is unexpected, but it's a relief".

Mrs. Smith: (frustrated) "Dr. Rice, you wanted a deeper excision, and now the results show it's benign. I can't go through more surgeries based on uncertainty".

Dr. Rice: (cautious) "I share your frustration, Mrs. Smith. However, this doesn't guarantee it won't turn malignant in the future. A more thorough excision could provide long-term assurance."

Mrs. Smith: (resistant) "Dr. Rice, I can't keep going through surgeries on "could be" scenarios. I need assurance, not more uncertainty."

Despite attempts to explain, trust was shattered.

Mrs. Smith sought medical care elsewhere after two years when the growth returned. Sadly, the biopsy confirmed malignant melanoma. Extensive surgery followed, but the disease had already spread, leading to severe complications and Mrs. Smith's eventual demise.

Before her death, Mrs. Smith urged her son, Mr. Dan, to sue Dr. Rice. Seeking justice, Mr. Dan enlisted the services of a medical malpractice lawyer, Mr. Toad. The lawyer, working on a contingency basis, assured Mr. Dan that he would only be paid if they won the case.

The legal battle unfolded over two years, with Dr. Rice finding himself in court alongside five other doctors facing similar lawsuits. During the trial, Mr. Toad grilled Dr. Rice on his handling of the case, emphasizing the importance of early detection for complete cure.

Mr. Toad: "Good morning, Dr. Rice. Let's get straight to it. Did you inform Mrs. Smith about the possibility of complete cure if melanoma is detected early?"

Dr. Rice: "Well, that's a hypothetical question."

Mr. Toad: (leaning in) "Did you convey this information to Mrs. Smith?"

Dr. Rice: "Multiple times. But she refused to understand."

Mr. Toad: (nodding) "Yet, nowhere in your notes is it mentioned that you discussed this possibility with the patient?"

Dr. Rice: "It's there, but maybe not explicitly."

Mr. Toad: (raising an eyebrow) "Why is it not explicitly mentioned, Dr. Rice?"

Dr. Rice: (pausing) "Well, the notes are a summary. I can't write down every detail in every case."

Mr. Toad: (smirking) "But isn't this detail crucial? A matter of life and death?"

Dr. Rice: (defensively) "I believed she understood the risks."

Mr. Toad: (leaning back) "Let's talk about the biopsy reports. Two different results from two different pathologists. Why did you not seek a third opinion?"

Dr. Rice: (sighing) "The second report indicated a benign growth. I chose to proceed cautiously."

Mr. Toad: (accusingly) "You were dependent on pathologists, Dr. Rice. But did you provide a radical approach to the patient?"

Dr. Rice: (hesitant) "I discussed the possibility of a deeper excision, but Mrs. Smith was resistant."

Mr. Toad: (addressing the jury) "Ladies and gentlemen, Dr. Rice's dependency on conflicting pathology reports led to a lack of decisive action. He should have either sought a third opinion or recommended a radical approach. He failed to do so, and though not a criminal, he was negligent."

The jury deliberates, and after a tense wait, they deliver their verdict.

Jury Foreperson: "We find Dr. Rice guilty of negligence. Mrs. Smith's version is absent, and relying solely on the doctor's account is not enough. We recommend holding him accountable."

The lawyer secures a settlement for Mr. Dan, taking a percentage of the amount.

Mr. Toad: (smirking) "Another win for justice. Let this be a lesson to all doctors – negligence has consequences."

The courtroom empties, leaving behind a sense of resolution and a lingering tension between the pursuit of justice and the complexities of medical practice.

Media Outrage Unleashed:

As the courtroom drama unfolded, the media wasted no time in seizing the narrative, crafting sensational headlines that painted Dr. Rice as the "killer doctor in a white coat." The public, always hungry for a story that blended tragedy and controversy, eagerly consumed the damning headlines.

Headline 1: "The Killer Doctor Unmasked!"

The first headline hit like a sledgehammer, questioning Dr. Rice's competence and expertise. "He does not know the difference between a normal wart and cancer. How can he miss such a big thing?" The media played the emotional card, emphasizing the patient's unfortunate demise and questioning the worth of any compensation paid to the grieving family.

Headline 2: "Paying for Malpractice: A License to Practice?"

The second publication took a more accusatory tone, suggesting that Dr. Rice's ability to pay for malpractice might grant him the license to continue practicing. "How can he be allowed to practice? He will pay and then practice. How many more victims?" The insinuation lingered in the minds of the public, fostering a sense of distrust in the medical profession.

Headline 3: "America's Descent into Medical Chaos!"

In a grandiose proclamation, the third headline proclaimed, "America is going from bad to worse because of these killer doctors." The media, in its pursuit of sensationalism, painted a bleak picture of the entire healthcare system, instilling fear and distrust in the hearts of the American populace.

The Ripple Effect:

The media's onslaught had a profound ripple effect. Fear now gripped patients across the nation, and the number of lawsuits against doctors surged. The very individuals sworn to heal were now viewed with suspicion, their every decision questioned. Doctors found themselves not only battling malpractice suits but also contending with a tarnished image in the eyes of the public.

The courtroom verdict, initially seen as a triumph for patient rights, had inadvertently cast a dark shadow over the entire medical community. The intricate dance between media sensationalism and public perception became a force capable of shaping the landscape of healthcare, leaving both doctors and patients entangled in a web of uncertainty and mistrust.

The Legal Gold Rush: Lawyers Pivot to Medical Malpractice

In the aftermath of high-profile medical malpractice cases, a paradigm shift occurred within the legal landscape. Lawyers, astute to the potential windfall, began strategically redirecting their practices toward the lucrative realm of medical malpractice. The allure of substantial settlements and the perception of doctors as vulnerable targets fueled this migration.

Understanding the Easy Money:

Lawyers keenly observed the media frenzy surrounding malpractice cases and recognized the gold mine that lay in representing aggrieved patients. The emotional potency of these cases, coupled with the promise of significant financial compensation, presented an irresistible opportunity for legal practitioners seeking high-profile and high-reward cases.

The Legal Landscape Transformed:

Seasoned attorneys, once immersed in various legal domains, swiftly adapted to the changing dynamics. They recognized that medical malpractice cases had become a powerful narrative, capturing public attention and sympathy. Consequently, these legal professionals strategically rebranded themselves as champions of patient rights, ready to take on the allegedly negligent medical establishment.

Mastery of the Law:

These lawyers, well-versed in the nuances of medical malpractice law, understood its complexities and how to navigate them for maximum impact. They knew that building a case against a doctor required a meticulous understanding of medical procedures, terminology, and the intricate details of patient care. Armed with this knowledge, they crafted compelling narratives that resonated with juries and the wider public.

The Art of Paperwork:

Crucially, lawyers realized that time was on their side. Medical malpractice cases were not only emotionally charged but also legally intricate. Lawyers, well aware of the psychological toll protracted legal battles took on doctors, employed a strategic use of paperwork. The constant filing of motions, requests, and subpoenas became a tactic to wear down the resolve of physicians.

Frustrating the Doctors:

Doctors, committed to their profession and the well-being of their patients, found themselves entangled in a legal web. The sheer volume of paperwork, coupled with the demanding nature of their medical practices, left them physically and emotionally drained. Lawyers exploited this vulnerability, understanding that frustrated and fatigued doctors might be more inclined to settle rather than endure prolonged legal battles.

The Legal Gold Rush Unleashed:

This shift in legal focus triggered a veritable gold rush in the legal community. Lawyers specializing in medical malpractice cases became sought-after figures, representing a growing clientele of patients seeking retribution for perceived negligence. The symbiotic relationship between media sensationalism, public perception, and legal opportunism reshaped the dynamics of medical malpractice litigation, transforming it into a powerful force that transcended the courtroom.

In this evolving landscape, the intersection of law, medicine, and public sentiment became a battleground where reputations hung in the balance, and the pursuit of justice became entangled with the pursuit of financial gain.

Add To This A Media Spices And The Dish You Cook Is Tasty

Mr. Stan was discharged from the hospital after being admitted in the emergency department on day 1 due to abdominal pain. He had suffered from fever and vomiting, which were initially treated as an infectious cause. It was discovered that he had consumed a significant amount of outside food on the same day, and the following day, he had indulged in excessive alcohol consumption with friends. Dr. Nale, attending physician, conducted a thorough history and examination, uncovering that Mr. Stan was also taking drugs. He admitted, "Dr., I had a few pain medications, so I took them myself. But instead of relieving the pain, they caused vomiting."

Dr. Nale promptly ordered investigations and initiated symptomatic treatment. When asked about the possible diagnoses, he explained, "It may be simple food poisoning, drug-induced gastritis, drug-induced perforation, or even appendicitis."

Mr. Stan, bewildered by the array of potential diagnoses, exclaimed, "Dr., you're telling me so many possibilities. How is it possible that you can't diagnose a simple abdominal pain?"

Remaining composed, Dr. Nale, a mature doctor with 20 years of experience, responded, "Sir, our stomach is like a miracle box. Considering your consumption of outside food, painkillers, alcohol, and drug abuse, each one has the potential to harm you."

Mr. Stan, growing frustrated, retorted, "Dr., don't teach me how to live my life. You better do your job and provide a proper diagnosis and treatment."

Despite the tension, the patient was eventually diagnosed with food poisoning and drug-induced gastritis. He received appropriate treatment.

As Mr. Stan lay in his hospital bed, Dr. Nale decided to involve both Mr. Stan's wife and the patient in a discussion about his health. Dr. Nale, a seasoned professional, recognized the need for a collaborative approach.

Dr. Nale: "Mr. Stan, I understand that you're frustrated, and I appreciate your concerns. Your wife is here, and I think it would be beneficial for all of us to discuss your health and the way forward."

Mrs. Stan, visibly concerned, took a seat beside her husband, holding his hand.

Mrs. Stan: "Doctor, we just want him to get better. Please, tell us how we can help."

Dr. Nale: "Certainly, Mrs. Stan. I believe a key part of Mr. Stan's recovery involves addressing his lifestyle choices. We need to work together to create a plan that ensures he's making healthier decisions moving forward."

Mr. Stan, still irritated, reluctantly agreed to participate in the discussion.

Mr. Stan: "Fine, but make it quick. I just want to get out of here."

Dr. Nale: "I understand, Mr. Stan. Let's discuss your daily routine, diet, and how we can make sustainable changes. Mrs. Stan, your support is crucial in helping him adopt a healthier lifestyle."

Mrs. Stan: "Of course, Doctor. I'm willing to do whatever it takes to help him."

Dr. Nale: "Good. Now, Mr. Stan, let's talk about your pain management. Instead of self-medicating, we can explore alternative treatments and therapies that won't jeopardize your health."

As the conversation continued, Dr. Nale encouraged both Mr. Stan and his wife to actively participate in the decision-making process. They discussed dietary changes, exercise routines, and methods to manage stress without resorting to unhealthy coping mechanisms.

Back at home, Mr. Stan persisted in his unhealthy habits. Just three days after his discharge, he resorted to heavy painkillers for leg pain, plunging himself into severe abdominal pain. Concerned, his relatives rushed him to the hospital. However, before they could reach the medical facility, he went into cardiac arrest and was declared dead upon arrival.

Devastated, Mrs. Stan went into shock, her grief pouring out in anguished cries. In her distress, she directed her anger towards the hospital and its staff, accusing them of her husband's demise.

Mrs. Stan: "This hospital killed my husband! He was here just a few days ago, and you people didn't treat him properly. Now he's dead. You're all murderers!"

The hospital manager, trying to diffuse the situation, approached Mrs. Stan calmly.

Manager: "Madam, I understand your pain, but creating chaos and shouting won't help. Please, come to my office, and we can discuss this."

Mrs. Stan, still engulfed in her grief, accused the manager of intending to bribe her.

Mrs. Stan: "You want to bribe me, calling me to your cabin now?"

The manager attempted to call her into his office, realizing the importance of addressing her concerns and maintaining order in the hospital. However, Mrs. Stan resisted, convinced that her accusations were justified.

In the midst of this emotional turmoil, the hospital staff tried to navigate the delicate situation, striving to provide comfort and address Mrs. Stan's grievances. The tragic turn of events highlighted the complex challenges faced by both healthcare professionals and grieving families in times of crisis.

As the tragic events unfolded, an unexpected twist added fuel to the already somber atmosphere. News of Mr. Stan's demise reached the media, and like a swarm of hungry vultures, three to four news channels descended upon the hospital, armed with cameras and probing questions.

The spotlight shifted to Mrs. Stan, who, in her grief, became the unwitting protagonist in this media frenzy.

Reporter: "Mrs. Stan, can you share your thoughts on what happened to your husband? Do you believe the hospital is responsible?"

Cameras rolled as Mrs. Stan, caught in the whirlwind of emotions, poured out her grievances, accusing the hospital of being a deathtrap.

Meanwhile, the news crews, sensing a sensational story, turned their attention to other patients in the hospital, desperate for any tidbit that could add drama to their breaking news segment.

Reporter 2: "We're here at the scene where a family is claiming their loved one was a victim of medical negligence. What do you have to say about the conditions in this hospital?"

Patients and their families, initially seeking medical attention, found themselves thrust into the media spotlight, sharing their experiences with a mix of shock and apprehension.

The elusive hospital manager stepped into the fray, attempting to control the narrative and present the hospital's side of the story.

Manager: "We deeply regret the loss, but we are investigating the matter. Please understand, we are committed to providing the best care to our patients."

However, the media circus continued its relentless pursuit, determined to uncover a villain in this tragedy. Dr. Nale, fortunately off-duty, narrowly escaped the probing questions, avoiding the storm brewing within the hospital walls.

In the midst of the media frenzy, one anchor's voice pierced the air like a siren of condemnation.

Anchor: "These killer doctors are on a rampage! Who will stop them?"

A sensational guest on the show seized the opportunity to amplify the drama.

Guest: "Hospitals and doctors are slaughtering more patients than a war can. They don't even know how to diagnose!"

A representative from the patient's side joined the cacophony, alleging negligence.

Patient Advocate: "Mr. Stan visited the emergency department three days ago. The doctor suspected stomach perforation but didn't order a sonography or standing x-ray. This is outrageous!"

The anchor, fueled by the sensational narrative, declared doctors as lethal machines.

Anchor: "These doctors have become killing machines, using their degrees to experiment on us and sentence us to death!"

A doctor, invited to the show to provide perspective, defended the medical profession.

Doctor: "Why are you saying such absurd things? The emergency doctor attended to the patient promptly. He recovered within an hour, so there was no need for an x-ray or sonography."

Unyielding, the anchor questioned the authority of medical decisions.

Anchor: "Who decides there's no need? It could have saved the patient's life. Doctors are playing with lives!"

The doctor, undeterred, fired back.

Doctor: "If doctors aren't needed to make decisions, why don't you go and treat? It's easy to criticize from the sidelines!"

In this sensationalized exchange, the narrative painted doctors as heartless experimenters, hospitals as death traps, and the anchor as the fiery advocate for justice in the face of perceived medical negligence.

The television studio crackled with tension as the heated exchange between the incensed anchor and the unyielding doctor reached a fever pitch.

Anchor, seething with anger: "You people have become rude! You don't have any grace left. For money and substandard care, our citizens are dying."

The doctor, undeterred, shot back with a scathing critique of the media's sensational tactics.

Doctor, accusingly: "What absurdity! The media has become a TRP-hungry monster. You're selling your soul, harping on people who have suffered or died, and blaming the very individuals who tried to save them!"

The anchor, persistent in his pursuit, challenged the doctor on the patient's tragic outcome.

Anchor, accusingly: "Doctor, isn't it true this patient would have survived if you had conducted radiography reports or endoscopy in time?"

The doctor, standing firm, clarified the circumstances surrounding the patient's demise.

Doctor, sternly: "Do you even know why this patient died? He died because of stomach perforation. That happens when it happens. When he came to the emergency room, he had gastritis due to painkillers and food poisoning."

The guest chimed in, suggesting that perhaps keeping the patient in the hospital would have made a difference.

Doctor, defensively: "If we keep the patient for observation, then this same media and you would be sitting here accusing us of looting. Extra bills, unnecessary admissions, and medicines. Make up your mind."

The anchor, infuriated by the doctor's stance, accused him of deflecting blame.

Anchor, angrily: "How rude! You do wrong, and still, you blame us."

The doctor, undeterred, responded with a stark reminder of the complexity of medical science.

Doctor, emphatically: "You people have no idea how complex medical science is and how unpredictable it can be."

The anchor, not to be outdone, recounted a tragic tale of medical misjudgement.

Anchor, accusingly: "Just the other day, a patient went to the doctor for chest pain. His report came back normal. He was sent home and died in his bed that night. The attending doctor later said he died of sudden cardiac arrest."

A guest added another layer to the narrative, sharing a heart breaking story of a surgical procedure gone awry.

Guest, emotionally: "Exactly! I know a patient who underwent cancer surgery and died a few days later due to bleeding from the site of the operation."

In a final flourish of sensationalism, the anchor called for drastic measures.

Anchor, passionately: "I ask the government to revoke the licenses of all these killers and don't allow them to practice!"

The doctor, with a touch of sarcasm, retorted with a challenge to the anchor's proposed solution.

Doctor, sarcastically: "Oh, then you'll go and treat the patients, or perhaps the government will send them to some other country?"

In the dark corridors of media sensationalism, a sinister dance unfolds as the public is led astray by distorted narratives. The media, hungry for attention-grabbing headlines, plays a pivotal role in fostering a victim mentality among patients, showcasing extreme cases as the norm in hospitals.

Not too long ago, a national newspaper in Italy splashed a shocking headline across its front page, declaring that giving birth in Italy had become perilous. The alarming assertion was grounded in individual cases of alleged mismanagement that led to the tragic deaths of newborns. This ignited a firestorm of panic and condemnation against the healthcare system.

In the aftermath of this sensational claim, a study scrutinized the child mortality rate in Italy. Astonishingly, the data revealed a stark reality: 63 children per 1,000 births in 1950, 30 children per 1,000 births in 1970, and a mere 3.3 children per 1,000 births in 2008. Contrary to the media's narrative, Italy emerged, alongside France, as the safest place in the world to give birth.

However, a mere handful of heartbreaking cases of infant mortality became the catalyst for a full-blown scandal, tarnishing a healthcare system that was fundamentally healthy and efficient. Journalists, in their pursuit of sensationalism, opted to bypass the real statistics and demonize an otherwise robust medical infrastructure.

This pattern of irresponsible journalism rears its head repeatedly, especially in the coverage of medical malpractice cases. Each legal dispute is transformed into a spectacle, devoid of context or an exploration of the genuine statistics.

In summary, the media's penchant for sensationalism perpetuates a distorted image of the healthcare system, manipulating isolated incidents to paint a grim picture that does not align with the broader statistical reality. This approach not only misguides the public but also undermines the confidence in a healthcare system that, despite its imperfections, stands as one of the safest places for childbirth in the world.

Media, the medical field, and the judiciary are integral components of society, each playing a crucial role. Accountability is paramount among these pillars, and they should hold one another responsible. However, when the media engages in demonization and broad-brush generalizations of entire professions, it poses a significant risk. Such actions have the potential to sow seeds of anarchy within these professions, eroding trust to a point where recovery becomes nearly impossible. Preserving trust is vital for the smooth functioning of these societal pillars, ensuring their continued effectiveness and positive impact.

Upholding Law Is Good But How Can You When You Don't Know The Human Science

In the heart of a medical drama, accusations of negligence loomed over Dr. Aster, a seasoned physician and emergency department doctor. The stage was set when Mrs. Stellar, a known case of hypertension and diabetes, staggered into the emergency room, gasping for breath. Her medical history revealed a recurrent battle with breathing issues, stemming from allergies and environmental changes.

In the throes of duty, Dr. Aster swiftly initiated nebulizer therapy and prescribed medications to address the apparent allergy and bronchitis. However, as the clock ticked away, a disheartening reality unfolded – there was no response to the treatment after three agonizing hours.

Mr. Stellar, fueled by anxiety and frustration, confronted Dr. Aster in the midst of the medical storm.

Mr. Stellar, accusatory: "Dr., what are you doing? Even after three hours, there's no improvement. It seems like you have no clue about her condition!"

Undeterred, Dr. Aster, like a calm protagonist facing a tempest, defended his approach.

Dr. Aster, reassuring: "Mr. Stellar, her history strongly indicates an acute bronchitis episode. The sounds in her chest align with this diagnosis. Please, exercise patience."

As the suspense thickened in the emergency room, the clash between a desperate family member and a dedicated doctor unfolded. The air crackled with accusations, skepticism, and the high stakes of a life hanging in the balance.

In this intense medical narrative, the line between life and death blurred, and the unfolding drama begged the question – would Dr. Aster's diagnosis stand the test of time, or would the accusations of negligence cast a dark shadow over the emergency department? Only time would reveal the true climax of this riveting medical tale.

In the pulsating emergency room, where life and death danced on a razor's edge, a chilling shout erupted from the nursing staff attending to Mrs. Stellar.

Nurse, urgently: "Dr., please come here. Mrs. Stellar is not responding to commands. She looks unconscious. Her oxygen level is also falling."

Dr. Aster, the protagonist of this medical thriller, sprinted to the bedside. A quick examination revealed a grim reality.

Dr. Aster, with urgency: "Sister, send ABGA and other reports. I'm writing. We need to intubate her and put her on a ventilator."

As the tension escalated, Dr. Aster turned to Mr. Stellar, the anxious husband, delivering a grave diagnosis.

Dr. Aster, resolute: "Sir, your wife has gone into hypoxic shock. Her oxygen levels have plummeted, rendering her unconscious. We need to put her on ventilatory support."

A desperate plea echoed through the chaotic room.

Mr. Stellar, in anguish: "No, Dr.! You cannot put her on that. She has refused to allow these things. Please, don't do that."

Dr. Aster, the voice of reason in the storm, attempted to sway Mr. Stellar.

Dr. Aster, pleading: "Sir, please allow me. It will save her life. And remember, there is no provision for 'Do Not Resuscitate' in our country as of now."

In a crescendo of emotions, Mr. Stellar's resistance intensified.

Mr. Stellar, defiantly: "No, I will not allow her to be put on all these deadly machines. I cannot see her suffer. You give whatever injection you can."

In the face of unwavering resistance, Dr. Aster found himself at a crossroads. The dramatic narrative unfolded, highlighting the clash between medical necessity and a husband's vehement refusal. The looming specter of life-saving interventions hung in the balance, as the characters grappled with the ethical complexities of medical management in the throes of an unfolding crisis.

In the dramatic twists of Mrs. Stellar's medical saga, the unfolding events took a surprising turn as the diagnostic reports arrived, revealing an additional layer to her complex condition – heart failure. Dr. Aster, the dedicated physician, swiftly pivoted to address this newfound challenge.

With urgency in his actions, Dr. Aster initiated heart failure therapy, administering medications in a bid to salvage Mrs. Stellar from the grips of this insidious ailment. As the drugs coursed through her system, a stroke of fortune emerged – Mrs. Stellar began to respond positively. The precipice of despair gradually gave way to a glimmer of hope as her condition stabilized.

Remaining under Dr. Aster's vigilant care for an additional ten days, Mrs. Stellar eventually earned her ticket to recovery and was discharged to convalesce at home. However, the respite was short-lived, as Mr. Stellar, driven by lingering resentment, seized the moment to unleash his pent-up frustration.

Mr. Stellar, brusquely: "Dr., you may have ten years of practice, but frankly, it's because of you that my wife suffered. You could have diagnosed heart failure immediately and treated her for that."

In the face of Mr. Stellar's accusatory words, Dr. Aster, calm and composed, offered his defense.

Dr. Aster, diplomatically: "Sir, you may be right. I apologize if you and your wife suffered. But remember, I have to adhere to medical guidelines. Additionally, don't forget that I suspected the possibility of heart failure, prompting me to order those crucial diagnostic reports."

The courtroom of emotions echoed with the clash of frustration and medical rationale, creating a sensational crescendo in this intricate tale of life, healing, and the often-thankless role of the medical practitioner. The lingering question hung in the air – in the unpredictable landscape of healthcare, where does accountability truly lie?

In the courtroom's charged atmosphere, Mr. Stellar's words reverberated with betrayal as he accused Dr. Aster.

Mr. Stellar, passionately: "No, sir, we came here with trust, but your actions have left us wounded."

Swiftly, Mr. Stellar wielded the legal sword, filing a medical negligence case against Dr. Aster. The stage was set for a legal showdown, with the truth hanging in the balance.

As the hearing commenced, both parties presented their versions of the harrowing tale. The courtroom, reminiscent of those seen in the legal landscapes of the USA or UK, housed a jury, poised to weigh the evidence and deliver a verdict.

The judge, a figure of authority, addressed the jury with a solemn charge.

Judge, emphasizing: "Jury members, you are here to determine whether there is negligence or not. Listen to both sides, evaluate the witnesses, and, in the end, render your judgment. Remember, Dr. Aster is not an extraordinary being; consider him as an ordinary person. You must unravel the entire scenario and decide whether negligence exists or not."

As the legal drama unfolded, the jury stood as the gatekeepers of justice, tasked with navigating the intricacies of medical practice, patient trust, and the elusive line between negligence and circumstance. The echoes of this courtroom saga resonated with the weight of responsibility, leaving the fate of Dr. Aster suspended in the balance of legal scrutiny and public opinion.

As the shocking accusations echoed in Dr. Aster's ears, a profound sense of disbelief and concern gripped him. He understood the inherent challenges of expecting jurors to grasp the intricacies of critical medical decisions, where the interplay of various factors often led to complex and nuanced choices, sometimes prone to misunderstanding.

As the legal proceedings unfolded, the courtroom became a battleground of expertise. Expert witnesses, summoned by both sides, took center stage. Those representing the patient's side presented a unified stance, claiming, "According to the history, we would have suspected heart failure as well."

However, the courtroom drama took a riveting turn during the cross-examination led by the defense lawyer.

Defense Lawyer, probing: "Doctor, suspecting heart failure is one thing, but would you have initiated treatment without confirmation?"

In a tense moment, not a single doctor on the stand agreed to such a course of action. Their collective understanding acknowledged the pervasive misuse of medical negligence laws, where anyone initiating treatment without a confirmed diagnosis risked facing legal repercussions under the act of commission.

The courtroom, now a cauldron of conflicting perspectives, underscored the precarious position in which medical professionals found themselves. The relentless scrutiny revealed the fine line doctors walked, balancing the imperative to act swiftly in critical situations against the looming specter of legal consequences.

In this sensational legal saga, the struggle for justice unfolded against the backdrop of a healthcare system grappling with the consequences of legal complexities, leaving Dr. Aster's fate hanging in the balance of legal interpretation and the intricate dance between medical necessity and legal accountability.

As the courtroom tension escalated, the prosecutor directed a piercing question at Dr. Aster, his voice cutting through the air like a blade.

Prosecutor, interrogating: "Dr. Aster, do you believe that if you had administered heart failure medicine early, it could have spared the patient from suffering?"

Dr. Aster, standing firm, responded with a calculated defense.

Dr. Aster, assertive: "The crucial point is that I suspected the condition. I promptly initiated the necessary tests, and it was only through those reports that I could commence treatment."

Undeterred, the prosecutor persisted, aiming to cast a shadow of negligence over Dr. Aster.

Prosecutor, accusingly: "But, Dr., she still suffered. As a senior doctor, by withholding heart failure treatment, isn't that an act of omission?"

Dr. Aster, unyielding: "For you, it might be an act of omission not to administer treatment without confirmation. However, the same action would transform into an act of commission if I had proceeded without confirmation, risking potential renal failure."

In a striking retort, the prosecutor attempted to undermine Dr. Aster's expertise.

Prosecutor, dismissively: "Dr., it seems like you've taken up the role of a lawyer. Leave that job to me. It would have been better if you focused on being a doctor."

Enraged by the insinuation, Dr. Aster fired back.

Dr. Aster, angrily: "It is because of people like you that these lawsuits are proliferating."

The judge, sensing the rising tension, intervened to maintain order in the courtroom.

Judge, sternly: "Dr., please refrain from making such comments. Our intervention is necessary because patients are suffering, and yet, they continue to bear exorbitant costs."

In this courtroom clash of words, the battle between legal scrutiny and medical practice unfolded with sensational intensity, laying bare the complexities and consequences that intertwine the realms of healthcare and the law.

In the climactic exchange within the courtroom, Dr. Aster, fueled by frustration and a sense of being misunderstood, unleashed a torrent of impassioned words.

Dr. Aster, with a hint of exasperation: "Sir, sorry to say, but how can you, this lawyer, and the jury presume to judge what I did in that split second to save a life? With all due respect, you are sitting here and judging the complex field of medical science as if we are dealing with TVs, fridges, and machines."

The prosecutor, seizing the opportunity to cast doubt on Dr. Aster's abilities, interjected confidently.

Prosecutor, dismissively: "See, Judge, this is beyond his scope. I think he is trying to hide his failure."

The judge, attempting to bring order to the discourse, clarified the court's purpose.

Judge, sternly: "Dr., we are not here to judge complex medical science. We are here to prevent harm to patients based on what you do or don't do."

Dr. Aster, undeterred, challenged the diversity of medical opinions within the case.

Dr. Aster, assertively: "Sir, even in this case, you have more than 10 doctor witnesses from both sides. Each has their own views. So, you should know that in the same situation, we all have different opinions, and frankly, we all are right."

The judge, acknowledging the complexity of the situation, expressed the necessity for justice.

Judge, grappling with the dilemma: " Frankly, Dr., none of us is saying that is not possible. But with increasing medical malpractice, we need to provide justice to patients?"

Dr. Aster, advocating for a more nuanced approach, countered the prevailing system.

Dr. Aster, passionately: "Any patient disgruntled by our service has the right to approach a proper forum. But the forum cannot be made up of lawyers and jurors. It should consist of doctor witnesses presenting their case in the presence of a legal expert – a judge."

Continuing with his argument, Dr. Aster emphasized the inadequacy of jurors in deciding intricate medical issues.

Dr. Aster, logically: "Juries are not optimally suited to decide the complicated issues of causation and duty of care. With respect to the major elements of liability – duty of care and causation – the parties must present expert testimony, which the jurors cannot evaluate independently."

Although the judge conceded that Dr. Aster had a point, he acknowledged the inherent limitations of the existing system.

The jury, shielded by the veil of secrecy surrounding their verdict, found the doctor guilty, leading to a compensation payout to the aggrieved party. The jury system's enigmatic nature prevailed, as jurors were not obligated to provide reasons for their decision.

In this riveting courtroom drama, the clash between the realms of medicine and law played out with intensity, highlighting the challenges and controversies inherent in the quest for justice within the medical malpractice landscape.

A Rectification Was Sought But Was Rejected. And Look How Much World Is Paying For That Rejection

In the harrowing tale of Mrs. Atalyah Gutbir's traumatic childbirth at Toronto General Hospital in 1984, the unfolding events painted a grim picture of medical complexities, lapses, and legal entanglements. Baby Zmora's birth left her in critical condition with permanent brain damage, setting the stage for a legal battle that spanned decades.

Mrs. Gutbir, in the throes of labor, experienced intermittent monitoring by a nurse using a "wooden stick." When her attending physician, Dr. Nicholson, performed an artificial rupture of membranes around 1:00 p.m., revealing meconium in the amniotic fluid, a potential sign of distress, the gravity of the situation escalated. Astonishingly, no electronic fetal heart monitor was employed, and Dr. Nicholson remained absent for three crucial hours.

As the labor progressed, Mrs. Gutbir was prompted to push without any indication of fetal distress, only to be relocated to another room abruptly. The anaesthetist was summoned to administer additional epidural medication, and Dr. Nicholson resorted to forceps for delivery. Panic ensued post-birth, leading to the baby's transfer to the Hospital for Sick Children.

The Gutbir family, back in Israel after Zmora's birth, remained silent about potential claims until 2001. Upon raising the issue, Toronto General had conveniently disposed of all records, while records from the Hospital for Sick Children hinted at a lack of continual monitoring during labor.

In the courtroom drama that unfolded, arguments echoed between the competency of medical practitioners, the intricacies of monitoring, and the evolving practices since 1984. Nineteen expert witnesses dissected complex medical jargon, shedding light on the nuances of patient monitoring, heartbeat assessments, and surgical techniques.

Amidst these complexities, the hospital sought to eliminate the jury, claiming that the scientific and medical evidence was too intricate for laypersons to comprehend. The judge, adopting a "wait and see" approach, recognized the challenge but preserved the right to a jury trial until necessity dictated otherwise.

The hospital and Dr. Nicholson faced successive defeats in both the jury court and the appeal court, culminating in a mandate to compensate. This case underscores the dilemma of judging acts of omission in the realm of medical science, where even with expert witnesses, differing opinions can muddy the waters. The potential repercussions of escalating investigations, increased medical scrutiny, and mounting costs underscore the fragile intersection of justice and the intricacies of healthcare.

BUT JUST A QUESTION TO THIS BOOK READERS COULD YOU COMPREHEND THE WHOLE MEDICAL COMPLEXITIES. BECAUSE THE PATIENT SUFFERED SO WAS IT MEDICAL NEGLIGENCE?

HOW CAN POLICYMAKERS AND JUDICIARY NOT UNDERSTAND THIS?

In the earlier decades of the twentieth century, when people filed medical malpractice lawsuits, they mostly claimed that doctors made mistakes in their actions – these are called errors of commission. For instance, a surgeon might perform a wrong procedure, a doctor could prescribe the wrong medication, or a healthcare provider might misinterpret test results, leading to complications.

However, something changed in the late 1960s and early 1970s. The number of malpractice lawsuits surged, and the nature of these claims shifted. Now, instead of being sued for actively doing something wrong, doctors were increasingly being sued for not doing something right – these are errors of omission. Negligence cases began to focus on instances where doctors failed to order necessary tests, missed crucial diagnoses like cancer, or didn't detect problems that should have been caught.

It's generally straightforward to understand when something is done wrong – a surgeon makes a mistake in surgery, a doctor prescribes the wrong medication, or a diagnosis is clearly incorrect. However, when evaluating negligence based on what a doctor didn't do, it becomes more challenging.

Consider this: A patient experiences shortness of breath, and the doctor treats it as a respiratory issue when it could be a heart problem. Or a doctor decides not to order specific tests that might have detected a serious condition. These are instances of errors of omission – things not done that should have been done.

It is easy to prove and comprehend if something is done wrong.

A surgeon cutting a wrong foot

A surgeon leaving something behind

A doctor seeing that it is attack still treating as gastritis

A doctor giving wrong pill

A doctor not seeing the fracture on xray or subdural hematoma on CT scan

Judging an act of omission after the fact can make any action seem negligent to a layman, be it a judge, lawyer, or juror. The level of education does not necessarily alter this perception. Even among the best experts globally, there can be a division of opinion on the same matter.

Consider scenarios such as a patient experiencing breathlessness, which could be treated as either a respiratory illness or a heart failure. A high heart rate might result from an infection or a cardiac issue. Administering medication to increase blood pressure could be a life-saving measure but might risk complications like gangrene if the patient already has a hand injury. Deciding whether to give antibiotics becomes a matter of preference or opinion.

Different medical professionals may advocate for a "wait and watch" approach in surgery, while others may favor a more aggressive surgical strategy. The choice of surgical approach in cases like fractures, knee replacements, or cancer can vary.

Determining whether an act of omission is serious or not requires the expertise of consultants in the specific field. Only these experts possess the knowledge and experience needed to evaluate the nuances of medical decisions and discern whether they constitute negligence.

The complexity arises because judging whether an act of omission is serious or not requires expert knowledge. Laypeople, including judges and jurors, may find it difficult to determine whether a doctor's decision to wait and watch instead of pursuing immediate surgery was negligent or a reasonable approach. Even among highly educated individuals, there can be differing opinions on whether a doctor's choice to prescribe a particular medication was appropriate.

In essence, the shift from errors of commission to errors of omission in medical malpractice cases highlights the challenges in assessing healthcare decisions, particularly when they involve what a doctor didn't do. Expert consultants, with specialized knowledge in the field, become crucial in determining whether a healthcare provider's actions – or inactions – constitute negligence.

The Tides of Change: A Tale of Doctors and Insurance

In the hallowed halls of the medical community, a palpable shift was underway. The once-trusted healers found themselves navigating treacherous waters as the specter of medical malpractice loomed large. Whispers of lawsuits and the echoing footsteps of litigators reverberated through the corridors, leaving doctors on edge and patients cautious.

The Secret Council: Many such happened everywhere

In the quiet corners of a renowned hospital, a clandestine meeting unfolded. A group of doctors, seasoned and weary, gathered to discuss the changing landscape of their noble profession. The air was thick with unease as they deliberated the rising tide of malpractice suits. One by one, they shared tales of colleagues facing legal battles, reputations tarnished, and the once unshakable trust between doctors and patients eroding.

The Paranoia Sets In:

As stories of legal woes circulated, paranoia seeped into the medical fraternity. Every diagnosis, every decision, became a potential litigation waiting to happen. The doctors, once revered for their expertise, found themselves second-guessing every step, haunted by the fear of being the next target in a courtroom drama.

The Cancer Screening Decree:

In a bid to shield themselves from the legal storm, a radical decision emerged from the secret council. They decreed a sweeping measure - every patient, regardless of symptoms or history, would be screened for cancer. The halls of the hospital echoed with the hum of X-ray machines and the whir of MRI scanners as a legion of patients underwent exhaustive tests.

The Proclamation of Possible Cancer:

Armed with an abundance of caution, the doctors, in their zeal to avoid malpractice accusations, started proclaiming the possibility of cancer with an almost prophetic fervor. Patients, once reassured by the healing hands of their physicians, now faced a barrage of potential diagnoses. The waiting rooms buzzed with nervous energy as individuals grappled with the uncertainty of their newfound medical destinies.

The Rise of Medical Indemnity:

Yet, amidst the chaos, a beacon of financial security emerged for the beleaguered doctors - medical indemnity insurance. A pact with these insurance guardians became a rite of passage for physicians seeking refuge from the storm of litigation. The once noble calling of medicine now bore the weight of insurance policies, a shield against the arrows of legal challenges.

The Dance with Uncertainty:

In this altered reality, doctors donned the cloak of caution, waltzing with uncertainty in each diagnosis and decision. The sacred trust between healer and patient strained under the weight of fear and litigation. As the medical landscape transformed, the story of doctors and insurance became a cautionary tale, a narrative where the pursuit of protection danced perilously close to the edges of overdiagnosis and an erosion of the very essence of compassionate care.

The escalating tide of medical malpractice cases unleashed a domino effect within the insurance industry, transforming what were once modest premiums into towering financial burdens for healthcare providers. Let's explore this progression with illustrative figures to grasp the gravity of the situation.

1. Initial Premiums:

- In the early days, when medical malpractice cases were relatively infrequent, insurance companies charged doctors and healthcare facilities reasonable premiums. Let's say, for instance, a doctor might have paid an annual premium of $10,000 for malpractice coverage.

2. Rise in Malpractice Cases:

- As the number of medical malpractice cases surged, insurance companies found themselves paying out substantial settlements and judgments. Suppose the annual payouts per doctor increased from an average of $50,000 to $500,000 due to the rising frequency and severity of cases.

3. Increased Payouts Reflect in Premiums:

- To cover these mounting costs, insurance companies had no choice but to raise their premiums. Let's assume the insurance companies, faced with a tenfold increase in payouts, raised the annual premiums for doctors accordingly. Now, a doctor might find themselves paying $100,000 annually.

4. Premiums Spiral Upwards:

- The cycle continued. As malpractice cases continued to surge, and payouts escalated, insurance companies faced the daunting task of sustaining their financial viability. Consequently, premiums continued their upward trajectory. The $100,000 premium might soar to $500,000 or even $1 million.

5. Financial Strain on Healthcare Providers:

- For hospitals and healthcare facilities, the financial strain was even more significant. A hospital that once paid a few hundred thousand dollars in malpractice insurance might now face premiums in the multi-million-dollar range. This staggering financial burden threatened the economic viability of medical institutions.

6. Industry-Wide Impact:

- The compounding effect of increased malpractice cases, rising payouts, and soaring premiums reverberated across the entire healthcare industry. Physicians, surgeons, nurses, and healthcare facilities, both large and small, found themselves caught in a financial quagmire.

7. Premiums as a Percentage of Revenue:

- To emphasize the gravity, consider a scenario where a small clinic generating \$1 million in revenue now had to allocate a significant percentage—perhaps 30% or more—towards malpractice insurance premiums, diverting resources from patient care, staff salaries, and facility maintenance.

In this whole financial chaos one can see the profound financial implications of the surge in medical malpractice cases. The compounding impact of increased payouts and rising premiums created an economic crisis within the healthcare industry, challenging the very foundation of patient care and medical practice.

Nutshell: Repel Effect, Vicious Cycle And Loss To All

The surge in medical malpractice cases triggered a chain reaction that significantly contributed to the overall increase in healthcare costs, ultimately impacting patients adversely. Here's a summary of the key points:

1. Rising Malpractice Cases: The increase in medical malpractice cases placed a substantial financial burden on healthcare providers, leading to higher payouts for settlements and judgments.

2. Escalating Insurance Premiums: Insurance companies, grappling with mounting payouts, responded by sharply increasing malpractice insurance premiums for doctors, surgeons, and healthcare facilities.

3. Financial Strain on Healthcare Providers: Doctors and medical institutions, faced with exorbitant premiums, had to divert substantial resources to cover insurance costs, limiting funds available for patient care, medical staff salaries, and facility maintenance.

4. Impact on Healthcare Institutions: Hospitals, clinics, and healthcare facilities experienced a significant dent in their budgets, with malpractice insurance premiums consuming a substantial portion of their financial resources.

5. Passing Costs to Patients: To offset the financial strain, healthcare providers, in turn, increased the overall cost of healthcare services. The expenses incurred in malpractice insurance premiums were passed on to patients through higher fees, charges for medical procedures, and increased costs for medications.

6. Ripple Effect on Reports and Medications: The financial strain prompted healthcare providers to seek additional revenue streams, contributing to an overall rise in the costs of medical reports, diagnostic tests, medications, and other ancillary services.

7. Erosion of Affordability for Patients: As healthcare costs soared, patients bore the brunt of the financial repercussions. The increased expenses for medical services, medications, and treatments made healthcare less affordable for the general population.

8. Vicious Cycle of Rising Costs: The interconnected cycle of rising malpractice cases, escalating insurance premiums, and the subsequent passing of costs to patients created a self-perpetuating loop. The more healthcare costs increased, the more patients struggled to afford necessary medical care.

In essence, the surge in medical malpractice cases not only strained the financial health of healthcare providers but also led to a systemic increase in the overall cost of healthcare. Patients found themselves caught in a vortex of escalating expenses, making access to quality healthcare increasingly challenging and underscoring the far-reaching consequences of the medical malpractice dilemma.

Did This Decrease The Cases: No But They Innovated To File More Cases On Different Pretext

Frustrated patients, fed up with prolonged wait times and delayed medical attention, sought legal recourse to address what they perceived as negligence in healthcare. One disgruntled patient expressed their discontent, stating, "I want to sue this hospital and emergency doctor. I was really sick. I went to the emergency room. It was full, and the doctor did not attend to me for 3 hours. How can they make me wait? I could have become seriously ill."

Media outlets seized on these grievances with headlines like, "These doctors have nothing better to do? Making patients wait for hours! Who will be responsible if a patient dies while waiting in the emergency room? Shameful!" The public narrative underscored the frustration of patients and fueled a growing demand for accountability in healthcare delivery.

A patient sought medical attention for an initial bout of fever, devoid of additional symptoms. The doctor, on the first day, recommended basic blood reports and prescribed paracetamol for the fever. However, as the days progressed, the patient developed cough, cold, and body aches. On the fourth day, experiencing vomiting and headaches, he rushed to the emergency room and was subsequently admitted, diagnosed with a viral flu. Upon recovery, the patient, spurred by an advertisement, contacted an attorney, seeking to sue the initial doctor for alleged delayed diagnosis of the flu.

In the ever-expanding landscape of medical malpractice litigation, lawyers navigated a complex terrain, strategically choosing cases with the potential for substantial compensation. Their decision-making process became a meticulous examination of various factors, creating a checklist that determined the viability and profitability of a case:

1. Extent of Damages:

   - The lawyers assessed the severity of the damages suffered by the patient. The greater the harm, the higher the potential financial compensation, making such cases more enticing.

2. Emotional and Mental Impact:

- Consideration was given to the emotional and mental toll on the patient. Cases that demonstrated significant distress and anguish promised a more compelling narrative in court, potentially resulting in higher compensation.

3. Social and Financial Standing:

- The social and financial standing of the patient became a crucial factor. Lawyers were inclined to take cases where the patient had a higher earning capacity, as this could translate into increased compensation for damages.

As lawyers compiled their lists of potential cases, the criteria for selection expanded. The spectrum of circumstances deemed as instances of omission broadened, leading to an influx of malpractice attorneys entering the arena. Simultaneously, juries and judges found themselves presiding over an increasing array of cases, each vying for compensation.

This surge in medical malpractice litigation created a dynamic environment where legal professionals strategically aligned themselves with cases that promised not only justice for the affected parties but also substantial financial gains. The interplay of damages, emotional impact, and the socioeconomic status of the patients became pivotal elements in shaping the landscape of medical malpractice lawsuits.

In the solemn halls of the courtroom, a hushed anticipation hung in the air as the small-time mechanic, burdened by the weight of his ordeal, prepared to share his heart-wrenching tale. His eyes, filled with a mix of sorrow and frustration, scanned the room, seeking empathy from those who held the power to bring him justice.

The mechanic took the stand, his voice trembling as he recounted the events that had forever altered the course of his life. "I trusted the doctor to fix me," he began, his words laced with anguish. "But instead, he left me broken. Broken not just physically but in every possible way."

With a heavy heart, he narrated how a seemingly routine surgery had transformed into a nightmare of prolonged hospital stays, endless rounds of tests, and a barrage of antibiotics that weakened his once robust immune system. The jury listened, some with misty eyes, as he painted a vivid picture of his life unraveled - a garage sold, a family's livelihood shattered, dreams of education for his children slipping away.

The mechanic's voice, filled with the raw emotion of a man who had seen his world crumble, echoed through the courtroom. "I am just a simple mechanic," he pleaded. "I had insurance, but it didn't save me. Now I am left with nothing. No work, no peace, and my kids are left with dreams they may never see."

As he spoke, tears streamed down his face, a powerful testament to the pain etched into every word. The jury, not immune to the human tragedy unfolding before them, found themselves moved by the sheer magnitude of his suffering.

In a dramatic turn, the mechanic's lawyer seized the moment, passionately arguing that no amount of money could fully compensate for the loss, but a substantial sum would serve as a small measure of justice. The media, always hungry for sensational narratives, swiftly embraced the heartbreaking saga, branding it with headlines that screamed "Killer Hospital" and "Killer Doctor."

In the end, the jury, swayed by the genuine emotion and undeniable injustice, delivered a verdict that spoke louder than words. The mechanic, though forever scarred, found a sliver of solace in the compensation awarded – a bittersweet resolution in a saga of shattered trust, lost dreams, and the relentless pursuit of accountability. And as the courtroom doors closed, the echoes of his cries lingered, leaving behind a poignant reminder of the human toll within the complex world of medical malpractice.

It was the year 1970, and a middle-aged man named Mr. Shan arrived at the emergency room in an American city. He had been experiencing high-grade fever, abdominal pain, and nausea for three days. His urine output was decreasing, and he complained of a burning sensation during urination. Dr. Renal examined him promptly, suspecting a urinary infection, and ordered necessary tests.

Dr. Renal prescribed medications, including injection paracetamol for fever, injection Buscopan for abdominal pain, and injection Ceftriaxone for the infection. Despite the treatment, the fever persisted, and antibiotics were adjusted. The doctor communicated regularly with the patient's relatives, keeping them informed about the situation.

As the medical bills accumulated, the family faced financial concerns. The billing department informed them that the bill had exceeded a certain limit. Worried about the escalating costs, Mr. Shan's son and wife contemplated discussing the matter with the doctor or considering a shift to a government hospital. The doctor empathized with their situation and assured them of efforts to manage the bill.

After ten days of treatment, Mr. Shan showed signs of recovery. However, when presented with the bill, the son expressed dissatisfaction, claiming exorbitant charges for consultations, investigations, and medicines. The argument escalated, involving hospital management, and eventually led to a confrontation with the doctor.

Mr. Shan's son, visibly upset, exclaimed, "This bill is outrageous! Look at the charges for consultations, investigations, and medicines. Why should we pay so much?"

The billing representative calmly responded, "Sir, these are charges for the treatments and services provided to Mr. Shan. We have not billed for anything that wasn't done."

Meanwhile, the doctor, Dr. Renal, arrived at the scene. "What seems to be the issue?" he inquired.

The son retorted, "Your visits were overpriced. You used to come, talk a few sentences, and leave. Why should we pay for that?"

Dr. Renal, maintaining composure, explained, "I'm your father's doctor, and the fees are for the medical care provided. It's my duty to treat and ensure his recovery."

The argument escalated, involving hospital management. The manager suggested, "Perhaps we can offer a discount to resolve the matter. He seems upset."

Dr. Renal expressed his disagreement, "This is not right. But if you think it will help, go ahead."

A discount was reluctantly offered to the patient's family, and they left the hospital. Outside, they encountered a person who handed them a card, saying, "I am Mr. Lawyer. I heard you weren't satisfied with the treatment?"

Engaging with the lawyer, they discussed filing a case of medical negligence. "The doctor prescribed antibiotics without waiting for a culture report, and he didn't consult specialists. This is misuse of antibiotics," argued Mr. Shan's son.

The lawyer nodded, "These are valid points. Let's proceed with the case."

Subsequently, a case was filed against Dr. Renal, and the courtroom became the battleground for allegations of malpractice. The court ruled in favor of the patient, setting a precedent with far-reaching consequences for healthcare practices in America and Western countries.

Dr. Smith sat across from his friend, Mark, a seasoned malpractice lawyer. The air was heavy with the weight of their conversation about the escalating malpractice cases across the country.

Dr. Smith hesitated before asking, "Mark, hearing about your cases, I can't help but worry. What if I have a patient who faces issues post-surgery?"

Mark leaned back, a wry smile playing on his lips, "Well, Doc, it depends on the damage, you know. The more damage, the more dollars in compensation."

The doctor sighed, "I had one patient with bleeding after a gallbladder removal. But I fixed it, and the patient was fine."

Mark nodded, "Sure, we can sue, but the payout might not be massive. Now, what if your patient gets hoarseness of voice after a thyroid surgery? Common, right?"

Dr. Smith chuckled, "Exactly! But what if the patient is, say, a teacher, or a musician, or even a lawyer whose whole career depends on their voice?"

Mark's eyes gleamed, "Ah, in that case, my friend, we're talking millions in compensation."

The doctor's smile faded, "Okay, what about a delayed cancer diagnosis? The patient refused a biopsy for months."

Mark leaned forward, "Now, that's a classic case. Not diagnosing cancer in time has the highest malpractice case percentage."

Dr. Smith, now visibly distressed, tried one last hope, "But Mark, I've been practicing for over 20 years. Thousands of successful surgeries without complications. Doesn't that count for anything?"

Mark's response was blunt, "Doc, what matters is what you did in the case in question. Your glorious past won't save you." As the reality sank in, Dr. Smith, with a newfound anxiety, called his hospital manager the next day – it was time to up that insurance cover.

NO ONE WILL EVER UNDERSTAND: I GUESS IT'S TOO LATE

In the intricate realm of medical malpractice, the crux often lies in discerning whether a doctor has breached their duty of care. Yet, if you were to query lawyers worldwide specializing in medical malpractice, a succinct mantra emerges: "If the doctor could have avoided something, then he or she is negligent."

For many doctors, this mantra is disheartening. Medicine is a dynamic field where practitioners navigate through a myriad of patient symptoms, employing a diagnostic approach to arrive at a differential diagnosis. In the pursuit of optimal care, doctors choose a course of action that best aligns with the patient's condition. However, the stark reality is that, given the complexity of numerous cases, including unclear diagnoses and delicate surgical procedures, unforeseen complications often arise. These complications, in the eyes of the legal system, might be deemed as avoidable, thus branding the practitioner as negligent.

Doctors are not merely treating textbooks or static cases; they are dealing with the intricacies of the human body, where each patient presents a unique puzzle. The path to a conclusive diagnosis is often fraught with uncertainties, and treatment decisions are made based on the best available information. The inherently unpredictable nature of medicine means that complications may occur, despite the utmost diligence and expertise exercised by the medical professional.

This disconnect between legal perspectives and the practical challenges faced by healthcare practitioners sets the stage for a complex and often contentious relationship. While lawyers seek accountability based on perceived avoidability, doctors grapple with the unavoidable uncertainties inherent in the practice of medicine. The clash between legal standards and medical realities underscores the need for a nuanced understanding of the challenges faced by healthcare providers, ensuring a fair and just appraisal of their decisions in the complex landscape of medical malpractice.

Indian Story

It Is Still Not 1989

Emergency Room – No laymen can ever understand what goes in our mind while we tackle emergency. But do they care?

The path towards the dangerous defensive medicine: We fail to learn

This is 1985 and yes it is India

Doctors own a duty of care. Supreme Court of India observed "Every doctor, at the governmental hospital or elsewhere, has a professional obligation to extend his services with due expertise for protecting life". So right but can it be judged in real sense qualitatively and quantatively. We will see.

The emergency room is a chaotic symphony of beeping machines and hurried footsteps. Dr. Kapoor, a seasoned physician, rushes between patients when the door swings open, revealing Raghav, a desperate man, half-dragging his unconscious sister, Pooja.

Raghav: "Doc, you have to help her! She's poisoned!"

Dr. Kapoor, glancing at the unconscious Pooja, replies sternly, "I need a police report before I can begin any treatment. It's protocol, I can't break the rules." Remember those movies which had this scene multiple times.

Raghav's eyes widen with panic. He grabs Dr. Kapoor's collar, a glint of desperation in his eyes.

Raghav: "Listen, Doc! I don't care about your rules. Save her now, or I swear..."

In an instant, Raghav pulls out a gun from his waistband and presses it against Dr. Kapoor's temple. The emergency room falls into an eerie silence, punctuated only by the distant beeping of machines. Oh you really think this is just a movie scene. Ask any doctor who has practiced in those days and you will be terrified to know how common this was.......

Raghav: "I won't hesitate to pull this trigger. You will treat my sister, or things are going to get ugly in here."

Dr. Kapoor, trying to remain calm, raises his hands in surrender. Majority of the doctor will be mentally disturbed for life time if there is oral abuse or physical abuse by relatives. But really no one cared.

Dr. Kapoor: "I understand your desperation, but violence won't help anyone. Let's find a solution together."

Just then, the emergency room door bursts open, revealing Officer Desai and two stern-faced constables. Raghav glances nervously at the new arrivals, his grip on the gun tightening.

Officer Desai: "What the hell is going on here?"

Raghav, still holding the gun to Dr. Kapoor's head, explains the situation with a shaky voice.

Raghav: "This doctor won't treat my sister without a damn police report!"

Officer Desai, assessing the situation, motions for the constables to stand back.

Officer Desai: "Lower the gun, son. We'll sort this out. But violence won't help your sister."

Raghav hesitates for a moment before reluctantly lowering the gun. Officer Desai takes control, instructing the constables to gather the necessary paperwork for the police report.

As the paperwork is hastily prepared, Dr. Kapoor, with a sense of urgency, begins treating Pooja, the medical team rallying around him.

However, the relief is short-lived. Days later, Dr. Kapoor finds himself facing a disciplinary inquiry. Officer Desai, adamant about upholding the law, explains the consequences of bypassing established procedures.

The scene concludes with a lingering sense of tension and moral ambiguity, leaving the audience questioning the fine line between doing what is right and adhering to the strict protocols in a system where life and death hang in the balance.

Let's see another instance: Still it is not 1989

Dr. Mehta, a compassionate physician working in a small town hospital in 1985, found himself entangled in an unexpected ordeal one stormy night. Shalini, a young accident victim, was rushed into the emergency room by a group of concerned bystanders.

Ignoring the raging thunderstorm outside, Dr. Mehta and his team immediately began providing life-saving treatment to Shalini, unaware of the bureaucratic storm that was about to unfold. As they battled to stabilize her, the hospital's entrance burst open, revealing Officer Singh and two stern-faced constables.

Officer Singh, a stickler for protocol, approached Dr. Mehta with a scowl. "You're treating a patient without a police report? That's against the rules, doctor!"

Dr. Mehta, in the midst of the life-or-death situation, explained, "I had to act quickly to save her life. We can sort out the paperwork later."

Ignoring the doctor's plea, Officer Singh declared, "This is a violation. You'll have to answer for this."

As Shalini's condition hung in the balance, Officer Singh, unmoved by the urgency of the situation, ordered one of the constables to fetch the necessary forms. The hospital staff, frustrated and bewildered, watched as precious moments ticked away.

In the cramped emergency room, Dr. Mehta continued to work tirelessly, navigating the chaos both inside and outside the hospital walls. The tension in the room escalated as the constable returned with the paperwork, and Officer Singh scrutinized every detail.

Finally, the paperwork completed, Officer Singh grudgingly allowed Dr. Mehta to resume treating Shalini. The doctor, fueled by a mix of frustration and determination, redoubled his efforts to stabilize her.

Days later, Shalini emerged from the shadows of critical condition, on the path to recovery. Dr. Mehta, however, faced a barrage of questions from the hospital administration and even a reprimand from Officer Singh for daring to prioritize a life over bureaucratic red tape.

The incident left an indelible mark on Dr. Mehta, who, despite the harassment, stood firm in his belief that a doctor's primary duty was to save lives, even if it meant facing the wrath of those who valued paperwork over humanity.

Repel effect: Repeat this instances, let the doctors discuss within themselves and you can see the massive damage happening.

At that time whenever this topic came up in debates or conference then doctors were frustrated about the situation. In a conference room a panel of doctors gathered for a heated debate at the All India Medical Symposium in 1986. The topic at hand was a contentious one - the challenges faced by medical professionals when treating accident victims without police reports, particularly in the face of harassment from law enforcement and the lack of legal protection.

Dr. Anand, a respected surgeon with a furrowed brow, took the podium. "Colleagues, we are encountering a grave dilemma. The recent incidents of police harassment for providing immediate treatment to accident victims are becoming alarmingly frequent."

Dr. Sharma, a vocal advocate for medical ethics, interjected, "It's our duty to prioritize patient care over bureaucratic hurdles. The Hippocratic Oath compels us to act swiftly in emergencies."

Dr. Kapoor, recalling the events of the previous year, added, "I faced legal repercussions for treating a critically injured patient without waiting for a police report. Our efforts to save lives are being obstructed."

Dr. Meera, a passionate advocate for change, stood up. "We cannot let fear of harassment dictate our actions. It's high time we address this issue collectively and lobby for legal protections for doctors in such cases."

The room buzzed with agreement as doctors exchanged concerned glances. Dr. Anand, with a thoughtful expression, proposed, "Perhaps we should form a committee to draft a petition, urging the courts and lawmakers to recognize the unique challenges we face in emergency medical situations."

Dr. Sharma nodded, "Yes, we need legal safeguards to shield doctors from unwarranted harassment. The courts must acknowledge that our primary concern is saving lives, not navigating bureaucratic red tape."

s the debate continued, the doctors forged a consensus to pool their resources and efforts. They envisioned a united front, pressing for legislative changes that would grant doctors the protection they needed to prioritize patient care without the looming threat of legal consequences.

Even the court did not came for help: They come only when it is too late…..Still it is not 1989

In the smog-filled city of Kolkata in 1988, Dr. Anirudh Kapoor, a dedicated physician known for his unwavering commitment to patient care, found himself entangled in a legal maelstrom that would shake the foundations of his beliefs.

It all began on a sweltering summer night when a critically injured man named Arjun was rushed into the emergency room of St. Mary's Hospital. Dr. Kapoor, recognizing the urgency of the situation, initiated immediate treatment without waiting for a police report.

Days later, the echoes of that fateful decision reverberated through the courtroom. Dr. Kapoor, dressed in a crisp suit that seemed out of place in the somber setting, faced a stern judge, a no-nonsense prosecutor, and an impassioned defense attorney.

The prosecutor, a seasoned legal veteran named Advocate Joshi, probed Dr. Kapoor relentlessly. "Dr. Kapoor, are you suggesting that you have the authority to bypass established procedures and treat patients without proper documentation?"

Dr. Kapoor, maintaining his composure, replied, "I believed it was a matter of life and death. The patient's condition was critical, and time was of the essence."

Advocate Joshi, with a skeptical tone, continued, "Are you above the law, Doctor? What gives you the right to make such decisions without adhering to proper protocols?"

As the intense questioning continued, the defense attorney, Advocate Rao, stepped in. "Your Honor, Dr. Kapoor's intent was purely to save a life. We cannot disregard the noble intention behind his actions."

The judge, a stern figure known for his no-nonsense approach, interrupted, "Noble intentions do not excuse a disregard for the law. Dr. Kapoor, you should have waited for the police report. Your actions are inexcusable."

The proceedings took a darker turn as Officer Gupta, the arresting officer, took the stand. He accused Dr. Kapoor of undermining the legal system and disrespecting law enforcement.

In a tense exchange, Officer Gupta exclaimed, "Your Honor, we cannot allow individuals, even doctors, to act above the law. Dr. Kapoor endangered the process of justice."

As the courtroom drama unfolded, Dr. Kapoor found himself at the mercy of legal scrutiny. The judge, unsympathetic to his justifications, delivered a scathing remark. "Dr. Kapoor, your actions not only endangered the legal process but set a dangerous precedent. I cannot condone such behavior."

In the end, the judge handed down a verdict that shook Dr. Kapoor to his core. The court ruled against him, imposing a fine and a temporary suspension of his medical license. The legal ordeal left Dr. Kapoor grappling with the consequences of his decision, a stark reminder that even noble intentions could not always shield individuals from the unforgiving grip of the law.

So since this was the stand of the police, lawyers and the court the doctors kept denying the treatment to the medico legal cases without police report. While this was done media and common people kept abusing the doctors and their work ethics. Not a single soul had a wisdom or intelligence to try to find the real issue. So every time a doctor refused the treatment rest of the doctors became villain. Seeds of hatred were sowed and it is going to hurt in future.......

It Is 1989- Parmanand Katara

Court gave direction but what about the accountability of state: And will someone ask about their accountability. For long they stood in silence.........It is 1989...

Then came the case and the judgement which defines duty of care in emergency.

The Parmanand Katara vs State case, decided in 1989, is a landmark judgment in Indian legal history that dealt with the duty of doctors to provide emergency medical assistance to accident victims, even in the face of potential legal consequences. The case brought attention to the delicate balance between medical ethics, legal obligations, and the right to life under Article 21 of the Indian Constitution.

In this case, Parmanand Katara, a lawyer, was seriously injured in a road accident in Delhi. He was taken to the All India Institute of Medical Sciences (AIIMS), but the doctors there refused to attend to him without a police statement. Unfortunately, Katara succumbed to his injuries during this critical delay.

The legal battle that ensued raised crucial questions about the duty of doctors to provide immediate medical aid and the conflict with legal formalities. The Supreme Court of India, presided over by Justice A.M. Ahmadi, delivered a groundbreaking judgment that emphasized the primacy of the right to life.

The court unequivocally stated that the **duty of a doctor is to preserve life,** and any hesitation or refusal to provide immediate medical assistance to a dying person in need is a gross violation of that duty. The court highlighted the ethical and professional obligation of doctors, emphasizing that the right to life takes precedence over procedural requirements such as filing a police report.

The judgment in the Parmanand Katara case reinforced the principle that the obligation to preserve life is paramount and cannot be compromised by legal formalities. It set a precedent for future cases involving the duty of doctors to provide emergency medical care and underscored the need for a compassionate and immediate response to save lives, irrespective of potential legal consequences.

This landmark case prompted a reevaluation of medical protocols and sparked conversations about the ethical obligations of healthcare professionals in emergency situations. It also served as a catalyst for legal reforms and discussions around creating a more conducive environment for doctors to prioritize saving lives without fear of legal repercussions.

While the Parmanand Katara vs State case in 1989 addressed the duty of doctors to provide emergency medical assistance, the judgment primarily focused on the ethical obligation of doctors to prioritize saving lives over procedural requirements. The court did not extensively delve into issues related to police harassment or violence against doctors.

The case primarily emphasized the immediate duty of doctors to provide medical aid and did not explicitly discuss the challenges doctors face due to police interference or violence from relatives. The judgment, while groundbreaking in recognizing the importance of preserving life, did not provide a comprehensive examination of the broader issues surrounding the safety and protection of medical professionals.

It's worth noting that discussions around the challenges faced by doctors, including police harassment and violence, have been ongoing in subsequent years. Cases and incidents highlighting these issues have prompted further dialogues and calls for legal reforms to address the safety concerns of healthcare professionals. While the Parmanand Katara case set an important precedent regarding the duty of doctors, subsequent legal and societal discussions have delved deeper into the broader context of ensuring the well-being and security of medical practitioners.

Repel effects which Court don't realise in medical profession

The situation described creates a complex and challenging environment for doctors, often referred to as the "repel effect." This effect arises from a combination of factors, including police harassment, legal consequences, and the threat of violence from the relatives of patients. Let's delve into the impact of each element:

1.   Police Harassment for Emergency Care:

- Doctors face a dilemma when providing emergency care without a police report due to established protocols or legal requirements.

- The fear of police harassment creates hesitation among medical professionals, potentially delaying critical care for patients in life-threatening situations.

- The implicit threat of legal repercussions can lead to a reluctance to act swiftly, despite the urgency of the medical situation.

2. Courts Pronounce Verdict of Guilt for Treating Without Report:

- The legal system's insistence on adherence to formalities before treatment puts doctors in a vulnerable position.

- Courts pronouncing guilt for providing immediate care without proper documentation can lead to professional and personal consequences for doctors.

- The fear of litigation and damage to professional reputation may deter doctors from prioritizing immediate medical intervention in emergencies.

3. Relatives Abusing and Beating Doctors for Non-Treatment:

- Doctors may face the wrath of distressed and emotionally charged relatives if they refuse to treat a patient without the required paperwork.

- This can result in verbal abuse, physical violence, and a hostile environment within healthcare settings.

- The repel effect intensifies as doctors find themselves caught between the duty to uphold medical ethics and the risks associated with potential harm from irate relatives.

Impact on Healthcare:

- The repel effect has a direct impact on patient outcomes, as delays in emergency care can lead to worsened conditions or even fatalities.

- It contributes to a culture of fear and uncertainty among healthcare professionals, affecting their ability to fulfill their primary duty of saving lives.

BUT FOR LONG WHO CARES. No one understood when the seeds of hatred became a small plant and when the fear in doctors sowed seeds for **defensive medicine**….. Don't worry you all we know what defensive medicine…..is

India From 1990-1996- Few Seeds Of Bitterness Are Sown

WHY DO YOU FORGET THAT WE WORKED UNDER SUBSTANDARD CONDITIONS

In the quaint town of Dhond, Dr. Anand Deshmukh, a well-respected medical practitioner, faced a tragic turn of events that would not only shatter a family but also cast a shadow over the practice of medicine in the Indian context.

On the 6th of May, the son of the first respondent, Mr. Kapoor, suffered a femur fracture. Initial aid was provided by a local physician, albeit with insufficient immobilization of the leg. Concerned about the severity of the fracture, Mr. Kapoor decided to transport his son to a hospital in Poona, a journey of about 200 miles.

Upon reaching the appellant's hospital, Dr. Deshmukh directed his assistant to administer two morphine injections. However, only one injection was given. The patient underwent a treatment process in the operation theatre, but unfortunately, his condition deteriorated.

Despite assurances given at 5:30 p.m. that everything was under control, the patient's health took a tragic turn by 9 p.m., resulting in his untimely death. Dr. Deshmukh, attributing the cause of death to fat embolism, issued a certificate to that effect.

In the legal aftermath, Mr. Kapoor filed a suit against Dr. Deshmukh, claiming negligence in the treatment provided to his son. The trial court and subsequently the High Court held Dr. Deshmukh responsible for the excessive force used during the reduction of the fracture, the lack of anesthesia during the procedure, and the resulting fat embolism that led to the patient's demise. Damages of Rs. 3,000 were awarded to Mr. Kapoor.

However, the judiciary's approach to this case raises significant concerns. The courts, perhaps unintentionally, viewed the incident through a prism of British healthcare laws, not accounting for the unique challenges and practices prevalent in the Indian healthcare system of that era. The British model, with its distinct legal and medical nuances, might not have been an ideal framework for evaluating the actions of Dr. Deshmukh.

This misalignment with the Indian healthcare context creates a repel effect in the medical profession. Doctors, already navigating a landscape with limited resources and differing medical practices, find themselves vulnerable to legal scrutiny that may not fully appreciate the complexities of their daily challenges. The fear of legal repercussions can hinder medical professionals from making decisions based solely on patient welfare, impacting the quality and efficiency of healthcare.

The case of Dr. Deshmukh serves as a poignant reminder of the importance of aligning legal judgments with the unique characteristics of the healthcare system in question. It underscores the need for a more nuanced understanding by the judiciary, one that considers the specific challenges faced by medical professionals in providing care within the context of the prevailing medical standards and resources of the time.

Indeed, the judiciary's failure to consider the significant aspect of the patient's travel for 200 kilometers reflects a lack of understanding of the medical nuances and the challenges inherent in the healthcare system of that time. The judge's ruling, seemingly divorced from the contextual realities, raises questions about the broader accountability and the systemic challenges faced by both doctors and patients.

In many cases, the accessibility and quality of healthcare facilities were—and still are—unevenly distributed, especially in regions farther away from urban centers. The judge's omission of the government's responsibility for ensuring robust healthcare infrastructure and accessibility might perpetuate a narrow view of the case.

Instead of acknowledging the constraints under which the doctor operated, the ruling appears to hold the individual practitioner solely responsible. This approach fails to consider the systemic factors, such as the availability of well-equipped hospitals and the challenges faced by patients in reaching them.

PLEASE MAKE UP YOUR MIND: A PLEA TO COURTS

In a quaint town nestled between rolling hills, Dr. Aarav Kapoor, a dedicated orthopedic surgeon, faced a challenging predicament. The recent legal landscape, shaped by a judgment reminiscent of Dr. Anand Deshmukh's case, had left a lingering fear among the medical fraternity.

One day, a distressed family rushed into Dr. Kapoor's small hospital. Their patriarch, Mr. Sharma, had suffered a complex leg fracture. Dr.

Kapoor, torn between his commitment to patient care and the fear of potential legal consequences, made a difficult decision.

"I understand the severity of the fracture," Dr. Kapoor began, his voice heavy with concern. "But considering the recent legal climate, I would strongly recommend shifting Mr. Sharma to a larger hospital with specialized facilities. It's in his best interest."

The family, bewildered and anxious, protested. "Why can't you treat him here, Doctor? We've heard you're the best in town!"

Dr. Kapoor, grappling with the weight of legal uncertainties, explained, "I want the best for Mr. Sharma. Given the complexities, a larger hospital with specialized services will provide the optimal care he needs. It's for his safety."

Reluctantly, the family arranged for an ambulance to transport Mr. Sharma to a distant city with a renowned medical facility. Little did they know that this seemingly prudent decision would soon be entangled in a legal quagmire.

A few weeks later, Dr. Kapoor found himself facing a courtroom filled with stern faces. The family had filed a case against him, alleging negligence and abandonment of duty. The judge, influenced by the prevailing legal sentiments, pronounced a judgment that left the medical community bewildered.

"You, Dr. Kapoor, are entrusted with the responsibility of providing medical care. If you cannot fulfill that duty, perhaps it's best to reconsider operating a hospital at all," the judge declared.

In the corridors of the hospital, doctors whispered in hushed tones about the injustice they felt. Dr. Kapoor, now burdened by the weight of a legal system seemingly punishing him from both ends, questioned the very essence of his profession.

The tale of Dr. Kapoor highlighted the conundrum faced by doctors who, out of genuine concern for patient welfare and fear of legal repercussions, find themselves caught in a cycle of uncertainty. The story underscored the need for a legal framework that understands the challenges of smaller healthcare setups, preventing scenarios where doctors are hesitant to provide care for fear of legal consequences.

YOU DON'T UNDERSTAND HUMAN BODY IS NOT MY FAULT…..

In the heart of a bustling city, Dr. Rohan Kapoor, an earnest and dedicated emergency room physician, faced a challenging night that would test the boundaries of his commitment to saving lives. One stormy evening, amidst the chaos of flashing ambulance lights and the steady hum of medical equipment, a critically injured patient, Mr. Arjun Malik, was rushed into the emergency department.

Arjun had been involved in a severe car accident, leaving him with multiple fractures and internal injuries. Dr. Kapoor, with a sense of urgency, led the medical team in providing immediate care. The trauma bay buzzed with activity as nurses prepped for surgery, and Dr. Kapoor orchestrated the delicate dance of emergency medicine.

Despite the team's best efforts, Arjun's condition remained critical. Dr. Kapoor, balancing on the precipice of medical uncertainty, made quick decisions and administered life-saving measures. Surgery was deemed necessary, but the severity of Arjun's injuries complicated the process.

As the hours passed, Dr. Kapoor worked tirelessly to stabilize Arjun before proceeding with surgery. However, despite his best efforts, immediate relief remained elusive. The patient's family, in a state of distress and fuelled by anxiety, questioned Dr. Kapoor's every move. The inability to provide instant relief, a consequence of the complexity of Arjun's injuries, led to mounting frustration.

Weeks later, as Arjun slowly recovered from the intricate surgery, his family chose a different path. They filed a lawsuit against Dr. Kapoor, alleging negligence in the delayed relief provided during the critical moments in the emergency room.

The court proceedings unfolded, and Dr. Kapoor found himself defending not only his medical decisions but also the inherent uncertainties of emergency medicine. The legal team argued that Dr. Kapoor failed to meet the standard of immediate relief expected in emergency situations.

The courtroom drama painted a complex picture. Dr. Kapoor, driven by a dedication to his patients, faced the challenging task of explaining the intricacies of Arjun's injuries and the limitations of immediate relief in certain cases. However, the family, clouded by their ordeal, sought solace in assigning blame.

In the end, the judge, lacking a deep understanding of the complexities of emergency medicine, ruled in favor of the family. Dr. Kapoor, despite his sincere efforts and commitment to his patient, found himself held liable for circumstances beyond his control.

The story of Dr. Kapoor serves as a poignant reminder of the challenges faced by medical professionals in emergency situations. It underscores the need for legal systems to appreciate the nuanced nature of healthcare decisions, especially in high-stakes scenarios where immediate relief may not always be feasible. The outcome of such cases can have a profound impact on the medical community, influencing the approach of healthcare providers in emergency settings.

ANOTHER VICTIM OF IGNORANCE

In the quiet town of Raipur, Dr. Aanya Sharma, a compassionate and diligent general practitioner, found herself entangled in a web of accusations that would test the very core of her dedication to patient care. One gloomy afternoon, Mr. Raghav Verma, a middle-aged man, visited Dr. Sharma's clinic with a persistent fever that had refused to subside.

Concerned about Mr. Verma's well-being, Dr. Sharma conducted a thorough examination, but the fever's origin remained elusive. Recognizing the need for further investigation, she ordered a series of tests to pinpoint the underlying cause. As the test results trickled in, revealing no conclusive evidence, Dr. Sharma decided to consult specialists to unravel the mystery of Mr. Verma's persistent fever.

With a genuine commitment to finding a solution, Dr. Sharma referred Mr. Verma to infectious disease specialists, internal medicine experts, and even a renowned hematologist. Each doctor conducted thorough examinations and prescribed different courses of treatment, trying to alleviate the stubborn fever that had eluded diagnosis.

Despite the collective efforts of Dr. Sharma and the specialists, Mr. Verma's condition persisted. Frustrated and desperate for answers, his relatives, fueled by anxiety and uncertainty, pointed fingers at Dr. Sharma. Allegations of negligence surfaced, with accusations that Dr. Sharma was prolonging the treatment to increase medical expenses.

The Verma family, fueled by mistrust and financial concerns, filed a lawsuit against Dr. Sharma, claiming negligence and malpractice. The courtroom became the battleground for a contentious dispute, where Dr. Sharma found herself defending not only her medical decisions but also her professional integrity.

The legal proceedings unfolded, and Dr. Sharma, in her defense, meticulously presented the chronology of Mr. Verma's case. She highlighted the collaborative efforts with specialists, the numerous tests conducted, and the evolving treatment plans aimed at resolving the persistent fever. The courtroom drama underscored the inherent uncertainties in medicine, especially when faced with complex and elusive medical conditions.

Despite the compelling evidence presented, the court, lacking a comprehensive understanding of the medical intricacies, ruled in favor of the Verma family. The narrative of financial motives overshadowed Dr. Sharma's genuine efforts to diagnose and treat Mr. Verma's illness.

The fallout was profound. Dr. Sharma, once regarded as a dedicated physician, found her reputation tarnished. The Verma family, disillusioned by the legal battle, struggled to find solace as they continued their quest for answers to Mr. Verma's persistent fever.

The story of Dr. Aanya Sharma serves as a cautionary tale, highlighting the challenges doctors face when navigating complex medical cases. It underscores the need for legal systems to approach medical malpractice cases with a nuanced understanding of the uncertainties inherent in healthcare, preventing unwarranted accusations that can have lasting repercussions on a physician's career and reputation.

COURT DID PROTECT BUT IT TOOK 11 YEARS...

Because The Patient Did Not Survive Means All The Efforts Were Of Negligence.......

Late Shri R.K. Sharma served as a Senior Operations Manager in the Indian Oil Corporation's Marketing Division. In June 1989, he developed high blood pressure, accompanied by significant obesity. He experienced complaints of swelling and breathlessness while climbing stairs. Seeking medical attention, he visited Mool Chand Hospital on 10.12.1989, but a conclusive diagnosis was not reached. Subsequently, the Indian Oil Corporation referred him to City Hospital on 14.3.1990.

At City Hospital, Dr. R.K. Mani and Dr. S. Arora examined Shri Sharma on 14.3.1990, recommending his admission for Anasarca (generalized swelling). Admitted on 18.3.1990, an ultrasound of the abdomen on 20.3.1990 revealed a left adrenal mass on the kidney. The following day, a CT scan confirmed the presence of the adrenal tumor, prompting the decision for surgical intervention.

On 2.4.1990, with the patient's and relatives' consent, surgery was performed to remove the malignant adrenal tumor. During the operation, due to Shri R.K. Sharma's obesity, the spleen had to be removed, and the tail of the pancreas suffered superficial, non-ductal trauma. This injury was promptly repaired during surgery and documented in the operation transcript and discharge summary.

Post-surgery, on 26.4.1990, ultrasound and CT scans were conducted to monitor the operative and pancreatic sites, revealing a pancreatic abscess. Seeking a second opinion, Shri Sharma's relatives sought treatment at another hospital, where an operation was performed in May to drain the abscess and repair the leak, still within City Hospital.

After discharge on 23.6.1990, Shri R.K. Sharma had limited contact with doctors until 9.10.1990, with a solitary visit on 31.8.1990 for a fitness certificate. During this period, he sought medical attention at various hospitals for different reasons, including fever, dressings for the operative site, and gluteal abscess drainage. Unfortunately, inadequate treatment for the gluteal abscess led to its spread, ultimately resulting in pyogenic meningitis.

In October, in critical condition, Shri R.K. Sharma was brought back to City Hospital, where he eventually passed away. Despite being advised to start chemotherapy promptly after surgical recovery, his relatives did not follow up with any doctor. The prolonged illness, known complications, the family consulting multiple doctors without consistent follow-up, and their lack of understanding of medical science led to legal complications.

The legal process took 11 years to reach a verdict, marked by media debates acting as both advocates and judges. Conferences were held, discussing the challenges doctors faced in dealing with frequent legal consultations. Despite the tragic loss of life, it is important to acknowledge that the doctors did not act with intent, raising questions about the need for such prolonged legal battles. This situation underscores the value of impartial judgment and the potential benefits of artificial intelligence, such as robots, in medical contexts.

Courtroom Scene: Cross-Examination of Dr. R.K. Mani, @ Hospital

Lawyer for the Victim (LV): "Dr. Mani, you were directly involved in the treatment of Shri R.K. Sharma at City Hospital, correct?

Dr. R.K. Mani (DM):"Yes, that's correct.

LV:" And it was under your care that Shri Sharma underwent surgery for the removal of the adrenal tumor?

DM:"Yes, that's correct.

LV:" Dr. Mani, can you explain why it took over two months to identify the pancreatic abscess post-surgery?

DM:" The postoperative care involved regular monitoring, and the abscess was identified during a routine follow-up.

LV:" Routine follow-up or negligence? The abscess wasn't identified until April, and by then, it had developed into a serious complication. Would you agree?

DM:" We were actively monitoring the patient, and the development of complications can vary.

LV:" Dr. Mani, the court has heard that Shri Sharma's family sought a second opinion at another hospital. Can you explain why they felt compelled to do so?

DM:" Seeking a second opinion is not uncommon, and patients have the right to explore alternative medical advice.

LV:" The need for a second opinion arose because of the pancreatic abscess, a complication that occurred under your care. Is that not correct?

DM:" The abscess was a known complication, and steps were taken to address it promptly.

LV:" Known complication or medical oversight? It took an additional operation in another hospital to drain the abscess. Why did your initial intervention not prevent such a severe condition?

DM:" The decision to perform another operation elsewhere was a choice made by the family. We addressed the complications as they arose.

LV:" Dr. Mani, let's talk about the gluteal abscess. Was it not your responsibility to ensure that all postoperative complications were addressed?

DM:" We provided comprehensive care, and the gluteal abscess was not initially identified as a direct result of the surgery.

LV:" So, you're suggesting that despite being under your care, Shri Sharma's condition deteriorated, and he eventually suffered from pyogenic meningitis due to factors beyond your control?

DM:" We did our best to provide appropriate care, but the spread of infection can be unpredictable.

LV:" Dr. Mani, is it not true that the prolonged legal battle and media debates were a result of the perceived negligence in Shri Sharma's treatment at @ Hospital?

DM:" Legal proceedings are often complex and involve multiple factors. Our focus has always been on providing quality healthcare.

LV:" Quality healthcare, or a series of medical oversights that led to a tragic loss? I submit that the responsibility lies squarely with the medical team at @ Hospital, and Shri R.K. Sharma paid the ultimate price for these lapses.

Judge:" The court will adjourn for the day. We will reconvene tomorrow at 10 a.m. for further proceedings.

Courtroom Scene: Cross-Examination of Shri R.K. Sharma's Relatives

Lawyer for the Doctor (LD):" Mrs. Sharma, can you please explain why there was a significant gap in Shri R.K. Sharma's follow-up visits with the doctors after his discharge from City Hospital?

Mrs. Sharma (MS):" Well, we were dealing with various complications, and we sought opinions from different specialists for his ongoing issues.

LD:" Complications that arose during his treatment at @ Hospital, correct?

MS:" Yes, but we wanted to explore all available options and ensure the best care for Shri Sharma.

LD:" Mrs. Sharma, it has been noted that Shri Sharma did not start the recommended chemotherapy after the removal of the adrenal tumor. Can you explain why that was the case?

MS:" We were overwhelmed with the multiple health issues he was facing, and the doctors didn't clearly explain the urgency of starting chemotherapy.

LD:" So, despite being advised to start chemotherapy for a malignant tumor, you chose not to follow the doctor's recommendation?

MS:" It's not that we chose not to follow it; we were dealing with several medical opinions, and things got a bit confusing.

LD:" Confusing or neglectful? Mrs. Sharma, you were aware of the risks associated with delaying chemotherapy, correct?

MS:" Yes, we were aware, but we were looking for the best course of action.

LD:" Looking for the best course of action while potentially compromising Shri Sharma's health. Can you explain why you did not maintain regular contact with any doctor for so many months?

MS:" We visited different hospitals for different reasons, seeking the right expertise for each issue.

LD:" Issues that may have been better addressed by consistent follow-up with a primary care provider. Would you agree?

MS:" We were doing what we thought was best for Shri Sharma.

LD:" Mrs. Sharma, did you or any family member attempt to clarify the importance of follow-up care with the doctors during this period?

MS:" We were dealing with a lot, and we thought the various specialists we consulted would guide us appropriately.

LD:" So, you relied on various specialists without a coordinated plan of care, despite knowing the critical nature of Shri Sharma's health?

MS:" We were trying to make informed decisions based on the information we received.

LD:" Informed decisions that resulted in a tragic outcome. It's evident that the lack of consistent follow-up and the delay in starting chemotherapy played a role in Shri R.K. Sharma's deteriorating health.

Judge:" The court will recess. We will resume tomorrow at 10 a.m. for further proceedings.

Courtroom Scene: Cross-Examination of Medical Witness by the Lawyer for the Doctor

Lawyer for the Doctor (LD):" Dr. Harish, you've been called as a medical witness to provide your expert opinion on the treatment of Shri R.K. Sharma. Is that correct?

Dr. Harish (DJ):" Yes, that's correct.

LD:" Dr. Harish, you mentioned in your testimony that a different approach could have been taken in Shri Sharma's case. Could you elaborate on what you mean by a different approach?

DJ:" Well, considering the complications that arose, there might have been alternative methods of treatment that could have been explored.

LD:" Alternative methods? Dr. Harish, can you specify what alternative methods you are referring to?

DJ:" For instance, a more aggressive postoperative care plan, different medications, or even alternative therapies could have been considered.

LD:" So, you are suggesting that the doctors at City Hospital did not explore all available options?

DJ:" I'm not saying they didn't explore options, but there might have been different avenues worth considering.

LD:" Dr. Harish, are you aware that the doctors at City Hospital followed established medical protocols in the treatment of Shri R.K. Sharma?

DJ:" Yes, I am aware, but sometimes protocols may need to be adapted based on the patient's unique circumstances.

LD:" Adapted or deviated? Dr. Harish, do you believe that deviating from established protocols in this case would have yielded a better outcome?

DJ:" It's hard to say for certain, but considering the complications, a more personalized approach might have been beneficial.

LD:" Dr. Harish, were you aware of the specifics of Shri Sharma's case at the time you provided your expert opinion?

DJ:" I had access to the relevant medical records and details of the case.

LD:" Access to records, but did you have firsthand knowledge of the intricacies of Shri Sharma's condition during the critical moments of his treatment?

DJ:" No, I did not have firsthand knowledge, but my expertise allows me to provide an informed opinion.

LD:" Dr. Harish, you understand the gravity of your expert opinion, and the impact it can have on the doctors involved. Would you agree?

DJ:" Yes, I understand.

LD:" By suggesting that a different approach could have been taken, are you not casting doubt on the decisions made by the doctors at City Hospital?

DJ:" I am merely offering an alternative perspective based on my expertise.

LD:" Dr. Harish, you must realize that your expert opinion, if unfounded, can be detrimental to the reputation and morale of the medical professionals involved. Do you feel any responsibility for the potential consequences of your testimony?

DJ:" I am here to provide an honest and professional opinion based on my understanding of the case.

LD:" An opinion that, if misguided, could lead to unwarranted consequences for dedicated medical professionals. Your Honor, I have no further questions for this witness.

Judge:" The court will adjourn for the day. We will reconvene tomorrow at 10 a.m. for further proceedings.

Courtroom Scene: Cross-Examination of Medical Expert by the Lawyer for the Victim

Lawyer for the Victim (LV):" Dr. Divyang, you've provided testimony asserting that the doctors involved in Shri R.K. Sharma's treatment exercised reasonable care and followed established medical standards. Is that correct?

Dr. Divyang (DA):" Yes, that's correct. The medical team adhered to standard protocols in Shri Sharma's case.

LV:" Dr. Divyang, you've emphasized that just because the outcome was unfavorable does not imply negligence. Can you elaborate on why you believe the doctors' actions were within acceptable standards?

DA:" Certainly. The medical team at City Hospital followed established protocols for Shri Sharma's condition. Complications can arise, and unfavorable outcomes, while unfortunate, do not necessarily indicate negligence.

LV:" Dr. Divyang, you've stated that the approaches taken are documented in medical literature and considered standard. Are these approaches infallible, or can deviations occur based on the patient's unique circumstances?

DA:" Standard approaches are based on extensive research and are generally effective. However, adaptations may be necessary depending on the specifics of the case.

LV:" So, while you claim the approaches are standard, you acknowledge that deviations might be necessary. Would you consider the complications in Shri Sharma's case as such a deviation?

DA:" The complications were addressed within the framework of standard care. Sometimes, despite best efforts, complications can occur.

LV:" Dr. Divyang, can you provide examples of circumstances where complications might be considered deviations from standard care?

DA:" Complications can arise due to unforeseen factors, patient-specific responses, or the progression of the disease. These are inherent risks that medical professionals consider.

LV:" In this case, we have an abdominal tumor removal surgery, a pancreatic abscess, and subsequent complications leading to pyogenic meningitis. Are these not significant deviations from the expected outcome?

DA:" The complications were unfortunate, but they were addressed promptly within the standard of care.

LV:" Dr. Divyang, given the complexity of Shri Sharma's case, would you agree that clear communication with the patient and family is crucial to ensure understanding and compliance?

DA:" Communication is important, but even with the best communication, complications can still occur.

LV:" Dr. Divyang, considering the unfortunate outcomes, do you believe there is any room for improvement in the standard approaches or communication protocols followed in this case?

DA:" Medical practice is always evolving, and there's continuous learning. However, the procedures followed were reasonable and within established norms.

LV:" So, despite the tragic outcome and the family's perception of negligence, you stand by your assertion that the medical team exercised reasonable care?

DA:" Yes, based on the information available and my expertise, I believe reasonable care was taken.

LV:" No further questions, Your Honor.

Judge:" The court will recess for the day. We will resume tomorrow at 10 a.m. for further proceedings.

Before the judgement day the **media headlines** were already pronounces their judgement. But whatever they pronounced in judgement they definitely did one thing, they provided the water and fertiliser for the plant of hatred in general public.

1. "City Hospital Horror: Docs Play God, Leave R.K. Sharma to Die!"

2. "Killer MDs: City's Medical Mafia Strikes Again, Mr. Sharma Sacrificed!"

3. "Negligent Butchers: City Docs Butcher Patient, Walk Away Unscathed!"

4. "Death by Design: City's Deadly Diagnosis Takes Another Innocent Life!"

5. "Hospital Hell: City's Deadly Duo Murders R.K. Sharma in Cold Blood!"

6. "Medical Mayhem Unleashed: City's Negligence Claims Another Victim!"

7. "Beyond Incompetence: City Docs Guilty of Premeditated Murder!"

8. "Sharma's Demise: City's Criminal Cover-up Exposed!"

9. "City's Black Day: R.K. Sharma's Death Linked to Doc's Devilish Plot!"

10. "Docs of Doom: City's Medical Team Accused of Cold-Blooded Killing!"

Final Judgment

In the matter of the allegations of medical negligence brought forth in the case of Late Shri R.K. Sharma, the court, having heard the arguments and evidence presented by both parties, renders the following judgment:

The court, after careful consideration, wishes to make it unequivocally clear that this judgment should not be understood to have held that doctors can never be prosecuted for medical negligence. The law recognizes that medical practitioners, like any other professionals, can be subject to legal scrutiny if their actions deviate from the established standards of care and competence.

However, in the present case, the court finds no evidence to suggest that the medical professionals involved, particularly those at City Hospital, failed to perform their duties with an ordinary degree of professional skill and competence. The medical team adhered to established protocols and standards, and their actions were in line with accepted medical practices.

It is imperative to acknowledge that medicine is a complex field, and even with the utmost care and diligence, adverse outcomes may occur. In the absence of gross negligence or a departure from the standard of care, medical practitioners cannot be held criminally liable for unfavorable results.

The court recognizes the need for doctors to perform their professional duties with a free mind, without the constant fear of legal repercussions for every adverse outcome. While accountability is essential, it must be approached judiciously, ensuring that the medical community can continue to provide the best possible care without the constant threat of unwarranted legal action.

In conclusion, the court finds no grounds to hold the doctors involved in the treatment of Late Shri R.K. Sharma guilty of medical negligence. The unfortunate outcome of Shri Sharma's case, while deeply regrettable, does not establish criminal culpability on the part of the medical professionals.

The court hereby dismisses the allegations of medical negligence against the doctors involved in this case. We trust that this judgment will not only bring closure to the legal proceedings but also encourage a continued commitment to excellence in medical care while maintaining a fair and balanced approach to legal accountability.

Judgement protected the doctor though it took 11 years to decide but the media destroyed the reputation.

Oh God, Now It Starts In India Also. - It's Just 1996

Finally the time arrives where the death to healthcare was pronounced. Easy path made chaotic and full of hatred

Debating the Inclusion of Doctors in the Consumer Protection Act: A Heated Exchange

The grand conference room echoed with the murmurs of policymakers, lawyers, and medical experts, all gathered to discuss the potential inclusion of doctors under the Consumer Protection Act of 1986. The atmosphere was charged with anticipation as the proponents and opponents prepared to present their arguments.

Lawyer in Favor (LF):" Ladies and gentlemen, today I present to you a case that exemplifies the need for including doctors under the Consumer Protection Act. In the matter of Dr. Abhinav, a registered Homoeopathic practitioner, we witness a situation where a patient suffered due to a questionable prescription. This incident emphasizes the necessity of holding medical practitioners accountable for their actions.

Opposing Lawyer (OL):" Hold on a moment! Are we seriously using a homeopathic case to argue for the inclusion of allopathic doctors under consumer protection? Homeopathy itself is a subject of debate in terms of scientific validity. How can we base such a significant decision on a practice that is still questionable

LF:*"Your Honor, the core issue here is not the specific medical practice but rather the accountability of practitioners. The Consumer Protection Act aims to protect consumers from unfair trade practices, and when a patient seeks medical care, they are consumers of a service. This case illustrates the potential harm caused by a lack of accountability.

OL:" But allopathic medicine is well-studied, well-regulated, and practiced by highly educated professionals. We have stringent standards and regulations in place. Using a case from a different medical paradigm to make a point about allopathic medicine is misleading.

LF: "Respectfully, I disagree. The principles of accountability and consumer protection are universal. While allopathic medicine is indeed well-regulated, it does not exempt it from occasional instances of malpractice or negligence. Including doctors under the Consumer Protection Act will ensure an additional layer of accountability for all medical practitioners.

OL:" But, by that logic, we could include any service provider under the act. Should we start holding lawyers accountable under consumer protection? What about architects or engineers?

LF:" Doctors are unique service providers; they deal with human lives. The stakes are higher, and the consequences of negligence can be severe. The Consumer Protection Act provides a framework for addressing grievances and holding practitioners accountable.

As the debate unfolded, the room buzzed with tension. Policymakers listened intently, weighing the arguments presented. The debate would influence the future of healthcare regulation, sparking discussions about the balance between accountability and the unique nature of medical practice.

Lawyer in Favor (LF):" Ladies and gentlemen, let's delve into the heart of the matter. Res Ipsa Loquitor — the thing speaks for itself. Take the case where no tests were conducted prior to surgery. The patient entrusted their life to a professional, and without diagnostic tests, the consequences were dire.

Opposing Lawyer (OL):" (Interrupting) Your Honor, these are grave cases of negligence, and they should be directly tried under criminal law, not consumer protection.

LF:" Your Honor, we're not suggesting that all cases should be handled under the Consumer Protection Act, but it provides an avenue for patients to seek redress without the burdens of a criminal trial. Now, consider foreign matter left in the body after an operation. Res Ipsa Loquitor again. The evidence is clear, and the patient shouldn't bear the burden of proving negligence.

OL:" Adding doctors under CPA will open a can of worms. They will be harassed, facing multiple cases for every adverse outcome.

Another Policy Maker in Opposition (PMO):" Lawyers, we must consider the consequences. This move could make doctors more fearful, and they won't practice medicine with confidence.

LF:" Fear? Confidence? Your Honor, the duty of a doctor is to prioritize the well-being of the patient. Breach of duty to maintain confidentiality — a patient's trust shattered. Shouldn't they be held accountable?

OL:" (Skeptical) But what about removing a normal organ or operating on the wrong side? These are clear cases of incompetence, not consumer issues.

LF:" (Nods) I don't dispute that, but the Consumer Protection Act provides a platform for expedited resolution. It's not about witch-hunting, but ensuring accountability.

PMO:" (Thoughtful) Lawyers, doctors, let's not forget the essence of our discussion — balancing accountability with ensuring that healthcare professionals can perform their duties confidently.

OL:" (Emphatic) I still believe criminal cases are the way to address gross negligence.

LF:" (Resolute) Your Honor, the Consumer Protection Act is not a tool for harassment but a shield for patients wronged by the very professionals meant to heal. We must consider a framework that upholds accountability while fostering a healthcare system where trust reigns supreme.

As the lawyers passionately debated, policymakers weighed the potential impact on both patients and doctors. The room buzzed with tension, and the decision on whether to include doctors under the Consumer Protection Act hung in the balance.

A Legal Turning Point: The Pandora's Box Unleashed: 1996

In the bustling city of Delhi, the Supreme Court of India became the stage for a legal drama that would reshape the landscape of medical accountability. The case of Indian Medical Association v. V.P. Shantha and Ors brought together legal minds, medical professionals, and policymakers in a courtroom charged with anticipation.

Dr. V.P. Shantha, a determined advocate for patient rights, stood as the symbol of change, challenging the status quo. The Indian Medical Association, representing the medical fraternity, sought to maintain the traditional boundaries, arguing vehemently against the inclusion of doctors under the Consumer Protection Act.

The courtroom, with its imposing decorum, witnessed a clash of ideologies as the legal teams presented their arguments.

Lawyer for Dr. Shantha (LFDS):" Your Honors, we stand at a crossroads of justice and accountability. The Consumer Protection Act is a shield for citizens against unfair practices. Why should doctors be exempt from accountability when every other service provider is not?

Lawyer for Indian Medical Association (LIMA):" (Defiantly) Your Honors, the medical profession is unique. We deal with matters of life and death. Including doctors under the Consumer Protection Act will open a Pandora's box of litigation, causing unwarranted fear among practitioners.

Chief Justice (CJ):" (Sternly) Let's focus on the merits. What is the basis of including doctors under the Consumer Protection Act?

LFDS:" Your Honor, it's about ensuring that medical professionals are held accountable for negligence or malpractice. We presented cases where patients suffered due to the lack of accountability — cases that fell under Res Ipsa Loquitor.

CJ:" (Thoughtful) Res Ipsa Loquitor... the thing speaks for itself.

Lawyer for Indian Medical Association (LFIMA): "Your Honors, distinguished members of the bench, we assert that medical practitioners, being part of a noble profession, are not to be brought under the Consumer Protection Act. The Indian Medical Council Act, coupled with the Code of Medical Ethics, serves as a comprehensive guide, outlining the standards of professional conduct and disciplinary actions against negligence."

Lawyer for V.P. Shantha (LFVS): "Your Honors, we respect the governance of the medical profession. However, it is crucial to acknowledge that the existence of regulatory bodies does not absolve medical practitioners of their responsibility towards patients who suffer due to their negligence."

LFIMA: (Assertively) "The District Forum, State Commission, and National Commission lack the expertise to comprehend the intricacies involved in medical cases. Their procedures are inadequate for determining the complex questions arising from medical negligence claims."

LFVS: (Counterarguing) "Your Honors, the Consumer Protection Act applies universally. Complexity should not serve as a shield against accountability. The relationship between a doctor and a patient, while based on trust, is not beyond the purview of consumer protection."

Another Lawyer for IMA (ALIMA):" (Stepping forward) Your Honors, the definition of 'service' under the Consumer Protection Act excludes services of personal nature. The doctor-patient relationship is based on trust, resembling a contract for personal service, and, therefore, should not fall under the Act."

LFVS: (Challenge in his eyes) "Your Honors, doctors render their services for a fee. This very transactional nature makes it a service under the Consumer Protection Act. We cannot ignore the monetary aspect; otherwise, accountability becomes a mere illusion."

ALIMA: (Fighting back) "Should lawyers be held accountable for every misadventure in court cases? We render our services for a fee too. Does this mean we stand trial for every failure in our representation?"

LFVS: (Firmly) "Your Honors, the key distinction lies in the nature of the relationship. A lawyer's duty is to the client, while a doctor holds a duty to life. The stakes are higher, and so should the accountability."

CJ: (Interjecting) Lawyers, doctors, let's maintain decorum. The court must consider the merits of the arguments.

As the courtroom simmered with tension, the legal minds passionately presented their perspectives. The fate of medical accountability hung in the balance, and the judges, with furrowed brows, pondered the intricate web of law, ethics, and societal expectations. The courtroom, a battleground of ideas, awaited the final pronouncement that would reverberate through the corridors of legal history.

Hon'ble Chief Justice (CJ): The matter under consideration pertains to the inclusion of medical practitioners under the Consumer Protection Act, specifically examining whether the services rendered by them fall within the ambit of 'service' as defined in Section 2(1)(o) of the Act.

Background: The Court has considered the arguments put forth by both the Indian Medical Association (IMA) and V.P. Shantha, along with the implications of including medical practitioners under the Consumer Protection Act.

Judgment: After due consideration, we find that the services rendered to a patient by a medical practitioner, except where the doctor renders service free of charge to every patient or under a contract of personal service, by way of consultation, diagnosis, and treatment, both medicinal and surgical, would fall within the ambit of 'service' as defined in Section 2(1)(o) of the Consumer Protection Act.

Rationale: The fact that medical practitioners belong to the medical profession and are subject to the disciplinary control of the Medical Council of India and/or State Medical Councils constituted under the provisions of the Indian Medical Council Act would not exclude the services rendered by them from the ambit of the Act.

The pronouncement sent ripples through the medical community, setting the stage for a seismic shift in the landscape of Indian healthcare. The decision, albeit intended to fortify patient rights, inadvertently unfurled a complex tapestry of consequences.

Medical Community Outcry:

The verdict echoed through medical associations and institutions, triggering a wave of discontent. Doctors expressed concerns over potential litigations, fearing a surge in malpractice suits that might lead to defensive medicine practices reminiscent of the American healthcare system.

Impact on Doctor-Patient Trust:

The once sacred bond between doctors and patients began to fray. The looming fear of legal repercussions cast a shadow over every diagnosis and treatment, eroding the trust that had been the cornerstone of the healing relationship.

Rise in Defensive Medicine:

Doctors, in a bid to shield themselves from potential lawsuits, embraced defensive medicine. Unnecessary tests and procedures became commonplace, driven not solely by patient welfare but also by the fear of litigation.

Overwhelmed Legal System:

The floodgates of litigation opened wide. The already burdened legal system found itself grappling with an inundation of medical negligence cases, further straining its capacity and delaying justice for both doctors and patients.

Erosion of Collegiality:

Once a fraternity, the medical community became increasingly divided. Collegiality gave way to caution, as doctors hesitated to collaborate or share insights, fearing that their professional opinions might be misconstrued in a courtroom.

Financial Strain on Healthcare:

The cost of medical indemnity insurance soared, causing a ripple effect on the overall cost of healthcare. As premiums skyrocketed, the financial burden was inevitably shifted onto patients, exacerbating the already strained economic disparities in access to quality healthcare.

Public Distrust:

The unintended consequence of the judgment was a surge in public distrust. The perception that doctors were now driven more by legal protection than patient welfare fueled skepticism and skepticism fueled a decline in public trust.

Calls for Reevaluation:

In the wake of the chaos that unfolded, voices rose from both within the medical community and the public, urging a reevaluation of the legal framework. The unintended consequences of the judgment became evident, prompting a national discourse on the need for a nuanced approach to medical accountability.

The verdict, while intending to fortify patient rights, inadvertently set in motion a chain of events that transformed the Indian healthcare system, introducing complexities, challenges, and an unanticipated paradigm shift. The journey ahead would require careful recalibration to restore balance, trust, and the true essence of the doctor-patient relationship.

Reasonable Care In Medical Field Is Subjective

And Who decides this?

Certainly, the concept of "reasonable care" is fundamental in the Consumer Protection Act, emphasizing that manufacturers, service providers, and professionals must exercise a reasonable standard of care in delivering products and services. Here are examples related to TV, cosmetics, and medical professionals:

TV Manufacturer:

- Scenario: A consumer purchases a new television, and within a week, it malfunctions due to a manufacturing defect.

- Reasonable Care Expectation: The consumer has a reasonable expectation that the TV should function properly for a reasonable period after purchase.

- Manufacturer's Responsibility: The TV manufacturer is expected to provide a repair, replacement, or refund in line with the reasonable expectations of a consumer purchasing a new television.

Cosmetics Company:

- Scenario: A consumer experiences severe skin irritation and allergic reactions after using a cosmetic product as directed.

- Reasonable Care Expectation: Consumers reasonably expect that cosmetic products are safe for use and won't cause harm when used according to instructions.

- Company's Responsibility: The cosmetics company is expected to ensure their products undergo rigorous testing for safety, and they should provide clear instructions and warnings. If harm occurs, they may be held responsible for compensating the affected consumer.

Medical Professional (Doctor):

- Scenario:A patient undergoes surgery, and post-operatively, complications arise that could have been avoided with proper care.

- Reasonable Care Expectation: Patients have a reasonable expectation that medical professionals will provide a standard of care consistent with their training and the prevailing medical standards.

- Doctor's Responsibility: The doctor is expected to exercise reasonable care in diagnosing, treating, and managing the patient's condition. Failure to provide an acceptable standard of care may lead to legal consequences under the Consumer Protection Act.

In each scenario, the overarching principle is that the provider—be it a manufacturer, cosmetics company, or medical professional—owes a duty of care to the consumer. This duty involves ensuring that the product or service meets a reasonable standard of quality, safety, and effectiveness. If the provider falls short of this standard, the consumer may seek remedies such as replacement, repair, refund, or compensation, as specified by the Consumer Protection Act.

While the principle of "reasonable care" in consumer protection is crucial, there are potential downsides, especially when courts misinterpret or apply it incorrectly. Here are some downsides, illustrated with examples:

1. Subjectivity and Interpretation:

- Example: A consumer sues a smartphone manufacturer claiming that the device's battery poses a fire hazard. The court, lacking technical expertise, may struggle to objectively determine what constitutes "reasonable care" in battery manufacturing, leading to subjective judgments.

2. Retroactive Assessment:

- Example: A consumer buys a car and, after a year, claims a manufacturing defect caused an accident. The court, without a clear understanding of when the defect occurred, may struggle to retroactively assess what level of care was reasonable at the time of production.

3. Diverse Industry Standards:

- Example: In the pharmaceutical industry, different drugs undergo varied testing standards. If a court applies a uniform definition of "reasonable care" across all drugs, it might not consider the industry-specific variations in testing and approval processes.

4. Impact on Innovation:

- Example: A tech company develops a cutting-edge product, and a consumer claims it causes health issues. If the court imposes a rigid standard of "reasonable care" without considering the innovative nature of the product, it could stifle technological advancements

5. Burden on Small Businesses:

- Example: A small-scale cosmetic manufacturer faces a lawsuit due to an alleged allergic reaction. The court, without considering the limited resources of the small business, might impose the same standard of care as a multinational corporation, leading to significant financial burdens.

6. Inconsistent Legal Precedents:

- Example: Courts in different jurisdictions may interpret "reasonable care" differently. A verdict in one case might set a precedent that conflicts with another court's ruling, creating confusion and inconsistency in legal outcomes.

7. Complexity in Professional Fields:

- *Example:* In medical malpractice cases, courts may struggle to navigate complex medical procedures and varying standards of care. Incorrect judgments might discourage doctors from taking on challenging cases for fear of legal repercussions.

8. Impact on Consumer Prices:

- Example: A court rules against a food manufacturer for not disclosing potential allergens. The company, to avoid legal risks, might increase product prices, impacting consumers who are not affected by allergies.

9. Fear of Litigation:

- Example: A doctor, fearing legal consequences, may order unnecessary tests or procedures to meet an arbitrary standard of care, leading to increased healthcare costs and potential harm to patients.

Now just think are doctors treating or repairing TV, mobile or fridge. Are all the humans same and have the same wiring and have no difference. A service which is provided with all the time with them be it manufacturing, marketing and so on have time with them. But doctors deal with humans how can they be put into same category as consumer and service. An English speaking and highly moralistic person thought of protecting patient from quacks or corrupt medical professional have put the whole health care under the bus. And they don't even realise this.

When Will They Accept That They Don't Know Medicine .....?

The courtroom buzzed with anticipation as Dr. Anuj Kapoor, a seasoned surgeon, took the witness stand. Across the room, the Verma family, anxious and aggrieved, sat with their lawyer, Mr. Prakash Sharma, who was known for his aggressive approach in medical malpractice cases. The Honorable Judge Malini presided over the case.

Judge Malini:" Dr. Kapoor, thank you for being here. We're here to discuss the surgery you performed on Mr. Raghav Verma. The family alleges negligence. Please walk us through the events leading up to the complications.

"Dr. Kapoor:" Your Honor, Mr. Verma presented with symptoms of acute abdomen and intestinal obstruction. Given his age and the urgency of the situation, I performed a surgery to address the obstruction.

Mr. Prakash Sharma, a formidable lawyer known for his zealous approach, rose to cross-examine Dr. Anuj Kapoor. The courtroom hushed as he approached the witness stand.

Mr. Sharma:" Dr. Kapoor, let's address the complications that arose after the surgery. Isn't it true that complications like infections and postoperative ileus indicate lapses in medical care?

Dr. Kapoor:" (calmly) Mr. Sharma, complications are inherent risks in surgeries, particularly in cases like Mr. Verma's. We took every precaution, but they can still occur.

Mr. Sharma:" (leaning in) Dr. Kapoor, would you agree that complications could have been avoided with more careful and precise surgical procedures?

Dr. Kapoor:"(steadfast) No, Mr. Sharma. We followed established protocols, and complications can arise despite the utmost care.

Mr. Sharma:" (with emphasis) Dr. Kapoor, the family believes that Mr. Verma's prolonged stay and subsequent costs were a result of negligence. Can you explain why the treatment extended for such a considerable duration?

Dr. Kapoor:" (clearly) Mr. Sharma, Mr. Verma faced complications that necessitated continuous monitoring and collaborative treatment. The extended stay was crucial for his recovery.

Mr. Sharma:" (raising an eyebrow) Dr. Kapoor, could it be that the complications arose due to inadequacies in your surgical technique?

Dr. Kapoor:" (firmly) No, Mr. Sharma. Our surgical technique followed standard procedures. Complications, especially in complex cases, are not indicative of negligence.

Mr. Sharma:" (pointedly) Dr. Kapoor, the family is concerned that the treatment decisions were driven by financial considerations. Can you assure the court that financial factors did not influence Mr. Verma's care?

Dr. Kapoor: (assertive) Absolutely, Mr. Sharma. Our decisions were solely based on medical necessity. We explored all viable treatment options for Mr. Verma's well-being.

Mr. Sharma: (smirking) Dr. Kapoor, are you suggesting that the family's concerns about the costs are baseless?

Dr. Kapoor:" (with conviction) The family's concerns are understandable, but every decision made was in the best interest of Mr. Verma's health.

Mr. Sharma:" (changing tone) Dr. Kapoor, do you acknowledge that Mr. Verma's family has suffered emotionally and financially due to the complications?

"Dr. Kapoor:" (empathetic) I understand the challenges the family has faced, but our actions were guided by a commitment to Mr. Verma's well-being.

As the cross-examination unfolded, Mr. Sharma aimed to cast doubt on Dr. Kapoor's decisions and insinuate negligence. The courtroom atmosphere remained charged, reflecting the tension between legal scrutiny and the complexities of medical practice.

In the solemn atmosphere of the courtroom, Judge Malini, known for her meticulous approach to cases, prepared to deliver the verdict in the medical malpractice suit against Dr. Anuj Kapoor and the medical team. The room was charged with anticipation as the judge, adorned in her black robe, addressed the assembled parties.

Judge Malini:" (gently) This has been a challenging case, and I appreciate the thorough presentations from both sides. The court has carefully considered the evidence and testimony presented.

The Verma family, seated with a mix of anxiety and hope, exchanged nervous glances. Dr. Kapoor, flanked by his legal team, maintained a composed demeanor as he awaited the judge's words.

Judge Malini: (solemnly) In cases such as these, we must weigh the standard of care against the unfortunate complications that occurred. It is not lost on the court that Mr. Raghav Verma faced significant challenges during his recovery.

Dr. Kapoor's legal team exchanged subtle glances, hoping for a favorable outcome. The judge continued, her words carrying the weight of impending judgment.

Judge Malini:" (deliberately) The court acknowledges that surgery, especially in cases of acute abdomen and intestinal obstruction, inherently carries risks. However, the family's concerns about the complications and prolonged treatment cannot be dismissed.

The Verma family leaned forward, hanging on to every word, while Dr. Kapoor's team exchanged concerned glances. The judge maintained a measured tone, aware of the gravity of her words.

Judge Malini:" (concluding) In light of the evidence presented and the concerns raised, the court finds that the standard of care fell short in this instance. Complications, while acknowledged as inherent, should have been more thoroughly addressed.

Dr. Kapoor's expression remained unchanged, masking any disappointment he might have felt. The Verma family, on the other hand, exchanged subdued smiles, finding validation in the court's acknowledgment.

Judge Malini:" (firmly) Therefore, the court rules in favor of the Verma family. Dr. Anuj Kapoor and the medical team are held liable for negligence in the standard of care provided to Mr. Raghav Verma.

As the judge pronounced the verdict, a palpable tension settled over the courtroom. Dr. Kapoor's team exchanged glances, recognizing the uphill battle they faced in challenging the ruling. The Verma family, while relieved to hear the court's decision, understood that the legal journey might not end with this judgment.

Media Debate on Medical Malpractice Verdict: TRP destroyed the reputation of whole medical field. Seeds got a new fodder……..

Anchor:" Good evening, ladies and gentlemen. Today, we bring you a heated debate following a recent court verdict in a medical malpractice case. Joining us are Mr. Prakash Sharma, the lawyer representing the Verma family, Dr. Alok Mehra, a fellow doctor, and Mrs. Verma, the relative of the patient.

Anchor:" Mr. Sharma, let's start with you. The court ruled in favor of the Verma family, finding the medical team negligent. Your thoughts on the verdict?

Mr. Sharma:"Thank you. This verdict is a victory for justice. It highlights the need for accountability in the medical profession. The family deserves closure, and this ruling provides that.

Anchor:" Mrs. Verma, how do you feel about the court's decision?

Mrs. Verma:" (emotionally) It's been a long journey, and we're relieved to have some acknowledgment. Our priority was always Mr. Verma's health, and we believe this verdict brings us a step closer to closure.

Anchor:"Dr. Mehra, as a fellow doctor, what's your perspective on this case?

Dr. Mehra:" While I sympathize with the Verma family, it's crucial to recognize that medicine is complex. The court's decision, while intended for justice, may inadvertently instill fear in doctors who are already navigating a challenging profession.

Anchor:" Mr. Sharma, the court acknowledged the inherent risks in surgeries, yet it ruled against the medical team. Your response?

Mr. Sharma:" The acknowledgment of risks doesn't absolve doctors of negligence. The standard of care must be upheld, and in this case, it was lacking. We need accountability to ensure patient safety.

Anchor:" Dr. Mehra, how do you think this verdict might impact the medical community?

Dr. Mehra:"It sends a chilling message. Doctors might hesitate to take on complex cases, fearing legal repercussions. We must remember that every medical decision involves uncertainties, and not every complication is a result of negligence.

Anchor:" Let's discuss the broader issue. There's a sentiment that doctors prioritize financial gain over patient well-being. Mr. Sharma, your thoughts?

Mr. Sharma:" While not all doctors are driven by financial motives, we must acknowledge that profit-driven practices exist. This case highlights the need for transparency and accountability in the healthcare system.

Anchor:"Dr. Mehra, your response to the generalization that doctors prioritize money?

Dr. Mehra:"It's disheartening to see such generalizations. Most doctors are dedicated professionals who prioritize patient well-being. We need a nuanced understanding of the challenges doctors face.

Anchor:"Closing thoughts, Mrs. Verma?

Mrs. Verma:"Our fight was for justice. We hope this case prompts a reevaluation of medical practices and ensures a safer environment for patients.

Anchor:" Thank you all for joining this intense debate. The court's decision has ignited discussions about the delicate balance between accountability and the challenges faced by the medical community.

REPEL EFFECT: Conference Discussion on Medical Malpractice Verdict- They still fail to realize.

They should have called their families or friends in USA and ask about the defensive medicine that has started there by now……..

In a conference room adorned with medical charts and diagrams, eight doctors from various specialties gathered for a discussion on the recent medical malpractice case that had stirred the professional community.

Dr. Suresh (Orthopedic Surgeon):" It's disheartening to see a fellow doctor facing such legal challenges. We dedicate our lives to healing, and yet, a single court ruling can cast a shadow on our entire profession.

Dr. Ananya (Pediatrician):" It's frustrating that people who don't understand the complexities of medicine are quick to point fingers. Every diagnosis and treatment involves a degree of uncertainty.Dr. Rajan (Cardiologist):"The legal system seems to disregard the fact that medicine is both science and art. We make decisions based on the best available information, but outcomes aren't always predictable.

Dr. Kavita (Neurologist):"It's not just about this case; it's the precedent it sets. Are we expected to guarantee perfect outcomes in every situation? That's an impossible standard.

Dr. Arjun (General Practitioner):" What baffles me is the lack of accountability for legal professionals. If a lawyer loses a case, there's no widespread blame on their entire profession. Why the double standard?

Dr. Meera (Gynecologist):"It's true. We're held to a standard that no one can consistently meet. Medicine is not always black and white. There are shades of gray, and that's something the legal system fails to understand.

Dr. Vikram (Oncologist):" The media doesn't help either. They sensationalize cases, painting us all with the same brush. The public is led to believe that every complication is a result of negligence.

Dr. Niharika (Psychiatrist):" The mental toll this takes on us is immense. The fear of litigation influences decision-making. We start practicing defensive medicine, ordering unnecessary tests just to avoid legal trouble.

Dr. Suresh:" So, what can we do about this? How do we bridge the gap between legal expectations and the realities of medical practice?

Dr. Ananya:We can learn law and read about every judgement. After this we need to change the way we practice. Before taking any decision we need to think whether our action will lead to litigation or not.

Dr. Niharika: "But it looks like whatever you do right or wrong anyone can take you to court. And once in court the language of law is beyond our understanding. In their nothing matters, only thing matters what the lawyer say and what the judge think.

Dr. Meera: But then there are acts and provisions. A judge will not give any judgement as per his wish. He need to say why he has given that judgement.

Dr. Suresh: You are right, but you need to understand our law. It is Judge made law. Whatever the judge say in a particular case will become a law for next case. So it is all the game of fundamental rights, human rights, philosophy, morality and legality. No one realise that in this they can never judge the decisions taken by a doctor.

This debate raged throughout the country for few months to year and the plants grew further. Now the root has become powerful and fruits of defensive medicine are seen......

The uncertainty of legal repercussions added an additional layer of stress to their already demanding roles.

Heated Debate in the City Garden: The seed of hatred has also grown to thick root plant.......

Underneath the shade of old trees in the city garden, a diverse group of citizens gathered to discuss the recent medical malpractice verdict that had stirred the community. Passions ran high as people from different walks of life expressed their opinions.

Rahul (Engineer):"I don't understand why these doctors are always given a free pass. They charge exorbitant fees and then mess up people's lives.

Asha (Teacher):" It's not fair to generalize. I've known doctors who work tirelessly for the well-being of their patients. Mistakes happen in every profession.

Arjun (Businessman):" Mistakes? This is beyond mistakes. It's about greed. They'll do anything for money. I've heard they get commissions from labs and pharmaceutical companies.

Neha (Journalist):"We can't paint all doctors with the same brush. There are certainly bad apples, but many doctors work ethically, putting patients first.

Rahul:"(nodding) I agree. But how do we know who's good and who's not? They should all be held accountable.

Sunita (Housewife):" It's true. We're at their mercy when it comes to our health. They should be more transparent about their dealings.

Vikram (Police Officer):" If they're found guilty, they should be sent to jail. It's not just about money; it's about people's lives.

Sneha (Social Worker):" We also need to consider the pressure doctors face – long hours, life and death decisions, and the fear of litigation. It's a tough job.

Arjun:" (dismissing) Pressure? What pressure? They make enough money to live comfortably. They're just using it as an excuse.

Asha:" (firmly) Let's not forget that doctors spend years in education and training. We can't undermine their expertise.

Neha:" The media also plays a role. Sensationalizing cases without understanding the intricacies of medical practice creates unnecessary fear.

Vikram:" (nodding) True. But accountability is crucial. If someone makes a mistake, they should face the consequences, no matter their profession.

Sunita:"And what about lawyers who lose cases? Do we blame all lawyers for that?

Rahul:" Lawyers don't deal with life and death. Doctors should be perfect every time.

Sneha:" (emphatically) Perfection is unrealistic. Mistakes happen in every field. The focus should be on learning and improvement.

As the debate raged on, opinions clashed, reflecting the complex sentiments of a community grappling with the complexities of the healthcare system and the human condition. The city garden, once a peaceful retreat, resonated with the echoes of a society struggling to find a balance between accountability and understanding in the realm of healthcare.

Heated Exchange with Doctors Entering the Debate: FRIENDS BECOMES FOES SO EASILY

As the debate in the city garden intensified, Dr. Anuj Kapoor and Dr. Meera Singh, both regular walkers in the group, decided to join the discussion. The atmosphere grew charged as the focus shifted to the medical professionals present.

Arjun: (pointing at Dr. Kapoor) Here comes one of them! How much money do you make from those surgeries, doctor?

Dr. Kapoor:" (calmly) Arjun, let's have a civil conversation. I'm here to listen and share my perspective.

Rahul:" (accusingly) Doctors like you charge a fortune, and when things go wrong, you blame it on uncertainties. It's a win-win for you.

Dr. Meera:"(defensively) That's not fair, Rahul. We don't choose this profession for easy money. We genuinely want to help people.

Asha:" (supportively) I agree. Doctors go through years of education and training, and it's not an easy journey.

Arjun:"(mocking) Education? Training? I've heard doctors get kickbacks from labs and pharma companies. Is that true?

Dr. Kapoor:" (firmly) No, Arjun. It's not true. Yes, there are bad practices in every field, but don't generalize based on anecdotes.

Vikram:" (pointedly) What about the unnecessary tests? I've heard doctors order them just to earn more.

Dr. Meera:" (explaining) Sometimes, tests are necessary for accurate diagnosis. It's not about money; it's about providing the best care.

Neha:" (defending) We can't blame all doctors for the actions of a few. There are unethical practices in every profession.

Sneha:" (nodding) And let's not forget the stress doctors go through. Constantly making life and death decisions is not easy.

Arjun:" (sarcastically) Stress? Maybe they should've chosen a less stressful job.

Dr. Kapoor:" (assertively) Arjun, we chose this profession to make a difference. Yes, there are challenges, but we work hard to save lives.

As the doctors tried to provide a balanced perspective, the heated exchange continued. Emotions ran high, reflecting the deep-seated mistrust and frustration within the community. The city garden, once a serene retreat, became a battleground for conflicting views on the healthcare system and the role of doctors within it.

It is so easy to be wise after the event and to condemn as negligence that which was only a misadventure. Benefits without risk is not possible

We ought to be on our guard against it, especially in cases against hospitals and doctors. Medical science has conferred great benefits on mankind but these benefits are attended by unavoidable risks. Every surgical operation is attended by risks. We cannot take the benefits without taking the risks. Every advance in technique is also attended by risks. Doctors, like the rest of us, have to learn by experience; and experience often teaches in a hard way.

Lawyers: No Disrespect Intended

Can we entrust the judgment of medical fraternity to them.

No insult intended but they are doing that insult day and day out.

Ananya Gupta, a young woman with a troubled marriage, found herself at a crossroads. Unable to navigate the complexities of her relationship, she sought the counsel of Mr. Rohit Verma, a reputed family lawyer known for his expertise in handling such cases.

Ananya's Visit to Mr. Verma's Office

Ananya entered Mr. Verma's well-appointed office, nervously clutching a file containing her marital woes. Mr. Verma, a middle-aged man with an air of confidence, greeted her warmly.

Mr. Verma: "Welcome, Ananya. Please have a seat. Now, tell me, what brings you here?"

Ananya: "Mr. Verma, my marriage is falling apart, and I need help. My husband and his family are making my life unbearable."

Mr. Verma: "I understand, Ananya. Let's go through the details. I assure you; we'll find a solution."

The Fabrication of Cases

As Ananya poured her heart out, Mr. Verma listened intently, his mind already formulating a plan that went beyond legal resolution.

Mr. Verma: "Ananya, considering the gravity of your situation, we need to play this strategically. We won't just file one case; we'll file multiple cases against your husband, his family, and even distant relatives. This will give us leverage."

Ananya: "But is that necessary, Mr. Verma?"

Mr. Verma: "Trust me, Ananya, we need to be proactive. Now, let's add allegations of violence and abuse to make our case stronger. It's time to turn the tables in your favor."

Exploiting Legal Loopholes

As the legal proceedings unfolded, Mr. Verma continued to guide Ananya, exploiting legal loopholes to their advantage.

Mr. Verma: "Ananya, we'll file cases not just in civil courts but also in criminal courts. We need to exert maximum pressure. And don't forget the medical council – let's question the competence of the doctors involved."

Ananya: "But I thought this was about my marriage issues."

Mr. Verma: "It is, Ananya, but we have to use every available avenue. Trust me; this will work in our favor."

Prolonging the Legal Battle

As time passed, the legal battle intensified. Mr. Verma employed delay tactics to prolong the proceedings, ensuring that the pressure on the opposing party remained constant.

Mr. Verma: "Ananya, slow and steady wins the race. We need to wear them down, make them more amenable to a settlement in our favor."

Ananya: "But isn't there a quicker and more straightforward way to resolve this?"

Mr. Verma: "Patience, Ananya. Rome wasn't built in a day. We're working towards a resolution that ensures your well-being."

As the legal battle unfolded, arrests were made, and innocent family members found themselves behind bars, facing charges based on false narratives. The once harmonious family was shattered, and the accused individuals endured harassment in jail while their reputation was tarnished in society.

The Settlement

Eventually, the prolonged legal battle took its toll on both parties. The accused family, exhausted and financially drained, sought an out-of-court settlement.

Mr. Verma: "Ananya, we've achieved our objective. They're willing to settle. This is the best outcome for you."

Ananya: "But at what cost, Mr. Verma? Wasn't there a more ethical way to resolve this?"

Mr. Verma: "Sometimes, Ananya, the legal battlefield demands tough strategies. We secured your future, and that's what matters."

In this exhaustive story, Ananya's interaction with Mr. Verma unveils the manipulative tactics employed by some lawyers, highlighting the ethical dilemmas faced by clients seeking justice through legal means. In conclusion, Mr. Verma's unethical and illegal practices not only exploited the vulnerability of his client but also wreaked havoc on the lives of innocent individuals. Filing false cases and fabricating evidence for personal gain not only violates the principles of justice but also undermines the integrity of the legal system. Such actions not only harm the victims but tarnish the reputation of the legal profession, emphasizing the importance of ethical conduct and the need for stringent measures against those who manipulate the law for personal gain.

Hippocratic world: Will they ever understand the medical science

In the heart of the bustling city, St. Mary's Hospital stood as a bastion of healthcare. Dr. Vikram Malhotra, a seasoned physician, found himself at the epicenter of a challenging case that would test the bounds of communication, health literacy, and the legal system.

Mrs. Mehta, a septuagenarian battling a complex array of health issues, was admitted under Dr. Malhotra's care. The family, grappling with health illiteracy, struggled to comprehend the intricacies of her condition. The ensuing saga would unfold as a tragic narrative of misunderstandings, miscommunications, and, ultimately, legal ramifications.

Dr. Malhotra made every effort to bridge the communication gap, using simple language and visual aids. However, Mrs. Mehta's family, steeped in anxiety, found solace in blaming the medical team.

Relative (Mr. Mehta): "Doctor, every day someone new comes in. Reports are being thrown around like confetti. We need answers."

Dr. Malhotra: "I understand your concerns. We're dealing with a complex case, and different specialists are providing their expertise to ensure we cover all aspects of your wife's health."

Despite Dr. Malhotra's earnest explanations, the family's frustration grew. Health illiteracy bred a lack of understanding about the fluctuating nature of Mrs. Mehta's condition.

Relative (Mrs. Mehta's Daughter): "Some days she seems fine, and others, it's like a nightmare. Why is there no improvement?"

Dr. Malhotra: "Mrs. Mehta's case is challenging. We are doing everything in our power, but her age and existing health issues complicate matters".

As days turned into weeks, the tension reached a boiling point. The family, tormented by grief and frustration, sought a scapegoat for their agony.

Relative (Mr. Mehta): "Doctor, despite all your explanations, our loved one is not getting better. You've added medicines, called in specialists, but she's deteriorating."

Dr. Malhotra: "I share your pain, but medicine isn't always exact. We adapt our approach based on the evolving situation."

Tragically, Mrs. Mehta succumbed to her ailments. Grief-stricken, the family sought solace in blaming Dr. Malhotra, convinced that negligence led to her demise.

Relative (Mrs. Mehta's Son): "She was fine before coming here. Your treatment killed her."

Dr. Malhotra: "I did everything in my capacity to help your mother. Her condition was critical from the beginning."

In the wake of Mrs. Mehta's passing, grief transformed into legal action. The family, propelled by sorrow and anger, filed both civil and criminal negligence charges against Dr. Malhotra.

Relative (Mrs. Mehta's Son): "We trusted you with her life, and you failed. We will see you in court".

The fight escalated that day where the relatives refused to pay the bill and take the body home. The doctor knowing the medicolegal subject advice for post-mortem but relatives bluntly refused on the pretext of culture and religion.

They filed civil and criminal case against the doctor within few months. Their lawyer prepared the affidavit where many allegations were put. They even charged with no communication, no consent and asking for money everytime. The lawyer even added many sentences and stories which never happened. But as usual the burden of proof remained on doctor. The case paper became the main stay of evidence and not the real treatment given by the team of doctor. The essence of lawyer argument was " If you have written then it is a proof and if not then you have not even visited the patient"

In the hallowed halls of justice, the air was charged with tension as the legal battle unfolded. Dr. Vikram Malhotra, a seasoned physician, faced relentless accusations from the fierce advocate, Raghav Sinha.

Raghav Sinha: "Your Honor, we are here today to expose a doctor who, driven by greed, failed to disclose crucial information to his patient. Dr. Vikram Malhotra intentionally kept the patient in the dark, leading to unforeseen complications."

Dr. Vikram Malhotra: "Your Honor, I assure you, my priority has always been my patients' well-being. I provided thorough explanations and the best care possible."

Raghav Sinha relentlessly grilled Dr. Malhotra, painting a narrative of deceit and corruption.

Raghav Sinha: (pointing) "Dr. Malhotra, did you or did you not conceal the potential complications and the need for extensive treatments just to increase your earnings?"

Dr. Malhotra: (firmly) "No, Mr. Sinha. My duty is to inform and treat my patients. I have never compromised their trust for financial gain."

Raghav escalated the accusations, accusing Dr. Malhotra of immoral and illegal practices.

Raghav Sinha: (addressing the court) "Your Honor, we contend that Dr. Malhotra engaged in unethical practices, receiving kickbacks from laboratories and pharmaceutical companies."

Dr. Malhotra's defense attorney vehemently challenged these sensational claims.

Defense Attorney: (assertively) "Your Honor, these accusations are unfounded. Dr. Malhotra's commitment to his patients is beyond reproach. We request concrete evidence for these allegations."

The intersection of medical complexities and legal intricacies often leads to challenges in the realm of healthcare. Lawyers, grounded in legal expertise, may struggle to comprehend the nuanced details of medical practices, just as doctors may find themselves grappling with the complexities of legal language. The disparity between these two domains can indeed create a scenario where legal processes, sometimes divorced from the intricate realities of medical care, take precedence.

Medical practitioners, while dedicated to their profession, are increasingly aware of the legal landscape that surrounds their practice. Fear of legal allegations has become a looming concern for many, and the need for meticulous documentation and adherence to legal protocols has heightened. This evolving landscape underscores the importance of interdisciplinary collaboration and effective communication between the legal and medical professions.

Lawyer Fails Even After Many Years Is Routine, A Doctor Fails It Is Negligence

One day, a police officer apprehended a person for the crime of theft. They saw him running and suspected him to be a thief. A complaint had been lodged from a nearby residence reporting a theft in an empty house. Upon arriving at the scene, they witnessed the individual running and subsequently apprehended him.

Upon capture, the person pleaded, "Sir, why are you catching me? Where are you taking me? I was running to catch my bus. My family will be waiting for me for dinner. Please let me go." However, the police constable, without consideration for the explanation, struck him with a stick on his heels, causing tremendous pain. The individual started crying, but the police, convinced they had solved the case, did not verify his story. They transported him to the residence from where the call originated. The neighbours, unable to identify him specifically, relied on the police's account, agreeing and signing wherever instructed.

The police proceeded to the opposite house, which had been forcibly opened. They summoned the owners and urged them to come as early as possible. The arrested person was taken to the lockup, where he was subjected to physical abuse, as the police believed there were more individuals involved in the theft. The inspector demanded information, shouting, "Tell me who was with you in the theft, and what items have you taken from that house? Where are the things?" The individual, in pain, responded slowly, "Sir, I am not a thief. I am a simple man who works nearby in a cloth shop. I was running to catch the bus so that I could reach home in time." However, before he could complete his statement, the stick struck his sole and then his heel. One of the constables seized him by the hair and began slapping him. This continued for several hours until the person, exhausted and in pain, became unconscious.

The police, fatigued from their actions, decided to rest for the day. The following day, the house owner arrived. They took him to his house, where the owner, unwilling to disclose the actual stolen items (cash and gold bars), provided a list mentioning jewellery and a few expensive items as lost. Armed with this list, the police returned, subjecting the accused to another brutal interrogation lasting two hours. He was left bleeding from the nose, with bruises on his head, arms, and stomach, in deep pain and semi-conscious.

The police, believing they had completed their task, took the accused to the magistrate court, where the court appointed a lawyer for him. Meanwhile, the family, now aware of their misfortune, rushed to the station. They cried and pleaded for help, recounting the same story to the police. However, the constable callously shouted, "All thieves are like this. Their families also know about them, and they have such stories. So don't waste your time. Your husband and father is now gone. He will rot in jail. Tell him to tell the truth and about his friends involved. Maybe we will ask the court to be lenient."

The son pleaded with folded hands, "Sir, please talk to the owner of the shop where my father works. He will tell you about my father's character. He is an honest person."

The people around the constable laughed and uttered a few cuss words, "All thieves are very honest. See how he is protecting his friends in crime." However, nobody paid heed to them, considering he was the sole breadwinner, and their school fees depended on him. It was anyone's guess that food became scarce, and their education turned into a distant dream.

He remained in jail for months before his case even came to trial. The lawyers took over the matter. The prosecution's lawyers examined all the files and noticed gaps in the case. The lawyer said to the police, "Bro, where are the fingerprints of this man at the crime scene."

The police responded, "Sir, it was chaos that day, and since we caught him running from the scene, we did not take the prints." The lawyer made a note in his diary, anticipating the defense would question this. He then inquired about whether the other persons involved were caught. They replied, "Sir, we tried to get all information from this fellow, but he keeps crying, getting unconscious, and saying only one thing: I was running to catch a bus."

He then asked, "Did you check any CCTV camera near the residence and the neighborhood?" They got excited, "Yes, sir, we did check, and we saw that three people went in and came out of the house with two bags." The lawyer now felt that the case was winnable. He asked for the footage, and when he saw it, he was shocked, "This footage has only the back of these people; their faces are so blurred."

The police explained, "Sir, you know how societies and shop owners are. They install CCTV cameras for their psychological benefit, but they are of substandard quality and are never maintained." Still, the police constable insisted, "But still, sir, see the color of the shirt of one of the thieves matches with this fellow's shirt on that day."

The lawyer made a note again in the pad. He then asked a pointed question, "Have you found any past crime of this person." The inspector replied, "No, sir, his past is clean." The constable intervened, "Sir, either he is very smart, or he is new in this field. The way the family behaved, he looks smart."

The lawyer then asked, "Have you gone to the shop where he said he works? Have you interviewed his son, a colleague?" The police responded, "What is the need to do so? He can have such an alibi. But he was found running, his shirt matches, and there is an actual theft. We thought that is good enough." The lawyer knew that there is a reasonable doubt. The fingerprints, the person's alibi, and his past crime mattered. The lawyer said to himself, "To me, he looks innocent." Still, he said to the police, "I can create a reasonable doubt in the mind of the judge. He will not get bail. Till then, try finding the other culprits."

After almost six months, the case had its first hearing. The prosecutor took leave, citing fever, and the next date was set for the following month. This continued for the next three months. When the arguments finally came, given that these were Indian courts with a pending list in crores (tens of millions), more than 30 cases were heard in a day. The accused individuals were made to stand at the back. Each lawyer for each culprit had only seconds to argue. What exactly happened remains unknown, but "bail rejected" was shouted for this fellow, and he was back in jail.

The defense lawyer was appointed by the court, so he was least bothered about the delay. He received his payment and didn't know the family or the culprit directly. He did ask for fees from the accused and mentioned that, in that case, he would expedite the matter. The person in jail pleaded, "Sir, I really have no money. Please help me. I will remain under your debt for life." However, the attitude was indifferent. The case went on for months, and then the actual argument day arrived.

The routine scene in such cases in our courts is at a snail's pace. A lawyer asks a question, the witness says something which is repeated multiple times for digitization. Then the lawyers ask another question, and hardly one witness's testimony gets over in 2 to 3 hearings. In fact, if the defense lawyer, prosecutor, witness, or the judge is absent due to reasons known to them, then the matter stretches like chewing gum.

These arguments went on for two years, and the person got bail in between. Now he was a free man but with a stamp on his forehead telling everyone that he is a thief. His job was gone, and the owner also had doubts now. The lawyer's argument had really created doubt. The judge, burdened with cases, wrote all notes and then actually forgot the real philosophy of the judiciary. Someone asked me once, "What is the philosophy of our judiciary?" I said, "No innocent should be punished, even if, for that, 100 guilty remain unpunished." He said, "Oh wow, that's a good one." I said, "Yes, it is only for cases fought in a movie or a TV serial." He asked, "Means?" I said, "In reality, the louder the lawyer, the more aggressive the lawyer, and if we have a downtrodden accused, then such philosophy is not there."

So in this case, too, the judge said, "There is a strong possibility that this fellow committed the crime. He was found near the scene in mysterious circumstances, his presence is possibly seen in CCTV footage, and the defense lawyer could not prove his alibi of being somewhere else when the crime happened. So I pronounce him guilty. He should serve three years in jail. Since he has served half a year already in jail, he will remain in jail for the rest of the time."

All hell broke loose on the family. They thought the judge would know this case is wrong. He would ask the right questions to the police and lawyer. He would ask the owner to come and say who their husband or father is, and since there is reasonable doubt, the judge will be lenient. Their defense lawyer came and said, "Don't worry; this happens. This is routine that a smaller court pronounces such judgments. We will appeal in a higher court. There the judge will see through the case."

They felt some ray of hope and asked about the expense. He said, "It will be a bit costly. The fees of lawyers will be a bit higher than this court. And since the case will go on for a few years, the cost can increase."

They said, "Just as the court appointed you as our lawyer, will we get a lawyer there also?"

He said, "No, it is an appeal from your side, and so the cost is yours."

They asked innocently, "Sir, please ask someone to fight for us. We will pay slowly every month until we can give all to him."

The lawyer laughed, "Beta, it does not happen like this."

The son asked, "Sir, can you help someone help us? Can we not ask the court to help?"

He said, "The court cannot do anything in this, as there are such crores of cases."

The wife asked, "But then can the government have any policy to help poor people like us?"

He again laughed, "Why will the government help people like you? You are fighting for justice for a possible criminal. Why would it waste money on you?"

The son shouted, "Sir, don't call my father a criminal. If you would have fought well and questioned the prosecutor, we could have saved my father."

The lawyer now got angry, "How dare you accuse me of this? Your father was caught running. I tried everything. The prosecutor could convince the judge; it is not my fault."

The son said, "But you never called the owner of the shop. You did not say that the CCTV camera has no clear picture."

The lawyer said, "Oh, now that's my fault. The owner could not prove that your father was at the crime or not. Your father only told he has left the shop. And I did not remember the CCTV camera part."

The mother cried, "Sir, let's go to the judge and say this, na. Still there is time. The judge will understand the mistake and free my husband."

The lawyer laughed, "First, you cannot go and meet the judge like this. And secondly, if you say to the judge that it is your mistake, then he will send you also to jail in contempt."

The family sat down in shock. They did not know where to go. The lawyer says that he forgot to say about the CCTV camera; the judge will not meet to rectify the mistake, they don't have money to file an appeal. Then they saw the prosecutor. They ran towards him and said, "Sir, it was a mistake to send my husband to jail. See, you ask the defense lawyer. He will tell you that the CCTV camera was not showing my father."

The lawyer laughed, "Go home. I have won the case. How does it matter if the image was not clear? The judge has no problem with that; then who are you to tell it a mistake."

They said, "But sir, when you knew that my father is not guilty, then why did you not tell the judge to release him? He would have listened to you."

The lawyer, "Why would I tell the judge to do so? I have won that case is what matters. I am a good lawyer who could prove your father guilty. If you want, you can appoint me your lawyer in appeal and see how fast I release him from jail."

The son asked about the fees, and hearing the amount, they knew they could not pay him even if they sold themselves.

They saw the judge coming out: "Sir, it's a mistake to send my husband to jail. Ask this prosecutor; he just told me that he also knows that he is not the culprit."

The judge saw the lawyer and said, "What is this you are telling? But then why did the defense lawyer poke holes in your theories."

The son pleaded, "Sir, see now you also know na that my father is not the culprit, then please release him. The police will listen to you."

The judge said, "What nonsense. I have already pronounced the judgment. If you want, then appeal in a higher court. Then appoint a good lawyer who can argue well."

The wife said, "Sir, but see what this prosecutor and defense lawyer did. They knew that my husband is not guilty, still, they did not fight well. You should punish them and not allow them to practice anymore."

The judge got angry, "This is absurd. The lawyer's work is to win the case. They do all to do that. If we start punishing them like this, then who will fight the cases? How will we know who is right and who is wrong?"

The family said, "But now can they knowingly misguide the court? This way they are punishing an innocent person."

The lawyer intervened, "Why are you arguing? This is our justice system. We give a chance to all to put their arguments. Then the judge looks into all that is present on his table and makes a right decision. And look how burdened we are. There are crores of cases and there are so many criminals in the country."

"But is it not the work of you people to help the innocent?" The lawyer said, "We are bound by client ethics. I have to do all to win the case."

The son pleaded with the judge, "Sir, you are so powerful. Even the police bow in front of you. Please tell the government to provide a free lawyer to fight in a higher court."

The judge laughed, "Have you gone mad? The government cannot pay for such things."

A doctor was standing nearby, hearing all this. He was summoned there as a case of negligence was filed against him as he could not save a person despite all his expertise and efforts. He said to the judge, "Sir, can they file a case against the lawyers for failing them in their case? The prosecutor for knowingly proving an innocent guilty and the defense lawyer as he did not prepare for the case well. And this too when they had almost 2 years to prepare for the case."

The judge shouted, "Who are you? Why are you speaking in between?"

The doctor said about his case. The lawyer shouted, "Oh, that case. Sir, don't worry. I am the prosecutor in this case also. I will see you in court. I will do all to prove your negligence and get maximum punishment for you."

The judge said, "These doctors of the present time are so careless. They get the degree, and when the time comes to save a patient, they act negligent. They cannot even save a person."

The lawyer pronounced the guilt judgment even before the case has started, "Sir, this fellow got this patient in the emergency room. He got an hour to decide what could be the diagnosis. He sent reports and did some diagnosis. He gave some treatment, but the patient died in a few hours. He had so much time, he was having the reports, and he knew the patient is very serious, but still, he could not save the person. How negligent he is? You wait; I will ask for a criminal case to be filed against you. I will make you pay a huge compensation to my client. They are already broken because the client's husband was a heavy drinker, and he lost money in gambling. He was already looted by some hospital when he had bad diabetes and suffered a major attack. They charged lakhs for putting some stent in him."

The story suggests hypocrisy within the legal system when it comes to applying the same standards to lawyers and doctors. While the legal system is portrayed as flawed and indifferent to the injustice faced by an innocent man, the same legal professionals are quick to pass judgment on a doctor facing a case of negligence. The lawyer, who failed to secure justice for the wrongly accused man, becomes the prosecutor in the medical negligence case, displaying a lack of consistency in the application of ethical standards. This highlights the story's theme of hypocrisy within the legal system and its practitioners.

Lawyers And Consumer Protection Act

Surprise Surprise: Jugglery of words: We will protect our own

In the bustling city of Bangalore, a legal drama unfolded as a complainant sought justice through the Karnataka High Court, only to be ensnared in a web of deceit and professional misconduct. The complainant, having engaged the services of an advocate for a civil writ petition, soon found himself entangled in a dispute that would eventually make its way to the National Consumer Disputes Redressal Commission.

The saga began with the complainant, driven by the pursuit of justice, hiring the services of an advocate in Bangalore. A consolidated fee of Rs. 2500 was agreed upon for the undertaking of a civil writ petition before the Karnataka High Court. To fulfill his financial commitment, the complainant allegedly issued two cheques, amounting to Rs. 2000, to the advocate.

As fate would have it, the initial court proceedings did not go as planned. The writ petition was passed over to the next day due to the absence of the respondent's counsel. Unfortunately, the case was not heard on the subsequent date either. It was during this time that the respondent, the advocate in question, allegedly demanded an additional Rs. 3000 from the complainant. However, faced with financial constraints, the complainant expressed his inability to meet this demand.

The situation took a turn for the worse when, on the day of the next hearing, the respondent failed to appear on behalf of the complainant. As a consequence, the court dismissed the complainant's writ petition. Shocked and aggrieved by the turn of events, the complainant, on being advised by the respondent, contemplated filing an appeal before the Supreme Court. The respondent, seemingly undeterred by his prior failures, offered to assist the complainant by introducing the case to his contacts in New Delhi, albeit for a fee of Rs. 10,000. However, the complainant, disillusioned by the advocate's actions, declined the offer and instead decided to file a formal complaint against the respondent for professional misconduct.

The case took a new twist as it entered the realm of consumer disputes. The complainant, seeking redress for the alleged professional misconduct, approached the National Consumer Disputes Redressal Commission.

The central question before the Commission was whether the services provided by the respondent fell under the ambit of the Consumer Protection Act.

In a surprising turn of events, the Commission ruled in the affirmative, stating that the service offered by the respondent to the complainant constituted a 'contract of personal service' and therefore could not be classified as 'service' within the meaning of the Consumer Protection Act.

We do not render any service to the litigants

In the intricate tapestry of legal affairs, a compelling case unfolded, shedding light on the complexities between clients and their advocates.

In 2006, Devendra Sharma, seeking resolution for a dispute, engaged the legal services of Mr. Mathai, an advocate with a reputation for legal acumen.

With Mr. Mathai's expertise, the dispute was successfully resolved in Devendra Sharma's favor. However, the triumph turned into turmoil when the settlement amount, rightfully belonging to Devendra, remained in the possession of Mr. Mathai. To Devendra's astonishment, Mr. Mathai not only withheld the funds but audaciously demanded an additional payment.

Frustrated and disillusioned, Devendra Sharma decided to seek justice through the legal system and filed a case before the Delhi State Commission.

To his dismay, the State Commission dismissed the case, asserting that advocates, including Mr. Mathai, were not subject to the Consumer Protection Act. It appeared that the legal fraternity enjoyed immunity from consumer disputes.

Undeterred by the setback, Devendra Sharma, propelled by a quest for justice, appealed to the National Consumer Dispute Redressal Commission (NCDRC).

In a surprising turn, the NCDRC reversed the Delhi State Commission's order, stating unequivocally that advocates, including Mr. Mathai, fell within the ambit of the Consumer Protection Act. The commission affirmed that clients had the right to file consumer disputes against their advocates for any deficiencies in services.

The NCDRC's decision reverberated through legal circles, prompting a group of advocates, led by Mr. Mathai, to appeal the decision at the highest court of justice – the Supreme Court. In the landmark case of "Bar of Indian Lawyers Vs. D.K. Gandhi ," the Supreme Court, in 2009, issued a stay on the NCDRC's order.

Since 2009 Supreme Court has not found time to hear this matter because it concerns their fraternity. Remember in V.Shantha case it took them few years to decide the fate of the community who faces violence day and day out because of their judgement.

Unfortunately, the apex court did not provide a definitive clarification on the fundamental issue.

The Unresolved Dilemma

In the hallowed halls of the Supreme Court, a crucial matter unfolded, centering on the accountability of lawyers under consumer protection laws. Advocate Mr. Chowdhary, representing the legal fraternity, argued passionately that holding lawyers accountable under consumer law would be unduly harsh.

As the Chief Justice of India (CJI), the honorable Mahesh Shah, listened intently, he contemplated the intricate balance between protecting lawyers from undue harassment and ensuring justice for clients who may suffer from professional deficiencies. Mr. Chowdhary vehemently asserted that lawyers should not be subjected to the Consumer Protection Act, emphasizing the absence of a mechanism to assess the quality of legal services.

However, the CJI, known for his astute reasoning, posed a poignant question. "If lawyers engage in delay tactics, demand money for their failures, neglect their duties, and settle cases without client consent, what recourse does the client have?" he queried. The lawyer maintained that clients were free to change lawyers and that lawyers, surprisingly, do not render any service to clients.

The CJI, visibly anguished by this revelation, remarked, "So, you mean clients have no one to turn to for justice? If that is the case, it is in bad taste." The courtroom fell into a momentary silence as the gravity of the situation sank in.

In an unexpected turn of events, the CJI did something unconventional. Despite the millions of pending cases and countless individuals suffering, he directed Mr. Chowdhary to withdraw the case. This decision, while seemingly abrupt, carried profound implications. It suggested a recognition of the complexities surrounding the issue, the lack of a clear legal framework, and the dire need for comprehensive legislation to address the grievances of clients facing professional misconduct by their lawyers.

The courtroom, steeped in a sense of uncertainty, awaited the implications of the CJI's directive. The unresolved dilemma of lawyers' accountability under the Consumer Protection Act continued to cast a shadow over the legal landscape, leaving both lawyers and clients grappling with the question of justice and fairness within the legal profession. The path to a definitive resolution remained elusive, and the plight of millions awaiting clarity in this matter endured.

BUT THEN DOCTORS ARE ALSO GOVERNED BY MEDICAL COUNCIL ACT THEN WHY THIS INJUSTICE

Justice Deferred - The Uncharted Struggle

In the corridors of justice, a battle unfolded that challenged the very essence of client-lawyer relationships. The case of Srimathi and Others vs The Union of India, And Others, on 6 March 1996, marked a poignant moment in legal history. The heart of the matter lay in the constitutional validity of Section 3 of the Consumer Protection Act, 1986.

At the center of this legal storm were practising advocates, the petitioners, who found themselves facing claims before the Consumer Disputes Redressal Forums. These forums, whether at the District or State level, became arenas where clients sought redress for grievances against their own legal representatives.

The petitioners vehemently contended that as advocates, they were governed by the Advocates Act and, therefore, should be exempt from answering claims under the Consumer Protection Act. Their argument rested on the assertion that the objectives of the Consumer Protection Act did not encompass legal services provided by advocates to their clients.

Amidst the intricacies of legal arguments, a broader narrative unfolded - a narrative of clients grappling with a sense of injustice. The very individuals seeking legal recourse found themselves entangled in a web of legal complexities. As the petitioners argued for exemption, clients faced a disheartening reality: the struggle for justice seemed uphill when pitted against their own legal representatives.

The essence of the story lay in the plea of the clients - individuals who had entrusted their hopes and legal matters to professionals only to find themselves at a disadvantage when seeking recompense for grievances. The narrative painted a picture of clients who felt abandoned by the very system designed to protect their rights.

The courtroom drama reflected the wider dilemma within the legal system - a system meant to uphold justice and fairness. Clients, already burdened by legal battles, were confronted with the harsh reality that their pursuit of justice against their own lawyers was met with legal arguments asserting exemption.

As the case of Srimathi and Others vs The Union of India, And Others continued, the question of justice lingered in the air. Would the courts acknowledge the challenges faced by clients who sought justice against their advocates, or would the legal intricacies prevail, leaving the clients in a state of disenchantment? The unfolding saga captured the fragility of trust within the legal system and the quest for justice that, at times, seemed elusive even within the hallowed halls of justice.

You Can Judge. Yourself Lawyer: It Is Not Our Fault Vs Doctors: It Is Only Your Fault

a.   As a doctor if you don't give favourable result you are negligent, But………

A client approached an advocate for a case. The advocate who is a senior counsel promises the client that he will represent him. He held out himself to be a very Senior Advocate in Bangalore and having connections with Senior Advocate of the Supreme Court . He promised he would introduce or refer the complainant's matter to an Advocate in Delhi and also that he would appear before the Supreme Court representing the complainant and get a favourable order for him. However, when the matter reached the Supreme Court, it was merely adjourned after hearing and no favourable orders were passed....

While deciding the instant petition(**BECAUSE THE LAWYERS WERE INVOLVED IT WAS A INSTANT HEARING- REMEMBER IT TAKES YEARS BEFORE GETTING OTHER HEARINGS IN COURT**) seeking quashment of complaint against a Senior Advocate, wherein it was alleged that he was not able to obtain orders in favour of client (the complainant); the Bench held that merely because a client did not succeed in the matter and orders favouring the him were not passed by a Court, the said client cannot make out a case that a fraud which has been committed by the advocate. It was observed that it is for all litigants to understand that an advocate can only make best efforts in the matter and the case would be decided on the basis of merits.

In India it is only Supreme Court that has followed this issue of merit and helped doctors achieve some protection against frivolous complaints. But lower courts and consumer court have kept doctors in dock. And it years and lots of money to reach to Supreme Court. By then the life is devastated.

b.   As a doctor you cannot refuse to patient discharge or files if he or she do not pay, But……..

Appellant, now a septuagenarian, has been practicing as an advocate mostly in the courts at Bhopal, after enrolling himself as a legal practitioner with the State Bar Council of Madhya Pradesh.

According to him, he was appointed as legal advisor to the Madhya Pradesh Bank Ltd. (Bank, for short) in 1990 and the Bank continued to retain him in that capacity during the succeeding years.

He was also engaged by the said Bank to conduct cases in which the Bank was a party. However, the said retainership did not last long.

On 17.7.1993 the Bank terminated the retainership of the appellant and requested him to return all the case files relating to the Bank.

Instead of returning the files the appellant forwarded a consolidated bill to the Bank showing an amount of Rs.97,100/- as the balance payable by the Bank towards the legal remuneration to which he is entitled.

He informed the Bank that the files would be returned only after setting his dues. The bank filed cases in Bar councils

In the reply which the appellant submitted before the Bar Council he admitted that the files were not returned but claimed that he has a right to retain such files by exercising his right of lien and offered to return the files as soon as payment is made to him.

c.   Fees delayed, Justice deferred.

In the quaint town of Rampur, where the whispers of justice often mingled with the winds of uncertainty, Mr. Chunnilal, a humble lower division clerk in the Central Excise Department, found his life upended by a notice terminating his services. Undeterred, he set forth on a journey to Allahabad, seeking refuge in the halls of justice.

In the bustling corridors of the Allahabad High Court, Mr. Chunnilal found solace in the chambers of Mr. Abhay, an advocate known for his legal prowess. The sunlit room became the stage where the fate of an unjust termination would be contested.

As Mr. Abhay meticulously prepared the legal arsenal, the clerk's hope swelled. Rs. 220 exchanged hands – a down payment for justice. An unspoken pact was forged, acknowledging that the remaining fees would be settled at the advocate's discretion.

Days turned into months, and Mr. Chunnilal, nestled in the anticipation of justice, penned letters inquiring about the progress of his case. Each letter, a plea for reassurance, found its way to Mr. Abhay's desk. The responses, a mix of promises and veiled assurances, echoed through time.

The advocate, navigating the intricacies of the legal system, juggled multiple cases. In the meantime, Mr. Chunnilal, his optimism waning but not extinguished, continued to seek updates. As the clerk made a second pilgrimage to Allahabad for signatures, he was met with vague affirmations of progress.

Yet, the turning point arrived like a storm on a quiet night. In August 1957, the order, a harbinger of despair, reached Mr. Chunnilal. His plea dismissed – the petitions filed late, a verdict that echoed the haunting footsteps of shattered hopes.

A moment of reckoning ensued. Frustration and betrayal, two unwelcome companions, took residence in Mr. Chunnilal's heart. Determined to unveil the truth, he confronted Mr. Abhay. The advocate, caught between the delicate dance of ethics and financial constraints, made a startling revelation – fees delayed, justice deferred.

Anguish and disappointment etched on Mr. Chunnilal's face, he made a choice – a choice not just to bear the brunt of bureaucratic injustice but to confront the shadows within the system meant to uphold righteousness.

d.   Part of the legal fraud but where is the evidence, and the case also if heard and judged at super speed.........

Once upon a time in a city called Raipur, there were some people - Mr. Radha, Mr. Uday, Mr. Kondal, Mr. Ramanaji, Mr. Sai Sita, Mr. Narayana, Mr. Ramdas, and Mr. Subba Rao. They got involved in a not-so-nice story of trickery and bad deeds. This is a story of a bank, false deeds, bad loans and bank crores of profit....

Mr. Radha and Mr. Uday, along with Mr. Kondal, decided to do something wrong. They worked in a bank and used their positions to break the bank's rules and help Mr. Kondal get a lot of money - Rs.1,00,68,050 to be exact. They did this by approving 22 housing loans that weren't okay.Then, Mr. Kondal got clever. He got Mr. Ramanaji and Mr. Sai Sita to pretend they owned some land. They even made fake papers and used fake people to pretend they were owners. Sneaky, right?

But wait, there's more! Mr. Narayana, the lawyer of the bank who was supposed to give honest opinions, decided to join the bad side. He gave false opinions and prepared false analysis and Mr. Ramdas, who was supposed to value the properties, also made up some false reports. All of this was done to fool Vijaya Bank into saying yes to those not-so-good housing loans.

But their story took a turn when the authorities found out. Now, they all faced charges like cheating, pretending to be someone else, making fake papers, and being part of a big plot. A criminal case was fiiled and arrest were made.

The surprise came with the judgement, "Merely because his opinion may not be acceptable, he cannot be mulcted with the criminal prosecution, particularly, in the absence of tangible evidence that he associated with other conspirators. Therefore it can be concluded that a lawyer acting in his professional capacity in good faith cannot be subjected to criminal prosecution. At the most, if it is found that the act is in violation of rules of the Bar Council, he may be subjected to disciplinary action by the Bar Council only.

Where did this common sense vanished when deciding the case against doctors……..

e.   Court has not power to punish the lawyer for misconduct only Bar council can……..

Once upon a time, in a small town, ten people applied for loans under the Kisan Credit Card scheme at the Dena Bank's Pulgaon Chowk Branch. They needed non-encumbrance certificates for their lands to secure the loans. A lawyer, an empaneled advocate of Dena Bank, was asked to verify and certify the borrowers' land titles. The lawyer provided, certified that the lands were clear and free from any issues.

However, as time passed, the borrowers didn't repay their loans. When the bank investigated further, they discovered that the documents submitted by the borrowers were fake. The certificates and land records were all fabricated.

The lawyer who had provided the non-encumbrance certificates found herself in trouble. She was accused of being involved in the fraud because she had certified the false documents. The case reached the court.

During the court hearing, the judge pointed out that just because the lawyer provided the certificates doesn't mean she was part of the fraud. The judge emphasized that only the Bar Council has the authority to take action against a lawyer. The court itself cannot revoke an advocate's license.

Oh really the Councils in Professionals are considered so powerful, but then what happened with the medical body or council.

A TSUNAMI IN MAKING: LOADS OF BITTERNESS AND HATRED

1997- Failure To Diagnose With Limited Resource, A Death And A Case

A mere deviation from normal professional practice is not necessarily evidence of negligence. Let it also be noted that a mere accident is not evidence of negligence. So also an error of judgment on the part of a professional is not negligence per se

In the sweltering heat of April 1997, a cloud of despair settled over the Verma household as Pramod Verma, the beloved spouse of Mrs. Poonam Verma, fell ill. It started with a persistent fever, leaving Poonam concerned for her husband's well-being. Seeking medical help, they turned to Dr. Ashwin Patel, a local physician known for his years of practice.

With an air of confidence, Dr. Patel diagnosed Pramod with a viral fever and prescribed medications to alleviate his symptoms. Days passed, but Pramod's condition only worsened. The relentless fever showed no signs of abating, prompting Dr. Patel to reconsider his initial diagnosis. The shift from viral fever to Typhoid Fever reflected the growing concern for Pramod's deteriorating health.

Despite the change in prescription, Pramod's condition failed to improve. Fearing the worst, the Vermas sought further medical intervention. The next destination on their journey for answers was Sanjeevani Maternity and General Nursing Home, under the care of Dr. Rajeev Warty.

Dr. Warty, a seasoned practitioner, examined Pramod and embarked on a three-day treatment plan. However, the shadows of uncertainty loomed large, and the situation took a grim turn. Dr. Warty recommended transferring Pramod to a more specialized facility, Hinduja Hospital, recognizing the gravity of his condition.

In an oblivious state, Pramod Verma was transported to Hinduja Hospital, where a team of medical professionals worked tirelessly to unravel the mysteries of his ailment. The clock ticked away as hours passed with the grim affirmation that Pramod's battle was nearing its end. Despite their best efforts, he succumbed to the relentless grip of the unknown illness after four and a half hours of desperate struggle.

Devastated by the loss, Mrs. Poonam Verma, the grieving widow, couldn't shake the haunting question – could Pramod have been saved if not for the twists and turns of the medical journey? Driven by this haunting doubt, she embarked on a legal battle, asserting that the carelessness of the doctors had cost her the love of her life.

The courtroom became the stage for the unfolding drama, where the tale of Pramod Verma's last days was narrated with a mix of sorrow and accusation. The quest for justice was not just a legal pursuit; it was an attempt to find closure for a grieving widow who sought answers to the questions that echoed in the corridors of her heart.

The courtroom is tense as RAVI SHARMA, the lawyer representing the Appellant, Mrs. Poonam Verma, steps forward to cross-examine Dr. Ashwin Patel. The atmosphere is charged with anticipation.

RAVI SHARMA

(smirking)

Dr. Patel, isn't it true that you, a supposed medical professional, failed to diagnose Pramod Verma's condition accurately?

DR. ASHWIN PATEL

(resolute)

I did my best to provide the appropriate care based on the symptoms presented.

RAVI SHARMA

(raising an eyebrow)

Your best? Mr. Patel, let's talk about the initial diagnosis. Viral fever, correct?

DR. ASHWIN PATEL

(nodding)

Yes, that was the preliminary diagnosis.

(raising voice)

RAVI SHARMA

(skeptical)

Preliminary, indeed. Two days pass, and the patient doesn't improve. Suddenly, you decide it's Typhoid Fever. A convenient shift, wouldn't you say?

(sarcastic)

Did you suddenly become an expert in infectious diseases overnight?

DR. ASHWIN PATEL

(defensive)

The change in diagnosis was based on the evolving symptoms and test results.

(raising voice)

RAVI SHARMA

(smiling)

Evolving symptoms? Or perhaps evolving guesswork? You, a homeopathic doctor, playing doctor with allopathic medications. Are you even qualified to make such decisions?

(looking at the jury)

Ladies and gentlemen, I question whether Dr. Patel even possesses a legitimate medical degree. How can we trust someone who blurs the lines between medical practices and appears to lack the necessary qualifications?

(raising voice)

RAVI SHARMA (CONT'D)

(accusatory)

Dr. Patel, your actions amount to more than negligence. They point to a complete disregard for the well-being of your patient. You failed to recognize the urgency of the situation, and your questionable qualifications cast a shadow over the credibility of your medical decisions.

(turns to the judge)

We're not just talking about medical malpractice; we're talking about the possible culpable murder by someone who might not even be fit to hold a medical degree.

(leaning in)

Are you truly the doctor you claim to be, or are you a danger to those who seek your care?

The cross-examination leaves the courtroom in a stunned silence, with the credibility of Dr. Ashwin Patel under scrutiny and the weight of the accusations echoing in the minds of the judge.

The judge then passes the judgement:

The court observes that the appellant contends that the medical care provided during this period fell below the expected standard, leading to the unfortunate demise of Pramod Verma.

In light of the evidence and the arguments presented, this court finds merit in the appellant's claim of negligence. The medical practitioners involved in the case, including Dr. Ashwin Patel and Dr. Rajeev Warty, are hereby held liable for their failure to provide timely and adequate care.

As a result, this court awards compensation to the appellant for the loss suffered due to the negligence of the medical professionals involved. The compensation amount will be determined in a subsequent hearing.

Once this judgement was passed the widow even filed a criminal case of negligence amounting to murder under section 304A.

Just remember this is just 1997.

Such cases were happening in heaps. The consumer forum were taking decisions more in favour of the patients after years of the trials. Then after on appeal only Supreme Court was giving a verdict of relief.

If the judges in consumer forum were so ill equipped to understand the uncertainties of the medical science then what was the remedy. Years and years of suffering and harassment for failure of treatment which is very much possible in any medical case.

"Unwanted Child"

In the quiet village of Lakshmanpur, nestled amid fields and humble dwellings, lived a woman named Radha Devi. She was a resilient laborer, toiling under the scorching sun to make ends meet for her large family. The burdens of life had led Radha to a decision that she believed would secure her future – she chose to undergo sterilization.

Dr. Ananya Sharma, a well-respected physician in the region, performed the procedure. The hope was that this would spare Radha from the challenges of additional pregnancies. The procedure, however, would unravel a tale of unexpected twists.

Months passed, and life in the village continued its steady rhythm. Radha went about her daily chores, confident that her decision for sterilization would bring her some respite. But life has a way of surprising even the most steadfast.

As the seasons changed, Radha began to feel a peculiar discomfort, an inexplicable shift in her body. Concerned, she sought the counsel of Dr. Vikram Singh, another respected doctor in the village, who confirmed what Radha feared – she was pregnant.

The news shook Radha to her core. How could this happen? She had entrusted her well-being to the hands of medical professionals. Dr. Vikram Singh, empathetic to Radha's plight, recommended a thorough examination to understand the reasons behind the failure of the sterilization procedure.

As the investigation unfolded, it became evident that the sterilization, performed with the best intentions, had not been entirely effective. Dr. Ananya Sharma, though highly regarded, had unknowingly overseen a procedure that failed to fulfill its purpose. The ramifications were profound – Radha Devi was expecting another child.

Dismayed by the shocking revelation, Radha Devi found herself standing at the crossroads of her life. The financial strain, coupled with the emotional toll of an unexpected pregnancy, weighed heavily on her already burdened shoulders.

In her pursuit of justice, Radha Devi, now known as Smt. Santra in the legal proceedings, took a courageous step. She filed a lawsuit seeking Rs.2 lakhs as damages for medical negligence. Her voice echoed through the court, a plea for acknowledgment of the pain, suffering, and unexpected hardship she faced due to a medical procedure gone awry.

The courtroom became the battleground where Smt. Santra confronted the medical negligence that had disrupted the course of her life. Dr. Ananya Sharma, faced with the consequences of an unintended failure, had to defend her actions.

The legal proceedings unfolded.

The courtroom is filled with an air of anticipation as the honorable JUDGE MALIK takes his seat. Smt. Santra, a woman of resilience, sits beside her lawyer, RAVI SHARMA. On the opposing side, Dr. Ananya Sharma and her defense attorney, KIRAN MEHTA, prepare for the legal proceedings.

RAVI SHARMA

(standing, addressing the court)

Your Honor, we are here today to address a profound injustice that has affected my client, Smt. Santra. She entrusted Dr. Ananya Sharma with a sterilization procedure, a procedure that failed and resulted in an unintended pregnancy.

(points at Dr. Sharma)

This case is not merely about negligence; it's about a substandard operation. Dr. Sharma, despite her standing, oversaw a procedure that did not meet the standards expected of a medical professional.

(turns to the judge)

We contend that Dr. Sharma's actions, or lack thereof, have caused significant suffering to my client. Smt. Santra sought a reliable solution, and what she received was substandard care, leading to an unexpected and unwanted pregnancy.

(raising voice)

RAVI SHARMA (CONT'D)

The evidence will show that the sterilization procedure was not performed with the diligence and precision expected of a medical expert. Smt. Santra deserves justice for the emotional and financial burden she has had to endure due to this substandard operation.

KIRAN MEHTA

(standing, addressing the court)

Your Honor, if I may, I'd like to present a perspective that contextualizes the situation. Sterilization surgeries, like any medical procedures, are not foolproof. Even the most skilled surgeons cannot guarantee a 100% success rate.

(presenting statistics)

Statistics indicate that failures in sterilization surgeries, as well as the use of condoms, are not uncommon. There's an inherent margin of error beyond the control of medical practitioners.

(turns to the judge)

We sympathize with Smt. Santra's plight, but we must consider the broader picture. Medical procedures, no matter how carefully performed, carry a degree of risk. Dr. Sharma is not culpable for an isolated incident that, unfortunately, falls within the statistical norms of such procedures.

(raising voice)

KIRAN MEHTA (CONT'D)

Your Honor, let us not place the weight of the world on the shoulders of our medical professionals. The unexpected, despite our best efforts, is an inherent part of life.

RAVI SHARMA

(responding)

Your Honor, while we acknowledge the statistical realities, we must also recognize when substandard care has contributed to those statistics. Dr. Sharma, in this case, did not meet the reasonable standard of care expected from a medical professional.

(turns to the judge)

Let us not forget that behind these statistics is a human being, my client, who entrusted her well-being to a doctor. We seek justice not just for Smt. Santra but to ensure that every patient receives the standard of care they deserve.

The courtroom atmosphere remains charged as the legal battle between justice for Smt. Santra and the defense of Dr. Ananya Sharma unfolds. The scales of justice hang in the balance as the courtroom drama continues before the honorable Judge Malik.

Trial Court Judgment:

The courtroom is tense as Judge Malik, a figure of authority, pronounces the judgment in the case of Smt. Santra against Dr. Ananya Sharma.

JUDGE MALIK

(After a thoughtful pause)

In light of the evidence presented and the arguments heard, this court finds Dr. Ananya Sharma negligent in her duty to provide reasonable care. The sterilization procedure, having failed to meet the expected standard, resulted in an unintended pregnancy for Smt. Santra. The court rules in favor of the plaintiff and awards damages for the pain and suffering caused by the substandard operation. Dr. Ananya Sharma is held accountable for this failure, and the compensation to be determined in a subsequent hearing.

The gavel strikes, marking the end of the trial court judgment.

Supreme Court Appeal Judgment:

The grandeur of the Supreme Court sets the stage for the appeal, where the esteemed justices, including CHIEF JUSTICE RAO, scrutinize the trial court's judgment.

CHIEF JUSTICE RAO

(after reviewing the case)

Upon thorough consideration of the trial court's judgment, this Supreme Court finds it necessary to reevaluate the conclusions drawn. Sterilization procedures, like any medical intervention, carry inherent risks, and the statistics presented indicate that failures can occur, even in the hands of skilled professionals.

(pause)

While the appellant, Smt. Santra, undoubtedly suffered due to the unintended pregnancy, we must acknowledge the complexities of medical procedures. The mere occurrence of an undesired outcome does not automatically equate to negligence.

(addressing the courtroom)

This court, therefore, overturns the trial court's judgment, emphasizing that the possibility of failure in medical procedures is recognized and cannot be solely attributed to negligence. Dr. Ananya Sharma, in this case, acted within the reasonable standards of medical care. The compensation awarded is hereby set aside.

The gavel strikes again, concluding the Supreme Court's revised judgment. The courtroom dynamics shift, leaving both parties to grapple with the legal nuances and the broader implications of the appellate decision.

Again this took 8 years to get the judgement. But by then all the reputation of Dr Sharma was finished as it was a small town. She never practised in that town then after as people feared to come to her for procedures.

Blame Is A Powerful Weapon

If the hands be trembling with the dangling fear of facing a criminal prosecution in the event of failure for whatever reason—whether attributable to himself or not, neither a surgeon can successfully wield his life-saving scalper to perform an essential surgery, nor can a physician successfully administer the life-saving dose of medicine

April 18, 1996

09:00 AM - Operation Commencement

Dr. Arjun Mehra, a skilled plastic surgeon, and his anesthetist, Dr. Nandini Kapoor, begin an operation to remove nasal deformity on a 38-year-old male patient with no history of illness. The patient, Mr. Vikram Singh, hopes for a positive transformation through this procedure.

09:30 AM - Unexpected Crisis

Midway through the operation, an unforeseen crisis strikes. Dr. Kapoor and Dr. Mehra notice Mr. Singh's alarming physiological changes. His blood pressure and heart rate plummet, signaling a severe complication.

09:35 AM - Emergency Response

Quick to react, Dr. Kapoor and Dr. Mehra halt the ongoing operation. Recognizing the urgency of the situation, they administer intravenous fluids and initiate procedures to stabilize Mr. Singh's deteriorating vital signs.

09:45 AM - Cardiac Arrest

Despite their immediate response, Mr. Singh experiences a sudden cardiac arrest, throwing the operation theater into chaos. Dr. Kapoor and Dr.

Mehra perform cardiopulmonary resuscitation (CPR) in a desperate attempt to revive him.

10:00 AM - Relatives Informed

With the situation critical, Dr. Kapoor contacts Mr. Singh's anxious relatives, updating them on the emergency. The gravity of the situation prompts a swift decision to transfer him to a larger hospital for specialized care.

10:30 AM - Transfer to Big Hospital

Mr. Singh is transported to a prominent hospital for further treatment. Dr. Kapoor and Dr. Mehra continue their efforts to stabilize him during the transfer.

April 19, 1996

08:00 AM - Medical Intervention Continues

At the bigger hospital, medical professionals intensify their efforts to ascertain the cause of Mr. Singh's sudden deterioration. Continuous monitoring and diagnostic tests provide crucial information.

April 20, 1996

12:00 PM - Tragic Outcome

Despite exhaustive medical interventions and the collective expertise of the healthcare team, Mr. Vikram Singh succumbs to the aftermath of the complications arising from the nasal deformity surgery. The cause of death is recorded as cardiac arrest and related complications.

Legal Proceedings:

The incident prompts legal action, with Dr. Arjun Mehra and Dr. Nandini Kapoor facing charges under Section 304A of the Indian Penal Code. The trial unfolds, exploring the circumstances leading to the tragic demise of Mr. Singh and scrutinizing the actions taken by the medical professionals during and after the operation.

The courtroom is charged with tension as the cross-examination of Dr. Arjun Mehra, the accused plastic surgeon, unfolds. RAVI SHARMA, the lawyer representing the deceased, Mr. Vikram Singh, steps forward with a determined expression.

RAVI SHARMA

(standing)

Dr. Mehra, let's begin with the basics. Can you confirm your medical qualifications and the degree you hold?

DR. ARJUN MEHRA

(somberly)

I am a qualified plastic surgeon with a degree from the prestigious All India Institute of Medical Sciences.

RAVI SHARMA

(raising an eyebrow)

Qualified, indeed. Now, let's discuss the surgical procedure. Is it not true that you made an incorrect incision during the operation, causing blood to enter Mr. Singh's lungs and resulting in a cardiac arrest?

DR. ARJUN MEHRA

(defensive)

No, that's not accurate. I followed the standard procedure, and complications arose unexpectedly.

RAVI SHARMA

(skeptical)

Complications, you say? Let's talk about the timeline. When did you realize something was wrong during the surgery?

DR. ARJUN MEHRA

(reluctantly)

Approximately thirty minutes into the procedure.

RAVI SHARMA

(smirking)

Thirty minutes. A significant time. Could it be argued that this delayed realization was due to a lack of attention or proper monitoring?

DR. ARJUN MEHRA

(frustrated)

No, it was an unforeseen complication. We acted promptly once we identified the issue.

RAVI SHARMA

(nods)

Promptly, you claim. Yet, Mr. Singh went into cardiac arrest. Did you initiate resuscitation immediately?

DR. ARJUN MEHRA

(looking uneasy)

Yes, we performed CPR without any delay.

RAVI SHARMA

(raising voice)

Dr. Mehra, let's talk about the decision to transfer Mr. Singh to another hospital. Why the delay in shifting him for further treatment?

DR. ARJUN MEHRA

(explaining)

We needed to stabilize him before transfer. It was a critical decision made in the best interest of the patient.

RAVI SHARMA

(smiling)

Best interest, you say? Now, isn't it true that Mr. Singh did not survive in your hospital itself? You shifted a lifeless body to another hospital, didn't you?

DR. ARJUN MEHRA

(defensively)

We did everything we could to save him, but the complications were severe.

RAVI SHARMA

(nodding)

Complications indeed. The patient, who entered your hospital alive, left lifeless. No further questions.

[END OF CROSS-EXAMINATION]

On the other side, KIRAN MEHTA, the defense lawyer, stands to counter the allegations and present the facts in a sequence that portrays a reasonable standard of care.

KIRAN MEHTA

(standing)

Dr. Mehra, let's establish the timeline of events. When did the cardiac arrest occur?

DR. ARJUN MEHRA

(weary)

It occurred approximately thirty minutes into the operation.

KIRAN MEHTA

(emphasizing)

Thirty minutes. Dr. Mehra, can you clarify what immediate actions were taken upon identifying the complications?

DR. ARJUN MEHRA

(looking composed)

We stopped the operation, administered intravenous fluids, and initiated CPR promptly.

KIRAN MEHTA

(nodding)

Prompt response. Now, regarding the decision to transfer Mr. Singh to another hospital, was this a calculated decision based on the patient's stability?

DR. ARJUN MEHRA

(assertively)

Yes, we needed to stabilize him before transfer to ensure the best chance of survival.

KIRAN MEHTA

(intrigued)

And was it not true that Mr. Singh, despite all efforts, succumbed to the complications?

DR. ARJUN MEHRA

(sincere)

Yes, unfortunately.

KIRAN MEHTA

(subtly)

Dr. Mehra, is it fair to say that the actions taken were in line with the standard of care expected in such situations?

DR. ARJUN MEHRA

(resolute)

Yes, we followed the appropriate protocols.

KIRAN MEHTA

(nods)

Thank you, Dr. Mehra. No further questions.

[END OF EXAMINATION]

The courtroom atmosphere remains charged as the contrasting narratives unfold, leaving the judge and those present to navigate through the complexities of the medical proceedings under Section 304A of the Indian Penal Code.

Trial court pronounced the doctors guilty. Appeal followed in various courts where they got no respite in judgements. Finally after 10 years of the case Supreme court is giving its judgement. Sadly long legal battle and depression of being accused of culpable murder took the toll and Dr Nandini died in between this phase of appeals.

IN THE SUPREME COURT OF INDIA

Criminal Appeal No. [XXXX] of 2006

The present appeal arises from the judgment of the Trial Court, which found Dr. Arjun Mehra and Dr. Nandini Kapoor guilty under Section 304A of the Indian Penal Code [IPC] for the death of Mr. Vikram Singh. The Trial Judge pronounced a sentence of imprisonment, leading to this appeal before the Supreme Court.

After careful consideration of the facts and arguments presented, this Court deems it necessary to revisit the standards for fixing criminal liability in medical negligence cases.

The Supreme Court emphasizes that for criminal liability to attach to a doctor or surgeon, the standard of negligence required to be proved should be exceptionally high, tantamount to "gross negligence" or recklessness. The Court asserts that mere lack of necessary care, attention, or skill does not automatically translate into a criminal offense.

The Court acknowledges the complexities of medical practice, stating that when a patient willingly seeks medical treatment or undergoes a surgical operation, every careless act of the medical professional cannot be categorized as criminal. The judgment underscores the potential chilling effect on medical practitioners if criminal liability were imposed for every unfortunate outcome.

In the present case, the patient, Mr. Vikram Singh, was a young man with no history of heart ailment. The nasal deformity operation, while not insignificant, did not involve a level of complexity or severity that would warrant criminal charges.

After a meticulous examination of the medical papers accompanying the complaint, the Supreme Court concludes that the act attributed to Dr. Arjun Mehra, even if considered negligent, does not rise to the level of recklessness or gross negligence required to invoke Section 304A of the IPC. The Court finds no evidence to compel Dr. Arjun Mehra to face a criminal trial for the alleged offense.

Tragically, Dr. Nandini Kapoor, the anesthetist, is no longer with us, having succumbed to depression during the protracted legal battle. The Court expresses its condolences and notes the toll the prolonged litigation took on her life.

In light of the above considerations, this Court allows the appeal, overturns the judgment of the Trial Court, and acquits Dr. Arjun Mehra of the criminal charges. The Court emphasizes the need for a careful balance between accountability and the understanding of the inherent risks in medical practice.

And remember the repel effect is now almost like a wild fire. Now the times have also changed. Media is becoming more aggressive. Day and night people beating the doctors, abusing them or applying black ink on their face was rampant. In fact it appeared as if media was arranging this things to increase the TRP. The seeds of hatred have now grown into a tree.

We have crossed the deadly path of disastrous effect of medical negligence tried under consumer protection act and criminal act in matter of few years which USA took more than 100 years. This time we are going to win the race……..

A Race For Higher Compensation Begins

A life lost but many more harassed. You file as many cases as possible and name all the doctors, at least one will break.

Even today friends in the USA and Europe feel we Indian doctors are inferior. Ask your patients first.

In the quiet, historical city of Baroda, India, the bustling streets came alive with the arrival of Dr. Mansi and Dr. Rahul, a couple from the USA, seeking a much-needed vacation. The date was March 3, 1997, and their journey had taken them through the vibrant city of Mumbai en route to their destination. Little did they know that their vacation would soon take an unexpected turn.

The couple, both accomplished doctors, reveled in the cultural richness of Baroda. The local cuisine, colorful markets, and historical landmarks fueled their exploration. As days passed, the city unveiled its charm, and the couple found solace in the simplicity of life away from their bustling medical practices in the United States.

However, on March 7, a subtle shift occurred. Dr. Mansi, an epitome of health, noticed the emergence of a skin rash on her hands and stomach. Accompanied by a mild fever, neck gland swelling, and a sore throat, the symptoms prompted initial concern. Dr. Rahul, her husband and a physician himself, took charge of her care in those early days, confident that the ailment would subside.

As days unfolded, the rash persisted. Concerned, Dr. Rahul decided to seek professional advice and, on March 10, took Dr. Mansi to consult with Dr. Kelkar, a local physician. After a thorough examination, Dr. Kelkar diagnosed a simple skin rash with a viral etiology. Reassured, he advised only antiallergics if necessary and recommended a follow-up visit in a day or two. Dr. Kelkar, who had plans to travel to the USA for a conference from March 25, assured Dr. Rahul that his wife's condition was not a cause for major concern.

Days turned into weeks, and the couple immersed themselves in sightseeing, cherishing the beauty of Baroda. Meanwhile,

However, on March 23, when Dr. Kelkar saw Dr. Mansi again, her condition had taken an unexpected turn. Despite feeling better after the initial visit, she now exhibited worsening symptoms after consuming cheese in a local restaurant. Concerned about the escalating rash and itching, Dr. Kelkar recommended hospital admission and diagnosed cheese-induced skin vasculitis.

Admitted under a friend of Dr. Rahul in a Baroda hospital, Dr. Mansi's care was handed over to a team of physicians, including a skin specialist. Dr. Kelkar prescribed steroid depomedrol, antiallergics, vitamins, and skin lotions. However, the situation didn't improve; instead, Dr. Mansi's skin continued to peel, leading to the tentative diagnosis of toxic epidermal necrolysis.

As the gravity of the situation heightened, Dr. Rahul, fueled by anxiety, intervened persistently in the treatment. Conversations with doctor friends in the USA prompted him to question and alter the treatment protocol. Tensions between the medical team and Dr. Rahul escalated as differing opinions clashed, reflecting the cultural and procedural disparities between healthcare practices in India and the USA.

With Dr. Mansi's deteriorating condition, Dr. Rahul decided to take her to Mumbai for further specialized care. However, the decision to discharge against medical advice presented a dilemma. Unfamiliar with such forms, the local doctors did not insist on signatures. Dr. Rahul, with insights from the USA, refused to sign, recognizing the potential legal implications.

In Mumbai, the couple sought refuge at Bombay Hospital, where Dr. Mansi was admitted under a plastic surgeon (a friend of Dr Rahul) and later referred to skin specialists, physicians, and critical care specialists. A provisional diagnosis of toxic epidermal necrolysis was made, and the medical team initiated aggressive treatment with antibiotics, steroids, and supportive measures.

Amidst the medical complexities, Dr. Rahul's involvement persisted. Fueled by a desire to align the treatment with the protocols he was familiar with in the USA, he sought constant interventions from his overseas connections. Arguments ensued, as the medical team grappled with the challenge of managing a critical condition while navigating the demands of an anxious and assertive spouse.

The healthcare journey reached its painful conclusion as Dr. Mansi succumbed to the severe effects of toxic epidermal necrolysis. The clash of medical practices, cultural differences, and the relentless pursuit of optimal care had, unfortunately, ended in tragedy.

Legal Actions by Dr. Rahul:

Dr. Rahul pursued legal action on multiple fronts, filing cases in civil court, criminal court, Gujarat Medical Council, and Maharashtra Medical Council. His allegations revolved around civil liability and criminal negligence leading to the death of his wife, Dr. Mansi.

Dr. Rahul's Allegations:

1. Unnecessary Steroid Use:

   - Claimed that the administration of steroids, specifically the dosage and necessity, led to infections and deteriorated Dr. Mansi's health.

   - Advocated for the application of medical protocols from the USA in an Indian medical setting.

2. Lack of Proper Paperwork:

   - Alleged insufficient documentation and paperwork, asserting that this compromised the quality of care provided to Dr. Mansi.

   - Emphasized the importance of paperwork standards akin to those in the USA.

3. Absence of Supportive Care:

   - Accused the medical team of failing to provide adequate supportive care, potentially contributing to the worsening of Dr. Mansi's condition.

   - Argued for the incorporation of support care protocols in line with practices in the USA.

4. Inadequate Dressing:

   - Pointed out deficiencies in the dressing procedures, suggesting a lack of attention to wound care and infection prevention.

   - Advocated for the implementation of dressing protocols consistent with practices in the USA.

Key Issues Overlooked by the Court:

1. Steroid Use as Life-Saving:

 - Failed to acknowledge the global acceptance of steroid use as a life-saving measure in certain medical conditions, even during the time of the incident.

 - Neglected to consider the contextual differences in medical practices and guidelines.

This is a 2002 article written by a Westerner. We Indians are considered inferior though half of the USA gets treatment from Indians. But the problem is our friends who go there and practice also feel that we who practice in India are inferior…

https://escholarship.org/uc/item/97d8t291

This is an article from Japan, the most sane healthcare in world. They respect their doctors and don't abuse them. This is 2016. Steroid is the mainstay in the early phase and read the dose.

https://www.sciencedirect.com/science/article/pii/S1323893016300661

2. Comprehensive Paperwork and Documentation:

 - Disregarded the fact that medical records demonstrated thorough and precise documentation, covering examinations, medications, and supportive care measures.

 - Did not recognize that the absence of certain forms did not equate to deficient medical treatment.

A case note from the case paper.

Date & Time Progress notes Treatment 23/04/1997 2-15 pm Maculo Papular Bullous lesion? Allergy to Exogenous toxin and Unlikely to be SLE/Allied disorder Adv Wysolone 50 mg once daily x 1week 40 mg daily x 1 week 30 mg daily x 1 week Inj. 'Depomedrol' 80 mg IM twice daily x 2 days Then 40 mg IM twice x days Omez 20 mg BD Baycip 500 mg twice daily Pepsigard liquid 1 tsf 4 times daily x 1 week Limcee 500mg twice daily Atarax 25 mg twice daily O To Consult Dermatologist May, I request

Dr. ARJ , MD. to see her Repeat : HC, TC/ DC ESR CRP SGPT, Urea, Creatinine, Total Protein, Uric Acid platelets, AN factor, DS-DNA, Complement. Eye check up Opthalmologist Dr. BR please arrange eye, dermatological check up Bed to change ripple bed Daily fluid intake 2 litres / a day To puncture blister and send fluid to School of Tropical Medicine, Virology Dept.

3. Supportive Care and Dressing:

- Overlooked the evidence in medical records indicating the provision of proper supportive care, nutrition, and dressing procedures.

- Failed to consider that dressing protocols were aligned with the accepted standards of care at that time.

4. Intervention by Husband:

- Did not scrutinize the constant intervention and interference by Dr. Rahul in the medical treatment of his wife.

- Overlooked the possibility that Dr. Rahul's actions might have contributed to the complications in Dr. Mansi's condition.

5. Root Cause Analysis of TEN (Toxic Epidermal Necrolysis):

- Neglected to delve into the root cause of Toxic Epidermal Necrolysis (TEN) and the potential impact of the treatment administered by Dr. Rahul, who lacked authorization.

Conclusion:

The court's decision to accept Dr. Rahul's friends from the USA as witnesses and the push for implementing USA-centric protocols without contextual considerations reflected a lack of understanding of the diverse and evolving nature of global medical practices. The court overlooked essential aspects of medical care, including the appropriateness of steroid use, the comprehensive documentation maintained, adherence to supportive care protocols, and the potential influence of external interventions on patient outcomes. This case emphasizes the importance of a nuanced understanding of medical contexts and the need for comprehensive evaluations in legal proceedings.

If someone wish to read the whole case in real time do read use this link

https://www.docplexus.com/posts/anuradha-saha-case-and-doctor-s-fault-quantum-of-compensation-and-debate-on-merit-of-treating-such-a-high-profile-case

But the real problem in world lies the half-truth and the hatred it builds around itself

https://www.indiatoday.in/magazine/health/story/20131111-supreme-court-medical-negligence-compensation-doctors-hospitals-768359-1999-11-29

Media Influence:

Sensational Headlines: The media, driven by sensationalism, portrayed the case with headlines like "Appointment with Dr. Death," fostering public mistrust and animosity toward healthcare professionals.

Selective Reporting: Media reports often highlighted allegations without providing a comprehensive understanding of the medical context and standards followed.

The Surge in Criminal Negligence Charges against Doctors (1996-2005): A Disturbing Trend

But then doctors are not human.

In the period spanning from 1996 to 2005 in India, there emerged a troubling trend where patient relatives and lawyers fervently sought to invoke Section 304A of the Indian Penal Code, dealing with death by negligence, against doctors. This wave of criminal negligence charges posed a significant challenge to the medical community, leading to a surge in arrests, mental abuse, and instances of violence against healthcare professionals.

Criminal Negligence as an Epidemic:

Patient relatives and their legal representatives increasingly pressed for criminal charges, aiming to categorize medical mishaps as instances of death not amounting to murder. This trend gained momentum, fueled by a rising mistrust in the healthcare system, heightened sensitivity to medical errors, and the influence of sensational media coverage.

Media's Role in Amplifying Tensions:

The media played a pivotal role in amplifying tensions, often sensationalizing cases and portraying doctors as villains rather than professionals navigating the complexities of patient care. Print and show media contributed to creating an atmosphere of fear, animosity, and public outrage against healthcare providers.

Supreme Court's Intervention:

Amidst this tumultuous period, the Supreme Court of India emerged as a beacon of reason and justice. The apex court consistently intervened to protect doctors, ensuring a fair and impartial examination of medical practices. The court's interventions provided a crucial safeguard against the unjust prosecution of medical professionals.

Violence and Mental Abuse Against Doctors:

The surge in criminal negligence charges translated into real-life consequences for doctors, physicians, and healthcare workers. Instances of violence against medical professionals became distressingly common. Doctors found themselves subjected to mental abuse, facing not only legal challenges but also physical harm at the hands of agitated relatives.

Protecting the Innocent, Punishing the Guilty:

Despite the challenges posed by this disturbing trend, the Supreme Court's unwavering commitment to justice became a crucial bulwark against the potential miscarriage of justice. The court, through its verdicts, struck a delicate balance—acknowledging the need for accountability while safeguarding innocent healthcare professionals from unjust prosecution.

Impact on the Medical Community:

The epidemic of criminal negligence charges left an indelible mark on the medical community. Doctors and healthcare providers faced heightened scrutiny, contributing to a culture of defensive medicine and fear of legal repercussions. This atmosphere had potential implications for patient care, as doctors grappled with the fear of legal consequences.

Some cases that happened

1.   Sudden Extubation Due to Violent Coughing:

Case: Patient died due to sudden extubation after violent coughing, resulting in cardiac arrest two days after surgery.

High-risk operation, displacement considered common in the medical profession.

Legal Perspective: Hospital held negligent for not mentioning the anesthetist's name in the operation notes. National Commission's decision questions the documentation practices.

2. Acute Pancreatitis and Multiple Organ Failure:

Case: Patient admitted with severe abdominal pain, fever, and vomiting diagnosed with acute pancreatitis.

High pulse and respiratory rate indicated severe pancreatitis with a survival rate of less than 10%.

Legal Perspective: Diagnosis and prognosis align with medical literature, suggesting a high-risk case with limited chances of survival. Raises questions about filing negligence cases based on expected outcomes in severe medical conditions.

3. Criminal Negligence Cases Against Gynecologists:

Case: Numerous criminal negligence cases filed against gynecologists in mortality during childbirth or high-risk gynecological operations.

Police involvement leading to doctor arrests.

Legal Perspective: Examines the rising trend of criminal proceedings against gynecologists and the impact on medical practice. Considers the complexities of childbirth and high-risk procedures.

4. Alleged Medical Negligence in a Gynecological Operation:

Case: Criminal case filed against Dr. Sulekha Pandey and Dr. L.K. Pandey after the death of a patient post-gynecological operation.

Allegations of killing the patient.

Legal Perspective: The case involves allegations of deliberate harm. The legal system needs to assess the evidence and expert opinions to determine the merit of the criminal proceedings.

The cases presented highlight the multifaceted nature of medical negligence claims in India. While some instances involve procedural issues and adherence to documentation standards, others revolve around the inherent risks of medical procedures and the challenges faced by doctors in high-risk scenarios. But as years passed by

The legal perspective varies, with some cases emphasizing the need for comprehensive documentation and transparency, while others underscore the importance of understanding the inherent risks associated with certain medical conditions and procedures. The role of the National Commission becomes crucial in determining whether the actions of medical professionals align with accepted standards and practices within the medical community. It prompts a broader discussion on the delicate balance between accountability and the understanding of medical complexities in the legal system

"Escalating Violence: Attacks on Healthcare Professionals in India"

In a disturbing trend that exposes the vulnerability of healthcare professionals, instances of brutal attacks on doctors have surfaced across India, shedding light on a disconcerting reality. One glaring example is the tragic incident at the Teok Tea Estate in Jorhat, Assam, where Dr. Deben Dutta, a senior citizen doctor, was mercilessly beaten to death by a violent mob of tea estate workers on August 31 of the previous year. Shockingly, the assailants even prevented the doctor from receiving emergency medical treatment.

These incidents extend beyond physical harm, with reports of doctors being subjected to degrading treatment such as being paraded naked, having their faces blackened, and even having human excreta smeared on them. The sheer brutality reached new heights in Thane, where Singhania Hospital, the sole multispecialty hospital, was razed to rubble following the death of a political leader. In this chaotic episode, patients admitted to the intensive care unit were not spared, and valuable medical equipment was vandalized, depriving tens of thousands of patients of essential investigations and treatments.

The point of contention lies in the stark contrast between these incidents and the nature of healthcare-related violence in India. Unlike other regions where the patient may sometimes become the perpetrator, in India, acts of violence are often orchestrated by groups. These groups, which may include relatives (beyond immediate family members), unrelated individuals, or local political leaders masquerading as social workers, take the law into their own hands with little fear of reprisal from authorities. Notably, individuals with known criminal records are frequently implicated in these attacks.

In smaller towns and villages, where healthcare facilities may be limited, the sole doctor becomes particularly vulnerable to intimidation and blackmail. The modus operandi involves the assembly of seemingly "spontaneous" groups comprising 100 to 200 people, fully equipped to unleash acts of extreme violence, catching the lone healthcare professional off-guard and defenseless.This alarming trend not only poses a severe threat to the safety of healthcare professionals but also raises questions about the security infrastructure and legal consequences for those perpetrating such heinous acts. Urgent measures are needed to ensure the protection of healthcare providers and to create an environment where they can carry out their noble duties

without the constant fear of violent reprisals. The collective responsibility of society, law enforcement, and policymakers is paramount to curbing this escalating menace and safeguarding the sanctity of the medical profession.

The Deceptive Orchestrators: Unraveling the Kolkata Hospital Racket

Once upon a time in the vibrant city of Kolkata, a shadowy family emerged as the puppet masters of chaos, weaving a deceptive web of deceit that ensnared five diverse hospitals. Their sinister plot unfolded each time tragedy struck, leaving the hospitals in turmoil and shrouded in the aftermath of orchestrated violence.

The family's intricate modus operandi was driven by a relentless pursuit of commercial gains, preying on the vulnerability of hospitals grappling with unforeseen patient deaths. Their target was clear: exploit the system for personal enrichment by any means necessary. Their tool of choice? The insidious art of manipulation.

In pursuit of their ulterior motives, the family offered their unlawful services to distressed families, promising a magical solution to their financial burdens. For a tempting cut—25% of the outstanding hospital bills—the family guaranteed to erase the financial strain that lingered like a haunting specter. Little did the unsuspecting victims know, they were being drawn into a malevolent plot that would unleash a torrent of chaos.

The family's playbook was well-crafted. Upon offering their services, they meticulously manufactured a ruckus, creating an illusion of chaos and despair within the hospital walls. Their trump card was the claim of medical negligence leading to the unfortunate demise of "their" patient. This claim, though baseless, served as the catalyst for a series of events that would push the hospitals to the brink.

Adverse publicity became the family's weapon of choice. Exploiting the power of public perception, they manipulated narratives and coerced the hospitals into a corner, demanding the waiving of hospital charges as recompense for the alleged negligence. The family's clandestine activities thrived in the shadows, their true motives hidden beneath a façade of grief and victimhood.

However, their web of deception eventually began to unravel. Proof emerged that exposed their involvement in inciting and participating in acts of arson and violence. The curtain was pulled back, revealing the orchestrators behind the mayhem. Law enforcement, armed with evidence, closed in on the family, determined to put an end to their sinister exploits.

As the family faced the consequences of their actions, Kolkata's hospitals could breathe a sigh of relief, free from the malevolent influence that had sought to exploit their dedication to healing. The tale of the Kolkata Hospital Racket serves as a stark reminder of the lengths to which greed can drive individuals and the resilience needed to safeguard the integrity of institutions dedicated to the noble cause of healthcare.But more than this in all this cases the police filed criminal cases agaisnt the doctor and hospital. For months and years they were harrased. Above this Breaking news media traumatised the doctors more.

Some Sanity- Jacob Mathew

Why Is That Everytime Supreme Court Have To Help?

Why The Lower Judiciary Do Not Help?

Punish me if it is gross but who will judge the gross negligence. Even real murderers are given a chance.

Once upon a time in a bustling city, lived Jeevan Lal, a man battling the relentless grip of advanced-stage cancer. His sons, well-aware of his terminal condition, faced the challenging decision of ensuring his final days were filled with comfort, care, and tranquility. However, their positions of influence in the government provided them with an opportunity that seemed improbable for most.

Jeevan Lal's sons approached the administrators of a renowned hospital, their plea echoing a mix of desperation and a genuine desire to alleviate their father's suffering. Despite knowing that no hospitals in the country would typically admit a patient in Jeevan Lal's condition, they fervently requested compassionate admission for their ailing father. The request was not based on hope for a cure, but rather a longing for controlled medical treatment, proper nutrition, and a serene environment.

The sons, driven by their love for their father and their influence, managed to secure admission, skillfully bypassing the usual channels. The hospital, recognizing the influential positions of Jeevan Lal's sons, welcomed the patient, acknowledging the family's wish for a dignified final journey for their beloved patriarch.

The family, including the informant, was well-aware of the severity and incurable nature of Jeevan Lal's illness. Despite this awareness, they chose the hospital setting, placing their trust in the hands of the medical professionals. Little did they know that this decision would become the foundation for a story of compassion, dedication, and unwavering commitment.

Jeevan Lal, admitted against the odds, became the focal point of attention for the hospital staff. Doctors and paramedical personnel, recognizing the terminal stage of his illness, dedicated themselves wholeheartedly to providing the highest level of medical care. Their attendance was not just a duty but a sincere expression of empathy for a family grappling with the impending loss of a loved one.

In the corridors of the hospital, compassion intertwined with medical expertise. The staff, despite knowing the limitations of medical intervention in advanced-stage cancer, ensured that Jeevan Lal received every ounce of care available. From controlling pain to providing emotional support, the hospital staff became silent companions on the family's poignant journey.

The Oxygen Crisis: A Medical Dilemma"

Characters:

Mr. Jeevan Lal (Patient)

Mr. Vijay Sharma (Elder brother of Mr. Jeevan Lal)

Nurse Attendant

Dr. Jacob Mathew

Dr. Allen Joseph

Another Doctor

Police Officer

Setting: CMC Hospital Ludhiana, Nighttime

Scene 1: Hospital Room, 22nd February 1995, 11 PM

Mr. Jeevan Lal lies in the hospital bed, visibly struggling to breathe. Mr. Vijay Sharma is anxiously pacing around the room.

Vijay Sharma: (Frantically) Nurse! Nurse! We need the doctor, it's an emergency!

Nurse Attendant: (Rushing in) What happened? I'll call the doctors right away.

Scene 2: Doctor's Arrival, 20-25 Minutes Later

Dr. Jacob Mathew and Dr. Allen Joseph enter the room.

Dr. Jacob Mathew: What seems to be the problem?

Vijay Sharma: (Panicking) My father is having difficulty breathing!

Dr. Allen Joseph: (Examining the patient) Get the oxygen ready!

Scene 3: Oxygen Cylinder Issue

The doctors attempt to administer oxygen, but Mr. Jeevan Lal is still struggling.

Vijay Sharma: (Observing) Wait a minute... that oxygen cylinder looks empty!

Dr. Jacob Mathew: (Surprised) What? Let me check.

Vijay Sharma rushes into another room, finds a gas cylinder, but faces difficulty fixing it.

Vijay Sharma: (Frustrated) Come on, come on!

Scene 4: Another Doctor's Arrival

Another doctor enters the room.

Another Doctor: What's happening here?

Dr. Allen Joseph: (Checking the patient) We're losing time; we need to act fast!

Scene 5: Patient's Declared Dead

Despite efforts, the patient's condition worsens.

Another Doctor: (Examining) I'm sorry, he's gone.

Vijay Sharma: (Angry and upset) What?! This could have been avoided!

Scene 6: Police Station

Mr. Vijay Sharma files an FIR against the doctors.

Police Officer: (Taking notes) So, you're alleging negligence in providing proper treatment?

Vijay Sharma: (Firmly) Yes! The oxygen cylinder was empty, and there was a delay in fixing the new one. They failed to save my father!

Scene 7: Courtroom

The court proceedings begin with lawyers presenting arguments.

Defense Lawyer: There was an attempt to provide oxygen promptly.

Prosecutor: But the cylinder was empty, causing a significant delay!

The case unfolds as witnesses testify, and the truth behind the alleged medical negligence comes to light.

Scene 8: Verdict

The court reaches a verdict based on the evidence presented.

Judge: In light of the evidence, the court finds the doctors guilty of criminal negligence under Section 304A of IPC.

"A Supreme Verdict: Balancing Justice and Medical Caution"

As the echoes of legal proceedings resonated through the corridors of justice, the two accused doctors found themselves entangled in a web of charges under Section 304A IPC. The judicial magistrate in Ludhiana had framed charges, and despite their efforts to challenge the order, their revision petition before the learned session judge was met with rejection.

Undeterred, the accused doctors decided to seek justice from the highest authority—the Supreme Court. Their appeal reached the pinnacle of the judicial system, where the apex court considered the gravity of the charges and the nuances of the medical profession.

In a landmark decision, the Supreme Court issued guidelines that sought to strike a delicate balance between justice and the protection of medical professionals. Recognizing the noble service rendered by the medical profession to humanity, the court emphasized the necessity of caution and care in handling cases involving recklessness or negligence.

The court acknowledged that while doctors could be prosecuted for offenses involving recklessness or negligence, it underscored the need to shield them from baseless or unjust prosecution. It cautioned against the misuse of criminal proceedings by some complainants who sought to pressure medical professionals into providing unwarranted or unjust compensation.

In its wisdom, the Supreme Court laid down specific guidelines for cases involving medical professionals accused of recklessness or negligence. The investigating officer, before taking any action, was mandated to obtain an independent and competent medical opinion. This opinion, preferably from a government-employed doctor with expertise in the relevant medical field, would serve as a critical assessment of the alleged negligence.

In the courtroom, the accused-appellants found solace in the Supreme Court's pronouncement. The judges, after careful consideration, concluded that even if all claims in the complaint were assumed true, they did not establish a case of criminal recklessness or negligence on the part of the accused-appellant.

Crucially, the complainant had not alleged that the accused-appellant was unqualified to treat the patient. The Supreme Court's verdict, therefore, not only protected the accused doctors from potential injustice but also set a precedent emphasizing the need for prudence and fairness when prosecuting medical professionals.

As the legal battle drew to a close, the accused doctors could exhale a sigh of relief, knowing that the highest court had weighed the complexities of their case and safeguarded the delicate balance between justice and the noble service they rendered to humanity.

In the aftermath of the Supreme Court's landmark decision, the medical fraternity found itself navigating a transformed landscape where guidelines for the prosecution of medical professionals were unveiled. The court, in its wisdom, had not halted the criminal proceedings; instead, it sought to instill a meticulous approach to the initiation of such proceedings.

As the legal community grappled with the implications of the judgment, Dr. Rahul, a vocal critic of the verdict, emerged as a prominent dissenting voice. He wrote: Indian Supreme Court ruling makes arrest of doctors harder. This verdict further shields the errant doctors from criminal negligence.

In a fervent critique, he contended that the guidelines did not exonerate doctors from potential charges but rather outlined a structured format for filing FIRs and conducting arrests. Drawing a parallel with the political class, he underscored the disparities in the treatment meted out to doctors.

The Supreme Court, through its guidelines, had aimed to strike a balance between justice and the protection of medical professionals. It emphasized the need for a cautious approach, ensuring that criminal proceedings were not initiated without substantial evidence and expert medical opinions. The court's decision reflected a commitment to the fundamental principle of ensuring that even if a multitude of criminals were left unpunished, one innocent should not suffer.

In the broader context, the Supreme Court's guidelines were perceived as a step towards ensuring fairness in the criminal proceedings against medical professionals. While the judgment did not absolve doctors from potential charges, it demanded a meticulous and evidence-based approach, upholding the cherished principle that no innocent individual should bear the brunt of a flawed system.

As the medical community grappled with the evolving narrative of justice, the debate spurred discussions on the intersection of law and medicine, and the delicate balance required to protect both the rights of patients and the integrity of medical practitioners.

Media could have written this headlines if they would have understood the verdict

"Supreme Court Crafts Precision: Landmark Guidelines for Medical Negligence Cases"

"Balancing Act: Supreme Court Issues Blueprint for Fair Prosecution in Doctor Cases"

"In the Name of Caution: Supreme Court Directs Thoughtful Process in Doctor Arrests"

"Judicial Precision: Supreme Court Charts Course for Fair Treatment of Doctors"

"Navigating Justice: Supreme Court Unveils Guidelines for Doctor Criminal Proceedings"

But they choose this headlines to spread more hatred and animosity....

"Supreme Court Ruling Raises Concerns: Fear of Injustice as Guidelines Favor Doctors"

"Patient Rights at Risk: Supreme Court Verdict Tilted Towards Errant Doctors"

"Medical Negligence Cases in Limbo: Patients Worry as Supreme Court Leans Pro-Doctors"

"Balancing Act or Injustice? Jacob Mathew Verdict Sparks Patient Advocacy"

"Patients Left Vulnerable: Supreme Court Decision Tilts Scales in Favor of Doctors"

"Errand Doctors Get Legal Shield: Patient Advocates Express Concerns"

"Patient Advocacy Groups Rally: Supreme Court Ruling Feared as Setback for Justice"

The story of cases can go on and on. This is the only profession were the victim is both the patient and doctor. But the real loser is PATIENT DOCTOR RELATIONSHIP.

In 2000 onward something sinister happened in INDIA that is still shaking the whole base of healthcare.................

The story continues

When Business Enters Healthcare

Is medical negligence so simple? Why doctors are only blamed

VICARIOUS LIABILITIY: A legal term.

In the bustling city of Metropolis, Clara Williams, a middle-aged woman, sought medical attention at City General Hospital for a routine knee replacement surgery. What was expected to be a standard procedure soon turned into a nightmare that shook the foundations of the hospital.

Clara, a retired school teacher, entered the hospital with optimism, hoping the surgery would alleviate her chronic knee pain. Dr. James Miller, a reputable orthopedic surgeon, was assigned to perform the operation. The hospital, known for its state-of-the-art facilities, had an impeccable track record.

The surgery appeared to go smoothly, and Clara was moved to a recovery room. However, as the anesthesia wore off, Clara realized something was terribly wrong. Severe pain engulfed her entire leg, and she found it challenging to move even a finger. Panic set in.

The nursing staff, alarmed by Clara's distress, summoned Dr. Miller. Investigations revealed a shocking error – a mix-up in medication dosages during the surgery had resulted in nerve damage. Clara's once hopeful outlook turned into a relentless battle against excruciating pain and physical limitations.

As Clara endured the aftermath, she decided to pursue legal action against City General Hospital. Surprisingly, her case wasn't directed solely at Dr. Miller but implicated the hospital as a whole. Clara's legal team argued that the hospital failed to establish and enforce adequate protocols to prevent such medication errors. They contended that the hospital's negligence in maintaining a safe and secure environment for patients had led to Clara's suffering.

The courtroom drama unfolded as Clara's legal team presented evidence of systemic failures in the hospital's procedures. They showcased instances of previous medication errors and highlighted the lack of a robust system for cross-verifying medication dosages during surgeries. The hospital's legal team, in turn, emphasized Dr. Miller's reputation and experience, attempting to isolate the blame on an individual rather than the institution.

The trial garnered media attention, and public opinion wavered between sympathy for Clara and skepticism about the hospital's responsibility. As the case progressed, the hospital faced intense scrutiny for its overall quality assurance and patient safety measures.

In a surprising turn of events, the court ruled in favor of Clara, holding City General Hospital accountable for negligence. The judgment acknowledged that the hospital's lax oversight and inadequate safety measures had contributed to Clara's suffering.

The case sent shockwaves through the healthcare community, prompting hospitals nationwide to reevaluate their internal procedures. Clara, though scarred by the physical and emotional ordeal, found solace in the fact that her pursuit of justice led to positive changes in healthcare institutions.

Substandard Staff: Who decides recruitment?

Nestled in the serene town of Chestland, Central General Hospital was known for its picturesque surroundings and the promise of quality healthcare. However, beneath the surface, a web of negligence was silently weaving itself through the corridors.

Dr. Maya Sharma, a seasoned surgeon, was dedicated to her craft. Her commitment to patient well-being was unwavering, but the hospital's recent cost-cutting measures threatened to compromise the quality of care. The hospital, facing financial constraints, decided to expedite the hiring process, neglecting the meticulous scrutiny that candidates usually underwent.

Among the new recruits was Nurse Linda Barnes, a recent addition to the hospital's nursing staff. Linda's credentials were shaky, and her past experiences hinted at a pattern of carelessness. However, the hospital, desperate to fill positions swiftly, overlooked these red flags in the interest of expediency.

One fateful day, during a routine appendectomy led by Dr. Sharma, Nurse Barnes made a critical error. Misinterpreting a dosage, she administered an incorrect medication to the patient, resulting in a severe allergic reaction. The incident, unfolding under the sterile glow of the operating room lights, sent shockwaves through the medical team.

As the patient's condition deteriorated, Dr. Sharma frantically worked to stabilize them, eventually calling for an emergency intervention to counteract the adverse effects of the wrong medication. The hospital's negligence in vetting and training its staff had set the stage for a medical catastrophe.

The aftermath of the incident was chaotic. The patient survived but faced prolonged recovery due to complications. Dr. Sharma, distressed by the avoidable error, filed a complaint against Nurse Barnes and, by extension, the hospital for its hasty recruitment practices.

Legal proceedings commenced, revealing the hospital's rush in hiring substandard staff to cut costs. The court, during the trial, learned about Nurse Barnes' questionable history and the lapses in the hospital's recruitment process. Dr. Sharma, despite being absolved of direct blame, testified about the hospital's negligence in ensuring a competent and qualified team.

The judgment, echoing the sentiment of the court, held Central General Hospital responsible for the medical negligence. The hospital was required to compensate the patient for the extended recovery period and undergo a thorough reevaluation of its hiring practices.

This incident served as a wake-up call. Hospitals nationwide should reevaluate their recruitment procedures, emphasizing the importance of meticulous scrutiny and training for healthcare staff.

What Degree, Any Doctor Will Do

In the vibrant city of Nayapur, where the skyline mirrored progress and prosperity, a seemingly reputable clinic operated by Dr. Arjun Verma caught the attention of many seeking medical assistance. Dr. Verma's clinic, adorned with glossy brochures and state-of-the-art equipment, projected an image of modern healthcare.

Amelia Singh, concerned about her father's persistent cough, sought the expertise of Dr. Verma after hearing glowing reviews from friends and colleagues. Little did she know that her family's life was about to take an unexpected turn.

Dr. Verma, with a charismatic demeanor and a welcoming smile, reassured Amelia that her father's condition was treatable. Prescribing a cocktail of medications, he projected confidence in his diagnosis. However, as days passed, Mr. Singh's health deteriorated, and Amelia grew increasingly alarmed.

Suspicion crept into her mind, leading her to investigate Dr. Verma's credentials. To her horror, she discovered that he was not a qualified allopathic doctor but held a degree in Ayurveda. The realization struck like a thunderbolt, shaking the foundation of trust Amelia had placed in Dr. Verma.

In a desperate attempt to rectify the situation, Amelia sought a second opinion from a licensed allopathic doctor. The truth unfolded – the medications prescribed by Dr. Verma were not only ineffective for her father's condition but were also exacerbating his health issues.

Fueled by a sense of responsibility and anger at the deception, Amelia filed a medical negligence case against Dr. Verma and his clinic. The court proceedings revealed a startling lack of oversight in the healthcare system, allowing individuals with alternative medical degrees to operate as allopathic doctors without proper scrutiny.

Dr. Verma, during the trial, argued that his Ayurvedic knowledge allowed him to provide holistic care. However, the court maintained that patients deserved transparency about the qualifications of their healthcare providers.

The judgment ruled in favor of Amelia, holding Dr. Verma accountable for medical negligence and misrepresentation. The court's decision sparked a broader debate about the need for stringent regulations and checks to prevent unqualified individuals from practicing allopathic medicine.

In the aftermath, Rivertown witnessed reforms in its healthcare regulatory framework, emphasizing the importance of verifying the qualifications of healthcare professionals. Amelia's courageous pursuit of justice served as a catalyst for positive change, ensuring that patients were no longer deceived by doctors masquerading under false credentials.

What Degree, Icu Is As Easy As Walk In The Park

In the heart of Dharampur, where the ebb and flow of life echoed through the walls of Tranquil Regional Hospital, a fateful night unfolded in the Intensive Care Unit (ICU). Dr. Aryan Kapoor, a practitioner of Ayurveda, found himself in an unexpected and challenging situation.

As the clock struck midnight, a critical patient, Mr. Anand Sharma, was rushed into the ICU. Suffering from severe respiratory distress, Mr. Sharma needed urgent intubation to support his failing respiratory system. The responsibility fell on Dr. Kapoor, the doctor on duty.

Dr. Kapoor, however, lacked the necessary training and expertise in critical care procedures like intubation. His Ayurvedic background, while valuable in its own right, was insufficient for the demands of the ICU. As the seconds ticked away, Dr. Kapoor attempted to stabilize Mr. Sharma with traditional Ayurvedic remedies, failing to recognize the immediacy of the situation.

The nursing staff, aware of the gravity of the patient's condition, frantically sought assistance from the hospital's allopathic doctors. However, the delay proved fatal. By the time an experienced doctor arrived to intubate Mr. Sharma, precious moments had slipped away.

Tragically, Mr. Sharma succumbed to respiratory failure. The grief-stricken family, already grappling with the sudden deterioration of their loved one, soon discovered the inadequacy of the doctor on duty. Shock turned into anger, and they decided to pursue legal action against Tranquil Regional Hospital.

During the court proceedings, it became evident that the hospital had erred in assigning Dr. Kapoor to a role beyond his qualifications. The judgment, while acknowledging the hospital's failure in maintaining a qualified staff for critical care, also highlighted the need for stringent checks and balances to prevent such situations.

The incident spurred reforms in the healthcare system of Tranquilville, emphasizing the importance of aligning staffing assignments with individual qualifications. The tragedy of Mr. Sharma, while irreversible, served as a catalyst for change, ensuring that patients in critical condition would receive appropriate and timely care in the future.

We Are Busy And So What If She Lost Her Hand

In the quiet town of Serenityville, nestled amidst rolling hills and blooming meadows, a tale of medical negligence unfolded within the walls of Serenity General Hospital. Emma Thompson, a vibrant young woman seeking treatment for an iron deficiency, found herself caught in the web of a medical catastrophe.

Emma, diagnosed with severe anemia, was scheduled for an iron infusion to replenish her depleted iron levels. Dr. Rachel Miller, an experienced hematologist, oversaw the procedure. Unbeknownst to both Emma and Dr. Miller, the stage was set for a series of unfortunate events.

As the nursing staff prepared Emma for the iron infusion, they failed to notice a critical detail – the venous flow wasn't established properly. The iron solution intended for Emma's veins instead seeped into the surrounding tissues, causing extravasation. The signs of impending disaster went unnoticed in the rush of daily hospital activities.

Days later, Emma began experiencing excruciating pain in her arm. The once-vibrant limb now bore the ominous signs of gangrene. Shocked and terrified, Emma rushed back to Serenity General Hospital, where the gravity of the situation unfolded. The extravasation of iron had triggered a cascading effect, leading to tissue necrosis and the onset of gangrene.

Dr. Miller, devastated by the unfolding tragedy, informed Emma that the extent of the damage necessitated amputation of her hand to prevent the spread of gangrene. The once-routine iron infusion had metamorphosed into a nightmare, altering Emma's life forever.

In the aftermath, Emma and her family decided to pursue legal action against Serenity General Hospital. The court proceedings uncovered systemic failures in the hospital's protocols for intravenous procedures, emphasizing the need for heightened vigilance and thorough training among the staff.

The judgment, while acknowledging the irreversible loss suffered by Emma, mandated a comprehensive review of hospital protocols to prevent such incidents in the future. Emma's resilience in the face of adversity inspired changes in healthcare practices within Serenityville and beyond, ensuring that the pain she endured would not be in vain.

Who Checks The Bill

In the bustling city of Urbanscape, where skyscrapers kissed the heavens and the hum of progress echoed through the streets, a reputed hospital named Metropolitan Medical Center stood as a beacon of healthcare. However, behind its imposing facade, a web of deception was carefully woven.

Rahul Malik, a middle-aged man with a history of respiratory issues, sought medical assistance at Metropolitan Medical Center when his condition worsened. His journey through the corridors of healthcare would soon turn into a nightmarish ordeal.

Upon admission, Rahul was assigned to a room equipped with various medical devices, including a nebulizer, a glucose monitoring system, and an oxygen concentrator. A team of doctors, led by Dr. Neha Kapoor, was supposedly overseeing his care.

Days passed, and Rahul's health showed no improvement. Puzzled, he began to question the necessity of the continuous billing for services and equipment that were seemingly untouched. The nebulous hum of the nebulizer was never heard, the glucose monitor never beeped, and the oxygen concentrator sat idly in the corner.

Growing suspicious, Rahul's family decided to investigate the hospital's billing practices. To their horror, they discovered a pattern of fraudulent charges – fees for consultations with doctors who never visited, bills for nebulizer sessions that never occurred, and charges for investigations that were either unnecessary or never conducted.

Outraged by the deception, Rahul's family confronted the hospital management and demanded an explanation. The hospital, caught in the crossfire of scrutiny, was forced to acknowledge the unethical practices that had victimized Rahul and many others.

Legal proceedings ensued as Rahul's family filed a lawsuit against Metropolitan Medical Center for fraudulent billing and medical negligence. The court, during the trial, uncovered a systematic scheme where patients were exploited for financial gain, tarnishing the hospital's once-pristine reputation.

The judgment ruled in favor of Rahul's family, holding the hospital accountable for its fraudulent practices and awarding compensation for the emotional distress caused. The case served as a catalyst for regulatory reforms, prompting authorities to tighten oversight on billing practices within the healthcare sector.

Metropolitan Medical Center, once considered a pillar of healthcare in Urbanscape, now faced public scrutiny and legal repercussions. Rahul's ordeal, while a painful chapter in his life, catalyzed a broader movement for transparency and accountability in the healthcare industry.

Governement Pays We Earn

In the bustling metropolis of Haripur City, where towering corporate hospitals stood as symbols of modern healthcare, a sinister alliance between medical professionals and profit-driven institutions threatened the well-being of unsuspecting patients.

Rajesh Kapoor, a government employee, was elated when he learned about a new government health care policy that promised free and efficient medical treatment. Little did he know that this seemingly generous initiative would become a pawn in a larger game of deception.

Diagnosed with a persistent backache, Rajesh was referred to EliteCare Hospital, a prestigious corporate healthcare facility participating in the government scheme. Dr. Malhotra, a renowned orthopedic specialist, greeted him with a reassuring smile. However, beneath the veneer of compassion lurked a nefarious alliance.

Unbeknownst to Rajesh, Dr. Malhotra and EliteCare Hospital had formed a clandestine nexus, driven by a shared goal – maximizing profits at the expense of patient welfare. The government-sponsored policy became a lucrative opportunity for this unholy alliance.

Dr. Malhotra, guided by financial incentives rather than genuine medical concern, recommended an array of unnecessary diagnostic tests and procedures for Rajesh. From MRIs to intricate spinal surgeries, the doctor's prescription seemed like a never-ending list of interventions.

Suspecting foul play, Rajesh's son, Arjun, decided to seek a second opinion from an independent healthcare professional. Dr. Mehta, an ethical and experienced orthopedic surgeon, was alarmed by the unnecessary procedures suggested by Dr. Malhotra. His diagnosis revealed that Rajesh's condition could be managed through conservative measures, without the need for invasive surgeries.

Arjun, determined to expose the malpractice, gathered evidence of the collusion between Dr. Malhotra and EliteCare Hospital. The evidence included falsified records, unnecessary medical interventions, and a trail of financial transactions indicating kickbacks.

Armed with this information, Arjun filed a complaint with the medical board and the legal authorities. The ensuing investigation uncovered the extent of the nexus between certain doctors and corporate hospitals exploiting government health care policies for financial gain.

In a landmark judgment, the court held Dr. Malhotra and EliteCare Hospital accountable for their actions, imposing hefty fines and revoking their licenses. The exposed nexus prompted widespread reforms in the implementation of government health care policies, emphasizing transparency and accountability.

Rajesh, spared from unnecessary medical interventions, became the unwitting hero in dismantling a network of deception. The incident served as a cautionary tale, prompting authorities to scrutinize such alliances and protect the integrity of healthcare systems designed to serve the public's well-being.

Hospital And Doctor And Commission Agents: Who Cares Then

In the sprawling urban landscape of MetroCity, where the pulse of progress echoed through towering skyscrapers, a nefarious alliance formed the backdrop of an elaborate scheme to exploit unsuspecting patients. The unholy nexus between Dr. Vikram Kapoor, Metropolitan Health Systems, and unscrupulous commission agents weaved a tapestry of deceit that would shake the foundations of healthcare ethics.

Dr. Vikram Kapoor, a once-respected physician, had succumbed to the allure of easy money. Enticed by financial incentives offered by Metropolitan Health Systems, a colossal corporate hospital, Dr. Kapoor found himself at the center of a clandestine network designed to maximize profits through unethical practices.

Act 1: The Temptation:

Metropolitan Health Systems, hungry for increased revenue, devised a strategy to inflate profits. The hospital engaged commission agents who were incentivized to bring in patients, promote unnecessary procedures, and ensure a continuous flow of revenue. Dr. Kapoor, enticed by financial rewards for each referred patient, willingly joined this dubious alliance.

Act 2: Exploiting Trust:

Patients like Mrs. Radhika Sharma, unaware of the dark forces at play, sought medical assistance for common ailments. Little did they know that their health concerns were commodified in a web of deception. Commission agents, posing as helpful intermediaries, convinced patients to consult Dr. Kapoor at Metropolitan Health Systems, downplaying alternative, less expensive healthcare options.

Act 3: Unnecessary Interventions:

Under the influence of the nexus, Dr. Kapoor, once a healer, began prescribing unnecessary tests and procedures to unsuspecting patients. From unwarranted surgeries to overpriced diagnostic tests, the hospital's revenue soared, leaving patients burdened with medical bills for services they never truly needed.

Act 4: Financial Kickbacks:

The commission agents, acting as middlemen between Dr. Kapoor and Metropolitan Health Systems, received hefty kickbacks for every patient they steered into the hospital's lucrative arms. The money trail flowed discreetly, hidden beneath layers of deceit, as patients continued to suffer both financially and physically.

Act 5: Exposing the Nexus:

Ravi, a diligent investigative journalist, stumbled upon irregularities in medical billing and treatment patterns. Digging deeper, he uncovered the nexus between Dr. Kapoor, Metropolitan Health Systems, and the commission agents. His exposé brought to light the exploitation of vulnerable patients for financial gain.

Act 6: Legal Reckoning:

Armed with Ravi's investigative report, legal authorities launched a thorough inquiry into the illicit practices. The court, horrified by the extent of patient exploitation, took swift action against Dr. Kapoor, Metropolitan Health Systems, and the commission agents. Licenses were revoked, fines imposed, and criminal charges laid against those responsible for tarnishing the sacred trust of healthcare.

Exploit The Trust And Earn Money

In the heart of Harmony City stood Serenity General Hospital, its façade echoing the promise of compassionate care and healing. However, behind the pristine walls of this medical institution, a dark conspiracy unfolded, betraying the trust of unsuspecting patients.

Act 1: The Illusion of Serenity:

Sophie Anderson, a middle-aged woman with a history of heart issues, sought solace at Serenity General Hospital when her symptoms escalated. Dr. Richard Turner, a seemingly compassionate cardiologist, welcomed her with assurances of expert care within the hospital's state-of-the-art facilities.

Act 2: The Deceptive Diagnosis:

Unbeknownst to Sophie, a nexus had formed between Dr. Turner and Serenity General Hospital. Driven by financial incentives, the duo exploited the trust patients placed in them. Dr. Turner, once a healer, succumbed to the allure of financial gain, prescribing unnecessary tests and procedures to boost the hospital's revenue.

Act 3: A Web of Exploitation:

Sophie, caught in the web of deception, underwent a battery of unnecessary diagnostic tests, each contributing to the growing medical bill. The hospital, complicit in the exploitation, fabricated reports to justify prolonged hospital stays and unnecessary procedures, all under the guise of comprehensive healthcare.

Act 4: The Financial Burden:

Sophie's trust, a sacred bond between patient and doctor, was shattered as she grappled with the mounting financial burden. The hospital, once viewed as a sanctuary, had become an accomplice in the betrayal of her well-being. Dr. Turner, motivated by financial incentives, callously continued the exploitation.

Act 5: The Unraveling:

As Sophie's health deteriorated, her family began questioning the escalating medical bills and the lack of improvement in her condition. Suspecting foul play, they sought a second opinion from an independent healthcare professional. Dr. Patel, a principled physician, uncovered the deception and realized the extent of the exploitation.

Act 6: Confronting Betrayal:

Sophie's family, armed with evidence of the fraudulent practices, confronted Dr. Turner and Serenity General Hospital. The hospital administration, caught in the web of their own deceit, attempted damage control but faced an imminent reckoning.

Act 7: Legal Consequences:

Legal authorities, apprised of the betrayal of trust, initiated an investigation into the hospital's exploitative practices. Dr. Turner and the hospital faced severe legal consequences, including fines, license revocation, and public condemnation for violating the sanctity of the doctor-patient relationship.

Conclusion:

The story of Sophie Anderson served as a stark reminder of the vulnerability patients face when trust is betrayed within the healthcare system. The once-hallowed halls of Serenity General Hospital were tainted by the stain of greed, prompting a reevaluation of ethical practices within the medical community. Sophie's journey, marked by deception and exploitation, ignited a call for transparency, accountability, and a reaffirmation of the sacred trust that should define the doctor-patient relationship.

The Actual Scenario: You Accept It Or Not Is Your Problem

Shadows of Deceit - The Sinister Meetings

Characters:

1. Mr. Arjun Mehra - Businessman and Hospital Owner

2. Dr. Ananya Kapoor - Eminent Surgeon

3. Dr. Raj Malhotra - Cardiologist

4. Dr. Naina Verma - Radiologist

5. Dr. Vikram Singh - Orthopedic Surgeon

6. Dr. Priya Sharma - Pediatrician

7. Dr. Sneha Patel - General Practitioner

8. Mr. Rakesh Verma - Commission Agent

9. Ms. Anita Khanna - Commission Agent

10. Mr. Vikas Sharma - Lawyer 1

11. Ms. Maya Desai - Lawyer 2

12. Mr. Aryan Kapoor - Lawyer 3

13. Mr. Karan Kapoor - Financial Analyst

14. Ms. Pooja Sharma - Billing Specialist

15. Pathology Head - Mr. Vikram Reddy

16. Radiology Head - Mr. Rahul Kapoor

Scene: A Lavish Boardroom

The room is adorned with opulence. Mr. Arjun Mehra, a charismatic but cunning businessman, sits at the head of the table. The doctors and commission agents gather, each with their ulterior motives.

Arjun Mehra: (Smirking) "Thank you all for joining this exclusive meeting. Beacon Medical Center is our ticket to unimaginable wealth. Dr. Ananya Kapoor, what ideas do you have to ensure patients keep coming back?"

Dr. Ananya Kapoor: (Confident) "I am an surgeon so more surgeries, Mr. Mehra. We can decide on charges which is win win for both you and hospital and in such a way that patients won't question us. I'll ensure my department contributes significantly".

Dr. Raj Malhotra: (Nodding) "Let's start the government scheme in our hospital. We will have patient directly being send by government. We can do all procedures in them. I have many plans to increase the number and also the revenue. We will have health check-up department and then you know how lucrative cardiology is. All fear death and heart attack. Cardiac procedures are a gold mine."

Dr. Naina Verma: (Smirking) "We are back bone of the hospital. More doctors and so more radiology reports and then now a days we can invest in many new machines. They are high end machines and the charges are also good for the hospital. We can decide on various model then after. Patients rarely understand the details."

Dr. Vikram Singh: (Chiming in) "Orthopedic surgeries are often subjective. Like cardiology we can tie up with government and hence get loads of patients. They will be coming here for surgery and not for right advice. So why care if they themselves want the surgery. Then every orthopaedic require loads of blood reports and radiology also."

Dr. Priya Sharma: (Slyly) "We can have high end paediatric intensive care unit and paediatric department. We need an Obstetrics and Gynaecology department. Now a days females are not ready to bear the pain of labour. They will always like to go for caesarean surgeries. Many are career oriented. Paediatric procedures are emotionally charged. Parents won't hesitate to pay for anything we recommend for their children."

Dr. Sneha Patel: (Cautiously) "General practice can play its part too. Now a days we are not that important branch. But if we do proper marketing around the residential areas then we can increase the walk in and then since it is a world of medico legal problems we can always increase the reference work to super specialists. Then they can do whatever they wish is right for patient and hospital business."

Arjun Mehra: (Grinning) "Excellent! Now, Mr. Rakesh Verma and Ms. Anita Khanna, your role is crucial. Commission agents will ensure patients keep flowing in, and we'll reward you handsomely for each one."

Rakesh Verma: (Smiling) "We'll lure patients with promises of top-notch healthcare, conveniently forgetting to mention the financial toll."

Anita Khanna: (Nodding) "The more patients, the more profits. We'll ensure our network keeps expanding."

The meeting continues as Mr. Arjun Mehra turns to the lawyers for their input.

Arjun Mehra: (Smirking) "Now, let's hear from our legal team. Vikas Sharma, Maya Desai, and Aryan Kapoor, how can we safeguard the hospital from possible negligence cases?"

Vikas Sharma: (Confident) "Mr. Mehra, we'll establish a robust consent process. Make sure patients sign off on every procedure, emphasizing the inherent risks. It'll be their word against ours."

Maya Desai: (Nodding) "Additionally, we'll discreetly encourage patients to sign arbitration agreements. This way, any disputes will be handled internally, away from the scrutiny of courts."

Aryan Kapoor: (Smirking) "We can also strengthen our legal team. The more skilled lawyers we have, the better equipped we'll be to manipulate the legal system. Delay tactics, appeals – we'll exhaust the plaintiffs until they give up."

Arjun Mehra: (Pleased) "Excellent strategies, team. This alliance will be impenetrable. With our increasing practices and your legal prowess, Beacon Medical Center will reign supreme."

Concerned whispers circulate among the doctors about potential legal consequences. Dr. Ananya Kapoor, representing the group, raises a question.

Dr. Ananya Kapoor: (Frowning) "What about us, Vikas, Maya, Aryan? How can you ensure our protection?"

Vikas Sharma: (Smirking) "Doctors, we have a plan for that as well. We'll ensure all procedures are well-documented, with emphasis on following established protocols. If a negligence case arises, we'll create an impenetrable defense around medical standards and best practices."

Maya Desai: (Chiming in) "Additionally, we'll discreetly influence expert witnesses. Our network will ensure that the medical experts testifying in court are sympathetic to our cause. Their opinions will carry significant weight."

Aryan Kapoor: (Leaning forward) "We will take indemnity covers for you and then we if any case arise then the payment will be done by the insurance companies. And remember this are civil liabilities and so maximum we will have to pay some money. This are not well circulated reports and so no issue on reputation also."

Arjun Mehra: (Smiling) "Doctors, you're in good hands. Our legal team will leave no stone unturned to protect you. Trust in our collective expertise, and Beacon Medical Center will remain untouchable."

Mr. Mehra, turns his attention to the commission agents, Rakesh Verma and Anita Khanna.

Arjun Mehra: (Leaning forward) "Rakesh, Anita, how do you plan to ensure a steady stream of patients to Beacon Medical Center?"

Rakesh Verma: (Smirking) "Mr. Mehra, our network is vast and persuasive. We'll establish ties with local clinics, offering them handsome commissions for referring patients to Beacon. Money talks, and soon, every medical professional in the vicinity will be singing our praises."

Anita Khanna: (Grinning) "Not just that. We'll create a brand of superior healthcare. Pamphlets, online reviews, and strategically placed advertisements will make Beacon Medical Center seem like the epitome of excellence. Patients won't be able to resist the allure."

Rakesh Verma: (Nodding) "Additionally, we'll employ community outreach programs. Health camps, free check-ups, and awareness drives – all aimed at creating a favorable image. We'll be seen as benevolent, caring for the community's well-being."

Arjun Mehra: (Pleased) "Excellent, Rakesh, Anita. You've thought this through. With such a comprehensive plan, we'll have a constant influx of patients. Beacon Medical Center will be the go-to choice for everyone seeking healthcare in the region."

Arjun Mehra turns his attention to the financial experts, Karan Kapoor and Pooja Sharma, seeking their insights on revenue generation.

Arjun Mehra: (Smirking) "Karan, Pooja, how can we ensure maximum revenue generation and inflate the bills without raising suspicions?"

Karan Kapoor: (Calculating) "Mr. Mehra, we'll implement a tiered billing system. Every service, test, or procedure will have multiple components, each with its own charge. This complexity will make it difficult for patients to scrutinize the bills."

Pooja Sharma: (Nodding) "Additionally, we'll strategically use medical codes. With a vast array of codes at our disposal, we can easily manipulate billing. Unbundling, upcoding, and charging for services not rendered will become common practice."

Karan Kapoor: (Explaining) "We'll also have a flexible pricing strategy. Based on the patient's appearance and willingness to pay, we can adjust the final bill. Insurance claims will be padded with unnecessary charges, ensuring maximum reimbursement."

Arjun Mehra: (Smiling) "Ingenious, Karan, Pooja. Your financial acumen will play a pivotal role in our success."

Arjun Mehra turns to Pooja Sharma, the billing specialist, seeking clarification on the strategy for sending inflated bills to insurance claims.

Arjun Mehra: (Leaning forward) "Pooja, can we send inflated bills to insurance claims without the patients knowing?"

Pooja Sharma: (Smirking) "Mr. Mehra, absolutely. We'll camouflage the inflated charges within the complexity of the billing system. Patients rarely understand the intricacies, and we can exploit that to our advantage."

Arjun Mehra: (Grinning) "Good, Pooja. Make sure the insurance claims reflect the maximum possible charges. We need every penny we can get."

Pooja Sharma: (Assuring) "Rest assured, Mr. Mehra. I'll ensure the billing practices align with our overall strategy. Insurance claims will be a significant source of revenue for Beacon Medical Center."

Arjun Mehra inquires about exploiting government schemes for maximum billing, turning to Pooja Sharma for an elaborate plan.

Arjun Mehra: (Scheming) "Pooja, how can we manipulate government schemes to our advantage? Where procedures are hard to track, and we can bill for more than what's actually done?"

Pooja Sharma: (Smirking) "Mr. Mehra, government schemes are our playground. We'll inflate the bills for major procedures, making it seem like a multitude of complex surgeries were performed. For example, for a simple stent insertion, we'll bill for additional procedures like IABP insertion, CABG, and even valve repair. The lack of oversight ensures we can get away with it."

Raj Malhotra: (Chuckles) "Ingenious, Pooja. The government won't scrutinize every case, and we'll exploit that to the fullest."

Arjun Mehra: (Nodding) "Good. Let's maximize our gains from every avenue. Beacon Medical Center will thrive under the guise of government schemes."

The discussion shifts towards creating a facade of commitment to healthcare professionals through clinical council meetings and renovations. Arjun Mehra seeks input from the group.

Arjun Mehra: (Thoughtful) "How can we create an illusion of commitment to healthcare excellence? Clinical council meetings, renovations – what are your views?"

Dr. Ananya Kapoor: (Smirking) "Regular clinical council meetings will be our stage for showcasing excellence. We'll invite renowned doctors, even pay them if necessary, to attend and speak highly of Beacon. Their testimonials will add credibility."

Dr. Raj Malhotra: (Nodding) "Renovations, too, will play a crucial role. We'll selectively upgrade areas visible to doctors – plush lounges, state-of-the-art conference rooms. It'll create an environment that suggests cutting-edge healthcare."

Dr. Naina Verma: (Suggesting) "Let's also have 'Doctor Appreciation' events. We'll shower them with accolades, awards, and recognitions. It'll create a perception of a hospital that values its medical staff."

Arjun Mehra: (Smiling) "Excellent suggestions. We'll orchestrate an atmosphere of excellence and commitment, even if it's just a facade. Beacon Medical Center will be the epitome of healthcare dedication."

Arjun Mehra: "In the realm of healthcare, perception is power, and we'll craft a narrative that makes Beacon Medical Center the symbol of unwavering commitment."

Dr. Ananya Kapoor: "Let the clinical council meetings be the theater where our commitment takes center stage, with influential voices singing praises for our supposed excellence."

Dr. Raj Malhotra: "Through renovations, we'll sculpt an ambiance of sophistication, ensuring that every doctor sees Beacon as the pinnacle of cutting-edge healthcare."

Dr. Naina Verma: "Doctor Appreciation events will be our canvas, painting an illusion of a hospital deeply appreciative of its medical staff, even if it's just a mirage."

Dr. Vikram Singh: "Let the facade of commitment be the backdrop against which we cast the illusion of a hospital genuinely devoted to the betterment of healthcare."

Dr. Priya Sharma: "Our meetings and events will be the stage where we act out the drama of commitment, playing our parts to convince every doctor of Beacon's unparalleled dedication."

Dr. Sneha Patel: "Through illusions of commitment, we'll project Beacon as a haven for general practitioners, a place where every doctor feels valued and appreciated."

Ms. Anita Khanna: "Through strategic events, we'll ensure the illusion of commitment permeates the medical community, securing Beacon's place as the commission agent's top recommendation."

Mr. Vikas Sharma (Lawyer 1): "Legalities aside, the illusion of commitment will be our shield against any skepticism, making Beacon seem like the epitome of ethical healthcare."

Ms. Maya Desai (Lawyer 2): "Our legal strategies will harmonize with the illusion of commitment, creating a fortress of defense around Beacon in the face of any scrutiny."

Mr. Aryan Kapoor (Lawyer 3): "The legal framework will dance in tandem with the illusion of commitment, ensuring that Beacon emerges unscathed from any legal challenges."

Mr. Karan Kapoor (Financial Analyst): "The financial aspects will be the invisible threads weaving through the illusion of commitment, ensuring Beacon's coffers are filled with unwavering trust."

Ms. Pooja Sharma (Billing Specialist): "Billing practices will align seamlessly with the illusion of commitment, ensuring that every financial transaction reflects Beacon's dedication to excellence."

Arjun Mehra addresses the group, seeking their views on handling a doctor who opposes unethical practices within the hospital.

Arjun Mehra: (Serious) "If any doctor raises objections or creates a ruckus about our practices, what should be our response? Let's hear your views."

Dr. Ananya Kapoor: (Confident) "We can hit them where it hurts. If it's a surgeon, we divert their patients to other specialists within the hospital. Make them feel the impact of their dissent."

Dr. Raj Malhotra: (Nodding) "Additionally, we can stop giving them new patients. If they're a source of income, cutting it off will surely make them think twice."

Dr. Naina Verma: (Suggesting) "Let's use our network to stop referrals to their clinics. If doctors don't refer patients, their practice will suffer."

Dr. Vikram Singh: (Smirking) "We can also tarnish their reputation subtly. Spread rumors or false complaints to erode the trust their patients have in them."

Dr. Priya Sharma: (Strategic) "Another approach could be using legal means. If they persist, we can exploit any minor legal discrepancies and initiate actions against them."

Dr. Rahul Mehra: (Psychiatric Perspective) "Isolation can be powerful. Create an environment where they feel like outsiders in their own workplace. It can break their spirit."

Dr. Sneha Patel: (Suggesting) "Financial pressure works wonders. Delay or reduce their payments, and watch them scramble to maintain their lifestyle."

Dr. Sameer Agarwal: (Cautioning) "But we must be careful. A unified front is essential, and we need to ensure they don't find support within the medical community."

Mr. Rakesh Verma: (Commission Agent's View) "Our network can play a pivotal role. Spread the word among doctors that collaborating with the dissenter is bad for business."

Ms. Anita Khanna: (Commission Agent's View) "Agreed. We can control the flow of patients and referrals, influencing their practice and income."

Mr. Vikas Sharma (Lawyer 1): (Legal Perspective) "While taking actions, let's ensure it's within legal boundaries. Any deviation could backfire on us."

Ms. Maya Desai (Lawyer 2): (Legal Perspective) "We should also monitor their communications. If they plan to expose us, we'll be a step ahead legally."

Mr. Aryan Kapoor (Lawyer 3): (Legal Perspective) "A legal battle can be protracted and costly. Dissenters must know we have the resources to outlast them."

Mr. Karan Kapoor (Financial Analyst): (Strategic) "Financially, we can cripple them. Make them dependent on the hospital, and they won't dare to jeopardize the relationship."

Ms. Pooja Sharma (Billing Specialist): (Practical) "Billing practices can also be a tool. Increase their expenses subtly, affecting their overall income."

Arjun Mehra gathers the heads of pathology, radiology, and billing, seeking a detailed plan on giving commissions to those who refer patients to the hospital.

Arjun Mehra: (Commanding) "Vikram, Rahul, Pooja, we need a meticulous plan on how we can give commissions to those who refer patients to us, be it doctors or laymen. Explain your strategies".

Mr. Vikram Reddy (Pathology Head): (Confident) "We can create a tiered commission structure for doctors based on the volume and value of referrals. The more they bring, the higher the percentage they receive."

Mr. Rahul Kapoor (Radiology Head): (Enthusiastic) "For radiology services, we can offer additional incentives for specific high-value procedures. MRI and CT scans will carry higher commissions to entice more referrals."

Ms. Pooja Sharma (Billing Head): (Practical) "From the billing side, we can discreetly add extra charges to the bills of referred patients. This additional amount will then be channeled back as commissions. It won't be easily traceable."

Arjun Mehra: (Smirking) "Good. Now, how about laymen who refer patients?"

Mr. Vikram Reddy: (Planning) "We can introduce a referral program for the general public. People who refer patients can receive vouchers or discounts for their own medical services or even cash rewards."

Mr. Rahul Kapoor: (Building on the idea) "Additionally, we can create partnerships with local businesses and offer them exclusive deals. When their customers refer patients, both the referrer and the local business receive benefits."

Ms. Pooja Sharma: (Calculating) "For laymen, we can subtly increase the overall bill amount and, in turn, provide them with gift vouchers or discounts on future hospital services. It ensures a continuous loop of referrals."

Arjun Mehra: (Pleased) "Excellent. Ensure the transactions are discreet, and the commission process remains confidential. We want a steady influx of patients without raising suspicions".

1. Mr. Arjun Mehra - Businessman and Hospital Owner

2. Pharmacy Head - Mr. Sameer Khanna

Scene: Private Meeting Room

Arjun Mehra sits down with Sameer Khanna, the head of the hospital pharmacy, to strategize on maximizing profits through pharmaceuticals.

Arjun Mehra: (Assertive) "Sameer, we need to discuss how we can enhance our revenue through the pharmacy. High MRP drugs will be our focus, and we'll negotiate better deals with the suppliers. Doctors will need to adhere to our preferred drug list. Let's hear your plan."

Mr. Sameer Khanna (Pharmacy Head): (Confident) "Absolutely, Arjun. To begin with, we'll categorize drugs based on their profit margins. The higher the margin, the more aggressively we'll push those drugs."

Arjun Mehra: (Nodding) "Good. Now, how do we ensure that doctors prescribe the medications we want?"

Mr. Sameer Khanna: (Strategizing) "We can implement an incentive program for doctors based on the revenue generated from the pharmacy. The more they align with our preferred drugs, the higher their incentives."

Arjun Mehra: (Sly Smile) "And for those who don't comply?"

Mr. Sameer Khanna: (Calculating) "We can subtly limit the availability of certain drugs. If doctors want those medicines for their patients, they'll have to play by our rules."

Arjun Mehra: (Approving) "Smart. Now, what about negotiations with drug suppliers?"

Mr. Sameer Khanna: (Explaining) "We'll negotiate deals where the apparent cost to the hospital is low, but the MRP remains high. This way, our profits increase, and doctors have little choice but to prescribe the more lucrative options. But we need to give bulk order and for that we need inflow of the patients".

Arjun Mehra: (Smirking) "Yes for that I have already devised a plan so do not worry on that front. What if some doctors resist?"

Mr. Sameer Khanna: (Confident) "We'll have regular training sessions disguised as educational seminars, emphasizing the benefits of our selected medications. Peer pressure can also be influential in making them conform."

Arjun Mehra: (Pleased) "Ensure that the pharmacists are aligned with this strategy. They should subtly guide doctors towards our preferred drugs."

Mr. Sameer Khanna: (Assuring) "I'll make sure the pharmacy staff is on board. We can also incentivize them based on the sales of targeted drugs."

Arjun Mehra: (Concluding) "Good. Let's make the pharmacy a lucrative arm of our business. The more profit we derive from medications, the better for Beacon."

Characters:

1. Mr. Arjun Mehra - Businessman and Hospital Owner

2. Chief Medical Administrator - Dr. Ananya Kapoor

Scene: Private Meeting Room

Arjun Mehra meets with Dr. Ananya Kapoor, the Chief Medical Administrator, to strategize on steering patient flow toward doctors aligned with the hospital's profit-driven agenda.

Arjun Mehra: (Direct) "Ananya, we need to ensure that our preferred doctors receive the majority of patients. From the emergency department to OPD referrals, we should guide patients to those in our pool. Let's discuss how we can make this happen."

Dr. Ananya Kapoor: (Nodding) "To achieve this, we'll need strategic coordination across various departments. Firstly, in the emergency department, we can designate specific doctors from our pool to admit all patients. This will create a direct flow to them."

Arjun Mehra: (Approving) "Good. Now, what about the OPD?"

Dr. Ananya Kapoor: (Explaining) "In the reception area, we can subtly guide walk-in patients to our preferred doctors. Receptionists can be trained to recommend these doctors for initial consultations, channeling more patients into their care."

Arjun Mehra: (Smirking) "That's clever. What about referrals from our own doctors?"

Dr. Ananya Kapoor: (Strategizing) "We'll encourage our doctors to refer patients internally, specifically to those within our pool. Subtle incentives can be offered to make this practice more attractive."

Arjun Mehra: (Intrigued) "And what if a doctor refuses to cooperate?"

Dr. Ananya Kapoor: (Assertive) "We can make it clear that cooperation will result in increased patient flow and career benefits. Those who resist might find themselves marginalized within the hospital hierarchy."

Arjun Mehra: (Calculating) "Perfect. How do we develop and maintain this pool?"

Dr. Ananya Kapoor: (Detailing) "Regular meetings with our preferred doctors, providing them with exclusive benefits, and creating a sense of camaraderie will ensure their loyalty. It's essential to keep them invested in the success of Beacon Medical Center."

Arjun Mehra: (Pleased) "Excellent, Ananya. Ensure that the entire staff, from emergency to reception, is aligned with this strategy. The success of our plan relies on seamless execution."

Dr. Ananya Kapoor: (Assuring) "I'll make sure the entire team is on board. We'll create an environment where our preferred doctors thrive."

Are You Really Serious That Filing Cases In This System Will Help The Patient Or The Doctor

Struggling for Justice: The Uphill Battle in Indian Medical Negligence Cases

In the labyrinth of India's healthcare landscape, patients find themselves entangled in a complex web woven by the nexus of corporate hospitals, complicit doctors, and legal professionals. The pursuit of justice for medical negligence victims becomes an arduous journey, with numerous roadblocks obstructing the path to accountability.

Scene 1: The Corporate Web Unveiled

In the heart of New Delhi, Mr. Kumar, a middle-aged businessman, found himself entangled in the intricate web woven by a corporate hospital and influential doctors. His journey began when a routine surgery turned into a nightmare of medical negligence.

Mr. Kumar had chosen one of the city's reputed corporate hospitals for a relatively straightforward procedure, unaware of the complexities that lay beneath the glossy facade. Dr. Mehra, a renowned surgeon with close ties to the hospital's administration, was assigned to perform the surgery.

As the surgery concluded, Mr. Kumar started experiencing excruciating pain and complications that he had not anticipated. Distraught and seeking answers, he approached the hospital's administration for an explanation. To his surprise, he encountered a stone wall of denial and deflection.

Unbeknownst to Mr. Kumar, the hospital's legal team swiftly went into action, crafting a narrative that absolved both Dr. Mehra and the institution of any wrongdoing. The hospital's management, well-versed in navigating legal intricacies, orchestrated a defense strategy that shifted blame onto unforeseeable complications rather than acknowledging negligence.

Behind closed doors, a clandestine meeting unfolded between hospital executives, Dr. Mehra, and their legal counsel. The hospital, driven by its financial interests and reputation, was determined to shield its assets and maintain its standing in the medical community.

The hospital's lawyers, skilled in the art of legal maneuvering, devised a strategy that aimed to prolong legal proceedings. Delays in court would wear down Mr. Kumar, testing his financial resilience and emotional fortitude. The corporate web had been intricately spun to protect the interests of those within its fold.

As Mr. Kumar sought legal representation, he soon realized the challenges ahead. The hospital's legal team, backed by considerable resources, outmaneuvered his lawyers at every turn. Legal complexities, adjournments, and bureaucratic hurdles became formidable adversaries, frustrating Mr. Kumar's pursuit of justice.

Should we not ask ourselves Is this the real solution? Or should we not think of something solid to cut down this web? And remember this is still the team fighting against the patient. But even in a one to one fight for medical negligence the cases go on for years with no relief in sight for both the doctors and patients. And the bitterness is ever increasing.

Think Of Some Alternative

Scene 2: The Legal Shield

Mrs. Reddy, a seasoned lawyer specializing in medical negligence cases, entered the narrative as a pivotal character shedding light on the challenges faced by victims in the Indian legal system.

As Mr. Kumar's case unfolded in court, Mrs. Reddy found herself representing him against the corporate giant. She was well aware of the labyrinthine legal processes that awaited her, intricately designed to protect the interests of hospitals and doctors.

The hospital's legal team, armed with experienced attorneys and substantial resources, began deploying a series of legal tactics to shield themselves from accountability. Mrs. Reddy faced a barrage of challenges, each aimed at prolonging the legal battle and dissuading Mr. Kumar from persisting.

Legal Maneuvering and Procedural Delays: The hospital's lawyers adeptly exploited the legal intricacies of the Indian judicial system. They filed numerous applications, seeking adjournments and exploiting procedural delays. Mrs. Reddy found herself constantly navigating a sea of motions designed to prolong the trial.

Expert Witnesses and Obfuscation: The hospital's legal strategy included hiring influential expert witnesses who attested to the standard of care provided by Dr. Mehra. Mrs. Reddy, however, faced the daunting task of debunking these witnesses and proving the existence of negligence.

Intimidation and Legal Jargon: The courtroom became a battleground of legal prowess. The hospital's lawyers utilized intimidating tactics, bombarding Mrs. Reddy with complex legal arguments and jargon. This deliberate strategy aimed to overwhelm, creating an environment where justice seemed elusive.

Financial Strain on Victims: Mrs. Reddy observed a recurring theme in medical negligence cases – the financial strain on victims. Legal battles required substantial financial resources, and the hospital's legal team exploited this vulnerability. Many victims, unable to bear the financial burden, were forced to withdraw their cases.

As Mrs. Reddy tirelessly fought for Mr. Kumar, she became increasingly cognizant of the uphill battle that victims of medical negligence faced in the Indian legal landscape. The intricate legal shield, carefully crafted by hospitals and their legal teams, created an environment where justice was not only delayed but often denied.

In this scene, the audience witnessed the power dynamics in the courtroom, where legal acumen and financial resources often determined the trajectory of medical negligence cases.

Now think both of them are lawyers who are fighting the case for their client. Whose ever is guilty the opposite party always find it difficult to match with the pace of the legal proceedings and legal terminologies. Do we think be it patient or be it doctor will get the real justice? But one thing is clear the bitterness is going to increase in general.

Think Of Some Alternative

Scene 3: A Victim's Dilemma

Amid the legal theatrics and convoluted proceedings, the focus shifted to Ms. Singhania, a victim of medical negligence who found herself entangled in a web of dilemma, facing a critical choice between justice and the protracted legal battle.

Ms. Singhania's journey began when her son, a promising young athlete, suffered irreparable harm due to a misdiagnosis. The hospital, desperate to protect its reputation, deployed a legal strategy that shifted blame and minimized culpability. Distraught and seeking answers, Ms. Singhania decided to pursue justice, unaware of the immense challenges that lay ahead.

The Emotional Toll: As Ms. Singhania delved into the legal process, the emotional toll became increasingly apparent. The constant reminders of her son's suffering, coupled with the adversarial nature of legal proceedings, weighed heavily on her psyche. The hospital's legal team, aware of this vulnerability, exploited it as a tool to dissuade her from persisting.

Financial Strain: Legal battles demanded significant financial resources, a fact that Ms. Singhania found out soon enough. The hospital's legal team, well-versed in prolonging proceedings, strategically drained her financial reserves. Legal fees, court expenses, and the sheer cost of sustaining the fight became a mounting burden, forcing Ms. Singhania to reassess her pursuit of justice.

The Dilemma: Caught in a vortex of emotions and financial strain, Ms. Singhania faced an agonizing dilemma. The protracted legal battle was taking a toll on her well-being, and the hospital's legal maneuvers seemed unending. The constant fear of an uncertain outcome loomed large, prompting her to question whether the pursuit of justice was worth the immense personal cost.

Legal Fatigue: As months turned into years, Ms. Singhania grappled with legal fatigue. The hospital's legal team, recognizing the toll on her resilience, intensified their efforts to wear her down. Adjourning hearings, filing additional motions, and employing a barrage of legal tactics, they aimed to create an environment where surrender seemed like the only viable option.

The Crossroads: At a critical juncture in her legal battle, Ms. Singhania found herself at a crossroads. The pursuit of justice, initially a beacon of hope, now seemed like an unending ordeal. The hospital's legal shield, fortified by delays and financial strain, cast a shadow over her quest for accountability.

In this scene, the audience witnessed the personal turmoil of a victim confronting the harsh realities of the legal system. Ms. Singhania's story epitomized the daunting choices faced by many victims of medical negligence, caught in a web of emotional distress and financial constraints, while grappling with the agonizing decision of whether to continue the fight or succumb to the overwhelming odds.

Is this not the reality of Indian legal system. The initial filing of replies and rejoinder are such that they can never bring the truth out. And then comes the delays in actual argument and even if they happen they are so short and so out of context that the victim will always feel depressed. After years of the process when the day of justice come then the relief would be in pennies. But then the most disturbing part is process of appeals. And more years. Do we really think this is how the medical negligence justice can be availed? But one thing is sure the bitterness increases.

Think Of Some Alternative

Scene 3: Dr. Anand's Agony: Navigating the Legal Maze

Dr. Anand, a dedicated physician, found himself ensnared in the legal complexities of a false medical negligence case. The plaintiff, Mr. Malhotra, claimed that Dr. Anand's alleged negligence led to severe complications after a routine surgery. Unbeknownst to Dr. Anand, this legal battle would become a distressing odyssey, unraveling the frustrations that many doctors face in such situations.

The False Allegations: Mr. Malhotra, prompted by avaricious intentions, sought the assistance of a shrewd lawyer notorious for filing inflated medical negligence claims. Unscrupulous in his pursuit of maximum compensation, the lawyer crafted a narrative that portrayed Dr. Anand as a reckless and negligent practitioner, despite the lack of substantial evidence.

Legal Maneuvering: The lawyer, well-versed in the art of legal maneuvering, inundated Dr. Anand with a barrage of motions, requests, and legal jargon. The goal was clear – to overwhelm Dr. Anand and force a settlement that would be lucrative for Mr. Malhotra and financially draining for the doctor.

Emotional Toll on Dr. Anand: The legal battle took an emotional toll on Dr. Anand, who was perplexed and frustrated by the unfounded allegations. As court hearings extended over months, Dr. Anand faced sleepless nights and mounting stress. The emotional anguish of being falsely accused of negligence gnawed at his sense of professional integrity.

Financial Drain: The legal expenses, coupled with the potential threat to his professional reputation, strained Dr. Anand's finances. The lawyer, aware of this vulnerability, strategically prolonged the proceedings, aiming to exploit the financial strain on the doctor and coerce a settlement.

The Guilt of the Innocent: Dr. Anand's frustration grew as he grappled with the irony of being held accountable for actions he never committed. The false narrative perpetuated in the courtroom fueled public scrutiny and cast a shadow on his years of dedicated service. The guilt of the innocent became a haunting theme in his professional life.

Navigating a Complex Legal System: Dr. Anand, frustrated by the seemingly endless legal battle, found himself questioning the efficacy of a legal system that allowed unscrupulous individuals to exploit it for personal gain. The intricacies of legal proceedings, often favoring the plaintiff in medical negligence cases, added to his disillusionment.

The Long Road to Vindication: As Dr. Anand continued to navigate the complex legal system, he clung to the hope of eventual vindication. He sought solace in the support of colleagues who understood the challenges faced by doctors in the current medico-legal landscape.

There is another side of coin also to this story of medical negligence. Due to high health illiteracy in our country and increasing numbers of media outburst against the doctors and increasing number of ambulance chaser lawyers, there are fury of cases against doctors for every misadventure. This also led to emotional, financial and mental toll on the doctor. This lead to repel effects. And so they start devising plan to avoid litigation in practice. Bitterness is increasing but so is the defensive medicine. And the ultimate loser is patient-doctor relationship. So is the system we want?

Think Of Some Alternative

Please Understand The Complete Failure Of The Present Situation

The scenarios portrayed in the four stories underscore the complexities and challenges inherent in the current medico-legal landscape in India. The system heavily relies on medical negligence cases as a means of seeking accountability, with lawyers and judges navigating the intricacies of healthcare without the necessary medical expertise. Here are some reflections on this situation:

1. Legal System Challenges:

- The legal system's reliance on medical negligence cases can be problematic, as lawyers and judges may lack the specialized knowledge needed to fully understand intricate medical details.

- Decisions made without a nuanced understanding of medical complexities may lead to unjust outcomes, potentially harming both doctors and patients.

2. Need for Expertise:

- Healthcare is a highly specialized field, and legal proceedings involving medical matters demand a deep understanding of medical science and practices.

- There is a need for legal professionals with medical expertise or collaboration between legal and medical experts to ensure a fair evaluation of cases.

3. Alternative Dispute Resolution:

- Exploring alternative dispute resolution mechanisms, such as mediation or expert panels consisting of both legal and medical professionals, could offer a more balanced and informed approach.

- These mechanisms might facilitate a nuanced understanding of cases, reducing the likelihood of unjust outcomes.

4. Continuous Education:

- Ongoing education for legal professionals and judges about medical advancements and practices can bridge the knowledge gap and foster a more informed decision-making process.

- This could involve training programs, workshops, or collaborations between legal and medical institutions.

5. Strengthening Regulatory Oversight:

- Strengthening regulatory bodies overseeing healthcare and legal practices can contribute to a more accountable and transparent system.

- These bodies can establish guidelines, standards, and protocols for handling medical negligence cases, ensuring a fair and informed process.

6. Public Awareness:

- Increasing public awareness about the challenges in the legal-medical interface can lead to a more informed society.

- Educating the public about the complexities involved in healthcare decisions and the potential consequences of filing unjustified cases can contribute to a more discerning approach.

In essence, while medical negligence cases remain an avenue for seeking accountability, addressing the inherent challenges calls for a multi-faceted approach. Collaborative efforts between the legal and medical communities, alternative dispute resolution mechanisms, and continuous education are essential components of creating a more just and equitable system.

Today, legal remedies for medical errors are not considered part of the continuum of care. If something goes wrong during patient treatment, the typical response is to call in the attorneys. Lawyers take over, and the patient's problem is no longer seen as situated in the health care system; rather, it is under the auspices of the legal system. The focus then shifts to limiting information flow, stating one's case, making the better argument, and proving the other party wrong. Very little in this endeavor fosters an environment of care, and no part of it readily leads to healing.

The history of the medical profession reveals a continued emphasis on care and healing. "The obligation of physicians to relieve human

suffering stretches back into antiquity. In taking the Hippocratic Oath, physicians throughout the centuries have sworn to apply their skills for the "benefit of the sick

Subsequently, societies maintained their high regard for the physician's powers of healing. In 18th century Germany, doctors ranked above knights. In the early 19th century, Thomas Carlyle wrote that "[t]he physician can abolish pain, relieve his fellow mortals from sickness. He is indisputably usefullest of all men."'

How the mighty have fallen, some might say

Yet today, physicians can cure patients of so many more diseases than just a few decades ago, let alone centuries ago. Despite this progress, patients today frequently question the expertise of doctors, and skepticism abounds over the motives of health care professionals. Some of the traditional paternalistic approaches of doctors negatively affected the patient experience.

Similarly, the current medical malpractice litigation system pays little attention to suffering. The highly contentious nature of medical malpractice lawsuits frequently does nothing to address patient suffering. In addition, as cases can languish in the courts for years, the suffering can be prolonged. Too often in a medical malpractice action, all parties-the injured patient, doctors and other health care professionals who provided care, and the community-suffer much more than they ought to.

In fact, studies of medical malpractice cases typically find that most victims of substandard care do not file claims or recover any compensation. The Harvard Medical Practice Study revealed that only 1/16 of patients, injured due to negligent acts actually received compensation through the medical malpractice litigation system.

According to the Physician Insurers Association of America, only 0.9% of malpractice claims result in jury verdicts for the plaintiff (27.4% are settled prior to trial; 67.7% are dropped or dismissed, and 4% result in a verdict for the defendant).

The fact that the majority of patients who suffer injury as a result of negligent care receive no remedy from medical malpractice litigation is a strong indictment of the system. Moreover, those who do receive compensation often must wait years to do so, and may or may not receive adequate compensation. When malpractice litigation fails to provide compensation for most of the injured, it not only fails with respect to one of its core tasks

Hopefully readers of this book would have realized by now that present system of medical malpractice is way beyond success. It has only increased the level of bitterness between the actual parties that is doctor and patient.

Solution

"We cannot solve our problems with the same thinking we used when we created them"

Act Of Commision: No Relief Only Punitive Action

In the field of medicine, there are instances where punitive actions should be taken against healthcare professionals due to various reasons, such as negligence, malpractice, ethical violations, or criminal behaviour. It's important to note that punitive actions are typically taken to ensure patient safety, uphold the standards of medical practice, and maintain the integrity of the healthcare system. Here are some examples of acts that should lead to punitive actions:

1. **Medical Malpractice**:

   - Example: A surgeon performs a procedure negligently, resulting in serious harm or death to the patient. The failure to meet the standard of care may lead to legal action, including lawsuits and revocation of medical licenses.

2. **Fraudulent Activities**:

   - Example: A healthcare professional engages in billing fraud by intentionally submitting false claims for reimbursement. This could lead to legal consequences, fines, and the loss of professional licenses.

3. **Patient Abuse or Mistreatment**:

   - Example: Physical or emotional abuse of patients by healthcare staff. Such actions can lead to disciplinary actions, lawsuits, and criminal charges.

4. **Violation of Ethical Standards**:

   - Example: Breach of patient confidentiality, engaging in relationships with patients that are considered unethical, or conducting medical experiments without proper informed consent. These actions may result in disciplinary actions by medical boards or professional associations.

5. **Criminal Offenses**:

   - Example: A healthcare professional involved in drug trafficking, theft, or other criminal activities. Criminal charges can lead to imprisonment, fines, and the loss of professional licenses.

6. **Incompetence or Impairment**:

- Example: Practicing medicine while impaired by drugs or alcohol, or demonstrating incompetence in providing appropriate care. Such cases may lead to investigations, sanctions, and license suspension or revocation.

7. **Failure to Report**:

- Example: Not reporting incidents of medical errors, adverse events, or colleagues engaging in unethical behaviour. This failure to report may lead to disciplinary actions for lack of transparency and accountability.

8. **Scope of Practice Violations**:

- Example: A healthcare professional performing procedures or providing care beyond their authorized scope of practice. This may result in sanctions by regulatory bodies.

Punitive actions vary and can include fines, probation, suspension, or revocation of licenses, and legal consequences. These actions aim to hold healthcare professionals accountable, protect patients, and maintain the public's trust in the healthcare system. It's essential for healthcare professionals to adhere to ethical standards, legal regulations, and best practices to avoid such punitive actions.

Can Any One Deny That Justice Is Needed For The Patient

MEDICAL MALPRACTICE

Serious acts of commission and malpractice in medicine often involve intentional or negligent actions by healthcare professionals that result in harm to patients. Here are examples of such serious acts:

1. **Surgical Errors**:

- Performing surgery on the wrong body part or patient.

- Leaving surgical instruments or sponges inside a patient's body.

- Operating on the wrong patient.

2. **Medication Errors**:

- Administering the wrong medication or dosage.

- Failing to review a patient's medical history for potential drug interactions.

- Providing medication without proper authorization or prescription.

3. Failure to Diagnose or Delayed Diagnosis:

- Failing to recognize and diagnose a serious medical condition in a timely manner.

- Neglecting to order necessary diagnostic tests or misinterpreting test results.

4. Birth Injuries:

- Improper use of delivery instruments leading to birth injuries.

- Failure to respond appropriately to fetal distress during labor and delivery.

5. Patient Neglect or Abuse:

- Ignoring or neglecting the needs of a patient, leading to deterioration of health.

- Physical, verbal, or emotional abuse of patients by healthcare staff.

6. Informed Consent Violations:

- Performing medical procedures without obtaining informed consent.

- Failing to adequately inform patients about the risks and benefits of a procedure or treatment.

7. Fraudulent Billing Practices:

- Submitting false claims for reimbursement.

- Engaging in upcoding or unbundling of services to inflate charges.

8. Unethical Conduct:

- Violating patient confidentiality.

- Engaging in a romantic or inappropriate relationship with a patient.

- Conducting medical experiments without proper informed consent.

9. Impaired Practice:

- Practicing medicine while under the influence of drugs or alcohol.

- Continuing to practice with a known impairment that affects patient care.

10. Lack of Supervision:

- Allowing unqualified individuals to perform medical procedures without proper supervision.

- Failure to oversee and manage trainees or subordinates, leading to patient harm.

These examples represent serious breaches of professional standards and should result in legal actions, disciplinary measures by medical boards, lawsuits, and damage to the professional reputation of healthcare providers. It is crucial for healthcare professionals to adhere to ethical guidelines, maintain a high standard of care, and prioritize patient safety to avoid involvement in such serious acts of commission and malpractice.

But Don't You All Think That There Should Be A Time Line For Justice. Think About It.

Justice In Time

Do You Think Only Doctors Would Be Involved Here? Punish All And Equally

Fraudulent activities in the context of medical negligence involve intentional deception or misrepresentation, leading to harm or financial loss. It's important to note that proven cases of medical negligence involve a breach of the standard of care, while fraudulent activities may involve intentional deceit beyond negligence. Some examples of fraudulent activities in the realm of medical negligence that may warrant punitive action include:

1. **False Billing**:

- Inflating medical bills with charges for services or procedures that were not performed.

- Billing for more expensive procedures than those actually provided.

2. **Kickbacks and Referral Fraud**:

- Accepting or providing kickbacks for patient referrals or the use of certain medical services.

- Improper financial arrangements between healthcare providers for patient referrals.

3. **Credential Fraud**:

- Falsifying credentials, qualifications, or licensure to practice medicine.

- Impersonating a licensed healthcare professional.

4. Fraudulent Research:

- Fabricating or falsifying research data to support medical claims or gain financial benefits.

- Misrepresenting research findings in publications.

5. Pharmaceutical Fraud:

- Marketing or promoting drugs for uses not approved by regulatory authorities.

- Concealing or misrepresenting information about the safety or efficacy of pharmaceutical products.

6. Patient Record Manipulation:

- Altering patient records to cover up mistakes or negligence.

- Falsifying medical documentation to support fraudulent claims.

7. Unnecessary Medical Procedures:

- Performing unnecessary medical procedures solely for financial gain.

- Recommending unnecessary tests or treatments to generate revenue.

8. Concealing Medical Errors:

- Intentionally hiding mistakes or errors that result in patient harm.

- Providing false information to patients or their families about the cause of adverse events.

9. Identity Theft:

- Using patients' personal information for fraudulent activities, such as obtaining medical services, prescriptions, or insurance benefits.

When such fraudulent activities are identified, legal authorities, medical boards, and regulatory bodies should take punitive actions, including license revocation, fines, and even criminal charges, depending on the severity of the misconduct. It is crucial for healthcare professionals and institutions to uphold ethical standards and provide accurate and honest care to patients.

By Punishing Only The Doctor Will Not Help As The Mechanism Of Fraud Will Conti Ue. So Punish All And Again In Time.

Punish All Partners In Crime

Certain Crime Which Are Subjective But Not Acceptable. Find Them And Punish Them. Medical Profession Is Not Any Profession

Patient Abuse, Mistreatment, Violation Of Ethical Standards: Not Allowed

Patient abuse and mistreatment in the context of medical care are serious ethical and legal violations that can lead to severe consequences for healthcare providers. Punitive actions may be taken against individuals or institutions that engage in such misconduct. Here are some examples of patient abuse and mistreatment that may warrant punitive action:

1. **Physical Abuse**:

   - Inflicting physical harm on a patient through actions such as hitting, slapping, or restraining inappropriately.

   - Using excessive force during medical procedures, examinations, or restraints.

2. **Verbal Abuse**:

   - Using offensive or demeaning language towards a patient.

   - Yelling, berating, or using threats to intimidate a patient.

3. **Neglect**:

   - Failing to provide necessary medical care, attention, or assistance to a patient, leading to harm or deterioration of health.

   - Ignoring patients' basic needs, such as nutrition, hygiene, or medication.

4. **Sexual Abuse**:

   - Engaging in any form of unwanted or inappropriate sexual contact with a patient.

   - Making sexually explicit comments or gestures that create a hostile or uncomfortable environment for the patient.

5. **Emotional/Psychological Abuse**:

- Engaging in behavior that causes emotional distress or trauma to a patient.

- Manipulating or intentionally frightening a patient.

6. **Financial Exploitation**:

- Taking advantage of a patient financially, such as stealing money or possessions.

- Pressuring or coercing a patient into signing financial documents or making payments.

7. **Informed Consent Violations**:

- Performing medical procedures without obtaining proper informed consent from the patient.

- Providing inaccurate or incomplete information about the risks and benefits of a treatment or procedure.

8. **Discrimination**:

- Treating a patient unfairly or differently based on factors such as race, gender, age, ethnicity, or disability.

- Denying necessary medical care or services based on discriminatory beliefs.

9. **Privacy Violations**:

- Inappropriately disclosing a patient's confidential medical information without consent.

- Allowing unauthorized individuals to access a patient's private medical records.

10. **Failure to Report Abuse**:

- Healthcare professionals who witness abuse but fail to report it to the appropriate authorities may also face consequences.

When instances of patient abuse and mistreatment are identified, punitive actions can include legal charges, license revocation, fines, and civil lawsuits. Additionally, healthcare institutions may implement disciplinary measures, and regulatory bodies may conduct investigations to ensure patient safety and uphold ethical standards in healthcare. Patients who experience abuse or mistreatment are encouraged to report such incidents to the relevant authorities and seek legal advice if necessary.

Every Doctor Should Remember That You Have Being Given Powers To Heal But That Power Is Not There To Abuse.

Power That Abuses Can Never Heal

If You Are Criminal Or Personally Disturbed You Need Help, You Cannot Help

In cases of medical negligence, punitive actions may be taken in response to criminal offenses, incompetence, or impairment on the part of healthcare professionals. It's important to note that medical negligence alone may not necessarily involve criminal conduct, incompetence, or impairment. However, when these elements are present, they can exacerbate the severity of the situation and lead to more severe consequences. Here are examples in each category:

Criminal Offenses:

1. **Drug Diversion**:

  - Healthcare professionals diverting controlled substances for personal use or sale.

2. **Fraudulent Prescription Practices**:

  - Prescribing medications for non-existent patients or for purposes unrelated to medical treatment.

3. **Healthcare Fraud**:

  - Billing for services not rendered or submitting false claims to healthcare insurance providers.

4. **Sexual Assault**:

  - Engaging in non-consensual sexual contact with a patient or anyone.

5. **Homicide or Assault**:

  - Intentionally causing harm or death to a person through actions such as physical assault or grossly negligent behaviour.

6. **Criminal Negligence**:

  - Engaging in actions that grossly deviate from the standard of care, resulting in criminal charges.

Incompetence or Impairment:

1. Substance Abuse:

- Impairment due to alcohol or drug abuse that compromises the ability to provide safe and effective medical care.

5. Mental Health Issues:

- Unaddressed mental health issues affecting a healthcare professional's ability to perform their duties competently.

6. Failure to Keep Current:

- Neglecting to stay updated on medical advancements, resulting in outdated practices.

7. Disregard for Safety Protocols:

- Consistently ignoring safety protocols and procedures, putting patients at risk.

Regulatory bodies and medical boards play a crucial role in investigating and addressing cases of incompetence and impairment. Criminal offenses may lead to legal proceedings and potential imprisonment.

It is essential for healthcare professionals to adhere to ethical standards, maintain competence, and seek help if they are facing personal challenges that could impact their ability to provide safe and effective care. Additionally, regulatory bodies and legal authorities work to ensure patient safety and uphold the integrity of the healthcare profession.

A Criminal Mind And An Incompetent Healer Will Always Harm

Trust Is Multi Layered. No Excuse And No Passing The Buck. Patient Knows Only You

Failure to report, especially in the context of medical negligence, can be a serious ethical and legal breach. Healthcare professionals are often obligated to report certain events or issues to appropriate authorities for the well-being and safety of patients. Failure to fulfill these reporting obligations may result in punitive actions. Here are examples of situations where failure to report could lead to punitive action:

1. Failure to Report Medical Errors:

- Not reporting significant medical errors or adverse events that occur during patient care, which could compromise patient safety and contribute to a lack of transparency.

2. Non-Compliance with Mandatory Reporting Laws:

- Neglecting to report incidents as required by law, such as cases of child abuse, elder abuse, or certain infectious diseases.

3. Failure to Report Impaired Colleagues:

- Not reporting colleagues who are impaired due to substance abuse or mental health issues, jeopardizing patient safety and violating professional standards.

4. Neglecting to Report Unethical Conduct:

- Failing to report instances of unethical behavior or professional misconduct by fellow healthcare professionals.

5. Failure to Report Suspected Abuse or Neglect:

- Not reporting suspicions of abuse or neglect of patients, especially vulnerable populations such as children, the elderly, or individuals with disabilities.

6. Non-Compliance with Quality Assurance Requirements:

- Failing to report deviations from established quality assurance protocols or standards, undermining efforts to maintain and improve healthcare quality.

7. Negligence in Reporting Infection Control Violations:

- Neglecting to report breaches of infection control practices that could lead to the spread of infectious diseases within healthcare settings.

8. Failure to Report Breaches of Patient Privacy:

- Not reporting incidents where patient confidentiality or privacy is compromised, such as unauthorized access to medical records.

9. Non-Adherence to Reporting Adverse Drug Reactions:

- Failing to report adverse drug reactions or side effects, hindering efforts to monitor and ensure the safety of pharmaceutical interventions.

10. Neglecting to Report Research Misconduct:

- Not reporting instances of research misconduct or ethical violations in scientific studies.

Punitive actions for failure to report can vary but may include disciplinary measures, fines, and legal consequences. Reporting mechanisms and obligations are in place to safeguard patients, maintain the integrity of healthcare systems, and ensure the accountability of healthcare professionals. Adherence to reporting requirements is crucial for promoting transparency, accountability, and patient safety within the healthcare industry.

With Advent Of Corporate Hospital It Is Seen That The Doctors Who Know Many Things Are Wrong Still Do Not Report To Protect Their Jobs And Secure Good Payment. A Patient Do Not Know Anyone And Has No Knowledge About The High Standards In Medical Care. Doctors Should Think Only And Only About The Safety Of Patient

No Excuse Means No Excuse. Period

So this part of law and punitive action carries no arguments what so ever. Only request is timely justice and appeal less system.

Act Of Omission Why There Is Need Of Alternative Way To Address Medical Negligence?

If You Feel There Is Need To Find An Alternative Then

Read Further.........

The use of an adversarial approach in healthcare presents a troubling scenario, where patients are thrust into a confrontational stance against their caregivers, including doctors, nurses, and hospitals. This occurs irrespective of whether the injury resulted from preventable causes, individual or systemic errors, or was simply an unfortunate outcome with no discernible error. The abrupt shift transforms caregivers into perceived adversaries overnight, creating an adversarial dynamic. In legal proceedings, direct communication between parties is forbidden, enforcing a channel of communication exclusively through legal counsel.

To illustrate, consider the case of a patient who undergoes surgery and experiences unexpected complications. Instead of a collaborative effort to understand the root cause and address the situation together, the adversarial system immediately positions the patient against the surgical team. Communication barriers prevent direct dialogue, and the patient, now facing the need for additional medical care, is forced into the challenging task of seeking alternative sources of treatment during a critical period.

In another scenario, a patient may suffer an adverse reaction to medication, leading to serious health consequences. Rather than fostering open communication to explore the factors contributing to the adverse reaction, the adversarial model isolates the patient from their healthcare providers. This lack of direct communication leaves the patient grappling with the aftermath of the injury, attempting to recover or adapt without clear explanations from medical professionals.

In both examples, the adversarial approach not only hinders collaborative problem-solving but also necessitates patients to establish new care relationships at a time when they are most vulnerable. The absence of direct explanations from healthcare providers further compounds the challenges, leaving patients to brace themselves for a prolonged legal battle that adds emotional and financial burdens to an already distressing situation. These narratives underscore the pressing need to reconsider and reform medical malpractice approaches towards more patient-centered and collaborative models.

Simultaneously, doctors find themselves without a conducive platform that encourages open discussions about medical errors and facilitates learning from mistakes. This absence of a supportive environment deprives them of crucial opportunities to enhance their skills and knowledge. It also hampers their ability to express empathy and maintain ongoing care for patients who have suffered injuries. Moreover, doctors operate under the constant shadow of potential litigation and escalating insurance premiums, all while having limited avenues for personal healing and growth following errors.

To illustrate these challenges, consider a scenario where a surgeon encounters a complication during a procedure. In the absence of a forum that encourages transparent discussions, the surgeon may miss out on valuable insights from colleagues and experts, hindering the opportunity to learn and refine their surgical skills. Furthermore, without an empathetic and open environment, the surgeon may struggle to maintain a supportive relationship with the patient, impacting the overall quality of care.

In another instance, a physician administers medication that leads to an adverse reaction in a patient. The lack of a conducive space for discussing errors prevents the healthcare professional from sharing experiences and gaining insights from peers who may have encountered similar situations. This limitation not only impedes the doctor's personal and professional growth but also obstructs the development of a more robust and error-resistant healthcare system.

Moreover, consider the emotional toll on doctors operating in an environment fraught with the constant fear of litigation. A physician who has made an error may face heightened stress and anxiety, impacting their mental well-being and, consequently, their ability to provide optimal care to future patients.

In essence, the current system not only deprives doctors of opportunities for improvement and learning but also places them in a precarious position where the fear of litigation hampers their ability to heal and contribute effectively to the well-being of the community. By incorporating examples and stories, we can better understand the real-world implications of these challenges and the urgent need for a more supportive and trusting healthcare environment.

Risk Reduction Vs Error Reduction

Risk reduction and error reduction are two distinct approaches in the context of medical negligence, each addressing different aspects of patient safety.

1. Risk Reduction:

- Definition: Risk reduction focuses on minimizing the likelihood of adverse events or errors occurring in the first place.

- Example: In a hospital setting, implementing protocols for proper hand hygiene among healthcare providers is a risk reduction strategy. By promoting and enforcing rigorous handwashing practices, the risk of transmitting infections between patients is significantly reduced, contributing to overall patient safety.

2. Error Reduction:

- Definition: Error reduction, on the other hand, centers on identifying and mitigating errors that have already occurred to prevent their recurrence.

- Example: Consider a scenario where a medication error has occurred due to confusion in drug names. Implementing a barcode scanning system for medication administration is an error reduction strategy. This technology helps ensure that the right patient receives the right medication, reducing the risk of medication errors.

Integration of Both Approaches:

- Effective risk management often involves a combination of risk reduction and error reduction strategies.

- Example: To address the risk of surgical errors, a hospital may implement pre-operative checklists (risk reduction) to ensure that all necessary steps are taken before surgery. Additionally, implementing a system for reporting and analyzing any surgical errors that do occur (error reduction) allows the hospital to learn from these incidents and implement changes to prevent similar errors in the future.

In summary, risk reduction aims to prevent adverse events proactively, while error reduction focuses on learning from and preventing the recurrence of specific errors. Both approaches are essential components of a comprehensive patient safety strategy in the complex landscape of medical negligence.

Only Risk Reduction

Risk reduction is often directly related to defensive medical practice. Defensive medical practice refers to healthcare providers taking precautions, sometimes beyond what might be medically necessary, with the primary goal of protecting themselves from potential legal actions or malpractice claims. In this context, risk reduction measures are implemented as a defensive strategy to minimize the likelihood of adverse events or errors that could lead to legal consequences.

Healthcare providers may engage in defensive practices due to the fear of litigation, rising malpractice insurance costs, and the potential impact on their professional reputation. Risk reduction becomes a defensive tactic when physicians and healthcare institutions adopt practices that may not necessarily enhance patient care but are implemented to mitigate the risk of legal challenges.

Examples of risk reduction measures that can be associated with defensive medical practice include:

1. **Excessive Testing**: Ordering unnecessary diagnostic tests or procedures to ensure comprehensive documentation and to demonstrate thoroughness in patient care, even if the clinical indication may not be strong.

2. **Overprescribing Medications**: Prescribing medications or treatments that may not be strictly necessary, but are done to address patient concerns or to avoid potential criticism.

3. **Defensive Documentation**: Thorough and defensive documentation practices, where healthcare providers document extensively to protect themselves legally, sometimes at the expense of clear and concise clinical communication.

4. **Avoidance of High-Risk Patients or Procedures**: Physicians may choose to avoid high-risk patients or complex procedures to minimize the chances of complications that could lead to legal challenges.

While risk reduction is a legitimate and important aspect of improving patient safety, it becomes problematic when it is driven primarily by legal concerns rather than a genuine commitment to enhancing patient care. Striking a balance between effective risk reduction for patient safety and defensive medical practices is essential for maintaining the integrity of the healthcare system. But is this possible when patient with a lawyer combination are standing in a way accusing at every possible error that occur in medical practice?

Dr. Sarah Mitchell, an experienced physician at City General Hospital, found herself caught in the complex web of defensive medicine. Over the years, the hospital had adopted a risk reduction model with a strong emphasis on mitigating potential legal risks. This approach, while aimed at improving patient safety, had inadvertently transformed the medical practice into a realm where defensive measures took precedence over patient-centric care.

In the bustling halls of City General, Dr. Mitchell encountered a patient named Mrs. Anderson, a middle-aged woman with a history of chronic back pain seeking relief. Mrs. Anderson had undergone numerous treatments, and Dr. Mitchell believed that a conservative approach, including physical therapy and pain management, would be most appropriate. However, mindful of the hospital's risk reduction model, she felt compelled to order a battery of diagnostic tests, including advanced imaging, even though the clinical necessity was questionable.

The test results revealed minor degenerative changes consistent with Mrs. Anderson's age and history, but nothing alarming. Despite this, Dr. Mitchell decided to prescribe a strong painkiller and refer Mrs. Anderson to a specialist, all in an effort to create an extensive paper trail showcasing a thorough and exhaustive approach to her care.

As Dr. Mitchell continued her rounds, she encountered Mr. Johnson, a patient with a common respiratory infection. Instead of relying on her clinical judgment, she opted for a broad-spectrum antibiotic and additional unnecessary tests to rule out any rare complications. The decision was motivated more by the fear of potential malpractice claims than by the patient's immediate medical needs.

The hospital, too, had implemented various risk reduction protocols. Extensive checklists were mandatory for even routine procedures, contributing to delays and impacting the overall efficiency of patient care. The fear of litigation loomed large, affecting the entire healthcare team's decision-making process. Defensive documentation practices became the norm, with physicians spending more time on meticulous record-keeping to safeguard themselves legally.

Over time, the hospital's risk reduction model had unintended consequences. Patient care, once focused on individual needs, became a series of defensive maneuvers aimed at avoiding legal pitfalls. The ethos of medicine as an art and science dedicated to healing and caring for patients was gradually overshadowed by the pervasive fear of litigation.

In this tale of defensive medicine, Dr. Sarah Mitchell and City General Hospital navigated the delicate balance between risk reduction and patient-centered care. The challenge remained: finding a way to prioritize patient well-being without compromising the principles of healthcare in an era dominated by the ever-present specter of legal repercussions.

Error Reduction: Need Of Medical Practice

Error reduction is widely regarded as a crucial component of best medical practices. While it may not be the sole approach, integrating error reduction strategies into healthcare delivery is essential for enhancing patient safety, improving outcomes, and fostering a culture of continuous improvement. Here are different steps and classifications related to error reduction in medical practice:

Steps for Error Reduction:

1. Identifying Potential Errors:

- Conduct thorough analyses of past incidents and near misses.

- Encourage reporting systems that allow healthcare professionals to identify and report errors without fear of punitive measures.

2. Root Cause Analysis:

- Investigate the underlying causes of errors to understand systemic issues.

- Utilize root cause analysis tools to identify contributing factors and implement targeted solutions.

3. Standardization of Processes:

- Develop and implement standardized protocols and procedures to reduce variability in care delivery.

- Ensure clear communication and understanding of standardized practices among healthcare teams.

4. Enhanced Communication:

- Implement effective communication strategies among healthcare providers, including standardized handoff protocols.

- Encourage open communication between healthcare professionals and patients to ensure a clear understanding of treatment plans.

5. Technological Integration:

- Integrate technology to streamline processes and reduce the risk of errors, such as computerized physician order entry (CPOE) systems.

- Utilize electronic health records (EHRs) to improve information sharing and reduce the likelihood of transcription errors.

6. Continuous Training and Education:

- Provide ongoing training to healthcare professionals on the latest clinical guidelines and best practices.

- Offer simulation training for high-risk scenarios to enhance preparedness and response.

Classifications of Error Reduction:

1. Preventive Errors:

- Implement strategies to prevent errors before they occur.

- Examples include checklists, safety protocols, and standardized procedures.

2. Detective Errors:

- Focus on identifying errors promptly after they occur.

- Encourage reporting systems, incident investigations, and routine monitoring for early detection.

3. Corrective Errors:

- Implement measures to correct errors and mitigate their impact.

- Involve root cause analysis to address systemic issues contributing to errors.

4. Adaptive Errors:

- Foster a culture of adaptability and learning from errors.

- Encourage healthcare professionals to adapt practices based on lessons learned from errors and near misses.

5. Proactive Errors:

- Anticipate potential errors and implement preemptive measures.

- Utilize risk assessments, simulations, and scenario planning to proactively identify and address potential risks.

Benefits of Error Reduction:

1. Enhanced Patient Safety:

- Reduces the likelihood of adverse events and patient harm.

2. Improved Quality of Care:

- Standardized processes and continuous improvement contribute to overall care quality.

3. Patient Trust and Satisfaction:

- Patients are more likely to trust healthcare providers and be satisfied with their care when errors are minimized.

4. Professional Development:

- Encourages a culture of continuous learning and professional development among healthcare professionals.

5. Financial Impact:

- Reduces the financial burden associated with legal consequences and compensations for medical errors.

In conclusion, error reduction is a multifaceted approach involving various steps and classifications. It is a vital aspect of best medical practices, promoting patient safety, improving healthcare quality, and fostering a culture of continuous improvement within the healthcare system.

SO THE BEST MODEL IS EITHER INTEGRATIVE APPROACH OF BOTH RISK AND ERROR REDUCTION OR ERROR REDUCTION MODEL

Error Reduction

In the bustling corridors of City General Hospital, Dr. Sarah Mitchell, a seasoned physician, was deeply committed to a patient-centric approach with a focus on error reduction. The hospital had implemented comprehensive measures to identify and mitigate errors, fostering a culture of continuous improvement rather than adopting defensive practices.

Mrs. Anderson, a middle-aged woman suffering from chronic back pain, sought Dr. Mitchell's expertise. The physician, adhering to the hospital's commitment to error reduction, engaged in a thorough examination and considered the patient's history. Instead of opting for unnecessary diagnostic tests, Dr. Mitchell recommended a conservative treatment plan, including physical therapy and targeted pain management. The emphasis was on providing personalized care rather than adhering to a one-size-fits-all approach.

Across the hospital, the commitment to error reduction was evident. Dr. Mitchell's colleagues diligently followed evidence-based guidelines and collaborated on regular case reviews to identify areas for improvement. The hospital had implemented technology to streamline communication, ensuring that medical teams could share critical information efficiently, reducing the risk of miscommunication errors.

As Dr. Mitchell continued her rounds, she encountered Mr. Johnson, who presented with a respiratory infection. Applying the principles of error reduction, she relied on her clinical judgment, prescribing a targeted antibiotic based on the patient's symptoms and medical history. Unnecessary tests were avoided, as the focus was on delivering precise and effective care tailored to the individual.

The hospital's commitment to error reduction extended beyond individual patient interactions. Robust training programs were in place to keep the medical staff abreast of the latest advancements and best practices. Regular simulations and drills were conducted to enhance the team's response to emergencies, reducing the likelihood of procedural errors.

In this environment of error reduction, the hospital had created a culture where physicians felt empowered to learn from mistakes and actively engage in collaborative efforts to enhance patient safety. The fear of litigation was replaced by a commitment to transparency and accountability.

As the hospital embraced a model centered on error reduction, Dr. Mitchell and her colleagues experienced a shift in their approach. The focus was no longer on defensive measures but on continual learning and improvement. Patient care became a collaborative effort where the hospital and its healthcare professionals worked tirelessly to provide the best possible outcomes while minimizing the risk of errors. The tale of City General Hospital became a story of dedication to patient safety through a proactive commitment to reducing errors in every aspect of healthcare delivery.

INTEGRATIVE APPROACH

In the heart of City General Hospital, Dr. Emily Reynolds exemplified a commitment to both risk reduction and error reduction in her day-to-day medical practice. The hospital had cultivated a culture that recognized the importance of minimizing risks while actively learning from any errors that occurred.

One day, Dr. Reynolds encountered Mr. Lewis, a patient with a complex medical history requiring surgery. Applying a risk reduction approach, Dr. Reynolds ensured that the surgical team adhered to a comprehensive pre-operative checklist. This checklist, a product of the hospital's risk reduction strategy, covered every detail from confirming the patient's identity to double-checking equipment readiness. By following these standardized protocols, the surgical team aimed to prevent potential errors and complications during the procedure.

During surgery, Dr. Reynolds encountered an unexpected anatomical variation. Despite the meticulous planning, this unforeseen challenge could have resulted in a potential error. However, the hospital's commitment to error reduction came into play. Dr. Reynolds immediately communicated with her team, initiating a collaborative effort to address the situation. The surgical team adapted their approach in real-time, drawing on their collective experience and expertise to navigate the unexpected challenge successfully.

Post-surgery, the hospital's risk reduction model continued to play a crucial role. Dr. Reynolds ensured that Mr. Lewis received personalized post-operative care, taking into account potential risks associated with his medical history. The patient's recovery plan was tailored to minimize risks and optimize outcomes.

In the weeks following the surgery, the hospital's commitment to error reduction became evident. Dr. Reynolds and her team engaged in a comprehensive review of the surgical procedure, analyzing the unexpected anatomical variation and identifying areas for improvement. This proactive approach to error reduction allowed the hospital to implement changes in their surgical protocols, enhancing future patient safety.

Meanwhile, another physician at City General Hospital, Dr. James Carter, was overseeing a patient, Mrs. Turner, with a chronic condition that required ongoing management. Dr. Carter applied risk reduction by ensuring that Mrs. Turner received regular check-ups and monitoring. The hospital's risk reduction model included the use of advanced technology for remote patient monitoring, allowing for early detection of potential issues.

Despite these preventive measures, Dr. Carter encountered a situation where Mrs. Turner experienced an adverse reaction to a medication. Applying error reduction principles, Dr. Carter promptly communicated with the hospital's pharmacy and therapeutics committee to review the incident. The hospital took immediate corrective action, adjusting medication protocols and enhancing communication channels to prevent similar errors in the future.

In this story, City General Hospital showcased the successful integration of both risk reduction and error reduction strategies into their day-to-day medical practices. The hospital's commitment to preventing potential risks while actively learning from and correcting errors contributed to a culture of continuous improvement, ensuring optimal patient care and safety.

Let's Discuss In Nutshell Various Options/Models

Arbitration And Mediation

In the realm of patient compensation through arbitration and mediation programs, there exists a nuanced landscape where improvements are observed, particularly in mediation, yet significant challenges persist. Let's explore this through stories that illustrate the complexities of the current system.

The Arbitration Dilemma:

Dr. Divyang, a skilled surgeon, found himself entangled in an arbitration case after a challenging procedure resulted in unforeseen complications for Mrs. Thompson. The arbitration process, following traditional tort law standards, provided limited avenues for appeal, leaving Dr. Divyang and Mrs. Thompson in a situation where resolution seemed elusive.

In this scenario, the arbitration model, relying on established legal frameworks, did not create substantial incentives for doctors and hospitals to prioritize risk management over error reduction. Dr. Divyang faced a situation where admitting any wrongdoing could potentially have legal ramifications, hindering the learning process for both himself and the hospital.

Mediation's Promise and Limitations:

On the other side of the spectrum, Ms. Ramirez, a patient who experienced complications post-surgery, opted for mediation as a means of seeking compensation. The facilitative and confidential nature of mediation allowed for open communication between Ms. Ramirez and the healthcare providers involved.

However, despite the potential improvements in standards of care through open dialogue, mediation still grappled with challenges. As a voluntary process, healthcare providers retained the looming threat of litigation. This fear influenced their degree of cooperation in individual cases, making it a strategic decision rather than a commitment to transparently address errors and enhance patient safety.

Furthermore, while mediation provided a platform for learning within the confines of a specific case, it lacked mechanisms to ensure that the lessons gleaned reached other healthcare providers. The confidential nature, while fostering openness, also restricted the dissemination of valuable insights that could contribute to system-wide safety enhancements.

Bit Better Than Complete Punitive Action But Still Falls Short

No Fault Liability System: New Zealand And Sweden

In the quiet town of Greenwood, the residents had long enjoyed a close-knit community and trusted their local healthcare providers. Dr. Rebecca Lawson, a dedicated physician at Greenwood General Hospital, found herself at the center of a paradigm shift in the medical landscape—one that would alter the dynamics of patient compensation and safety promotion.

News had arrived that the state was contemplating the adoption of a no-fault liability system, challenging the traditional framework that required a finding of physician negligence for patients to receive compensation. Dr. Lawson, respected for her commitment to patient care, couldn't help but wonder how this shift would impact both healthcare providers and the patients they served.

As the system underwent transformation, a patient named Mr. Harris became a pivotal figure in the unfolding narrative. Mr. Harris had undergone a routine surgical procedure that, unfortunately, led to unexpected complications. Under the traditional model, the burden of proving physician negligence loomed large, adding stress to an already distressing situation for both Mr. Harris and Dr. Lawson.

However, in the new era of no-fault, Mr. Harris found solace in a simplified process. He needed only to demonstrate that he had been injured due to medical care, and his case met the established compensation criteria. The emphasis shifted from pinpointing negligence to addressing the undesirable outcome resulting from medical intervention.

This change brought relief to Dr. Lawson, who, under the traditional model, would have navigated a complex legal process to defend against allegations of negligence. The no-fault system spared her from the stigma associated with malpractice claims, allowing her to focus on patient care without the constant fear of litigation.

Yet, as the town adapted to this new paradigm, questions lingered regarding safety promotion. Would a no-fault system incentivize improved care and contribute to a reduction in medical errors? Dr. Lawson, known for her dedication to continuous improvement, pondered the potential implications.

Some argued that without the deterrent effect of negligence claims, physicians might not feel the pressure to enhance their practices. On the other hand, proponents believed that the absence of stigmatization would foster a culture of open communication and learning, ultimately benefiting both doctors and patients.

As the discussions unfolded, Dr. Lawson found herself grappling with the dual nature of the no-fault system. While it addressed the immediate concerns of compensation and reduced the adversarial nature of medical disputes, it did not inherently address the emotional healing journey of patients who had experienced undesirable outcomes.

In the heart of Greenwood, the adoption of the no-fault system marked a significant departure from the traditional approach. It promised a more streamlined process for compensation but left an open question regarding its impact on safety promotion and the holistic healing of patients. Dr. Lawson, ever committed to her patients' well-being, observed the evolving landscape with a sense of cautious optimism, recognizing that the true success of the no-fault system would lie in balancing the interests of patients, healthcare providers, and the pursuit of continuous improvement in medical care.

In the lively town of Greenwood, the media debate on the proposed no-fault liability system took a dramatic turn, transforming the community center into a battleground of conflicting opinions. The panel, chosen for their fervent beliefs and strong voices, unleashed a torrent of sensationalism and impassioned arguments that captivated the entire town.

As Dr. Jessica Barnes stepped onto the stage, her words dripped with charisma and conviction, igniting the flames of enthusiasm among supporters of the no-fault system.

Dr. Jessica Barnes:

"Ladies and gentlemen, welcome to a new era of compassion! The no-fault system is our ticket to a world where patients no longer suffer the indignities of proving negligence. It's time we prioritize healing over litigation, and let our healthcare providers breathe without the constant shadow of malpractice claims. Let's break free from the chains of an outdated system and embrace a future of empathy and continuous improvement!"

On the opposing side, Mr. Richard Thompson countered with a fiery determination, his arguments piercing the air like thunderclaps.

Mr. Richard Thompson:

"Hold on, Greenwood! Are we so quick to abandon accountability in the pursuit of convenience? The no-fault system might seem like a beacon of fairness, but what about the very essence of medical progress? Without the threat of negligence claims, what incentive do our doctors have to strive for excellence? We're jeopardizing the very foundation of our healthcare system, trading it for a mirage of compassion!"

As the panelists clashed, the audience erupted into a cacophony of cheers, jeers, and impassioned shouts. The debate was no longer a civil exchange of ideas but a full-blown spectacle, each side vying for dominance in the court of public opinion.

Audience Member #1 (shouting):

"Dr. Barnes is speaking the truth! We need a system that understands the pain of patients without the burdensome legal circus!"

Audience Member #2 (counter-shouting):

"Thompson's right! Accountability matters! We can't just let doctors off the hook; we need checks and balances to ensure the best care possible!"

Amidst the chaos, the town's residents engaged in impromptu debates of their own, passionately defending their chosen sides. Emotions ran high, transforming the once-respectful town center into an arena of passionate clashes.

Takes Care Of Compensation Part But Over All Healing Is Still Not There

Enterprise Liability Model

In the bustling town of Rivertown, a shift in the way hospitals handled medical liability sparked both curiosity and concern among its residents. The town was known for its tight-knit community, and the latest development in healthcare practices set tongues wagging.

Dr. Sarah Thompson, a respected physician at Rivertown General Hospital, found herself caught in the midst of this transformation. The talk of the town was the introduction of an enterprise liability system, an approach that aimed to restrict liability to hospitals rather than individual doctors.

One evening, as the townsfolk gathered at the local community center, Dr. Thompson took the stage to explain the intricacies of this new system. She used a story to break down the complex concept into something everyone could understand.

"Imagine our hospital as a big ship sailing through the challenges of healthcare," began Dr. Thompson. "In the past, when something went wrong on this ship, individual crew members were held responsible. But now, with enterprise liability, the ship itself, our hospital, will bear the responsibility for any mishaps during the journey."

As she continued, she delved into the benefits proponents claimed this system would bring. "You see, one of the advantages is that it takes the blame away from individual doctors. It encourages open discussions about mistakes, helping us conduct internal reviews and improve our practices for the benefit of everyone on board."

The audience listened intently, nodding in understanding. However, Dr. Thompson didn't shy away from the concerns surrounding this new approach.

"Now, some worry that this shift might prioritize avoiding risks over learning from mistakes, especially at the institutional level. It's like ensuring the ship doesn't encounter storms but not focusing enough on teaching the crew how to navigate them effectively," she explained, using a metaphor that resonated with the maritime setting of Rivertown.

She went on to highlight a crucial point of contention. "There's also the question of whether hospitals will be willing to share information about mistakes with the passengers—the patients. This system might not do much in terms of emotional healing, and we need to be sure that it leads to fair and efficient resolutions that satisfy everyone involved."

As Dr. Thompson concluded her explanation, she opened the floor to questions and concerns from the audience. The townspeople, now equipped with a narrative that painted a vivid picture of enterprise liability as a ship navigating the waters of medical responsibility, engaged in a thoughtful dialogue about the implications of this new approach on their healthcare journey.

In Rivertown, the story of enterprise liability became a tale of navigating uncharted waters, where the community grappled with the balance between avoiding risks and learning from mistakes, all while ensuring transparency and emotional healing for everyone aboard the ship of healthcare.

As Dr. Sarah Thompson concluded her explanation of the enterprise liability system in Rivertown, the community center buzzed with murmurs and discussions. The townspeople, now armed with a better understanding of the new approach, engaged in a lively conversation about its implications.

John, a local business owner: "I get it now, it's like the hospital taking responsibility for the whole team, right? But what about the individual doctors? Don't they need to be accountable for their actions too?"

Mary, a school teacher: "That's exactly what I was thinking! It sounds good for transparency, but will this make doctors less careful? If the hospital is the one on the hook, what's to stop doctors from being a bit lax in their practices?"

Tom, a retiree: "Dr. Thompson mentioned that one of the benefits is removing blame from individual doctors to encourage open discussions. But what about us, the patients? Will we still know what went wrong if something does go awry?"

Emily, a young mother: "I'm all for improving practices, but what about emotional healing? If something goes wrong, I want to know the whole story and how it will be resolved. Will this new system give us that transparency and closure?"

Charlie, a local farmer: "It's like they're steering the ship, and we're just passengers. But I want to know if this will lead to better care or just cover things up. What's in it for us, the ones relying on the healthcare system?"

As the discussion unfolded, various concerns and questions surfaced among the townspeople. The metaphor of the hospital as a ship navigating through healthcare challenges resonated, but there was a collective desire for more clarity on how this system would impact individual doctors, patient information, and overall healthcare quality.

Dr. Thompson, sensing the need for further clarification, patiently addressed each question, emphasizing the importance of finding a balance between accountability, transparency, and continuous improvement in healthcare practices. The townspeople, though still uncertain about the uncharted waters ahead, left the community center with a sense that their voices had been heard and their concerns acknowledged.

The story of enterprise liability in Rivertown became not just about the metaphorical ship but also about a community actively engaging in the dialogue about the future of their healthcare journey.

Increasing Expertise-Screening Panels & Medical Courts

SCREENING PANELS

In the quiet town of Meadowville, Sarah found herself facing an unexpected challenge. A routine medical procedure had gone wrong, leaving her with more questions than answers. Frustrated and seeking justice, she decided to file a medical malpractice claim against the hospital and the attending physician.

Little did Sarah know that her quest for answers would involve navigating a complex system. Meadowville had a medical screening panel in place— a group of experts who would review her case before it even reached the courts. It was like a checkpoint in her journey for justice.

As Sarah presented her case to the screening panel, she felt a mix of hope and anxiety. She recounted the details of the procedure, the unexpected complications, and the impact it had on her life. The panel listened attentively, asking questions and jotting down notes.

After what felt like an eternity, the panel delivered their verdict. They concluded that Sarah's case had some merit and could proceed to the next stage. It was a small victory for Sarah, but the road ahead remained daunting.

As her case moved through the legal system, Sarah realized that the screening panel, meant to filter out frivolous claims, added an extra layer of complexity. It was like a game with rules that seemed to favor the system rather than the individuals seeking justice.

Sarah's frustration grew as the process continued. The legal battles prolonged her suffering, and the emotional toll was undeniable. The screening panel, while intended to streamline the process, felt like an obstacle course—another hurdle in her pursuit of truth and compensation.

Meanwhile, in Meadowville, Dr. Divyang, the physician involved in Sarah's case, faced his own set of challenges. The screening panel didn't necessarily motivate him to reflect on his practices or share information about the incident. The fear of legal consequences overshadowed any potential for a collaborative learning experience.

The community, observing these legal battles and screening processes, grew skeptical. The panels were meant to save costs, but they did little to rebuild trust between the people and their healthcare providers. Instead, they conveyed the message that there were more barriers to overcome in the pursuit of truth and justice.

In Meadowville, Sarah's story became a symbol of the complexities within the system. The screening panels, intended to bring clarity, often left individuals like Sarah feeling like they were lost in a maze of legalities. The town grappled with the question of whether these panels were truly serving justice or merely adding more layers to an already intricate game.

In India Such Screening Panels Are Used As Medical Boards When There Is A Possibikity Of Criminal Negligence Against The Doctor. This Has Helped Prevent Frivelous Complains And False Arrest Of Doctors. But Overall To Replicate In All Cases Is Just Addition Of One More Tedious And Emotionally Burn Out Phase.

Medical Courts

Pros of Specialized Medical Courts:

1. Expertise: Specialized judges with medical knowledge can better understand the complexities of medical cases, leading to more informed decisions.

Example: Just as Judge Anderson's tech expertise transformed how technology cases are handled, medical courts could bring a similar level of understanding to healthcare litigation.

2. Decision Speed: Specialized courts may expedite the legal process, providing quicker resolutions for both patients seeking justice and healthcare providers aiming to improve practices.

Example: In cases like rapid technological advancements, having specialized judges could keep pace with evolving medical standards and practices.

3. Uniformity and Coherence: Medical courts may offer consistency in decision-making, ensuring a standardized approach to medical claims.

 Example: Unlike traditional courts where judgments can vary, medical courts could establish a coherent set of principles specific to healthcare litigation.

Cons of Specialized Medical Courts:

1. Political Pressures: If judges in medical courts are elected rather than appointed, they might succumb to political pressures and special interest influences.

Example: A case where a judge, influenced by pharmaceutical lobbyists, ruled in favor of a drug company raises concerns about the impartiality of elected judges.

2. Compensation Objectives: Specialized courts might not fully address the compensation objectives of the healing-centered framework, potentially falling short in providing holistic relief for patients.

Example: While medical courts could minimize frivolous cases, they may not ensure that compensation accurately reflects patients' needs.

3. Risk Reduction over Error Reduction: Healthcare providers in medical courts would still face the same pressures as in traditional courts, possibly prioritizing risk reduction over learning from errors.

Example: Despite specialized expertise, the fundamental dynamics of legal pressures in healthcare might persist, hindering a shift towards a more error-reducing culture.

As communities weigh the pros and cons of specialized medical courts, the challenge lies in finding a balanced approach that leverages expertise while safeguarding against potential pitfalls.

Restorative Justice, The Dawn After Darkness

Restorative justice, when applied to the realm of medical malpractice cases, emerges as a unique process. It serves as a transformative approach where all relevant parties connected to a particular medical error join forces to collectively address its aftermath and consider the implications for the future of patient care.

In the context of medical malpractice, restorative justice prompts crucial inquiries: Who has been adversely affected by the medical error? What are their specific needs for recovery and understanding? To whom do the obligations and responsibilities for the incident belong, both among healthcare providers and the affected patient? Who holds a stake in the overall situation, including potential improvements in medical practices?

Rather than solely focusing on assigning blame or punitive measures, the process of restorative justice in medical malpractice cases centres around engaging all stakeholders. This inclusive approach involves doctors, nurses, hospital, the affected patient, and possibly even family members in a shared journey toward finding a comprehensive solution. It transcends the conventional legal framework, emphasizing a collective effort to not only address immediate consequences but also to collaboratively shape a path toward healing, improved patient care, and a more empathetic healthcare system.

Let's first understand the process in a simple way

Once upon a time in the quaint town of Harmonyville, a crime unfolded that shook the community to its core. The victim, Emily Thompson, a beloved schoolteacher, had her home vandalized, and her cherished possessions were stolen. The townsfolk were shocked and angered by this act of violation against someone who had dedicated her life to educating the town's children.

As the police investigation commenced, it became evident that the perpetrator was a young man named Jake Simmons, a troubled teenager grappling with personal challenges. The evidence pointed to Jake, who soon found himself facing not only legal consequences but also the disdain of the community.

However, instead of pursuing a traditional legal route, the town decided to explore the concept of restorative justice. A community meeting was called, bringing together Emily, Jake, their families, local leaders, and even some of Emily's students who were deeply affected by the incident.

The gathering took place in the town hall, a space usually reserved for civic discussions but now transformed into a forum for healing. The air was tense as Emily, with a mix of apprehension and determination, faced Jake, who sat with remorse etched across his face.

The facilitator, a seasoned mediator named Grace Miller, initiated the restorative justice process. The fundamental questions were posed: Who had been hurt? What did they need? Whose obligations and responsibilities were at play? Who had a stake in this situation?

Emily expressed her pain and the emotional toll the crime had taken on her sense of security. Her students shared how they felt violated in their safe space, and Jake's family acknowledged their role in his struggles.

As the dialogue unfolded, a surprising shift occurred. Rather than focusing solely on punishment, the conversation shifted towards understanding the root causes of Jake's actions and how the community could contribute to his rehabilitation.

The town collectively brainstormed ideas for restitution. Jake, eager to make amends, offered to perform community service, assist in rebuilding what was damaged, and participate in counseling sessions. Emily, in turn, expressed her willingness to mentor Jake and guide him towards a more positive path.

In the months that followed, Jake actively engaged in his restitution commitments. Slowly but surely, the Harmonyville community witnessed a transformation. The once-vandalized home became a symbol of resilience, painted by community members who came together to rebuild.

Through restorative justice, the town of Harmonyville not only mended the immediate wounds caused by the crime but also cultivated a sense of empathy, understanding, and shared responsibility. It became a story of redemption and healing, proving that sometimes, justice isn't just about punishment but about restoring the fabric of a community torn by wrongdoing.

Restorative justice, often associated with cases of brutal torture and egregious human rights abuses, has demonstrated its efficacy in fostering reconciliation even in seemingly irreparable situations. If it can be successful in such extreme circumstances, then there is a strong argument that restorative justice principles should be harnessed to address the complexities within the context of a physician-patient relationship damaged by medical error.

In healthcare, the bond between doctors and patients is built on care and trust. When medical errors happen, it can strain this relationship. Restorative justice, known for healing extreme situations, can be valuable here too.

In healthcare, compassion is crucial. Restorative justice, focusing on accountability and rebuilding trust, fits well. After a medical error, patients may feel hurt and lost. Restorative justice, emphasizing open communication and empathy, aligns with healthcare values.

Healing from a medical error isn't just about legal action. It involves the emotions of both patients and healthcare providers. Restorative justice, with its emphasis on communication and shared decision-making, fits the healthcare profession.

As we push for a patient-centered approach in medical cases, embracing restorative justice is vital. It promotes dialogue, understanding, and a culture of improvement. In a time where empathy matters, incorporating restorative justice is necessary for a compassionate and patient-focused healthcare system.

Let's Start Understanding The Process

Patient

Patient And The Needs: Not All Are After The Money. Majority Wants Healing

In the quiet town of Serenity Falls, a place known for its close-knit community, lived Rachel Mitchell, a dedicated nurse, and her patient, Mr. Henry Turner. Their lives intertwined one fateful day when a medical error occurred, leading to unforeseen complications for Mr. Turner.

Rachel, deeply affected by the incident, was determined to find a way to address the harm caused. The town, valuing its community spirit, decided to embark on an innovative path – restorative justice.

1. Information: Unraveling the Truth

A community meeting was arranged, bringing together Rachel, Mr. Turner, their families, and local leaders. The air was tense as they discussed the incident openly. Restorative justice began with providing the victims, Rachel and Mr. Turner, with the information they sought – an understanding of what went wrong.

Mr. Turner, during the meeting, expressed his fears and confusion. Rachel, in turn, candidly explained the situation, acknowledging the mistake and detailing the steps taken to prevent a recurrence. The transparency in communication started the process of healing.

2. Opportunity to Participate: A Shared Journey to Resolution

In Serenity Falls, community involvement was not just a concept but a way of life. Restorative justice facilitated a dialogue where all involved parties had an opportunity to participate actively. Instead of feeling isolated, Mr. Turner and Rachel were integral parts of the solution.

Community members suggested various ways to enhance patient care, ensuring that Mr. Turner's experience led to positive changes. This collaborative effort empowered the victims, giving them a sense of control over the resolution process.

3. Emotional Restoration and Apology: Mending Hearts

Emotional restoration was a crucial element in the restorative justice process. Rachel, recognizing the emotional toll on Mr. Turner, offered a sincere apology. She expressed genuine remorse, and the community witnessed a heartfelt exchange that started the process of emotional healing.

The town rallied behind Mr. Turner, organizing support groups and counseling sessions. As the emotional wounds began to mend, a palpable sense of compassion enveloped Serenity Falls.

4. Material Reparation: Rebuilding Trust

While financial compensation couldn't undo the past, the community rallied to provide material reparation. A fund was established to cover Mr. Turner's medical expenses and future healthcare needs. The town's collective effort to rebuild trust went beyond words, showcasing the genuine commitment to making amends.

5. Fairness and Respect: A Restored Sense of Dignity

Fairness and respect were paramount in Serenity Falls. The restorative justice process ensured that Mr. Turner was treated with dignity throughout. By involving him in decision-making and acknowledging his experiences, the town restored a sense of fairness and respect.

As time passed, the scars of the incident healed, and a renewed sense of trust emerged. Serenity Falls, through the application of restorative justice, showcased the transformative power of empathy, collaboration, and community-driven solutions. Rachel, once at the center of the incident, became an advocate for patient-centered care, emphasizing the importance of learning from mistakes to create a safer and more compassionate healthcare system. The town's commitment to restorative justice not only repaired the immediate harm but also laid the foundation for a stronger and more interconnected community.

LAW TEACHES DON'T APOLOGISE AS IT MEANS YOU HAVE ACCEPTED GUILTY. REALLY????

In the bustling city of Rivertown, Dr. Sarah Reynolds, an experienced surgeon, found herself at a crossroads after a medical procedure resulted in unexpected complications for her patient, Mr. James Henderson. The air in the hospital became heavy with tension as whispers of potential litigation circulated.

Angle 1: The Silence of Liability

Dr. Reynolds, guided by years of medical training, hesitated to offer an apology. In the realm of conventional wisdom within the medical profession, admitting fault was often synonymous with legal liability. The fear of litigation loomed large, and Dr. Reynolds, like many doctors, opted for silence. This silence, however, left Mr. Henderson feeling abandoned, questioning the empathy of the person he had entrusted with his health.

As the days unfolded, the absence of an apology left a void in the doctor-patient relationship. Mr. Henderson, grappling with physical and emotional distress, yearned for acknowledgment and reassurance. The silent treatment fueled frustration, amplifying the perceived lack of caring from his physician.

Angle 2: The Healing Power of Apology

Contrastingly, in a neighboring town, Dr. Emily Turner faced a similar situation involving a medical error. Drawing inspiration from restorative justice principles, Dr. Turner recognized the potential of an apology in the healing process.

Understanding that an apology need not be an admission of legal guilt, Dr. Turner approached Mr. Samuel Rodriguez, her patient, with sincerity and compassion. She expressed genuine remorse for the unforeseen complications, emphasizing her commitment to his well-being. This act of vulnerability transformed the atmosphere, creating a space for open communication.

In this scenario, the apology served multiple purposes. Firstly, it demonstrated Dr. Turner's remorse, acknowledging the emotional toll on Mr. Rodriguez. Secondly, it expressed her intent to ensure Mr. Rodriguez received the necessary support for recovery. Lastly, the apology became a bridge toward restoring harmony in the doctor-patient relationship.

Reflection on Cultural Perspectives: Japan's Apology Tradition

In the distant land of Japan, the significance of apology in the justice system has deep roots. For Hiroshi Wagatsuma and Arthur Rosett, an apology in Japan serves a triple function – indicating remorse, showcasing the intent to compensate, and, if accepted, restoring harmony between the victim and offender. This cultural perspective highlights the transformative power of an apology in fostering healing and rebuilding relationships.

Conclusion: A Tale of Two Approaches

The tale of Dr. Sarah Reynolds and Dr. Emily Turner paints a vivid picture of the contrasting perspectives on apologies in the medical field. While one chose silence driven by legal considerations, the other embraced the healing power of acknowledging mistakes. In a world where the dynamics of healthcare are evolving, the story of these two doctors reflects the ongoing debate within the medical community on the role of apologies – whether they are perceived as admissions of guilt or as essential components of compassionate and patient-centered care. The outcome of each approach, both for the patients and the doctors, underscores the nuanced complexities embedded in the delicate dance between accountability and empathy in the realm of medicine.

India Has Always Believed In Apology And Forgiveness.

So Think About This

"Restorative Justice: Where Apology Is An Art And Forgiveness, A Masterpiece"

Financial Compensation Is Also Important But It's Just A Part Of Justice

In the bustling city of Mumbai, the Deshmukh family thrived as a close-knit unit. Raj Deshmukh, the sole earner of the family, worked tirelessly to provide for his wife, Priya, and their two children, Aarav and Diya. The Deshmukhs led a comfortable life until an unexpected turn of events changed everything.

Raj, experiencing persistent headaches, sought medical advice from Dr. Anika Patel, a well-regarded neurologist in the area. Unfortunately, a series of oversights and misdiagnoses led to a delayed diagnosis of a severe medical condition. By the time the correct diagnosis was made, irreversible damage had occurred, leaving Raj incapacitated and unable to continue working.

As medical bills piled up, the financial strain on the Deshmukh family became overwhelming. Raj's lost wages, coupled with the escalating costs of ongoing medical care and rehabilitation, put a considerable burden on their once-stable finances. The family faced the harsh reality that material compensation was not just a desire but a necessity to navigate this unforeseen crisis.

The legal battle that ensued highlighted the importance of material compensation in cases of medical negligence. The financial aspect encompassed not only the direct medical costs but also factored in Raj's lost wages and the emotional toll on the family's well-being.

In court, the Deshmukh family's lawyer argued passionately for comprehensive material compensation to address the immediate financial challenges they faced. The judiciary, recognizing the extent of the negligence and its impact on the Deshmukh family's livelihood, awarded a substantial settlement to cover medical expenses, rehabilitation costs, and the loss of income incurred by Raj.

However, as the legal proceedings unfolded, it became evident that material compensation alone couldn't address the emotional and psychological toll on the Deshmukh family. Raj's inability to contribute to the family income left him feeling a sense of loss, and the once-vibrant family dynamics were strained.

In the pursuit of a holistic resolution, the Deshmukh family, inspired by the principles of restorative justice, requested a meeting with Dr. Patel. In this dialogue, beyond the legal discussions of compensation, the family sought an acknowledgment of the emotional impact of the medical error. They expressed their need for Dr. Patel to understand the void left in their lives due to the substandard care Raj had received.

Dr. Patel, recognizing the gravity of the situation, offered a heartfelt apology. She expressed genuine remorse for the oversight that had led to such significant consequences for the Deshmukh family. The apology, while not diminishing the need for material compensation, became a crucial component of the resolution. It provided a sense of closure and acknowledgment, helping the family embark on the journey of emotional healing.

In the end, the Deshmukh family's story emphasized the critical role of material compensation in addressing the tangible consequences of medical negligence. However, it also underscored the importance of acknowledging the emotional impact and fostering a sense of empathy and understanding in the pursuit of a more comprehensive resolution. The tale of the Deshmukhs highlighted that while material compensation is a crucial step, it must not stand alone but should be

accompanied by efforts to restore not just the financial stability but also the emotional well-being of the affected individuals and their families.

In Present Justice System Only Money Is What Is Provided And That To If Lucky

Doctors

DOCTOR: Majority have good faith for patient. And not err intentionally.

And remember about human body, complex behaviour of human body and also of the medical procedures and medicines.

In the bustling medical hub of Mumbai, Dr. Aryan Khanna, a dedicated cardiologist, found himself grappling with an unexpected turn of events after a cardiac procedure for his patient, Mrs. Nalini Shah, resulted in complications. The conventional route of medical malpractice litigation loomed, a restorative model that could reshape the narrative around medical errors was in place in INDIA

Recognizing the need for a comprehensive approach, Dr. Khanna and the hospital initiated a restorative process that extended beyond the patient-doctor dialogue. The hospital's internal audit and fact-finding team played a pivotal role in objectively assessing the events leading to Mrs. Shah's complications. This internal scrutiny aimed not at assigning blame but at understanding the systemic factors that contributed to the incident.

The audit team, consisting of medical professionals, patient advocates, and a neutral third party with no affiliations to the hospital, convened for a pivotal interactive session. Dr. Khanna, Mrs. Shah, her concerned daughter, and the neutral third party gathered to delve into the details of the incident, creating a charged yet constructive atmosphere.

Dr. Khanna commenced the discussion by providing a thorough account of the cardiac procedure, openly acknowledging any unexpected complications. Mrs. Shah, accompanied by her daughter, listened intently, seeking clarity and reassurance amidst the complexities of the medical scenario.

The neutral third party, a seasoned mediator well-versed in facilitating restorative processes, skillfully guided the conversation, ensuring a focus on uncovering the facts rather than assigning blame. This mediator encouraged each participant to share their perspectives, concerns, and questions.

Mrs. Shah, visibly distressed, expressed her anxieties about her health and the emotional toll the incident had taken on her family. The neutral third party provided a compassionate space for her to voice these concerns, emphasizing the importance of emotional healing alongside the pursuit of truth.

The audit team meticulously examined medical records, scrutinizing procedures, communication protocols, and any deviations from standard practices. The neutral third party facilitated a dialogue between Dr. Khanna and the Shah family, allowing them to ask questions, seek clarifications, and articulate their expectations for resolution.

As the interactive session unfolded, a collaborative atmosphere emerged. Dr. Khanna acknowledged any communication gaps and shared his unwavering commitment to learning from the incident. The neutral third party facilitated an agreement for ongoing communication between the medical team and the Shah family, fostering a sense of partnership in Mrs. Shah's recovery.

The hospital audit concluded with a comprehensive report outlining findings, recommendations for improvement, and a plan for continuous support for the Shah family. The neutral third party ensured the report's impartiality, fairness, and accessibility to all parties involved.

By engaging key stakeholders and introducing a neutral third party, the process not only sought to uncover the facts but also aimed at building trust, understanding, and a shared commitment to improvement within the healthcare system.

Simultaneously, insurance companies conducted their own audits, seeking to establish the veracity of the medical procedures and the extent of liability. This multifaceted examination aimed to provide a holistic view, involving all stakeholders in the quest for truth.

An interactive session unfolded with representatives from the insurance company, hospital administrators, Dr. Aryan Khanna (the cardiologist), Mrs. Shah, and her family gathering to explore the intricacies of the billing process. The neutral third party, who facilitated the hospital audit, continued to guide the session, maintaining a focus on uncovering facts rather than assigning blame.

The insurance company representative presented the findings of their audit, meticulously examining billing records and charges for medical procedures. Dr. Khanna, accompanied by the hospital's financial team, provided insights into the billing practices, emphasizing the hospital's commitment to fair and transparent financial transactions.

Mrs. Shah and her family, eager to understand the financial aspects of her medical care, raised questions about specific charges and the overall billing structure. The neutral third party ensured that the dialogue remained constructive, encouraging open communication between the insurance company, hospital representatives, and the Shah family.

As the session progressed, it became evident that there were no indications of overbilling or financial irregularities related to Mrs. Shah's care. The insurance company audit confirmed that the charges aligned with industry standards for the procedures performed, providing a sense of financial transparency to the Shah family.

However, the insurance company representative also highlighted areas for improvement in billing communication, suggesting clearer explanations for patients regarding the breakdown of charges. This constructive feedback served as a valuable takeaway for the hospital's financial team, aligning with the commitment to continuous improvement.

The session concluded with a collaborative understanding between the insurance company, hospital administrators, and the Shah family. An agreement was reached to enhance communication about billing practices, ensuring that patients and their families receive transparent information about the financial aspects of their care.

In a unique twist to the conventional narrative, Dr. Khanna, guided by the principles of restorative justice, took the courageous step of offering a sincere apology to Mrs. Shah. This apology, far from admitting legal guilt, became a cornerstone in the healing process. Mrs. Shah, touched by the doctor's empathy, found a sense of closure that transcended the financial compensation sought in traditional litigation.

Dr. Khanna, motivated by a commitment to continuous improvement, actively engaged in Mrs. Shah's ongoing care and recovery. The restorative approach extended beyond compensation, focusing on the patient's well-being and the doctor's dedication to learning from the experience.

The hospital's internal audit and fact-finding process revealed areas for improvement in protocols and communication, the findings subsequently forwarded to the Medical Board of Maharashtra for external evaluation.

The Medical Board, comprising experienced healthcare professionals, legal experts, and patient advocates, convened to review the reports and oversee the steps taken by Hospital. The neutral third party, who facilitated the previous audits, played a pivotal role in presenting the information to the Medical Board, emphasizing the collaborative and restorative nature of the process.

The board meticulously examined the hospital audit, focusing on the medical procedures, communication protocols, and the hospital's commitment to learning from the incident. Simultaneously, the insurance company audit findings were reviewed to ensure that financial aspects were in line with the quality of care provided.

To ensure a fair determination of compensation, the Medical Board enlisted the expertise of a legal professional appointed by the government. This legal expert, with no affiliation to the hospital or the insurance company, provided an impartial evaluation of the situation, considering both medical and financial aspects.

The board determined a fair compensation for Mrs. Shah, considering the physical and emotional impact of the incident on her life. The compensation package included coverage for medical expenses, ongoing care, and additional support for emotional healing. Importantly, the Medical Board ensured that the compensation process was transparent, fair, and aligned with the principles of restorative justice.

The final report, summarizing the hospital and insurance company audits, the patient's response, and the Medical Board's determination, was made public. It served as a valuable resource for other healthcare institutions, promoting a culture of transparency, accountability, and continuous improvement in the medical community.

As per the norm every hospital was to have an internal clinical council meet every month to discuss various cases, complications, unusual occurrences and any case of medical negligence or error. The goal was clear: to learn from mistakes, rectify errors, and elevate patient safety standards.

During one of these sessions, Dr. Khanna found himself in the spotlight about Mrs.Shah's case. The meeting room hummed with anticipation as fellow doctors prepared to question and gain insights from the incident.

Dr. Khanna, standing before his peers, commenced by recounting the events leading to Mrs. Shah's cardiac surgery complications. The internal audit findings, presented by the hospital's fact-finding team, illuminated areas for improvement in communication, procedural adherence, and postoperative care.

Dr. Kapoor, a senior surgeon known for his meticulous approach, raised a hand to pose a question. "Dr. Khanna, could you shed light on the communication gaps identified in the audit? How do you plan to address them to prevent similar issues in the future?"

Acknowledging the significance of open dialogue, Dr. Khanna elaborated on the specific communication challenges and outlined steps to implement clearer communication protocols, enhance patient-family interactions, and ensure a more comprehensive informed consent process.

Dr. Gupta, an anesthesiologist, contributed, "In incidents like these, the coordination between surgical and anesthesia teams is crucial. How can we strengthen that coordination to minimize the risk of complications?"

The conversation delved into interdisciplinary aspects of patient care, with Dr. Khanna and his colleagues actively engaging in discussions. The Internal Clinical Council meeting evolved into a collaborative platform where doctors shared insights, posed relevant questions, and collectively worked toward enhancing the hospital's standards of care.

A young resident, Dr. Patel, eager to learn, inquired about lessons from the incident and their integration into the hospital's medical education programs. Dr. Khanna outlined plans for ongoing training and professional development, highlighting the hospital's commitment to a culture of continuous learning.

As the meeting concluded, MumbaiCare Hospital's Chief Medical Officer, Dr. Arjun Singh, praised the collective effort to address challenges and learn from each case. He underscored the importance of transparency and announced that detailed audit reports, discussions, and action plans would be made public on the hospital's website every month.

Crucially, the lessons learned from this incident were not confined to the hospital's internal circles. The findings, along with Dr. Khanna's approach and the subsequent actions taken, were published for all doctors. The transparent sharing of information became a cornerstone in preventing future errors and fostering a culture of continuous learning within the medical community.

In the end, the story of Dr. Aryan Khanna, Mrs. Nalini Shah, and the collaborative efforts of the hospital, insurance companies, and the medical board showcased the transformative potential of a restorative model. It illustrated that by prioritizing understanding, healing, and continuous improvement over blame, the medical field could evolve into a more resilient, patient-centric, and learning-oriented community.

JUSTICE IN TIME IS JUSTICE WELL SERVED: OTHERWISE IT IS FARCE

The importance of a continuous and timely restorative justice process in healthcare cannot be overstated. Both for the patient and the doctor, a swift and ongoing resolution is crucial for several reasons:

1. Timely Closure for Patients:

Patients who have experienced medical complications are already navigating physical and emotional challenges. A swift resolution, coupled with transparent communication, provides them with a sense of closure. This timeliness ensures that they can focus on their recovery without the prolonged stress of legal battles or uncertainty about the outcome.

2. Emotional Healing:

For patients, emotional healing is a vital aspect of recovery. The timely resolution of a medical error allows for open communication, an apology if necessary, and a clear path forward. This process helps in rebuilding trust, mitigating emotional distress, and supporting the patient's overall well-being.

3. Preventing Prolonged Legal Battles:

A continuous and timely restorative justice approach minimizes the risk of prolonged legal battles. Traditional litigation can be time-consuming and emotionally draining for both patients and healthcare providers. Swift resolution through restorative processes reduces the burden on all parties involved.

4. Learning Opportunities for Doctors:

From the doctor's perspective, a timely resolution allows for immediate learning opportunities. Addressing errors promptly ensures that corrective measures can be implemented swiftly, preventing similar incidents in the future. This approach fosters a culture of continuous improvement within the medical community.

5. Preserving Professional Reputation:

For healthcare professionals, a timely resolution is crucial for preserving their professional reputation. Swift acknowledgment of errors, active engagement in the resolution process, and a commitment to improvement contribute to maintaining trust and respect within the medical community and among patients.

6. Facilitating Ongoing Education:

The continuous nature of the restorative justice process supports ongoing education for healthcare providers. Monthly internal clinical council meetings, as seen in the previous story, provide a platform for doctors to share experiences, discuss errors, and collectively work toward improving patient care. This continuous learning culture becomes ingrained in the hospital's ethos.

7. Building Trust with the Public:

A hospital's commitment to continuous improvement, transparency, and timely resolution is essential for building and maintaining trust with the public. By regularly sharing audit reports on the hospital's website, the institution demonstrates accountability and reinforces its dedication to patient-centered care.

In essence, the continuous and timely nature of the restorative justice process ensures that both patients and doctors can move forward constructively. It minimizes the emotional toll on patients, facilitates ongoing learning for healthcare providers, and contributes to a healthcare environment built on trust, transparency, and a commitment to continuous improvement.

Community: Medical And General Public

Punitive only legal option has led to lot of bitterness. Time to correct.

The current punitive action-oriented medical negligence system has precipitated a divisive atmosphere, fostering bitterness between the medical community and the general public. This adversarial approach, akin to a battleground, has engendered a perception of doctors as infallible gods who are immune to scrutiny and patients as potential adversaries resorting to legal battles at the drop of a hat. Such a polarized dynamic is detrimental to both parties, as doctors and patients are interdependent entities in the realm of healthcare.

Doctors, who may perceive themselves as omnipotent, need a paradigm shift in their perspective. Acknowledging errors and accepting accountability are critical for fostering a culture of continuous learning and improvement. The prevailing system, often marked by defensive medicine and a reluctance to admit mistakes, hampers the medical community's ability to actively participate in meaningful ways beyond serving as expert witnesses during legal proceedings.

On the other side, patients should recognize that the pursuit of justice doesn't always align with the punitive legal battles that have become commonplace. Instead of seeking retribution, a more constructive approach involves involving the medical community in a manner that promotes learning, empathy, and collaborative problem-solving. The aim should be to help doctors comprehend and rectify the harm caused to patients, fostering a culture where errors are viewed as opportunities for improvement rather than as grounds for legal warfare.

Furthermore, integrating the general public into initiatives aimed at enhancing healthcare offers the prospect of empowering communities. By giving the public a greater voice in policies that directly impact their well-being, there's an opportunity to bridge the gap between doctors and patients. This inclusivity fosters a sense of shared responsibility for healthcare outcomes, steering away from the acrimony inherent in the current punitive model. Ultimately, a shift toward a restorative and community-focused approach has the potential to reshape the doctor-patient relationship, engendering a system where trust, collaboration, and a commitment to continuous improvement prevail.

Imagine a medical malpractice liability system that goes beyond mere legal battles and paperwork, envisioning a realm where healing takes centre stage.

In this ideal system, compensation is not just a financial transaction but a means to restore balance and justice.

Safety becomes a shared commitment, preventing harm before it occurs, and reducing the overall impact.

Information flows freely, creating a collaborative environment where lessons learned from each case contribute to the collective knowledge of the medical community.

The system doesn't stop at compensation; it extends a hand towards restorative opportunities, acknowledging the emotional and psychological aspects of healing for all parties involved.

This vision transcends the adversarial nature of traditional liability systems, ushering in an era where empathy, transparency, and a commitment to continuous improvement guide the path to true healing.

Epilogue

In the illustrious kingdom of Ayodhya, ruled by the wise and just King Ram, a common man named Gopal approached the royal court with a grievance. Gopal had undergone treatment from a renowned healer, but complications arose, leaving him distressed and seeking justice.

Gopal, his voice trembling with a mixture of frustration and desperation, addressed the mighty king, "Oh, Raja Ram, the guardian of justice, I seek your wisdom and fairness. I have undergone treatment from a healer, a supposed savior, only to find myself entangled in a web of complications. My life, my well-being, everything hangs in the balance."

King Ram, sitting atop his majestic throne, observed Gopal with a calm and discerning gaze. The courtiers and spectators awaited the king's response, sensing that this encounter would be no ordinary affair.

With a measured tone, King Ram beckoned Gopal to speak his truth. Gopal, pouring out his heart, narrated the challenges he faced, the pain he endured, and the shadows that now haunted his life. The echoes of his grievances resonated through the grand hall.

Raja Ram, known for his commitment to justice and fairness, decided to address the matter with a comprehensive approach. He summoned not only the aggrieved Gopal but also the healer in question, Gopal's family, the council of ministers, another respected healer from the town, and a few notable individuals from the community.

King Ram, his gaze unwavering, addressed the healer, "Esteemed healer, Gopal has brought forth grievances of complications arising from the treatment you provided. We are here to seek the truth, unravel the complexities, and find a path to resolution. Speak freely, and let justice prevail."

Healer: Your Majesty, I humbly present the details of Gopal's case. The treatment began with the utmost care, but as we navigated the complexities, unforeseen complications arose.

King Ram: Explain, healer. What challenges did you encounter?

Healer: Your Highness, the ailment was intricate, and decisions were made based on the best medical judgment. However, the human body, as complex as it is, sometimes responds in unexpected ways.

Gopal: (interjecting) Unexpected ways that left me in agony! Your Majesty, I just sought relief, not more suffering.

King Ram: Gopal, your pain is acknowledged. Let the healer continue.

Healer: Indeed, Gopal, your suffering pains me. I assure you, every decision was made with your well-being in mind. Unfortunately, healing is not always a linear path.

Gopal: (with frustration) But what about the complications? Did you not anticipate them?

Healer: Your Majesty, complications are inherent in the practice of medicine. While we strive for perfection, we must also accept the limitations of our knowledge.

King Ram: (nodding) The healer speaks truth. Continue.

Gopal: (softening) I understand the challenges now, but the pain...

Healer: Gopal, your pain weighs on my conscience. I am committed to your recovery, and I extend my deepest apologies for the hardships you've endured.

King Ram: (addressing the healer) Apologies are a step toward healing wounds. Now, let us work toward a resolution that ensures Gopal's well-being and fosters understanding in our kingdom.

King Ram: (turning to the other healer) Healer Vasuki, I seek your insights. How do you view the medical intricacies in Gopal's case?

Healer Vasuki: Your Majesty, healing is an art as much as it is a science. I've reviewed the case, and I concur with my colleague. The challenges faced were formidable, and unforeseen complications can arise even with the most meticulous care.

King Ram: (thoughtful) So, what are your thoughts on the decisions made during the treatment?

Healer Vasuki: Your Highness, considering the circumstances, the decisions were rational. Medicine, despite all its advancements, is not without uncertainties.

King Ram: (addressing both healers) It is clear that the intricacies of healing are complex. Yet, Gopal's pain cannot be overlooked. How do we reconcile these perspectives?

Healer: Your Majesty, I propose a collaborative approach. Let us work together to alleviate Gopal's suffering and, in the process, enhance our understanding of healing.

King Ram: (nodding) Collaboration is indeed the path to resolution. Gopal, are you open to this collaborative effort?

Gopal: (with hesitation) Your Majesty, I just want the pain to end. If this collaboration ensures that, I am willing.

Healer Vasuki: (addressing Gopal) Your well-being is our priority. Together, we shall explore avenues to bring relief and healing.

King Ram: (decisive) Let this collaboration begin. We shall strive for a solution that not only addresses Gopal's pain but also advances the knowledge and practice of healing in our kingdom.

King Ram: (addressing the respectful citizen from the town) My friend, you have witnessed the impact of Gopal's condition on our community. Can you share your insights into the hardships he has faced?

Respectful Citizen: Your Majesty, Gopal is a respected member of our town. His illness has not only burdened him physically but has also affected the harmony of our community. He was the sole breadwinner for his family, and the financial strain has been palpable.

King Ram: (reflecting) Indeed, the ramifications are far-reaching. Gopal, can you elaborate on how this illness has affected your day-to-day life and your family?

Gopal: (with a heavy heart) Your Majesty, my family depended on my work. With the illness, I've not only suffered physically but have seen my family struggle. It's been challenging to make ends meet and provide for my children's education.

King Ram: (compassionate) These are critical aspects to consider. Healing is not just about treating ailments; it's about restoring lives. We must address Gopal's immediate needs while ensuring that such hardships are minimized for others in the future.

Respectful Citizen: Your Majesty, may I suggest a community-driven initiative to support families during times of illness? This way, we can collectively ensure that no one bears the burden alone.

King Ram: (appreciative) Your suggestion is wise. We shall work towards a framework that fosters community support during challenging times.

Gopal, rest assured, we aim not only to heal but to fortify our community against such adversities.

Gopal: (grateful) Your Majesty, I am thankful for your understanding and support.

King Ram: Together, we shall embark on a journey of healing that encompasses not just the individual but our entire community.

King Ram: (addressing his council of ministers) My esteemed ministers, we are faced with a challenge that goes beyond the individual – it touches the very fabric of our community. I seek your counsel on how we can allocate funds to support those facing illness and hardships.

Minister 1: Your Majesty, perhaps we can establish a dedicated fund for medical emergencies. This fund could be accessible to citizens facing unexpected health crises, providing them with financial assistance.

Minister 2: Additionally, we could create a streamlined process for citizens to approach us with their needs. Establishing a committee that reviews and assesses the circumstances could ensure a fair and transparent allocation of resources.

King Ram: Your suggestions are sound. A designated fund and an accessible mechanism for citizens to seek support will indeed fortify our commitment to the welfare of our people. How can we ensure that the process is known to all citizens?

Minister 3: Your Majesty, we can organize community outreach programs, disseminate information through town criers, and have a dedicated section on the town's notice board. This way, everyone will be aware of the support available.

King Ram: (nodding) Excellent. Let it be known that our commitment to the well-being of our citizens extends beyond the walls of this palace. Together, we shall weave a safety net that embraces every member of our community.

King Ram: (addressing both healers) Wise healers, your skills are invaluable to our kingdom. However, with great power comes great responsibility. I urge you to send a message to all healers in our kingdom, emphasizing the importance of working safely, maintaining clear communication, and seeking assistance from fellow healers when needed.

Healer 1: Your Majesty, we understand the gravity of our responsibilities. We shall craft a message that highlights the principles of safe and collaborative healing, ensuring that it reaches every healer in our realm.

Healer 2: Furthermore, we will encourage a culture of continuous learning among our peers. This incident has shown us the importance of staying updated and seeking guidance from others when faced with medical intricacies.

King Ram: Your commitment to the well-being of our citizens and the enhancement of healing practices is commendable. I trust that your message will resonate with every healer in our kingdom. Let it be a reminder that in the pursuit of healing, collaboration and knowledge are our greatest allies.

King Ram: (addressing everyone present) In the face of challenges, we have come together to find solutions that not only address individual grievances but strengthen the very foundation of our kingdom. The incident involving Gopal has shown us the importance of unity, compassion, and continuous improvement. Let this be a testament to our resilience and commitment to creating a kingdom where every citizen's well-being is of paramount importance. As we move forward, let us embrace the spirit of restorative justice, learning from the past to build a brighter and healthier future for all.

"In the healing tapestry of life, King Ram's justice stitches understanding, compassion, and fairness, crafting a narrative where the threads of truth mend the wounds of medical negligence."

In conclusion, King Ram's vision of restorative justice, as witnessed in the intricate tapestry of medical dilemmas, illuminates a path for India to forge its own narrative in the field of healthcare. By fostering open dialogue, understanding, and collaborative solutions, this model beckons towards a future where the healing touch of justice is felt by both patients and healers alike. India, with its rich history and diverse culture, has the potential to adapt and adopt such a compassionate approach, paving the way for a medical system that values restoration, transparency, and the holistic well-being of its citizens. In embracing this ethos, India can shape a narrative where healthcare becomes a beacon of empathy, turning moments of crisis into opportunities for healing and growth.

GOD WILL SHOW THE PATH

About the Author

Dr. Yogesh Gupta

Dr. Yogesh Gupta, a distinguished Senior Consulting Physician in India since 2003, is a seasoned professional and keen observer of the evolving landscape of medical practice in the country. His extensive experience and profound insights into the trajectory of healthcare in India have made him a respected figure in the medical community.

Dr. Gupta's perspective on medical negligence is shaped by his commitment to learning from errors, fostering a culture of continuous improvement within the medical field. As a compassionate practitioner, he goes beyond treating individuals, emphasizing the interconnected nature of health and well-being within entire families. His holistic approach to patient care extends beyond the clinical realm, emphasizing the importance of earning the trust and confidence of the families he serves.

In addition to his professional journey, Dr. Gupta attributes much of his success to the unwavering support of his intelligent and beautiful wife, who has been his pillar of strength in all endeavors. Blessed with two angelic daughters, they serve as the guiding light in his life, inspiring him to continually strive for excellence in both his personal and professional spheres.

An accomplished author, Dr. Yogesh Gupta has penned two insightful books in the past. ""COVID Diaries: Virus vs We"" provided a unique perspective during the challenging times of the pandemic, while ""We

Learn as We Grow"" encapsulated his wisdom gained over the years. In his upcoming third book, he delves into the historical background of present healthcare challenges, offering solutions and emphasizing the need for India to forge its own path in healthcare and medical negligence law. Dr. Gupta advocates against blindly adopting the models of the USA or Europe, proposing a tailored approach that aligns with India's unique context and envisions a more effective and just healthcare system.

In addition to his roles as a practicing physician and author, Dr. Gupta is a Professor of Practice at the esteemed Institute of National Forensic Science University in Gandhinagar, Gujarat. He is a sought-after speaker and writer, sharing his knowledge and insights with the wider community. Furthermore, he leads the Gifted Hands Foundation, an NGO dedicated to teaching CPR to school students, contributing to the community's well-being beyond his clinical practice. Dr. Yogesh Gupta's multifaceted contributions make him a notable figure in the medical and healthcare landscape in India.